W9-CQH-556

Forge Books by Meredith Blevins

The Hummingbird Wizard
The Red Hot Empress
The Vanished Priestess

The Red Hot Empress

An Annie Szabo Mystery

Meredith Blevins

A Tom Doherty Associates Book
New York

This is a work of fiction. All the characters and events portrayed in this book are either products of the author's imagination or are used fictitiously.

THE RED HOT EMPRESS: AN ANNIE SZABO MYSTERY

A Forge Book
Published by Tom Doherty Associates, LLC
175 Fifth Avenue
New York, NY 10010

www.tor.com

Forge® is a registered trademark of Tom Doherty Associates, LLC.

ISBN-13: 978-0-765-34690-2
ISBN-10: 0-765-34690-7

First edition: September 2005
First mass market edition: September 2006

Printed in the United States of America

0 9 8 7 6 5 4 3 2 1

Dedicated to

My mom ~ Lying under your baby grand, my fingers wrapped around the piano leg, your melodies shifted reality, making the world rounder and warmer. Music made our home—thank you.

and . . .

My husband, Win ~ Rock and roll and rumble and purr—all your tones are home sweet home.

Spirit of Monkey

I am the ancient wanderer
    of mysteries, dark and light.
Wizard of the animus,
    singing shapeless forms to life.
Pound of rhythm, drum of dance,
    my breath is brilliant mischief,
And my heart brews yin jing magic
    that can cure one hundred ills.
I am built for heat, for living.
    LISTEN . . . I AM THE MONKEY.

—Cerena Woo, *Chinese Animal Guides*

The Empress travels through the great mysteries, past and future, protecting The Monkey. She cannot avoid this obligation to him.

—Hao, traditional Chinese herbalist

The Red Hot Empress

One

I smelled Chinatown before I got there. Steamy and rich, ripe and rotting, it is kodo juice laced with pale green danger. The present smells boom box energetic, and the past is slick cod dying on a side street.

I'd escaped the ancient civilization of trees and headed to the nearest patch of wild, San Francisco. My income over the past several months had tapered to the leaky drip of a farmhouse faucet—that's what happens when the drama of other people's lives unfolds across your workspace. I rented the quiet solace of an urban hotel room with a large desk and a fast Internet connection.

Ninety-three languages are spoken in San Francisco, a city of seven square miles. Understanding comes hard and people are often angry, causing spectacular behavioral displays. Vegetarian shoes are a hot item. Metrosexuals are old news. The newly rich clash ideologies with the old rich, but they live and shop in the same places; in a small city it's impossible to avoid people you don't like. People who remind you too much of yourself—where you've been, where you're going.

This whole human and geographic mess is a breeding ground

for more potential *National Eye* stories than you can shake a stick at. A gold mine of heroism and lunacy, it was the perfect place to plant myself and collect interviews.

I'd inherited an office building and I'd put it on the market before San Francisco's real estate bubble burst. One sucker bit, offering a ridiculous price. Two others jumped in, creating a bidding war. When the battle ended, and the last bloodied warrior was left standing, I was told escrow would close in thirty days. I planned to celebrate by blowing money I didn't have yet, and doing it in a big way. I rented the fourth-floor studio at the Bay View Hotel on Fisherman's Wharf.

It wasn't just my premature and hopeful millionaire status that got me moving to the city. A phone call from Madame Mina precipitated my exodus from quiet culture to urban chaos.

"Come down here," she said, skipping anything resembling hello. "I've got the story of the year for you. It's about a Chinese kid. Maybe you'll even win a fancy award to stick on your wall."

Nobody who works for *The Eye* gets an award, maybe an egg splattered on their windshield, but no award.

Mina said, "You know my new place in Chinatown? There's a neighbor kid here, Jimmy. You won't believe this, but the boy tones."

The toy bones . . . Now what had Mina gotten herself into?

"*The Eye* wouldn't do a story on toy bones unless they're for underprivileged dogs," I said, "a warm, fuzzy angle. If it's something else, you know I don't do gruesome."

"Annie Szabo, you need to get your hearing checked. I said, THE BOY TONES."

"I have no idea what you're talking about."

"That's what makes this story great," she said. "Jeez! I shouldn't have to tell you about your own business."

I heard the *prrring* of an old-fashioned doorbell, the kind that lets a shopkeeper know when a client has walked in.

"You're busy," I said. "I'll be down soon, and you can tell me about the toning boy."

She muffled the receiver. I heard her, bossy, telling someone to take a seat and wait.

"Look," she said, "toning is an ancient healing method. Jimmy hears people the same way we hear music. When they're sick, he tones them. It sounds like chanting—he even cured Mrs. Liu's arthritis."

Not bad. If I could make this sound anywhere close to the truth, Jimmy would make good copy. With luck, he had a winning smile. If Jimmy looked like a kid who tortured bugs, the story wouldn't wash.

"Is there an adult," I said, "other than you, who'd give me permission to put Jimmy's picture in *The Eye*?"

"Hao, an herbalist. Jimmy's uncle. They live up the street. We're happy to be in *The Eye* with Jimmy. You know," Mina said, "the smiling grandparents?" She hung up the phone.

There it was. Mina had been trying to weasel her way into *The Eye* ever since she'd weaseled her way back into my life. I was more than skeptical, but after some quick research I discovered that toning was real. I dug up a house-sitter, packed my bags, and drove south. I'd spend money, I'd earn money, and in between I'd dig up a few great stories. I did not expect Jimmy to be one of them.

I was wrong. Jimmy was twelve years old, *almost*, he'd said, and he was happy to report that he could blow up my car in ten minutes flat using a book of matches, red dye from a pack of cigarettes, and the lead foil from a wine bottle. Then he smiled. He was dazzling, I was hooked.

At his suggestion, we visited a hospital two miles from Chinatown, Hao tagging along. The sick-sweet scent of antibacterial spray was a wrench. Jimmy and Hao didn't seem to notice. I watched Jimmy tone a girl sunk deep in her wheelchair. I snapped a few photos, then I put my camera away. It was intrusive, wrong.

Holding the girl's hand, Jimmy closed his eyes, swaying slightly. A chant, low and deep, rose from the center of his belly. The chant picked up volume, filling his throat. His voice vibrated across the linoleum of the sterile hall, its pink heat rising through the soles of my shoes; I could almost hear the germs give up and die. Jimmy was beyond dazzling. He was a miracle.

I whispered to Hao. "Is he curing that child right now?"

"Western mind." Hao narrowed his eyes, searching for words. "Sometimes there is no cure, but there's a healing. Time will tell us which has occurred."

Jimmy visited another patient, a man attached to a mechanical octopus. Undaunted by the pulsing lights and plastic tubing, Jimmy rested his forehead against the man's forehead. Jimmy closed his eyes and hummed, holding the man's box-bone face between his hands. I asked Hao what I was witnessing.

"Music is made of sound waves, the same way that colors are light waves. Music is energy." Hao stopped talking and cocked his head.

"Go on," I said, "you haven't lost me yet."

"What will make sense for you?" Hao looked at me as if he were trying to communicate with the dead. "That man," he said to me, "has cancer. Probably no cure for him, but a reduction in pain will occur. After that, acceptance of the outcome. Peace."

"Acceptance is the healing."

"Exactly!" Dawn spread across his face. I was not a lost cause. "Cancer cells are our own body cells gone mad. When the cells are rumpled by disease, our inner music sounds like bad jazz played by a drug addict. Health sounds like a Mozart sonata. Like Jimmy, Mozart was a terrible pest, but the universe gave him a door open only to a few."

"How do you . . ."

"Know Mozart? Because I'm Chinese? My grandfather played in the San Francisco Symphony."

"No, no. How does Jimmy know about toning? Did you teach him?"

"My talent is tonics and herbs. Jimmy works with my brother, Ike Qi. Ike hears the same way Jimmy does, but his healing ability is greater than Ike's."

"It's a rare gift."

"Very. I didn't want this article on Jimmy," Hao said, "but Mina feels it will help the sick. I believe she just wants her picture taken with one of the Qi brothers."

I'd been drinking a grape soda that I'd bought from a hospital vending machine, and the bubbles backed up and almost flew out my nose.

"Pardon me?" I said.

"Mina has a crush on us"—his eyes picked up a twinkle—"but usually not both brothers on the same day."

There he stood: quiet, serene, wearing a baggy shirt and matching trousers, black slippers, and lines around his deep, kind eyes. No dramatic flair, and he didn't seem bent on personal destruction. If his brother were cut from the same cloth? Definitely not Mina material.

Jimmy found us. He was wrung out and ready to leave. I promised him a trip through a fast-food joint and a giant Slurpee. He perked up a little, but when we reached the car he slid in beside Hao, resting the weary weight of his body against his uncle. Clowny Drive-Thru was just around the corner, and I bought heavy-carb fortification.

I thought Jimmy had fallen asleep while holding a half-eaten burger. He hadn't. Slumped between me and Hao, his voice slurring with fine irritation, Jimmy said, "I climb inside people to work, but lots of them *want* to be sick. It makes me tired."

"What do you do when you're inside?"

He shrugged and took a hefty suck of Slurpee. "I bend waves until they're straight, same as when the guy next door tunes his guitar—no big deal. When I was a kid, being inside people scared me, seeing little strands coiled around each other, weird voices running up and down their wires. . . ." Jimmy's face went soft and he swirled his straw around the bottom of his cup.

"I believe he's hearing DNA," Hao said. "The voices of a patient's ancestors."

Jimmy rolled his eyes. "Whatever. I'm learning how to ignore them."

I said, "Do you really hear voices?"

"People never shut up inside. It's so annoying."

"It poops you out, and sometimes people get on your nerves. Why do it?"

Jimmy sat up straight, regaining some of his shine. "You know the sound a bat and ball make when they connect, and you know it's GONE without even looking?"

"A solid knock that feels like *YES.*"

He relaxed into his seat. "When I tune someone just right, it's the same feeling."

Excitement and exhaustion both—sounded like Jimmy's gift shinnied up and down the same greasy pole.

Jimmy glanced at me. A grin tiptoed across his face. He studied my car's headliner, slipping his fingers under the edge of the fabric, then he eyeballed my backseat. He faced forward again, content.

"I really like fixing babies." He rattled the straw around his empty plastic cup. "No jabber inside, they just want to feel good. Easy."

There it was. A perfect story for *The Eye.*

I parked in front of Mina's. I lined them up, my camera in hand. Mina wedged herself between Jimmy and Hao. All three stood in her doorway, the name and address of her business capping the top of the photo, her phone number painted on the window to her right. Mina's smile was glorious, Hao's smile was horrified.

I wasn't sure if everything I'd seen and heard was true, but when

I left Chinatown everyone was happy—not so common after an interview. Jimmy was an auspicious beginning to my month in San Francisco.

Ten minutes after I turned off Grant, a shrill shriek blasted my eardrums, just about wrapping me around a Monterey pine growing in the median strip on 19th Avenue. A minor stink bomb had exploded on my backseat. At the first red light, I checked out the damage. My seat was sooty, and the air steamed yellow sulfur. A knockoff Rolex watch bubbled beneath a melted glob of lead. Pretty impressive. I hoped Jimmy's wild spirit would offer him protection from whatever life had waiting in its batty attic.

I pulled in front of the Bay View. Adjusting my rearview mirror, I flicked away flakes of mascara, smiling at myself. I had work lined up. Soon I'd be able to pay off my credit cards and take a trip and start racking up debt all over again. For the moment Mina liked me, and she liked her new home, which was sixty miles away from *my* home. Life felt pretty good.

A slow week for movie star gossip, Jimmy made the paper's next edition. No word from Chinatown, and it's true that no news is good news. When the world's gone very wrong, news becomes a continuous mantra of misery, repeated until your eyes glaze over like an Easter ham.

Two

Pending the close of escrow, four days was the latest theory, I was juggling low-interest credit card balance transfers left and right. I'd given up trying to figure out what expenses were deductible and exactly how much I owed who. Whom. Just in case the sale fell through, or an earthquake leveled my financial freedom, I'd spent the month in San Francisco working my behind off.

My oldest daughter, E. B., was meeting me at the Bay View that afternoon. I'd be wrapping up an interview, and she'd have fresh money in her pockets. It had taken her three months to wind artsy streams through Isis Oasis, prime land tucked in the hills south of San Francisco. Her watery installation now oozed the sweet ozone of peace as far as a fat cat's checkbook could hear.

Forty-two hundred dollars per week buys Isis women the freedom to walk around naked, read poetry to trees and other trapped botanicals, and to journal their paths. Sharing is encouraged, all goddess aspects are open for inspection, and during the full moon a few guests run with the wolves. Others simply bathe in the moon's soft illumination, city streetlights far and muted. All things they could do without spending one dime, but some people have to fork over a lot of dough to feel the full value of an experience. I'd interviewed the Isis owner. Hard to imagine—she was too odd for *The Eye*. A set of twins as legendary as the Coit Tower were up last on my work schedule.

Jean and Jan are impossible to miss, equally impossible to pin down, but I'd gotten lucky. One morning, as they were leaving the Cafe Rafael, I ran into them. Literally. One sister chuckled as I brushed pastry from the other sister's elegant jacket.

Dressed in vintage Dior with sable piping, they were size eight mirror images. The awkward Italian girls, raised on a chicken farm in Petaluma, grew into stunning women. They ran to Hollywood during its golden age. Tall and voluptuous, they sizzled like Sophia Loren gone sassy. They'd modeled for *Vogue,* they still did ads for everything from swanky "senior living communities" to Metamucil. It was rumored that they had serviced an occasional alpha male who hankered after twins. It was rumored that they still did. A delicious tidbit, none of my business, and I hoped it was true.

Their last official interview being sometime around the death of RFK, they'd made it clear to the press that their lives were off-limits. I'd already spilled my breakfast all over one of them. Having nothing to lose, I introduced myself and asked if they'd like to talk. Eureka! The women answered *YES*. They bubbled like Sunday champagne—the time was right, they weren't getting any younger, and, as everyone does, the twins loved *The Eye*. We'd made a date, shook hands, and they turned on their alligator heels, the last crumbs scattering on aged Italian tile.

I was pumped for the interview. What secrets were the twins ready to shed? I dressed in a sage green suit, conservative and cool, and caught a cab downtown. I was running late.

I waited in the lobby of the Rafael, just left of the café. No twins. Ten minutes spent pacing, my absolute outer limit. Still no twins. I asked the young woman at the reception desk if there was a message for me. Raising her eyebrows and asking for my identification, she told me that I was expected in Room 223. Considering her youth, she had a real knack for eyebrow-raising. A vision of her life stretched out before me, one bad Hallmark moment: marriage to a well-groomed man, producing two children and a home filled with escalating feuds. The inevitable divorce. Nursing her disappointment in men, she'd retreat to Isis Oasis, the burble of E. B.'s peaceful waters soothing her troubled brow.

I took the Rafael's elevator up and Jan opened their door. The twins wore flowing caftans of pale turquoise film. The room smelled like marijuana. I'd expected vermouth, not pot.

We spent three hours together. A contact high plus two shots of beautiful blue Bombay gin kept me afloat on their rollicking sea. Yes, they'd worked standard modeling jobs, starting when they were kids during the Depression. Their fees were steep. They did the movie gig, then they returned home, tired of glamour and pretty boys. Hollywood called them back several times, but they thumbed their noses. They had plenty of money and no one poking around their lives—the best of both worlds.

Jean and Jan worked as spies during the McCarthy Era, ratting on supposed Communists, sometimes giving our government a bum steer toward men who'd been disappointing lovers or bad business partners. They liked danger and they didn't care about politics. They had known, in the biblical sense, three presidents, several governors and senators, each man harboring a twin fantasy. They joked that they'd been privy to more government secrets than J. Edgar Hoover. Hoover was not one of their clients, Jean told me, straight-faced—he'd lusted after different physical equipment. Jan hooted out loud. After the McCarthy nonsense was over, they worked a few real spy jobs behind the Iron Curtain. That career was brief but successful.

The twins laughed as they related escapades, partly because they were funny, partly because the ladies were loaded. I tried to hold my own, telling tales of Madame Mina, her vision of my future varying depending upon how much she liked me that day, my pet giraffes. It all sounded pretty tame.

I had loads of material on the twins, and there wasn't much of it I could use. Not much that I *would* use. The juicy parts sounded tawdry, but there was nothing tawdry about them. They'd created a spectacular life and they'd enjoyed every inch of it. I'd hit them at a time when they had an urge to unload, but no real desire for press. I flopped back on their couch.

Not only were they naughty . . . they had . . . terrific instinct. . . .

That was the last thought that I remembered roaming around my balmy brain.

Filtered afternoon light hit the room like a neighbor's shoe slamming against a paper-thin wall. I stumbled into the bathroom and splashed water on my face, my head spinning with leftover smoke.

I called out to the twins, their names having wriggled through my Swiss cheese mind.

"Hello, twins? Twins?"

No answer. I explored their suite.

They had dumped me, leaving not a trace of our tryst other than my own shoes in front of the amber couch where I had, basically, passed out, and my purse, which had fallen off the couch, spilling a rabble of gum wrappers and spare change on the carpet.

There was a note for me on the coffee table. They'd enjoyed my company—I looked at my rumpled clothing and hoped they hadn't enjoyed me too much—and said if I was in a pinch or simply wanted to have a good time, they could often be found at the Rafael. Under the last name Duette.

Those two would never fit into Isis Oasis. Not even the trees would believe the stories I'd heard.

Leaving the hotel, I thought a man wearing a black trench coat slipped into the thin alley, squeezing between the Rafael and the theater, when I spotted him. I peeked between the narrow gray buildings. No one but a frail gargoyle wearing silt. Walking into a cafe across the street, I ordered a cup of French roast coffee, strong and black. Hallucinations do not make for safe driving.

When my head was clear, I drove to the Bay View, imagining dinner, entertaining my daughter with tales of the twins over two lobster dinners.

Three

E. B. said, "I don't feel like fish."

"Lobster is *not* fish."

"I am trying to diet and I can't eat lobster without butter."

"What are those jeans? A size six?"

"I'm having trouble zipping them up."

"Then buy a size eight. As life gets bigger your body expands so you can hold your experiences. Unless something's wrong," I said, "people don't get thinner as they age."

"You are the ultimate queen of justification."

"Thanks. Listen," I said, "while we stand here arguing, two lobsters with our names on them are waiting to be eaten."

"Mother, there must be something you want that doesn't involve two thousand calories."

I sat on the couch in my living room at the Bay View Hotel. I was letting go of lobster; I was wondering if my daughter and I would survive a small vacation together. Wondering if we could agree on just one meal. Her invocation of the MOTHER word was not a good omen.

I said, "Okay, you decide, but I'm not eating anything resembling yard clippings covered with a tangy vinaigrette."

"I had enough of that at Isis."

"Sweetie, all that hard physical labor. You need real food, protein." It's not as if she couldn't eat the damned lobster with just a little butter.

"Hey! Let's go to Chinatown and watch New Year's unfold," she said, all chipper and happy. "We can see Grandma Mina first, get the visit over with, then pig out on dumplings."

I had never considered dumplings a diet food, but I was done arguing. My taste buds realigned. There was one plus here—I could wear comfortable clothes to Chinatown.

"Good," I said, "dumplings and Tsingtao beer."

E. B. tilted her head. She looked at me as if I were a pole lamp she'd buy if I didn't clash with every single thing she owned. "Chinese beer . . . Have you noticed that your pants are starting to, I don't know, stretch the limits?"

I had noticed. "Is it that obvious?"

"Only because you're wearing pants with elastic waistbands." She gave me her artist's unyielding eye again. "Maybe you're pregnant."

"You are sick," I said, "truly sick."

"You and Leo are pretty active."

That was the last straw. "How would *you* know?"

"Your alfresco thing doesn't leave much to the imagination— must be something about fresh air that really gets to you. Have you been careful?"

Nothing strains the seams of a mother-daughter relationship like the truth, but she was the one who'd started down this road.

"E. B., I'm leaving the baby-making business. Forever."

I waited until the light went on above her head. Her face changed. She understood.

She leaned forward, patting my knee with her caring little hand. I could almost hear her fretting about brittle bones and the rising cost of nursing homes.

"That," she said, "would explain the extra pounds and the way you've been acting. Sensitive, cranky, moody."

"You're absolutely right. Let's eat."

"But you've always been cranky."

"Did I ever once spank you?"

"No."

"I probably would now. Let's get dinner."

"After Mina."

"Maybe you'd like to stay with her," I said. "You're her favorite grandkid." A few days with Mina would be an antidote to anything resembling thought. It would certainly vanquish any Isis leftovers.

She laughed, told me I was not getting rid of her that easily. She picked up her car keys, and I handed her the directions to Mina's new place.

Reading the scrap of paper, she said, "We're going to the Jade Emporium?"

"It's the Jade Palace now. Mina thinks Palace sounds classier than Emporium."

"Tell me she hasn't gone into retail."

"She thought keeping the storefront was a good cover for her fortune-telling business."

"Why does she need a cover? Sometimes I worry about her."

"You're the only one who does. That's why you're her favorite anything."

The buildup for Chinese New Year's is long, and red is a must. I changed into a red dress, silky and soft. E. B. wore bright red leather jeans, a matching cropped jacket, and a deeper red skintight top. If there was one extra inch of flab on her, I didn't see it. I also didn't see where she was going to put dinner, but that was her problem.

She read the directions and shoved them in her back pocket.

I stuffed a giant Snickers bar in my purse. Unless Mina was with a client, we were doomed to at least an hour of dire predictions and juicy gossip.

My daughter and I had found our comfort level—we were breathing and friendly-acting again. She'd hang out with me for a few days, and I'd stay in town until the Bay View month ran out and Chinese New Year's Eve came in. Fireworks, the dragon parade, welcoming in the year of the monkey. Leo Rosetti, my oversexed dancing bear, would be my partner at the parade. E. B. would be gone by the time he arrived, and I couldn't think of one good reason to tell her he'd be joining me.

Four

Family scandal does not go out.

—Confucius

Family protection can only be given when you know exactly
what your relative is doing. If necessary, slippery elm can be used
to loosen the loved one's lips. Slippery elm also pulls secrets out
of your enemies, but be careful—there are some things you'd
rather not know.

—*The Gypsy Guide to Wisdom*
Zlato Milos, 1902

*C*hinese laborers built the great railroads, they came and went
from the Mother Lode, and they could not return to China.
So, in the state they called Golden Mountain, the Chinese settled
along Stockton Street, the only place they were allowed to rent
rooms. It was an iceberg-sized chunk of Shanghai that had broken
off from Mainland China, drifting across the wide, wild Pacific until it hit *Gum San Ta Fow.*

The Chinese did what they do many places—they prospered
and took care of each other.

The Chinese had no desire to assimilate. Surrounded by *fan
kwai,* foreign devils, they needed protection from within and without. Local merchants formed the Chinese Six Companies to maintain order and to handle contacts with the outside world—
meaning the rest of San Francisco. The Chinese Six grew up and
got tough. They became the tongs. Like the Mafia, the tongs took
care of their own. And, like the Mafia, they took care of people
who got in their way.

In the eastern part of the United States slavery had ended, but in

San Francisco Chinese girls who'd been kidnapped from the Mainland were stripped and put up for auction. Once in America, their lives were short and brutal, each worth about three thousand dollars.

California became a dangerous place for Asians, but it was home.

A few whites ventured into the dark womb of San Francisco, courting addiction and death, longing to get lost among opium dens and prostitution and slavery.

Then Mother Nature, sick of the whole mess, picked up the remote control and pressed her index finger on the button marked *shake*. The city did. In April of 1906 San Francisco, including Chinatown, looked as if it had been leveled by a troop of bulldozers belonging to a vengeful goddess's personal wrecking crew.

The Chinese called the disaster Opportunity. They rebuilt their community, and a few timid outsiders poked their noses inside the gates. Chinese shopkeepers, calling the whites *pig faces* in Cantonese, smiled as money dove into their cash drawers. The residents went on a decorating frenzy geared to attract more tourists. New plaster dragons coiled around bank buildings, phone companies, and furniture stores. Rooflines were folded up at the ends like dinner party napkins. Red, green, and yellow paint exploded up twenty-four square blocks with one hundred thousand residents. Grant Street sizzled.

This was where Madame Mina, once again, planted her fortune-telling enterprise. As chaotic and cantankerous as Chinatown, the neighborhood fit her like a silk slipper.

E. B. zipped up Grant, nearly taking out two old Chinese ladies. They gave her the finger; she smiled angelically in response, waving hello. We drove past a train wreck of underground movies, music, and luggage stores. An old man, sitting on a black box covered with duct tape and bumper stickers, played a one-string zither to an audience of none. Magic and verbal abuse swirled up the street past statues of cultural heroes honored by pigeons with bird graffiti.

Lacquerware and girlie magazines, herbal physicians and antler bins. Live fish roiling in plastic sidewalk tubs flipped water onto the sidewalk, soaking bamboo gardens and serene porcelain Buddhas.

E. B. parked at an angle, turning her wheels toward the curb. If the parking brake failed, we'd run over pedestrians instead of important things like BMWs parked across the street. She'd parked in front of a bakery. Pork buns, mooncakes, glazed almond cookies . . . I'd never make it until dinner.

Three doors down from Mina's, the adult fortune cookie factory rolled out cookies, hot and fresh. We bought her an X-rated bag of them.

Mina's front door wore a fresh coat of purple paint and one copper star hung above it. I knocked. Footsteps approached, fast and urgent. The door blew open.

"It took you long enough to get here," she said.

Mina grabbed the front of my dress with one hand, and the front of E. B.'s top with her other. Pulling us both inside with one move, she poked her head back out the door, scanning the tattered alley. Mina bolted the door and leaned her back against it, sighing her relief.

"I have been sending *both* of you messages for two hours."

"You could have just used the phone."

"And you could have ignored it. Messages sent through the head are hard to ignore."

I couldn't argue, there we were, but now I was certain we should have eaten first. This smelled like trouble, and trouble takes time.

"What are you so worked up about?" I said. "The FBI finally catch on to you?"

Mina went white and led us down a few stairs into her living room. The previous owners had left behind kitchen goddesses, small erotic Chinese carvings, and faux-jade necklaces in a dusty glass case. We were looking at our Christmas gifts for years to come.

She bent, peering out a low alley window, checking the side street. She lowered her blinds with a fast crash.

"Hey," I said, "I was joking about the FBI."

"It's no joke. An agent was here, he even showed me his badge. He's all over my life, Jimmy's life, and probably yours, too." Lowering her voice to a whisper, she said, "There's trouble about Jimmy."

I had a flash, sudden and sick.

Little Jimmy, an illegal immigrant, bouncing his way back to China in a small boat, and I had flushed him out with that stupid article. After the US handed him over to China, he'd be warehoused in a concrete world devoid of human rights. What had I done? Then I thought, *Get real—a Chinese kid in Chinatown. His family's probably been in the US longer than mine has.*

"Will you please put a blanket over your brain?" Mina covered her ears with both hands. "You're making me crazy and I'm out of aspirin. We've got to come up with a solution."

"Solution to what?"

"To Jimmy," she said. "I swiped him."

Five

I thought back to the man in black outside the Rafael, disappearing between buildings. That ratty coat . . . he looked like government. I could not begin to imagine what the FBI wanted with us. One thing was certain—someone who'd been assigned to tail me, and Mina, and one skinny kid? I could only begin to imagine the bounds of his ineptitude. I should have known trying to please Mina by sticking her picture in *The Eye* would backfire.

I surveyed our future gifts in the glass case, pressed tight to the wall. I wondered if any of the necklaces were real jade, how much we could pawn them for, and how much money it would take to get Mina out of the country. It wasn't a solution to government intrusion. It was a pipe dream built for my own pleasure.

Her Jade Palace was freshly decorated—a new rug here, a framed photo of an ice-cream cone standing in front of the Eiffel Tower there. No longer into zebra, her couches now wore tiger stripes and brown suede. They were eight-footers. A plasticine camel loped across the base of one lamp. In one corner, heavy draperies created a nook in which to tell her clients that disaster beyond their wildest dreams or long-term bliss was waiting just around the corner.

Tossing Mina's stack of sales brochures on her coffee table, I sat down on one of the tigers. I said, "Do you have any wine around?"

"The last tenants might have left some. You want me to check?"

"No, that's okay."

I didn't care what anyone had to say about my waistline. I pulled out my giant Snickers bar and tore it in half, handing the larger part to Mina.

Punctuating the air with her candy bar, Mina said to me, "Know what? You ruined Jimmy's life."

"I did that? All by myself?"

"Okay, okay, I was partly to blame," she said. "I wanted fame and glory. I guess it made me go a little nuts."

Chewing my candy bar, I was as solemn and thoughtful as the loping camel.

"There *is* an upside," she said. "I've never been so busy. It was nice of you to put my phone number and address in the paper."

As if I'd had a choice. "I don't know what you're so uptight about. One FBI nitwit is not going to put a dent in our lives. It won't take long for the man to get bored and take off."

"I hope you're right, but there's more than one nitwit looking for Jimmy," she said. "This has been a big lesson for me—fame is not all that it's cracked up to be."

I looked around. No jacket, no backpack, not one sign of a twelve-year-old kid. "Where have you stashed Jimmy? I'm assuming you didn't lose him after you stole him."

"He's upstairs watching television, and I told him to stay put. I can't sense if he's here or gone. My power is going right down the tubes," she said, "and I think I'm getting hives."

"Mina, calm down. Let's start at the beginning."

"Sort of a dumb place to start, when we're already in the middle."

"Humor me. Why did you steal him and from who? Hao knows where he is, right?"

"Why, who, and how?" E. B. stood, pulling her jacket across her shoulders. "I think I'll come back later."

My dim sum was walking out the door, and so was my lifeline to sanity.

I said, "Wait a minute. Where are you going?"

"I might visit friends," she said, "maybe family. Don't worry about me. You're in more danger with present company than I would be walking alone in the Tenderloin district."

"*What* family?" I asked her back, as she closed the door behind her.

"I've got family all over," Mina said, "which means *she's* got family all over. Maybe she's picking up protection herbs for Jimmy."

I didn't want to think about E. B. consorting with any known Szabos. From the moment I was pregnant, I knew the Szabo genes had spent a maximum of two minutes charming my genes before they'd beaten them senseless and swiped their genetic markers. Nothing to do about it now. She was an adult, and my allotted worry-time for her had expired.

I said to Mina, "Who else is after Jimmy?"

"Who isn't? Besides the FBI guy, there's an environmental person. He wants Jimmy to listen to dolphins and translate their vibes—do not ask me what that means. A Russian ballet group wants him to write dance music. One rich family wants him to move in with them and write a symphony about their family. Gads, he's just a kid," she said, sounding bluer than blue. "I should have been a bookkeeper instead of a counselor . . . all those neutral numbers and no people."

"You hate numbers."

"Right now I'm not so crazy about people, either."

"It'll pass in a week or two."

"There are other government people, but it's kind of hard to remember them. They all look alike, including the women." Pulling out a cigarette, she said, "Why can't they work together and play connect-the-dots? No wonder this country is such a mess."

She lit her cigarette, blowing smoke straight up to the smoke alarm. Nothing.

"This other group of government snoops," she said, "they're doctors. They want Jimmy to live in Atlantis and cure diseases. Do you believe it? People who waste their entire lives working for a health plan and a pension think *I'm* crazy enough to believe in Atlantis! That place landed on the bottom of the ocean ten thousand years ago."

"Not Atlantis. Atlanta."

"You've heard of it?"

"Atlanta, Georgia. It's packed with doctors and scientists. The agency is called the CDC. They're not bad guys."

"Anyone who was in Nazi Europe during World War II has a right to get nervous over government doctors."

Another puff of smoke toward the alarm, followed by another nothing. "Jimmy's got to pull out some batteries from his backpack and fix that thing," she said. "I could fall asleep watching the late movie and never wake up."

"You could stop smoking."

"Why bother when Jimmy can BUILD an alarm from the junk he carries around in his backpack, never mind fix one?"

She was so practical.

"I haven't told you about the biggest kook who landed on my doorstep."

"No wonder you look pooped."

"I need stronger women's herbs from Hao," Mina said, fiddling with her wrinkles. "The supreme kook is that religious nut who's up the street, just off Columbus. Flora Something."

Flora Light, a Sunday morning media angel tending the spiritually hungry. Her TV show came complete with plush carpeting and a humanoid Ken doll, feeding her canned questions about the scriptures. I'd seen her broadcast once. Nursing a hangover, I'd flipped on the tube. It only took her ten minutes to convince me I was going to hell, sent by a wrathful and ticked-off God. Of course I was wrong—I'd created my own temporary hell the night before by mixing my liquors.

I said, "What in the world does Flora want with Jimmy?"

"Some hooey about Jimmy's duty to the world. What she really wants is healing sessions so people will donate money to her church. I heard her say to her assistant that Jimmy would make good television. Like I said, she's full of hooey."

I remembered thinking that Jimmy would make good copy. I cringed to be anywhere near the same thought process as Flora Light.

"Annie. She calls herself an evangelist. Is that related to being an angel?"

"How would I know?"

"You knew about Atlantis."

"I think I'll go upstairs and talk with Jimmy."

"You'll have to knock on his head to get his attention. He's playing video games and eating junk food. Hao won't let him eat junk. Hao's not very American, probably why he's so thin."

And then my brain skipped backward. "Why, exactly, isn't Jimmy with Ike and Hao?"

"Because the protective society is interested in Jimmy, too. They'd like to use his chanting tones to neutralize people."

"Protective society?"

"The tongs. Don't you know what *neutralize* means? The uncles don't want Jimmy near them."

"Oh, for God sakes. Your imagination needs to get off the playground and take a long nap."

"This is not my imagination. I think maybe Ike or Hao worked for the tongs when they were young. They keep tabs on people," she said. "You're never really out."

"Where do you come up with this stuff?"

"I've been listening to people's lives for at least two hundred years. I know everything."

Chewing my last bite of Snickers, I walked upstairs. After I had his attention, I wanted to ask Jimmy what Mina's brain sounded like. I was pretty certain she'd gone around the bend. Maybe more than once.

Six

"I saw my picture in your newspaper," Jimmy said. "It was way cool."

"Easy, you're a cool guy," I said. "Jimmy, do you want to be here?"

"I don't mind. Madame Mina's got popcorn and rental movies, and I've got my video games."

"You know about all the people who want you?"

He focused his attention on his GameBoy, his thumbs playing the hand control faster than a fire dance.

"Talk to me," I said.

"Wait a minute. I just reached level eight and I've never been this far before."

That line must come with all video game instructions. He stared at the screen, mesmerized. It was hard to imagine how disease could sound worse than an electronic war.

I waited until the first phase of level eight ended. I grabbed the hand control, putting it on pause, so he wouldn't lose his place.

"Jimmy, what about the lady up the street? The one with the church."

There was silence, the kind that pushed alarms inside my head.

"Jimmy?"

"Flora. I'm supposed to go to church tomorrow and help her."

I held his chin, urging his eyes away from two frozen superheroes. "Let's have a slumber party up here tonight," I said. "You can tell me about Flora if you want to. If not? No sweat. We'll watch movies and eat Mina's popcorn."

He asked if I wanted to play SuperMonstro with him. I said I was a lousy loser. He smiled at me with those incredible eyes—ancient, wise, sly and childish, charming and smooth. I agreed to play a video game, and he promised to go easy on me. I didn't believe him. Jimmy likes to win. I know the look. I wear it, too.

I'd watchdog Jimmy, and I'd try not to think about E. B. mixing it up with her Gypsy family members—she was odd enough without encouragement. Next morning I'd take on Flora Light, reigning evangelical diva of old-time religion mixed with affluent New Age guilt.

After trouncing my superhero back to sublevel one, Jimmy fell asleep on a fluffed nest of cushions. I smelled sage wafting up the stairs, and I heard Mina speaking to the four directions of her home, purifying us, protecting us. *Go for it,* I thought. *Can't have too much protection.* Pulling out the hideaway bed, I intended to sleep lightly, ready to keep Jimmy safe from government agents, tongs, and ideological fanatics of every sort.

Often, in my dreams, I am tall, lean and almost beautiful. But not that night.

Wandering through scalded images of saints and numbed by their voices swirling me dizzy, I was lifted up and sucked into a broken vortex. Jagged shards of colored glass spun against the walls inside my skin, angry and red, pounding my body, shaping it from the inside out. Flattened and captured by a thin bead of lead, I was looking down on the prayers of many, unable to help anyone. I was trapped inside a stained-glass window.

Maybe I was part of an old California mission—an earth-rolling jolt jiggled the lead loose. I rolled over, but I couldn't move again. Unintentional, but it placed me in perfect position to moon the pews and the altar. A thought wafted by, written in bold letters—*If my views about religion have to be captured for all eternity, at least I am facing the right direction.*

More jiggling, and I could turn my head. I saw my companions in the colored-glass window. They had learned to move within the frame, to live with prayers floating up, and to ignore the pain inside them.

Joan of Arc had called a warrior's time-out. She was lying nude on a chaise lounge, her sword on the floor beside her. She laughed with a black saint who covered her body in flowers. The petals grew from his skin, and he scattered them on her with loving kisses. One of the three wise men towered over them, tall and fierce. He held his lantern of myrrh above them. He loved them, he did not approve of them, and he took care of them. Moans and wet sounds— things were getting hot and heavy between the pair on the couch. I turned my head. A saint deserves privacy as much as the next guy.

A fat Italian man, certainly no saint, more in the realm of a priest gone ribald with life's possibilities, pulled me toward him. The pull was a wade through warm Jell-O. He was skin-rich, and his laugh made no sound, but I could feel it. He kissed me, and I loved the taste of him, an electric eel teaching me to live and take care of myself in the middle of pain. I understood—it was possible. I wanted to eat him whole. I did. Then he slid out the other side of me, twisting. I sighed beneath his cold-glass skin gone hard, listening to countless confessions drift to the ceiling. Plenty of joy. Even inside the pain of confession, there was joy. The secret of the saints.

Another hard jolt, an aftershock. Our glass ripped like torn cellophane. The black man fell off Joan of Arc, his loss twisting his face sour, full of grief. He reached out once, stretching his arm, trying to take her with him. Too late. She was left with the wise man, each terrified, for different reasons, to lose the man tumbling to the floor. I held close to my bawdy priest, wrapping my body tight around his. When the next temblor hit, we dropped to the floor of the church.

The fallen black saint was slipping between the cracks in the wood floor, no way to save him. He'd been lost when he let go of Joan. Joan and the wise man, still above us, were holding hands, curling in the glass-turned-cellophane. They were rippled with heat, edges burning. The fire jumped beyond the frame, licking the walls of the church. Sweating and afraid, I was as wet as if I'd slipped in a rainstorm and couldn't get up. I heard drumming, it was the footsteps of my round priest following them into the fire. I found my legs. I ran to save him. Lost in smoke, I followed his sound until there was nothing left to follow. The church kept shaking.

But there was no earthquake, and there was no church. No sainted lovers, no alchemists changing people's pain to newborn, wriggling life. When I awoke, I was sprawled across Mina's Hide-A-Bed, my grown daughter sitting on the edge of the mattress, shaking my shoulders as gently as powdered plaster falling from the ceiling.

She asked, "Are you asleep?"

I tugged my eyes into blurry focus. "Not anymore."

"Sorry."

"GADS." I rubbed my eyes. "I was trapped for all eternity inside a church."

"Peaceful."

"Terrible. I was part of the building, a solid chunk of fired cherry Jell-O. Then there was incredible sex, loving saints, and a burning church."

"Your idea of hell is being stuck inside a burning church after great sex. It figures."

"I'm sure it's only one of my many personal versions of hell. What are you doing here?"

In the half dark her face glowed pale. She said, "I came in late and fell asleep in Mina's extra room. Then I had The Dream."

"Flying monkeys from *The Wizard of Oz* . . ."

"I woke up," she said, "and thought I saw their shadows outside my window." E. B. rested her head between her hands. "This is too pathetic," she said. "A bad dream, and I run to Mom."

"I should never have let you see that movie. You've been dreaming about those damned monkeys since you were five."

"You didn't know it would scar me for life. I'm going back downstairs."

One of the downsides of parenthood—the ability to scar someone for life. One of the downsides of raising someone to speak their mind—they show you the scars.

"Sure you're okay?"

"I'm fine." She looked around the room strewn with popcorn and a pizza box and videotapes. "Could I just crawl into bed with you for a few minutes?"

My daughter is six inches taller than I am. I put my arm around her, we arranged ourselves, and she snuggled into the covers, falling toward sleep. I was glad for the company, but I was not about to risk sleep and another shot at being a religious one-dimensional object gone wild. I lay awake, staring at the ceiling. Mistake. Opaque saints floated peacefully above me.

"E. B.," I said, shaking my daughter, pointing to the ceiling, "open your eyes and tell me what you see."

She opened her eyes a tiny crack. "Eggshell white paint splattered with spiders."

"No, the saints. Flying overhead."

"Mom? They're all yours."

My voice was a hushed, sleeping virgin. "Did you know the

word *hag* originally meant a woman who studies saints and miracles?"

In reply, E. B. rolled over and stuck her head under a pillow. I answered her reply with my elbow.

"If you'd *really* wake up," I said, "you'd see them hovering above us."

She flung aside the pillow, rolled onto her back, and propped her eyes wide open, using her fingers. "Nothing, but if it makes you happy," she said, "I'll start calling you a hag."

"Go back to sleep."

She did.

I watched the saints' slow procession, weightless as water above me. That night I had been torn and shaped by colored glass. I had become part of sacred architecture and spinning, sacred lust. Trapped with a few religious icons, I'd heard their love, and I'd witnessed their deaths. Then I saw them float, soft as smoke, above my head, through the ceiling. Up to the heavens.

I waved good night to the saints. One turned and winked at me, and my dreamscape became a total blank for five solid hours.

Next morning, E. B. sat at Mina's kitchen table drinking coffee, sketching in her notebook. Mina brewed herbs on the stove. E. B. apologized for waking me during the night. I looked over her shoulder, catching a glimpse of her work.

I said, "Forget what I said about letting you see those flying monkeys. Without your psychic scar, you might not have your art."

"Do you believe that?"

"I'm glad you have an outlet—leave it at that."

She laughed, but I wasn't kidding. Keep that clutter stuffed in your closet, and you could be looking at real trouble.

Jimmy was still asleep upstairs, clutching an old stuffed bear. There was a taste, not quite as strong as a taste, more like a tease, of spring in the air. Something sensuous, something whispering, *You have survived another winter* . . . I leaned in Mina's doorway, drinking my coffee. Soon I'd be ready to face Flora Light.

An excited hum cruised the early alleys. Chinese New Year's decorations were going up, and red envelopes filled store windows. People wore their smiles a little wider. They were welcoming the year of the monkey, something I wouldn't mention to E. B. Something I wouldn't have to mention. Soon posters of monkeys would be everywhere. She'd probably leave sooner than planned.

Mina stood in the doorway with me, a touchy, restless animal. She gave the street a quick up-and-down. She sipped her brew, and it smelled god-awful. Three neighbors stood on ladders, stretching a banner above the alley. A giant blessing for this new year—a five-foot monkey wearing a red smile, a red bottom, and a curved tail surrounded by laughing paper children.

"You know," Mina said, tapping the side of her mug with a freshly manicured fingertip, "monkeys are complex creatures. Not as frightening as humans, what animals are? I'm not sure monkeys even eat meat. But they're devious. A vegetarian monkey could change its mind any minute, and I always think those baboons would have sex with anything. Are baboons monkeys?"

E. B. swacked her sketchbook closed and climbed the stairs. Probably finding her purse. I'd suggest we meet later at the Bay View. The room was, after all, paid for. I still harbored a fantasy of spending quality time together, with or without a lobster.

Yep, here she came, footsteps down the stairs, heading straight for us and the front door. If I were surrounded by images of my life-long nightmare, I'd leave, too.

I handed her the Bay View room key. "Why don't we meet at the hotel?"

"I think I'll catch up with friends for a few days, then go home. You need to hang around long enough to make sure Jimmy's okay."

"Jimmy's not going to take that long."

She looked at her grandmother, considering, I was certain, all the time-eating possibilities involved with Mina and a kid.

"Let's play it by ear," she said. "You have your cell?"

"Yes. Call me."

I understood, she understood, and we kissed good-bye. E. B. walked to her car—the very car that had delivered me to Mina's. I had too often been in her presence without means of escape. I'd take care of the crazies ASAP. Then I'd rescue Jimmy, even if it meant adopting him. A twelve-year-old boy with a supernatural gift and a talent for explosives was a piece of cake compared to Madame Mina.

I asked Mina for directions to Flora's church.

"Right at the edge, where Chinatown meets the girlie shows at North Beach. In the big old building."

"Near City Lights?"

"I don't know what that is."

"Ferlinghetti's bookstore."

"Black-and-white posters on the walls with poems that don't rhyme?"

"Right . . . You've gone inside the bookstore?"

"Once. By mistake. I thought it was a dress store. Some guy was in the window changing the display. He was wearing a nice dress. I went inside to shop, and we started talking. That's when I found out he was a man, and the place wasn't a dress store."

"Which big old building is Flora's?"

"Next to the good Italian bakery on Columbus. The person who owns it has one of the cutest behinds I've ever seen. I'm certain he's a man."

Maybe I'd stop in for calories and caffeine. You can't have too much of either, and a nice behind is a bonus.

"Hey. When you see Flora Light," Mina said, "don't mention that you know me."

"You two have a run-in?"

"Sort of. She pretends she has the only hot line to the Great Unknown, and it makes me mad."

"What did you do? Tell her to go to hell?"

"Don't drink any more coffee. It makes you kind of goofy," Mina said, patting my head. "I haven't said anything too rude, but it's coming. I put a bumper sticker on my car to ward her off—it made me feel better."

"You marred your beloved Lincoln?"

"This was important. The sticker says, *God, protect me from your followers.*"

"I like it."

"I have nothing against God, but his groupies drive me nuts."

Mina underestimated Flora. She was no groupie. She was God's saleswoman of the year, putting a marketing spin on everything from money to misery.

I set my coffee cup down and slung my purse over my shoulder. "Don't let Jimmy escape."

"No problem."

"He's a special kid."

"You've only seen his present, but I've seen his future. I'm not letting one thing happen to him."

She bustled around the kitchen, making tea, pulling out herbs.

"Mina," I said, "do you have clients coming?"

"Mercury must be retrograde. I'm booked solid all day."

"You know what? I'm taking Jimmy to Hao and Ike's."

She turned around, slow and thoughtful. "I guess that's okay," she said, "but tell them to watch every person who comes into their shop. Bad things are waiting for the entire family."

"I'll pick Jimmy up when I'm finished with Flora, then I'll disappear him for a little while."

"Watch yourself at that woman's place. If her idea of God rubs off on you, take a shower before you come back here telling me I'm going to rot in hell."

If I ever told Mina she was going to hell, I'd be several continents away. And I'd do it by telegram.

"You know what?" I said. "I think hell is just the inner city of heaven."

"What does that mean?"

"That death used to be a very pleasant place until an interstate called DinkyMinds tore through, dividing it in half. The inner section became hell, the suburbs became heaven. Before the interstate," I said, "everyone spent death together in one, big happy community."

Mina lit another cigarette. "Boy, those were the good old days."

Seven

Music sets up a certain vibration that unquestionably results in a physical reaction. Eventually the proper vibration for every person will be found and utilized.

—George Gershwin

When harmony in the universe is lacking, disaster comes to the world. When harmony in the body is out of whack, that person gets sick or dies. If someone you know is sick, and you don't know why, apply guitar music and dance, dance, dance. . . .

—*The Gypsy Guide to Wisdom*
Zlato Milos, 1902

*E*ast on Waverly, north up Stockton, it was only a three-block walk to Hao and Ike's shop. Jimmy didn't say much, but he seemed happy. Mina had filled him with Trix cereal. He'd dropped a packet of Pop Rocks into his third bowl, and the green-and-pink milk fizzled and sputtered. Mina clutched her chest, certain his food had been possessed.

Morning street life unfolded without tourists. Temples and alleys yawned and opened their shutters. Herbalists and vegetable vendors swept sidewalks and chatted. Two old men sat on folding chairs outside a market, passing a newspaper back and forth. A sexy poster of actress Zhang Ziyi was taped to their window. A couple of housewives argued over barrels of white peaches, litchi, and bitter melon. New Year's excitement made people a little more mouthy, a little more everything.

Jimmy wanted figs, and I gave him a few bucks. We passed beneath a market's doorway festooned with figures of children, protecting us from flying devils. A Chinese woman sold him the figs.

She wore a red T-shirt decorated with a flying bullet that read, *Today may be the first day of the end of your life.* I didn't clown around with her.

The woman spoke to Jimmy in Chinese. He answered her, making a funny face. She laughed, handing him a red envelope. Speaking English, she told me that Jimmy was a smart boy, very smart. She said all children born in the year of the monkey are full of energy and mischief. Very loyal.

The Chinese New Year's celebration happens during the second new moon after winter solstice. A spring festival, it's a time to sweep away grievances, to wear gold for wealth and red for luck in the coming year. Good children receive red envelopes filled with money, and all children are good. Fireworks, firecrackers . . . I noticed Jimmy eyeballing a box of stink bombs. I tugged him out of the store, his mouth filled with two ripe figs.

We walked up to Jackson, acting silly. Jimmy stopped two storefronts down from his uncles' shop. He cocked his head and stood frozen, his arm stretched in front of me.

"Hear that?" His voice was reverent and full, the voice of someone struck numb by the sound of an ancient organ huddling in a cathedral.

I listened. What I heard was a busted garbage disposal of churning city noise. I shook my head. "I hear everything. Nothing."

"Listen," he said. "Those sirens, maybe two or three blocks over. They're coming this way."

Sirens are urban wallpaper—everywhere. I tried harder. Then I had them.

Jimmy looked at me with an age older than mine. "You'll never hear those two tones again. Not exactly like that. Put your hand on your stomach."

I did.

He put his hand over mine. "Is this where you feel the siren sounds?"

"I hear them, I don't feel . . ."

But I did feel them, and my insides vibrated. Baby churgles, but very real.

"Sounds rattle us," he said, "and it happens every minute. Sometimes that's why we have headaches. A sound jiggles the inside of our heads, and it causes pain until our tissues slip back into place."

Tossing his backpack on the sidewalk, he found a pack of Fun-Snaps. He pulled out three powdered wads and hid them inside the doorway of Qi Dragon.

"When Uncle greets us, he'll step on these."

Jimmy hollered hello, and his uncle walked through the shop and around the gunpowder snaps.

"I know your tricks," he said, ruffling Jimmy's hair.

Smiling, Ike said that no introductions were necessary, he knew all about me. That's about the last thing anyone wants to hear from a stranger. I didn't see Hao, and I asked for him.

"Every morning," Ike said, "like clockwork, Hao walks these streets listening to life. He pretends he doesn't like gossip, but he does."

Jimmy said, "Hao even likes hearing people fight. He thinks it's funny."

"Me, I like quiet," Ike said, raising his arms to the benevolent and quiet sky above his roof, smiling to that distant country of gentle blue.

"Uncle Ike Qi hears like me," Jimmy said. "There is never *really* quiet."

"You talk too much. Go out back and play."

"Does out back have a fence?" I asked.

Ike said, "Today *out back* is the kitchen. Okay, Jimmy?"

Ike walked with him to the rear of the house, speaking to him in Cantonese. I didn't understand the words, but I understood the tone. *There are plenty of chores, stay out of trouble. I'm worried about you . . .* All tones of parent love are the same and the words are incidental.

While they talked, I explored. Dried herbs stored in jars and wooden barrels. Very few signs in English, most written in Chinese characters with prices taped to containers. Some items were pricey, $1,200 for a bird's nest. Ginseng, $5.99 a pound—must have been a bumper crop that year.

No mistaking one barrel's contents, and if you didn't believe your imagination, you could read the sign—it was written in plain English: Dried Deer Penis. The wooden barrel was loaded with them, and they weren't cheap. Neither is Viagra, and I assumed they were for the same thing. Shark fins, antlers, scores of items for increased fertility and virility. Look at the population of China—you can't argue with success. I picked up a penis. It was the color of a dried apricot. I turned it in my hand.

Behind my right shoulder, Ike said, "Would you like that?" He was wearing a sassy grin.

I put the penis down. "No thanks."

"Maybe a gift for your boyfriend?"

"How did you do that? I didn't even hear you coming."

"Your mind was occupied."

Jimmy's shadow crossed the doorway, and the mischievous gleam ran out of Ike's eyes. He drew the curtain closed between his shop and the kitchen, as if the fabric could cover our voices.

"Jimmy tells me that you want to come back for him after you talk to the preacher. But I don't know you, and suddenly everyone wants Jimmy."

"It's my fault," I said. "If I could take back the article I wrote about him, I would."

He waved his hand as if erasing a blackboard. "Please, no fault. Guilt makes for bad decisions and bad actions."

He tapped his chin with the tip of his index finger. "Even a stranger can earn trust. No guilt here, but there is responsibility and obligation."

Uh-oh. I had a feeling I was going to prefer guilt to obligation.

"Jimmy isn't safe in our home," he said. "I'm certain of that."

"Ike, I'm confused. Should I come back for Jimmy and watch him, just for a little while, or not?"

"He's not easy. He's everywhere at once."

"You and Hao do it."

"We love Jimmy. Would you mind giving me your right hand?"

Standing in a store filled with shark fins, birds' nests, antlers, and assorted anatomical parts made his request seem normal. His shop made lots of things seem normal.

Crooking my arm, Ike placed my hand in the center of my chest, putting his hand over mine. He laid his left hand on my lower back and he hummed. Rhythmic, a human drum. I felt him deep along my thighs and legs. Higher, lighter, inside my chest. He shifted his voice several notes lower, and my head buzzed.

"Look at your beautiful back . . . you love music. Use it for yourself and for Jimmy," Ike said. "He heals, but he also needs healing."

I started to tell him that none of this was my concern. Or problem.

Ike placed one finger over my lips. "Hush. You have no choice in this."

He chanted again, two notes at once. Looking into Ike's eyes, I was fully connected to him and to my blood and to my bones and every strange bin in the shop. Falling into a primal world, far away, and mine alone. I had no desire to stop the fall.

"I feel memories," I said, "and an empty ache."

"Your bones are letting go of secrets, bringing you to truth. Let that be."

I let that be.

Corridors stretched, and I heard whispers whirling down halls, around rooms, and out shattered windows. Beyond the windows, I heard orchards grow and shed their fruit, a landslide, an ocean slapping sand against a pool of starfish. Hungry, salty mouths. Love like a cannon spewing fire, a storm-torn river tearing up trees and boulders. Fire and water, the end of life, circling back to the beginning of silence. One breath, one sound was born, a low hum, close to the ancient om, and *in the beginning was the word* . . .

It all started, it all ended, and it was all due to start again. I got the picture.

I found my voice. "Ike, is Jimmy outside time when he chants people to health? The truth."

Ike laughed, small and delighted. "Now you want truth, good for you," he said. "Here it is—forget time, it's everywhere at once. Each life has its own force. Music, all sound, lifts that force up, and it lets it down. Jimmy's music is a miracle, a river. He uses it like a baptism, cleansing the spirit. This baptism is our healing tool."

"How'd you teach this to a kid?"

"I've learned much of what I know from Jimmy. After I grew up, my brain got in the way. Jimmy doesn't realize what he's doing, and I want to keep it that way as long as possible. You understand?"

"I don't understand one thing."

I wasn't kidding. And I was beginning to believe Mina had underestimated the number of kooks in Jimmy's life.

"The technique is simple," he said. "We tone a healing vibration that realigns the diseased body part. We're very careful. A slight wobble or too much volume can be a disaster."

Two aging men were raising one young man who could hum a human being into health or obliteration. I wasn't sure anyone was up to the task.

"Where are his parents?"

Ike sighed. "His father is our nephew. He left our culture far behind, and he was a negligent parent."

"He just sort of gave Jimmy to you?"

"When Jimmy arrived at an emergency room, our address was in his pocket. We'd seen him the month before, and we were worried, telling him to keep the paper in his pocket at all times. We said it was a lucky charm.

"They called us. When we arrived at the hospital, Hao cried— I'd never seen him do that. We barely recognized Jimmy. Lying on a cot in the ER hallway, he was sucking his thumb, rocking, humming. Malnutrition, living on the streets for two weeks, and five years old.

"A social worker buzzed by, saying Jimmy would be taken someplace. We asked where. Juvenile detention, then a foster home. Reading her clipboard, filling out her forms, she told us not to worry, rules had changed, rubber bullets were no longer used to keep children under control. They only used Mace, and soon they'd get rid of mesh cages. Zip, zip, paperwork finished, and she was gone."

Ike made a face and swallowed; something bitter was in his mouth. I tasted it, too.

"When the coast was clear, we wrapped Jimmy in a blanket, carrying him out of the hospital. Any stranger could have taken him. We gave him a home, and we healed him. Hao used herbs and food, I used music and toning bells. He became our Jimmy.

"Someday he'll be a great healer. Now, for a reason we don't understand, you've come into Jimmy's life. I've heard your heart, and I know you'll be good for Jimmy. Hao's a dragon—he thinks nothing will get Jimmy while he's on guard. Typical dragon arrogance." Ike said, "We can use your help."

"My hands are tingling," I said, "and my scalp and back. How did you do that?"

Ike ignored me. "Jimmy wants to please people too much, that's no good. He needs protection, and he must also learn self-control."

"You know he blows things up, right?"

"I believe he likes the sound."

"You're kidding."

Ike laughed. "Jimmy is a mystery."

No mystery there, Jimmy liked causing trouble. I looked at my watch, remembering Hao. This was an awfully long stroll around the neighborhood.

"Shouldn't Hao be home?"

A cloud crossed Ike's face. "Another worry. Our pasts won't make Jimmy's future easier."

"Okay," I said, "keep a leash on that kid until I get back. I'll watch him until the dust clears. Hopefully, I won't collapse."

Ike told me I was funny, but I wasn't kidding.

I heard Jimmy rustling around the kitchen, standing near the curtain. He'd probably heard every word. I was digging in the bottom of my purse for my lipstick—how it always gets stuck inside the lining, I don't know—when Ike turned me around and did his eyeball-to-eyeball thing again.

"You know that you're the Red Empress, a fertility goddess?"

"WHAT!"

"I mean in the way of helping people birth their true natures and teaching them how to nurture themselves."

"Ike, excuse me for saying this, but you are slightly out of your mind."

Handing me a dried deer penis, Ike said, "When you see Mina, give this to her. She likes me either way, in or out. Of my mind, that is."

Jimmy was a rascal, and it was obviously genetic. I hadn't blushed in years, but I could feel hot pink running up my neck, spreading across my cheeks like a case of chicken pox.

Jimmy sauntered in from the kitchen, sucking back a grin.

"Any message for Flora?" I asked Jimmy.

He didn't have to think long. "Tell her that I like her, but not what she wants me to do. It's too hard."

"Do I hear another *but,* or an *and* in there?"

"And I want her to leave me alone."

So far so good. Jimmy and I were straight with each other, and our position on Flora was the same. This might work.

"Ike," I said, "now that you've been inside my skin, can I ask you a personal question?"

"Sure."

"How'd you get your name?"

"I may be the only Chinese-American named after Dwight David Eisenhower. A genuine war hero—my parents loved him."

We laughed together. Ike, still laughing, said, "Please give Flora a message for me, too." His laughter stopped dead in its tracks. "Tell her I would kill anyone who hurts Jimmy."

Eight

Between two latex-infested adult stores, directly across from Ferlinghetti's bookshop, stood the Church of All Light, a beautiful gray-stone dowager. It was the former home of two churches and one temple that had dispensed religion and moved on.

I rattled the front doorknob. It was locked. I walked around the side of the church and read a sign planted in the grass: *Do you think God has forgotten you? Sorry—you're wrong.* I didn't know if that was supposed to cheer me or scare me. The side doors were locked, too. Steps climbing up the rear of the building to an office door were boarded up.

Walking around to the front again, looking at that sign, I decided my best shot for a happy eternity was if I simply fell through the cracks in God's memory.

This time I gave the front door a two-fisted pounding. A blowzy woman answered, puffy bags and smudged mascara under her eyes. She was struggling into a white robe. If it was intended to impart a heavenly aura, it missed the mark.

No words, but she tried on a smile. Even that looked bleary and distracted.

I said, "Are you Flora Light?"

"Dear, services aren't until tomorrow evening. Sunday mornings and evenings, Wednesday nights."

She handed me a brochure, turned, and started to close the door. Jimmy's face was on the front of her brochure, black-and-white vague, smiling like a milk-carton kid. Under his picture was a caption that read, *Jimmy Qi heals body and spirit, thanks to the Almighty.* Suggested donations for healing sessions, guided by Flora, were printed along the bottom. No surprise—the prices were Bay Area astronomical. Checks and credit cards were accepted, all payable to Flora's church. Over the ages, the Almighty has chosen some pretty interesting bankers.

I pushed my way inside, shutting the door behind me. "This can't wait, Flora."

I didn't know what I was going to say, but I was sure it would be blasphemous. I wanted her holy walls to receive the full impact.

Flora called toward the back of the church. "Wagner?"

"Is Wagner a bodyguard?"

"Wagner!"

A large black man appeared. He looked as if he'd just crawled from Flora's smudgy love nest, the mist of her Jungle Gardenia cologne clinging to him. I watched their body language, complete with a string of meaningful looks and mute expressions. I had the impression that guarding her body was not Wagner's number one duty.

I grinned and stuck out my hand. "Hi, Wagner," I said. "I've come with a warning for Flora."

He stuck out his hand, and we shook.

"Wagner, for God's sake!"

"Flora," I said, "this kid who's pictured in your brochure."

"Jimmy."

"He's my . . ."

My what? I should have worked this out with Ike before I'd left the shop. Forget Ike. I should have worked this out with myself.

"I'm Jimmy's social worker." I'd have to remember to tell Ike and Hao who I was.

She said, "Jimmy never mentioned . . ."

"Why would he? This is just a warning, a strong warning, but you may find yourself in trouble because of Jimmy."

"What was that?" Wagner said.

"Trouble," I said. "Time to wake up, Wagner."

He pumped the muscles in his arms without moving the rest of his body. I don't know how he did it, but he looked damned good doing it.

I said, "Jimmy's no longer allowed to participate in the events at this facility."

Flora's turn. "This," she said, "is not a facility. It's the house of the Lord. Who says Jimmy can't participate?"

"The State of California, but I'm the one you have to worry about. I can shut you down citing abuse, child labor laws, I don't know, just about anything I feel like tossing in the pot."

"Maybe you should ask for her ID," Wagner said.

Flora was busy being outraged, and she didn't hear her bodyguard's reasonable suggestion. I shut up, hoping she'd spin out of control. I was glad Wagner was there. I had a feeling Flora enjoyed performance art and that Wagner was her front-row fan.

She waved in Wagner's direction. "Go bolt the door."

"Wagner," I said, "don't. By federal law, if you lock me inside a building against my wishes, you are guilty of kidnapping."

I had no idea if that was true, but it sounded right.

Flora nearly shouted at me. "You're the one who pushed your way in here. And this is not a building," she said, "it is a church!"

"Your church may be exempt from federal taxes, but you are not exempt from federal laws."

I did know that was true.

Flora took a deep breath and deflated. It was similar to watching a blowfish lose its steam. "I apologize. It's not like me to fly off the handle. Your arrival disrupted my morning meditation."

I checked out Wagner, and he was closing in on a smirk. Morning meditation was a new euphemism on me. Looked like it was a new one on him, too.

"Do you understand what you're asking Jimmy to give up?" she said. "Wagner, would you bring us coffee? In the office?"

Yes, Wagner, and let's hope your robe stays stuck to your bottom because you look very nice from behind. Right then I was certain there was a God.

I followed Flora to the front of the church, weaving between rows of pews. I walked behind the altar, down a hall, and up eight stairs to a plush and private office. Flora asked me to take a seat while she dressed. She disappeared behind a deep red velvet curtain, and I settled into an overstuffed leather chair. She could take all the time she needed. My feet were killing me, and it really wasn't fair to verbally assault a woman wearing no makeup and the previous night's perfume.

I kept up a running conversation with Flora, asking questions that required answers. I didn't want her skipping out through a back window. Unless she left Wagner. I was beginning to wonder if, through osmosis, I'd absorbed a few chemical wonders from the dried deer penis. I felt pretty frisky.

Wagner brought coffee. He straddled the chaise lounge as if it were a kitchen chair, rearranging himself more than once. Difficult to manage the guard dog routine while sitting upon a water-silk chaise.

Flora flung the curtain open, entering her office with a flourish. I swear she must have applied glitter; she was positively radiant. I hadn't approached radiance, not in a room by myself, for quite a number of years.

"Now that we've relaxed . . . Pardon me, what was your name?"

A social worker's name. "Margaret Little," I told her.

Turning to Wagner, she said, "When faced with a dilemma, we find it helpful to pray." She offered one of her hands to him. She held out her other hand to me. Her pale skin was highlighted by a couple of liver spots.

"I don't want to hold hands with you," I said, "and I can't pray. You understand, separation of church and state. I'd get into trouble with my supervisor."

"We all must answer to a Higher Power."

"My boss thinks he *is* the higher power," I said. "Truth is, I've only prayed when desperate. Assuming there's someone up there fielding all those messages, that doesn't seem quite fair. So I quit praying."

"Maybe we can help restore your faith."

I said, "Let's cut the celestial baloney and talk about Jimmy."

"He's part of God's plan."

"Aren't we all," Wagner said, a note of sarcasm edging his voice. I didn't think he was any more comfortable with Flora's heavenly business than he was sitting on the silk couch. She narrowed her eyes in his direction, but Wagner held his ground. His furniture.

Flora said, "Jimmy was sent here to heal."

"And you collect money for his services."

"Donations are made to the church. It's a way of showing gratitude for Jimmy's gift."

"Does Jimmy get money from you?"

She was deciding if the state would be happier if Jimmy received money from the church, or if he didn't. I certainly didn't know.

"I buy Jimmy clothes," she said.

"Bought him one jacket," Wagner said.

I really liked Wagner. Not for the obvious reason, that he was stunning, but because Wagner was hovering somewhere near reality.

I made a state policy decision. "If you're paying Jimmy, we've got real trouble. He's too young to be employed. Period."

"The clothing was a gift."

"Not clothing, just one jacket," Wagner reminded her.

Flora exhaled her exasperation with me and with her bodyguard. "How far," she said, "are social workers allowed to stick their noses into a person's life?"

"When the person is a kid, the nose is allowed all the way in."

Flora leaned back in her seat. She closed her eyes, pressing her hands together. I watched her, and Wagner watched me. A good thing Wagner was on guard. I had a sudden urge to whomp Flora upside the head. I couldn't be trusted to behave any better inside a church than anywhere else in the world.

Flora prayed out loud, it sort of went on and on, and I tuned out.

She stopped talking to God and started talking to me without missing a beat. She said, "You do know that Jimmy's uncle gave him permission to work with me?"

"Which uncle?"

"Hao, his guardian."

"His uncle Ike asked me to come and get you out of Jimmy's life," I said, "and so did Jimmy." What was wrong with this woman? "Flora, he is a kid."

"Jesus was the same age when he began teaching in the temple."

"What can I tell you? I guess people matured sooner during the first millennium."

Wagner almost laughed, but he caught himself.

Flora stood up. I was dismissed.

She said, "Healing is his duty."

"Have you told him that?"

"Of course. But I believe he comes here because I buy him things his family can't provide. That's not the same thing as a salary, or of knowing your duty."

"He's not working because he wants things. He wants to make you happy, and he wants to help people. But it's too much."

Flora snorted. Suddenly she didn't look so radiant. "He likes the attention he gets. Jimmy is a heathen just like most of his kind."

Wagner's turn to do the eye-narrowing. I was absolutely certain that after I left he would ask her if *his* type were also heathens. Flora was one piece of work.

"About one-third of this city's population is Chinese-American," I said. "That's a healthy chunk of heathen flock."

Flora blanched. "I was not speaking about his ethnic heritage. I was speaking about his lack of spiritual guidance."

"My mistake."

She smiled at me. Reaching over, she squeezed Wagner's hand. He let her squeeze, but he wasn't buying it. If Wagner became available soon, I had any number of friends who'd like to meet him.

Wagner unwrapped himself from the chaise. He caught his foot on one of the scrolled mahogany legs and almost went over.

"Shit!"

"Wagner. Remember where you are."

One reprimand too many, Wagner went frozen-cold. It'd be a while before Flora experienced anything resembling radiance thanks to Wagner's meditative techniques.

"Flora, your flock will have to buy plane tickets to Lourdes instead of sticking money in your collection plate for Jimmy. Are we clear about that?"

"Miss Little, I assume it's *Miss,* this church has friends in every walk of life. Friends who may feel that Social Services has no business here."

I hate it when people pull out their kings and queens too early in the game. It ruins the suspense. But I did want to know something, and I'd just received the final boot, so I asked what I didn't really want to know.

"How did you find Jimmy?"

She looked in her lap. "We needed a healer, and Jimmy appeared. Divine intervention."

"She read about the kid in *The Eye*," Wagner said. "She never misses an issue."

I felt the weight of obligation heavy on my back, and I willed Ike's voice to be still.

When I walked out, leaving the two alone, the quiet between them was dense. The mother of all arguments had been placed on hold until they were sure I was gone.

I opened the front door. Jimmy was sitting on the church steps, waiting for me.

Nine

$\mathcal{H}$e was hungry. We stopped for kid fuel.

I tried calling Qi Dragon to let them know Jimmy was with me. The shop's phone was busy. Two more tries, the phone rang through. Ike sounded strained, distant, and unconcerned about Jimmy. About anything. I did my duty, told him Jimmy was safe, and that we'd stop and get his clothes, enough for a few days. I felt Ike's relief, but I still felt the strain. Something was wrong, but Ike would have to buck up and be okay. I could only handle one ordeal at a time.

I had a temporary plan for Jimmy. He'd hole up with me at the Bay View, play video games, and I'd get busy, wrapping up the last, straggly ends of work. My hotel wasn't within walking distance of Flora's church; that was a bonus. I didn't know if Hao had given Jimmy permission to work for Flora. If he had, I didn't like it. And I still wanted a small slice of quality time with my daughter. I hoped, given the wharf's lack of monkeys, she would show up.

I called her next. "I can't hear you," E. B. said. "My phone's been funky since I dropped it."

She said she'd find a real phone, one with a cord. One minute, two, then my cell rang. There was E. B., loud and clear, and there was a familiar number on my phone's tiny screen. The 415 area code; she was still in San Francisco.

Before I could ask where she was, she said, "Where are you?"

"McDonald's in Chinatown, but I spent the morning in church."

Silence.

"Are you there?"

"Still a bad connection," she said. "I thought you told me you'd gone to church. Then I thought you said McDonald's, and I imagined a huge wire sculpture called *McJesus and Fries.*"

"Forget the sculpture," I said, "and church wasn't a total loss. There was a terrific-looking man there."

"What about Leo?"

"Sometimes members of the opposite sex are like museum-quality art; they're nice to look at, but it doesn't mean you're taking them home. You want to have lunch?"

"I haven't eaten breakfast yet."

"It's almost noon."

"Late night. But, sure, let's get together."

"I'll come pick you up."

"That won't work."

"You're not a teenager, and I don't care what you're up to. I just want to see you," I said. "I won't even mention lobster."

"You can't pick me up because I drove us to Mina's, and you probably don't have your own car," she said. "You are such a drama queen."

In this case, guilty as charged. "Meet me at Mina's. We'll have Jimmy with us, so no place fancy."

"Mom, why were you at church? You didn't go there to ogle men."

"True," I said. "Wagner was a happy accident. You know that Buddhist saying, *If you meet the Buddha on the road, kill him?*"

"Sure."

"One more self-proclaimed Buddha, this one's a television evangelist, and I tried to deep-six her on behalf of Jimmy."

"Good for you."

"I don't think I was successful."

"Can't get all the bad guys," she said. "I'll see you in a few." E. B. hung up.

A few what? Minutes, hours . . . Days? I hadn't asked her if she was dressed yet. My guess was *not*. I'd count on seeing my daughter when I saw her. When I was her age, I certainly didn't check in with my mother. When I was her age, I had three tiny kids. I still hadn't figured out how that had happened.

Ten

I bought a green tea soda pop, taking the first glug at the counter. It was too sweet and I didn't drink it. Jimmy didn't want it, either.

I'd made the clerk unhappy. "You don't like the tea drink?"

"It's kind of sweet."

"You still got to pay for it."

"Not a problem."

"People order things and if they don't like them, they don't want to pay. We're not giving away free stuff around here."

I handed her two bucks, telling her to keep the change and the attitude.

Walking the streets, I noticed each new decoration going up or coming down. People ignored commerce—something remarkable in Chinatown. Families and friends gathered inside shops, watching satellite television direct from China. We stood inside one shop, joining four others in front of a thirteen-inch television. Hard to imagine Chinese stand-up comedy, but the locals were laughing their heads off. Two solid weeks of preparation for that night. Excitement was burbling like a monsoon-heavy sky, and the climax was approaching.

My cell phone rang again. Probably E. B. telling me she was just getting into the shower.

I said, "Hi, Honey."

"What's all that laughing?"

"Is this Mina?"

"Yes. Don't call me 'honey' again. It scares me."

"What do you want?"

"I have a break between clients. Mrs. Dok just canceled. You want to go out for lunch?"

"I just ate, and I'm waiting for E. B. We're going out to breakfast or lunch. I think."

"Good. We'll eat and wait for her together."

"I'll be there in two blocks," I said, pressing the *end* button.

"I've never spent much time around grown-up ladies," Jimmy said. "You sure eat a lot."

The dining room was packed with round tables, each with a lazy Susan loaded with bottles of sparkling cider, ginger ale, and Johnny Walker Red. Mina ordered four items from the menu. They spread out, taking over the table. After Jimmy finished eating, he played with the steamed chicken's feet, dancing them around his plate. I made him stop. It was disgusting.

He pulled out his handheld GameBoy. Since he was busy, it seemed like a good time to present Mina with her gift from Ike.

She turned it over in her hands and smiled. "He is so romantic," she said. "What kind of smile is that on your face?"

"I'm wishing I wrote fiction so I could create a scene where I handed someone a deer penis over lunch."

"You write for *The Eye*. You want to tell me there's a big difference between that and fiction? What happened when you saw Flora Light?"

I ran down our meeting, telling Mina I'd lied, saying I was a social worker. Mina was amazed that I'd come up with a false identity so quickly. I gave her the credit, saying my snappy lie was due to spending too much time around her. She took it as a compliment and patted my cheek. Sometimes being on Mina's good side is as bad as being on her bad side.

"I told Flora that Jimmy wasn't allowed to work for her anymore."

"He shouldn't be working for her, but it's a good thing for a kid to earn a little spending money."

"Mina, he didn't get one dime, and Flora is taking in a lot more than pocket change for his work."

"How much more?"

"We're talking thousands of dollars per healing."

Mina played with her food and sighed. "Pretending I could translate the language of God, raking in all that dough . . . I never had it in me to be such a big phony. Boy," she said, "what an idiot."

"You could still do it if you wanted to."

She didn't believe me, but it cheered her up.

"Flora said she has San Francisco money-muscle behind her," I said. "She made it clear that she knew what she wanted, and nobody was going to get in her way."

"I've got plenty of my own connections, but here's what makes someone in her line of work successful—she's ruthless. That requires concentration. My attention wanders, and I lose interest," Mina said. "I wonder if we need to worry about her getting mean."

"I have a queasy feeling that it's a possibility."

When the check landed on our table, Mina pulled out a wad of cash from the front of her blouse. Who knew what she had hidden in that brassiere? It was only a bit smaller than a Korean car cover.

"We'd better get going," I said. "Ike and Hao will think Jimmy ditched me."

She smiled at Jimmy, pinching his cheek between two fingers. "The best people are a handful when they're kids."

"Speaking of kids, I think E. B.'s avoiding me. Did I do something to tick her off?"

"You're her mother—that always ticks kids off," Mina said. "Where was she when you last talked?"

"A San Francisco number. It came up on my cell phone."

"So, call her up and tell her to get moving. Being embarrassed about having a mother is one thing. Being rude about it is something else."

"How embarrassing would *that* be to have your mother call?"

"Give me the phone. Grandmothers aren't embarrassing."

Pressing the *recall* button, E. B.'s last number came up on the display.

"This is where she called you from?"

"Yep." I pressed the *send* button.

A few seconds passed. Mina spoke into the phone. She said, "Uh-huh. Okay. All right. Make it snappy. Bye."

A pretend conversation, no one on the other end, staged for my benefit. Mina had recognized the phone number, too. Unlike me, she knew who it belonged to.

"She says something came up, she was about to call you, she'll do her best, but don't wait for her."

"Okay," I said.

"Sounds like a new romance." Mina looked at her watch. "YIPES! I've got to run. There is a pair of new clients, and the one I talked to sounded old. Old people think if you're fifteen minutes early, you're coming in just under the wire."

I was zapped by intuition. "Is the pair a set of aging twins?"

"When someone calls and makes an appointment, I don't ask a lot of questions. I just get a credit card number so I can charge them if they don't show up. If they're twins, they'll pay double. You don't get off paying for one person just because you look alike."

We parted, Mina trotting back to her Palace. Following Jimmy, I trudged up the hill to the Qi brothers, my lungs aching. I told myself I'd feel better if I stopped smoking. Then I remembered that

I'd quit twenty years before. When you've dumped an enjoyable habit, time stands still.

Walking into Dragon Qi, I tossed my purse on the counter, and Jimmy threw his backpack in the middle of the floor. It looked as if it weighed twenty pounds, and the kid wasn't even out of breath.

I hallooed to Ike and Hao. Nothing.

We walked up the stairs. Not one thing.

Jimmy turned on the television, switching the channel to All China World. I dialed the shop's number from their home phone, hoping to flush out Ike and Hao. I stood next to their business phone. It rang. It kept ringing, and the empty jangle spun around antler bins, dried eels, and dusty cans of jasmine tea.

"Where the hell is everyone?"

"Maybe they went to a neighbor's house to watch TV."

"Maybe." But I didn't think they'd go anywhere until they'd seen me haul Jimmy to the other side of town.

I walked into their kitchen, and I smelled sweet cologne. Flora? The door at the far end of the kitchen stood open a crack.

"Jimmy, what's behind that door?"

"Our yard. Not a really big yard, a place we park when we have a car. But there's a small fish pond and bamboo, a nice square of grass."

It was a tired door, it was splintered wood, painted red, narrow, with an ancient bronze knob. The knob was wobbly, one screw hanging loose. Jimmy stood next to me. I tried to hold him back, but it was too late.

Hao was lying on his back, round stones by the bubbling pond cradling his body. Ike was toning over Hao, a litany of anguish that picked Ike up from the sidelines of human experience, plopping him smack in the center of it all.

Eleven

I was at Ike's side in one second flat, kneeling over Hao. I felt his wrist, I checked his carotid. A delicate crucifix rested on the place where there should have been a pulse. I worked on his chest—up and down, up and down—no response. No blood on his shirt, none on the stones beneath him. Some red-turning-to-bruise on the side of his neck where he'd hit the stones. Maybe he'd had a heart attack or a stroke.

"Ike. Call 911. Hurry!"

"No strangers," he whispered. "Too late, too late . . . Hao's gone."

"I'm calling."

"We don't do that." Ike's eyes lit fire. "Outsiders are trouble."

"They might be able to save him."

But searching again for a pulse, feeling Hao's skin cooling, I knew Ike was right. Too late, too late . . .

I put my arm around Ike. "What happened to him?"

Ike pushed me away. He squatted on his haunches, rocking, singing, chanting sounds and words. Ike's eyes closed. He turned silent, then he began again. The new music he chanted crawled under my skin and into a dark cave, making my blood ache to be born again, causing me to lose time and trouble and place.

The place Ike had crawled to with his brother, dragging me along with him, frightened me. I placed my hand on his shoulder, lighter than the weight of a dragonfly's wing.

"Ike?"

He came back just long enough to instruct me.

"Please be quiet," Ike said. "Sounds that surround our body at the time of death are our soul's living blanket. The sound wraps us, carrying us to a city by cool waters, the place we reside after death. Chants remind the newly dead that they are no longer alive. As my voice grows dimmer, Hao's soul will understand it is moving away from the earth. It's necessary for peaceful transition—he'll know his death isn't a dream."

"Ike, Hao's body . . . someone has to get him for Jimmy. This is too much."

"I've been walking the bridge between life and death since I was a child," he said. "I won't leave my own brother unattended."

Last I remembered, Jimmy was standing next to me in the kitchen doorway. I looked around, expecting to see him in a small corner of the garden, crying, helping Ike chant Hao home. But I didn't see him. I knew fear, harsh and overbright, and my fear coiled itself around Jimmy.

"Ike!" I yelled in his ear. "Where's Jimmy?"

Lifting his head, Ike slid a note down to a slim A that hummed just behind my ear, the palest of good night kisses.

He repeated to me. "Where is Jimmy?"

"He was right here. Now I don't know where he is."

"You don't know . . ."

"Ike. Take a guess. Please."

Ike came back, raising his eyes to meet mine. "Where is Flora? She was here, angry that you'd gone to her church and started trouble. She thought you were from the government. But she described the woman to me," he said, "and I knew it was you. Do you hear Jimmy crying?"

"I don't hear one damned thing, and I'm scared to death."

"Hao wasn't home when Flora arrived. She was yelling, so I came out here for peace. She followed me, still yelling. Hao walked through the gate from the alley, you see our back gate? It's wonderful to have your own yard. She ran to him. Talking, talking, some yelling. Quiet. I thought they were kissing, making up. I didn't want to spy. Then Hao collapsed."

"Does Jimmy have hiding places?"

Ike was puzzled, hazy. "I thought Jimmy was next to me, singing his uncle home. I guess not."

I put my arms around Ike again, this time he didn't shake me off, and I walked him into the house. I told Ike that I'd had a quick glimpse of Hao, very quick, but I saw him sitting peacefully by a stream. He was home already, smiling and happy to be there.

Ike looked into my face. "Did you see a dragon on his shoulder?"

"No. Only cool water running down both arms."

"Then Hao is happy, content."

"Ike, Hao wants us to find Jimmy. He doesn't want Jimmy to join him."

"I should have thought of that."

But Ike was a shadow puppet, and a shadow puppet can't think. I needed help. I eased Ike into a comfortable chair.

I thought if I rang her phone off the wall, Mina would take a quick break from her fortune-telling session. No luck. I tried again. She'd turned on her answering machine. Slipping into a heavy German accent, I left a message, leaving no name, saying I'd give her ten thousand bucks if she'd see me immediately. I made the message a long one, hinting at more money, giving Mina time to pick up the phone.

"Wait a minute, wait a minute, I'm picking up the phone." She was out of breath. "Whatever your big disaster is, I don't want to take advantage of it. Five thousand, that'll clear my evening for you."

"Mina, it's me."

"Was that you a few minutes ago, too?"

"Yes."

"This better be . . . What's wrong? Is it E. B.?"

"Hao. Mina," I said, no way to soft-pedal it, "he's dead."

"What happened?"

"I don't know, and I don't know what to do with his body. Ike is destroyed, and Jimmy is missing."

"Have Hao's body taken from the house. Jimmy won't come out from under his bed until the body is gone."

"Ike won't let me call 911."

"Of course not," she said. "How long do you think it's been since Hao saw a doctor? Death certificates, autopsies. It's barbaric."

"Who should I call about the body?"

"St. Theresa's Catholic Church, seven blocks away. You remember—the place we went to steal Jerry's body."

"I remember. Are you sure?"

"That Catholic Church has no more use for the government, or paperwork, than you or me or anyone else in Chinatown. They'll take care of Hao in a decent way."

"Mina, Ike said that Flora was there when Hao died. I didn't see her, but I smelled her perfume."

"God help us. I'll get rid of my clients. You were right," she said, "they're twins, and it's a strange session. I'm talking as much as they are. I almost feel like I ought to be paying them."

"Paying *them?* You must be in shock."

"Of course I'm in shock. But they're fun and even older than me. There aren't that many of us left who still have brains and sex appeal." Her voice got small, stretching down a long hall. A child's voice. "Annie, why Hao?"

"Mina, I'll take care of Hao and find Jimmy. You should get rid of the women and rest."

"It's okay." One long blow into a Kleenex. "I can fall apart later. You find Jimmy, and I'll take care of Hao and Ike. Don't let Flora within one solar system of Jimmy. If he's already with her, grab him. Shoot her," she said, "if you can get away with it."

"Don't tempt me. Flora would like Jimmy to be the organ grinder's monkey, picking money off the streets for her."

"Ridiculous. Hao would never stand for that."

"He's not around to stop her anymore."

Twelve

They had always welcomed his words of healing and freedom, but now the women and children supported *him*. He learns the mystery of facing the separation of death.
—*The Eighth Station of the Cross*

We've got to think of death as something we can get through, or else living is too hard. Death is just another place where people eat and drink and make babies and then die. Except that when you die on the other side, you get born again down here. It sounds crazy, but it's true.
—Madame Mina, as learned from her grandmother

Ike was in bad shape. He was back over Hao's body, humming, smiling at him, kissing his forehead. It would only be a matter of minutes before Mina's arrival—she could be depended upon in times of death or natural disasters. And, like me, she didn't want Jimmy on the loose with Flora. I told Ike that Mina would be there soon to keep him company, but he didn't hear me.

No city in the world has hills that are as enthusiastic about their slope as San Francisco. I pulled off my low heels, running to St. Theresa's in my stocking feet. Two women placing delicate bamboo shoots in water gardens pointed at me, laughing. I often admire the freedom with which ridicule is hurled in Chinatown.

I knew of two places to look for Jimmy: Flora's church and St. Theresa's. Flora might have grabbed Jimmy during the confusion at the Qis' home, taking him with her. Jimmy was vulnerable, and he'd need comfort. And St. Theresa's . . . I was counting on the fact that it was the only church in the neighborhood handling death without paperwork. Jimmy would know that's where Ike, and Hao, would eventually show up.

St. Theresa's is small and lovely. Stonemasons built a perfect church, one where silence wore handwoven white cotton, miniature with gracious grandeur, more a cathedral than a church. Fourteen transparent cut-glass windows, and fourteen small alcoves, held the Stations of the Cross. A woman practiced the organ beneath virgins and angels, gold-leafed stars, and the sun painted on a domed ceiling.

Sitting cross-legged, Jimmy was nestled close to the organ inside the eighth station. The niche was small enough to crawl inside without being noticed. Jimmy was another small dark-eyed saint, waiting for a miracle and longing for peace.

The organist paid no attention to me. I walked quietly to Jimmy's nest, climbing inside with him. I was certain no saint or God would be disturbed by a woman with her arms around a child.

One of Jimmy's palms was resting on the inside wall. I put my hand over his and felt the organ's vibration rippling through it, smooth as gentle lupine covering a mountain meadow. Opening his eyes, he sent me his need, and I sent him a holding. You don't often get such clarity with kids. You get it less often with adults.

Together, we were silent. Closing his eyes again, running his hand along the cool plaster, he spoke to me. "I want to crawl inside these walls and live here."

I brushed the hair off his forehead. "Life's not that easy."

"I know," he said. "Neither is death. After I climbed in here, I fell asleep and had a dream."

"What did you dream?"

"Annie? I dreamed I was normal."

I held him against me. We sat, feeling the organ roll its notes up our backs, and I didn't let him go. "Jimmy, normal is not all it's cracked up to be."

"How would *you* know about normal?" He smiled at me.

Whatever normal was, we were getting back to it. I said, "We've got to leave. I don't want Flora to find you."

"She doesn't have one clue where I am."

"Good."

"Is she one of the bad guys?"

"I don't know."

"She was at our house when Hao left the earth. She kept tugging my arm, pulling me out the gate with her. I told her to let me go. She did," he said, "and Flora's a lot bigger than I am. She didn't have to let go."

"Since we don't know the bad guys from the good guys, we have a better chance of keeping you safe if no one knows where you are. No one includes Flora."

He leaned his head against the white plaster wall, staring up at the stained-glass windows. "She bought me a jacket, also a couple of video games."

"That was nice."

"Lots of her friends need help. She's not making that up. Sometimes she asks Hao for herbal medicines for herself," he said. "She doesn't sound so great inside. Flora believes in our skills. Not all white people do."

"Jimmy, she wants you, not Hao."

"I don't know. They liked each other a lot. I thought they might be in love."

"Maybe he let you work at her church because she was especially nice to him."

"He told her it was okay for me to work there, but she had tons of sick people waiting. I couldn't do it, and they got into a fight about me."

Jimmy's voice was squeaky and getting louder. He didn't like the idea of people fighting over him. Who does? The organist looked at us, frowning. Too bad. She was a lot louder than we were.

Jimmy's eyes went wide and huge. "Flora's other boyfriend wouldn't like it if he found out that Flora kissed Hao. Wagner's so big he wouldn't even need a gun to kill someone."

"Jimmy, your uncle was worn-out, and he decided it was time to leave."

I didn't quite believe that, but I hoped Jimmy could.

We dozed in the eighth station for fifteen minutes. When I woke up, the organist was gone, and a priest, paying no attention to us, readied the altar for afternoon mass. Climbing out, I dragged Jimmy with me. Deadweight, he was in no hurry to leave. I threatened to carry him out, and he found his legs. A few yards down the cold-stone aisle, we picked up our pace. I stuffed a ten-dollar bill in the wooden offertory box near the door. It was a small price to pay for sanctuary, a place where time had wrapped us in fuzzy-toned tranquillity.

"Annie," he said, "Ike needs me."

"Mina's staying with Ike. He'll be okay."

Deep sigh of relief. "Definitely okay. I *know* he and Mina are in love."

"You think everybody's in love."

"They really are. I've seen the two of them . . . *You Know.*"

Thirteen

Ant is widely used in China to increase sexual desire and sexual function. So is the silk moth. They are both very rich in zinc.

—Qi Lucky Dragon product brochure

Male silk moths should be eaten during the full moon to increase men's lust. Silk moth infusions also fight aging, and it's rich in juices that make men strong. Women shouldn't eat silk moths unless they want to grow a beard.

—*The Gypsy Guide to Health*
Zlato Milos, 1902

Mina and Ike. Together?

I didn't want to visualize that one, and I could not believe those two had left an unlocked door between them and the rest of the world.

"Forget *You Know*," I said. "I'm sure they're waiting for a priest to arrive."

But then I remembered the circumstances regarding the conception of Mina's child number four. She'd said it happened right under a casket; there was something about death that made her want to dance the juicy-life mambo. I wondered if we should call and tell them we were on our way.

Jimmy said, "I guess Ike's still singing Hao home, but I bet he'll kiss Mina again sometime."

"Is kissing *You Know*?"

"What did you think?"

"Holding hands."

He shook his head. "That's no big deal. Kissing is."

Jimmy had slipped into the same angelic pose he wore just be-fore one of his teeth-rattling pyro events.

I said, "Jimmy, never kid a kidder."

"What does *that* mean?"

"*You Know* is more than holding hands, it's more than kissing, you're not that naive, and I hope you never walked in on Ike and Mina while they were doing more than kissing."

"GAG. Seeing them kiss was gross enough."

We walked to Ike's. By the time we'd climbed one hill, run down the next, and repeated the routine, my heart and lungs were about to blow. I stopped and felt the pulse in my neck, a neurotic impulse when I expect impending death. The heart beating against my fingertips was a locked door whapped by an angry mob. When we reached the first corner of level ground, Jimmy patted my back.

"You don't have to keep up with me," he said. "I'm used to hills. Also, I'm a kid and you're not."

He'd just seen the man who rescued him from life on the streets, die. He was holding steady. I could, too. I hurried my step, ignor-ing the crew of neck-drumming fanatics.

Near the end of the block, we watched a hearse drive from the direction of Qi Dragon, passing us on its way to St. Theresa's. Probably Hao. Jimmy went quiet. We didn't speak until we reached the shop.

Mina was keeping Ike on the earth, their heads together over a cup of steaming brew.

Ike said, looking up at us, "They collected Hao in broad day-light. Now the tongs will know he's dead."

"The cover of night is best for removing bodies," Mina said. "It's not good to advertise death all over the neighborhood."

"But that's exactly what I want," he said.

I agreed with Mina. Why advertise death of the guard dog? On the other hand, theirs was a different world, and I was a foreigner.

Maybe Ike wanted all tongs to know that Hao had moved on, but I could not imagine why.

Jimmy ran to Ike, giving him a fast hug. He climbed a stool. Reaching up, he jammed his hand inside a wide jar of buff-colored flakes above the counter. Handing some to Mina, she stirred it into her already revolting brew. Ike did the same.

Jimmy said to me, "You want some hops? It's calming."

I'd rather have my hops in the form of beer, but Jimmy poured us each a cup of hot water, shaking a fist of hops in each cup, letting the flakes do their thing. He loaded his own tea with sugar. So much for calm.

I said to Ike, "You think the tongs killed Hao?"

"I don't know," he said, "but I'm glad they know he's gone. Looked like a classic black spider death. Used by tong martial artists, also a few highly trained private and government agents. Hold the neck, apply pressure, then let go. Blood rushes to the brain, and the vessels explode like fireworks—death in four, five minutes. Slight neck discoloration. Hao had many friends, also many enemies. He was," Ike said, "a complex man."

"Hao was old enough to have suffered a natural death. That's why we should have called the police."

"Annie, death's private," Mina said. "Cops are anything but."

"An autopsy would have given us answers."

Mina, Ike, and Jimmy—all three—looked at me as if I didn't have one clue about real evil. I wished they were right.

According to statistics, a person has to be pretty interested in someone to come up with the nerve, or the money, to kill them. I asked Ike why the tongs gave two hoots about Hao. Ike sighed, and Mina looked as if she wanted to fall into the middle of last week. There are some histories you'd rather not know.

"Maybe," Mina said to Ike, "you should rest."

"No more hiding," Ike said to Mina. She tumbled into the gray place that filters words and stories, a safe piece of inner geography. I could read it on her face. She'd hear what she wanted to hear, nothing more.

"When you're young and you live in this neighborhood," Ike said to me, "the tongs are very seductive. You probably know that."

"I thought the tongs were a relic."

"Not even close, but they're not interested in your world. It makes sense they don't exist for you. Anyway," Ike said, "when Hao was a young martial arts student, they enlisted him."

"Why not you, too?"

Ike smiled, small and frail. "Look at the difference between us."

Of course I couldn't look at the difference between them, because Hao's body was at St. Theresa's, being prepared for farewell observances.

Mina came around, offering a flat-line, "You're beautiful inside."

"That's a nice way of saying I'm a wimp." Ike put his hand on top of Mina's. She smiled, vacant, and her brain went *adios* again while I heard the short version of the Qi brothers' history.

Hao was a talented martial artist, a ferocious foe. But as he aged, he sought fewer physical tools and more powerful ones. He learned traditional medicine.

Herbalists are on every block. Like the winning housewife in a 1950 Betty Crocker bake-off, Hao used the same recipes as his neighbors, but his tonics produced superior results. He became a master, working exclusively for the tongs. In return he was given protection, status, and money.

Years passed, he wanted out. Hao was pacing the cage the tongs had built around his life. He took it easy, played possum, and as younger men came up, Hao slowly backed out of tong society. He knew a portion of peace, but it was never complete. He'd been in too deep to stop looking over his shoulder. When Jimmy came along, Hao cranked up his vigilance.

One spring day his paranoia was stamped and validated.

A young man oozing lust for old-time power, showed up at the Qi brothers'—he was an obvious mental case. Hao had worked for his father, and the young man remembered him. The young man assumed there was still loyalty. He was wrong. He assumed he could exert pressure. He was right.

He pestered Hao, requesting strength and power; he refused to go away. Hao and Ike discussed their options. Killing him was a possibility. The kid was spared—Ike and Hao didn't think they'd get away with the murder, so they chose to work on the young man's spirit. Hao would regularly dose him with a shen tonic that encourages seeking a spiritual path. With only two weeks of tonic under his belt, the regimen came to a screeching halt.

"The young man fell in love," Ike said, "and it was a hopeless situation."

Hearing the 'L' word, Mina emerged from her gray zone. "Let me guess. He wanted herbs to slip the woman, something to make her fall in love with him."

"Cornus," Ike said, "a powerful aphrodisiac. He wanted it for himself and for the woman he loved. Hao refused to sell it to him. When our backs were turned, the man stole it and ran to the young woman's house."

"Sometimes," Mina said, "men forget the basics like flowers and candy and dressing up nice."

"We get excited, and we forget about those things."

"I've had lifetimes *filled* with men. I know very well what you remember and what you forget."

Mina sparkled a little, and Ike sparkled back. Jimmy was right. They liked each other.

"The girl belongs to a powerful merchant family," Ike said. "They think tongs are scum, so he had to sneak inside her house."

"Maybe," Mina said, "she liked him and invited him over—no sneaking involved. I don't know why so many parents got to meddle in their kids' love lives."

I must have looked like a squeeze toy under a boot heel. I could feel my eyeballs popping out of my head.

"What?" she said to me.

"I'm registering this moment so I can toss it back in your face at a later time."

"You see what I have to put up with?" she said to Ike.

"You're a very patient woman."

Their mutual admiration and occasional pat-and-coo routine was producing a heavy desire to be back in the twins' hotel room, zonked out on something a lot stronger than Pepto-Bismol and a hot bath.

Ike shrugged. "Mina, maybe the young woman did let him in. Who knows? What she wanted was not relevant to her family or, for that matter," he said, "to the young man.

"When we noticed the cornus was missing, and it was enough to damage even the healthiest person, Hao ran to warn the young man's family. No need. Before he was out the door, everyone was here, in our own home, spewing smoke and anger."

I said, "Hao wasn't to blame for the nutty son."

Another one of those looks from all three. I was living in an old Disney movie, complete with singing dwarves and a pink fairy godmother.

"Of course they blamed Hao—for the theft, for the inappropriate attachment, for the young man's lunacy. The truth was too hard for his mother and father. The young man's world was already tilted, and eating that drug tipped him upside down. The stupid young man had tried to kill himself. His mother cried, and his father was deep red, yelling words I hadn't heard since I was a boy. Some curses are very instructive."

"Wait a minute," I said, "did he try to kill himself *here?*"

"No," Ike said. "He never had the chance to slip the woman the aphrodisiac, but he'd taken plenty of it. He made his case to her, pleading undying love, threatening suicide. To prove his devotion, he beat his head against her parents' freshly painted dining room walls—it was a big bloody mess. Both families carried him here," Ike said, pointing to the front door, "and laid him right over there."

Mina said, "Let me get this straight. He wanted to impress the young woman, so he beat himself senseless against her house?"

"Part of her house. Yes."

"Did he survive?"

"Don't rush me," Ike said. "Hao's face . . . I could tell he was thinking maybe he should forget herbs and sell fish. He's always liked fish."

"Ike!" Mina said. "Did Hao let the crazy kid die?"

"Hao worked on him, not easy in the middle of all that carrying on, deciding if he should let him slip away. Then we had real trouble. Jimmy walked in."

"And Jimmy solved the problem," I said, "by sending both families to kingdom come with a case of TNT."

Mina said to me, "Jimmy's a nice kid. You or me, now that would be different. We're practical women."

"Jimmy went right to work," Ike said. "He rushed to the stupid man's side, holding his head. Jimmy toned."

I'd almost forgotten that Jimmy was sitting there, drinking his tea, revisiting the day a nutty neighbor whapped himself on the head over love.

"It was the first time I really felt the inside of someone," Jimmy said, "and it was weird. I wanted to shift things inside him, but while I was humming, I felt the inside of my own head buzz. I didn't want to wreck my brains, so I was pretty careful."

"Did the guy come around?" I asked.

"Unfortunately," Ike said, "he made a full recovery. Two big families, one of them tong, one commerce, and both were present. You can imagine the outcome."

"Everyone wanted Jimmy."

"To cause injury here, to create healthy business there. We talked to the merchant family, and they eventually backed off. Not the tongs. Protecting Jimmy over the past two years has been a full-time job."

Jimmy's face was a gloomy sky. Time to change the curve of this conversation.

"Hao spent a lot of his life mixed up with the bad guys. That," I said, "had nothing to do with Jimmy."

"True. Hao had the power to battle devils, to meditate on death, and to cause it. I believe Jimmy hears only the angel's voices. Angels are stronger than devils or tongs."

For two full years, Hao had been in the way of something the tongs wanted—Jimmy. And they weren't the only ones Hao had to keep an eye on.

"Ike, did Flora ever cross paths with the tongs?"

"That's not . . . She's white."

Apparently even the tongs would only sink so low.

"You think it was a coincidence that she was here when Hao died?" I asked. "I don't."

"She was here a lot lately." Ike sighed. "They were falling in love, that's what my brother believed, and it may be true. She clouded his judgment in ways that occur only when people are deeply troubled or in love."

"I thought Flora was involved with someone," I said. "Her bodyguard."

"Oh. Wagner."

He spoke Wagner's name as if the man was a zit-ridden weakling.

"Wagner was work," he said, "but Hao was different. And some women, here and there, a butterfly among flowers—that's their nature. My brother had never believed in God, plenty of demons, but he started wearing a cross around his neck for her."

"Did Wagner know about them?"

"Hao picked Jimmy up after a healing session at Flora's—something he never would have allowed in his right mind, and something he had decided to put an end to. Wagner discovered them whispering together, flirting with each other. At least they were fully dressed." Ike rested his head in his hands. "What a mess," he said. "I've been in love many times, and it has always led to disaster."

Mina gave him more than a mild version of the stink-eye, but he didn't notice.

I thought of Wagner, his immense pride, his immense . . . everything. Hard to feature him letting go of Flora without a fight. Could be that Wagner thought a little bit of Flora was better than nothing. Could be he decided to make sure that Hao was a temporary blip on their screen.

Wagner had said that Flora tracked Jimmy and Hao down after reading my article in *The Eye,* but Ike told me differently.

"A female twin—tall white woman, a twin, energy split, a very bad omen—introduced Hao to Flora. She has bought expensive beauty products here for years. Chinese women only need pearl soap and water."

"Does the twin want Jimmy, too?"

"I believe she's one of the few people who DOESN'T want Jimmy. She knows him! But she got involved in that crazy church and started feeding it money. She and Flora are very close."

I wondered which twin was Flora's buddy, and I wondered if I'd sold Flora short. If her brand of religion welcomed wild women and high times, I might consider signing on. I also wondered if the twins were drifting apart, one twin having heard the eternal clock ticking down the days. When some people hear that sound they get desperate, searching for a religion that will save them from whatever they think they deserve.

I didn't know what had caused Hao's death. The tongs were angry because he wouldn't serve them, and he wouldn't let them use Jimmy. Ike said Hao had decided Jimmy wasn't going to work for Flora again; I didn't see that making her a happy little evangelist.

And Wagner—I found it hard to believe that he was cool with sharing Flora. But I've found a lot of things hard to believe, and most of them were happening right in the middle of my own life.

I said to Ike, "If the tongs still want Jimmy, you'll have a hard time standing in their way. Flora's just as tough. She'll pull out her credit card and wave it under Jimmy's nose all the way from your door to hers."

"Hao's death is a bad situation for Jimmy," Ike said. "Very bad. Please. Take Jimmy away and keep him safe until we discover who killed my brother and why."

"Have you ever heard of unsolved crimes? I'm not taking care of Jimmy until he's an adult."

Ike smiled. He kissed my forehead three times, as gentle and beneficent as small white petals falling from a branch.

Fourteen

Jimmy didn't want to leave Ike alone. I didn't want to leave Ike alone. Mina did not think it was a good idea to leave Ike alone. He wouldn't listen to any of us, and he shooed us on our way, assuring us he'd be fine. He had to attend to Hao's services. It wouldn't be an easy task with friends and neighbors busy with New Year's rituals and celebrations. Ike was strung out on Mina, ant juice, and fear. There was no arguing with him. He and Hao had a lot in common: They were healers, they both loved Jimmy, and they were two of the most stubborn men I had ever met, which is saying a lot.

The three of us walked to Mina's. I spotted the skinny white guy, same shabby coat, slipping between two buildings when our eyes met. This was ridiculous. The man was completely pathetic at his job. Pathetic or not, I didn't like being tailed. I'd deal with him soon. From what I'd seen, he was a purebred geek, someone easy to intimidate.

We turned into Mina's alley and were hit by an extraordinary sight. A huge papier-mâché lion puppet, with three pair of human legs sticking out from the belly, was careening in circles, bells jan-

gling, in front of Mina's place. The paper lion's head was almost
four feet across, trailing streamers and shiny beads.

Jimmy clapped his hands and whooped.

Mina said, "Oh for God sakes. Do you believe it?" Same tone of
voice you'd use if you looked out your window and saw unex-
pected company—boring relatives—and now you'd have to put
your life on hold and feed them.

"Discreet," I said to her. "Good planning."

"I didn't plan this, and there's that guy who looks like he
stepped out of a bad spy movie. I've decided he's all yours."

"Thanks. I only want to be noticed when *I* want to be noticed.
Is that asking so much?"

"Annie, yes. We're two sexy women with a Chinese boy who's
throwing snappers on the sidewalk like a half-wit orphan leaving a
loud trail in the forest."

Another round of snappers hit the ground. "Jimmy! Knock it
off. My eardrums," I told him, "are completely shredded."

"Hao ordered this," Jimmy said, pointing to the spectacle, "a
few days ago. It was a gift to you, Mina."

"Hao did this? Why?"

"A new business has to have a lion dance performed out front. It
attracts money and attention."

People waved at the lion, cheering him on. They offered us beer
and porkbuns. They used Mina's bathroom. She ran inside to get
business cards, and she chased out a couple of teenagers who were
playing poker with her tarot cards. She locked her door. I hoped
Hao was close enough to get a kick out of this. Us.

The dance was a liquid lion-snake, smooth as rainwater licking
the pavement, sensuous as the curve of a lover's thigh, performed
by martial artists.

Mina and I sat on her front steps with Jimmy. She smiled to her
neighbors, a plastered-on little smile. I waved. Jimmy whistled between his fingers, proud of Hao for arranging this gift. The weight

he carried looked lighter. He'd always feel guilty about Hao's death—he deserved to know the truth. Until he knew, he'd assume he was responsible.

Mina's phone rang. She unlocked her door and ran inside. Jimmy and I chewed candied ginger, enjoying the pranks and contortions of the dancers. We oohed and ahhhed in all the right places.

He said, "I want to do that when I grow up."

"You can do anything you want."

"I'm supposed to be a healer."

"That's what it seems like."

"But I don't want to be."

"Then don't."

"Because I want to be what I dreamed inside the church. Normal."

Mina walked out her door, cordless phone in hand. "Jimmy," she said, "the stars impel, they do not compel. I didn't make that up, someone told it to me. It means you get to do whatever you want, and that includes eating junk food your whole entire life."

Handing me the phone, she shrugged, saying, "I don't know how the woman knew you were here."

The woman? Looking around, I didn't know how anyone within ten miles didn't know where I was.

I said, "Hello?"

"This is Jan."

"Twin Jan?"

"The very one."

"How did you find me?"

"That doesn't matter. Here's what matters—Hao died because he was protecting Jimmy. Also, Hao was up to his ears in Flora and Wagner, not to mention the neighborhood bullies."

"How do you know this stuff?"

"We told you that we like you. Do you want to listen or not?"

"I'm listening."

"Now you're the one who's protecting Jimmy."

In response, I was silent.

She said, "I hope you're being quiet because you're putting two and two together."

The math was easy. "Anyone who protects Jimmy is in trouble."

"Bingo," she said.

And the phone went dead.

Fifteen

$\mathcal{T}$ he escrow officer had left a message on my cell. The pest control guys were taking care of minor damage. No biggie, a little rot and mildew on the siding, nothing unusual for a building about two inches from the ocean.

It sounded like a scenario that precedes *We have a problem here . . .* My troubled pots were already brewing, so that one went on the back burner.

Jan's *BINGO!* was sinking in hard and raw. I didn't want to do this alone anymore. I needed an emotional mattress, a warm cushion. I called Leo Rosetti, and I called him from Mina's house. Leo wouldn't be home. His teaching schedule at the women's shelter, trapeze arts and a ropes course for confidence building, was full. But hearing his recorded voice, leaving him a message, would give me a patch of personal ground to stand upon.

The machine cranked on, and he spoke, his voice chocolate brown, solid, and smiling. Why had I come to the city for an entire month? Was I nuts or something? I missed my house, I missed my Leo. I even missed the stray dog that showed up on my porch every morning to eat the cats' food and wander off.

Leo picked up after he heard my voice. "What's wrong?"

"You're home."

"Short day."

"I don't know where to start."

"Uh-oh," he said, "Just tell me what's going on right now."

I did.

Leo said he'd pack and head right down. "Besides, I raised a boy. I know how they are."

"Was Angel fascinated with explosives?"

"Kind of. He was more into starting fires."

"You're kidding."

"He also built thread webs in doorways, and wrapped cellophane over the toilet seat, under the lid. You get the picture."

"I'm glad I had girls."

"Here's the thing about raising a boy—if they're still alive when they're eighteen, you've done your job."

"I'm not raising him. I'm watching him for an unspecified time."

"You know what I mean."

"Safety is a high expectation."

"Between explosives and faith healing? I'd say it's very high."

Once again I found myself with an enormous desire to disappear. When the going gets tough, the tough run for their numb of choice. Leo was my current numb of choice, one hell of an improvement over Chunky Monkey ice cream, but he wasn't creating much of a buffer between me and reality.

"Meet me at the Bay View," I said. "I'm asking Mina to take Jimmy tonight. After that, I guess he's mine until he can live in his own house without worrying about getting snatched or witnessing another death."

"Annie?" he said. "Call Detective Lawless."

"Forget it."

"I know you hate to ask for help, but you could use some serious protection."

"I'd love to ask him for help"—a sure sign of my anxiety level—"but Ruth dragged him on a tour of Europe. She wants one decent vacation before retirement from SFPD kills him."

"For God's sake, don't say that to Ruth."

"Those were her words, not mine. Three of her friends have been widowed this year."

"I guess you're stuck with me for protection," he said. "Mostly you're just stuck with me."

"Leo, I don't need you for protection. I need sane company."

"You got it."

"Good," I said. "Wait. Did I tell you that a man in a ratty trench coat is following me? He's FBI."

"FBI? Are you sure?"

"Positive, and the man is everywhere. I'm going to use him."

"What are you talking about?"

"He must carry a gun. If there's trouble, he can cover my back," I said. "He'll be my protection."

"You're giving me the creeps."

"Next time I see him, which should be any minute, I'm going to introduce myself and work out some kind of deal."

"Don't do that!"

I could almost smell beads of sweat popping out on his forehead. What was Leo getting so worked up about?

He said, "When did you first notice him? Was it after the article ran on Jimmy?"

I tried to remember, but the past two days were a mush of music and death and curing and a missing daughter. And then I had it.

"I spotted him right after I met the twins."

Long silence. "Annie, I don't like it."

"The twins? I told you, they're on my side."

"You partied with them, and they're great old gals, and they've lived a big life with lots of color. That doesn't mean you can trust them."

Leo's sanity was kicking up trouble. "Actually," he said, "they could be major trouble. They love the edge."

"And," 1 said, a dim bulb igniting over my head, "maybe they miss it."

"Three hours," he said. "Tops."

Sixteen

I walked into Mina's kitchen, carrying her cordless, tossing it on the table. There was Mina, and there wasn't Jimmy.

"Relax," Mina said. "He's upstairs. Why he wants to kill videoed aliens I don't know. I told him they might be a lot nicer than human beings even if they *are* funny-looking."

"How's your client load?"

"Forget the clients," Mina said. "Sometimes life has other plans than the ones written on your calendar."

"I want that on my tombstone."

"PHAAA . . . What a thing to say!" She spit on the floor, grinding it into the old wood with the heel of a bright red pump.

"You want me around for while. I'm touched."

"You're entertaining. That's more than I can say for most people—dogs and Jimmy excluded."

Felt like a good time to ask for a favor.

"Mina, I need time alone. I want to nose around, maybe meet the fed face-to-face. I'd also like to find out what the pest guys are doing at my building."

"Your building has bugs?"

"Mold. I want to make sure they're not giving it a power wash and charging me for new siding."

"I had one client licensed by the state to kill bugs. A champion liar. His own wife told me that if Jesus Christ came back to earth as a pest control man, she wouldn't believe a word he said. She was very religious. When is Leo coming down?"

"Who said anything about Leo?"

"No one gets the soft glow you're wearing because they can't wait to meet mold and government agents."

"Leo's on his way," I said. "Don't get bent out of shape, but I don't want to leave you alone with Jimmy. He's too much to handle, and I'm not sure . . ."

She waggled her finger at me. "I'm one step ahead of you. I don't want to be alone with him either, and not because he's a big responsibility. We're sitting ducks in this place," she said. "After I eavesdropped on your conversation with Leo, you are *so* easy, I called E. B. She'll help with Jimmy."

"You called E. B.? I was using your phone."

"You've never heard of having two lines, home and business? Don't worry over details. A breather will do you good—you may end up with this kid forever."

"That's impossible."

"Of course it's possible, but one thing at a time," she said. "I'm taking Jimmy someplace we'll all be safe."

I waited for her to continue. She didn't.

"You going to tell me where that is?" I said.

"The Mystic Café. E. B.'s over there cleaning up, sorting through things. You know."

"The Mystic is the last building left standing on the south side of Haight, and the wrecking crew is coming anytime. Why clean it?"

"There are things in there I'd like to keep, maybe a few things she wants, too."

"Not the art, don't keep the art."

"No room for it. And, just between you and me, a big photo of a naked man wearing a fruit bowl on his head while he's holding a Chihuahua does nothing for me at all."

"What happened to those kids who were staying there? Rent-free as I recall."

"They're still there."

"E. B.'s made friends with them, and that's where she's been. Am I right?"

"Yep, but you didn't hear it from me. You two have to learn to communicate."

"I don't care who her friends are. She's shown remarkably better taste in choosing companions than I have."

Mina looked at me, anger building. That was the last thing I needed.

"I didn't mean your son," I said. "He was a great husband, fabulous-looking, and a terrific dad. One of the few good decisions I've ever made."

We both had the sense not to mention the other family members I'd been involved with. Before falling from grace, I was saved by a knock on her door.

"You answer it," I said, "and I'll tell Jimmy to keep killing aliens."

Soon this nightmare would end, and Jimmy's life would return to what it had been, minus one beloved uncle. But Jimmy could dream with the saints every night, and he'd never be granted the gift of normalcy. No huge loss. From what I know of life, which grows slimmer every year, normal douses an awful lot of spark.

I told Jimmy to stay put. No problem, he was approaching electronic level nine—that boy was not moving one inch. His thumbs danced on the pad, and his eyes were glued to the screen, but I was pretty sure he'd heard me. He'd turned down the volume when I started talking. More horrendous game music blooped—if life made any kind of sense, Jimmy would have been a total basket case.

I told him to rampage away until Mina was ready to leave. He shook his head in my direction, indicating understanding.

I placed a new video on the couch in case he obliterated that particular world and needed another part of the galaxy to conquer. I waved good-bye, he shook his head at the screen.

Seventeen

I walked downstairs to the kitchen, yammering all the way. I told Mina that Jimmy was a zombie, the noise upstairs was terrible, she'd better get packed soon, and I shut up when I noticed the expression on her face. Her chin was resting on the palm of her hand. She wore her grin slightly askew. By the bottom stair, I got a load of where her grin was aimed. There was a man sitting across from her. A man earnest in the way only a person who bears the weight of world-saving can be.

"Hello?" I said to him.

"Hey! This lady tells me you're the person who wrote the article about the kid who has the power to save life on earth as we know it."

I hoped Jimmy would stay upstairs.

Mina looked at him, and said, "We met the other time you were here, but I forget your name."

"Skip," he said. "I'm a water sign. My name used to be Rain, but I stopped using it. People always misspelled it. Now I'm plain Skip. Like someone the world is trying to skip over."

Mina excused herself, saying to me, "Skip is your territory. I'm an air sign. Later."

"Air. Very cool," said Skip. "Continuous mutuality. We breathe to live, we live to breathe."

She rolled her eyes. "You might find other things to live for as you get older. I'm going to take a nap."

Mina climbed the stairs, carrying a box of Triscuits and a can of Cheez Whiz to keep Jimmy from raiding the refrigerator and running into Skip. Jimmy was on a ten-minute feeding schedule.

Skip called out to her. "That food will kill you!"

Mina, turning slowly on step three, said to him, "This is pure protein and fiber."

"It's pure poison."

She narrowed her eyes. "Good. I am almost three hundred years old. I could use some help getting off this planet." Mina turned, continuing her ascent.

"WHOA . . ." Skip followed her with his eyes. "She doesn't look nearly that old. What a trip."

"Why are you here for, I gather, the second time?"

"When I read that article in *The Eye,* I knew you'd understand," he said. "I had to find you."

Disappearing into the Mystic Café with E. B. and her rent-free friends was looking better by the minute. I'd get rid of Skip, quickly and politely. You never know when a perfectly nice nut is going to turn.

"Skip, what can one boy do to save life on earth as we know it?"

"Water creates peace."

I already knew that. My daughter had earned an extraordinary sum of money for spawning sloppy-wet calm left and right. Knowing she could make good money had created a sincere sense of peace for me.

I waited for Skip's explanation concerning peace and water, but nothing happened. I studied him while he studied the air inside his head.

My first hit on Skip was that he'd been raised by hippie

parents—his mom ingesting many legal and illegal substances during her pregnancy, people who'd never recovered from the Grateful Dead and embroidered jeans. But, sitting there watching him, feeling him, I was granted a piece of intuitive understanding. Skip was spacey, but he was layered, possibly complicated. And he was smart. Not a great combination. I'd lead him by the hand to a place that was neutral and benign—no conversations concerning weather, global warming, acid rain, or other potential land mines. Then I'd lead him out the door.

I said, "Have you lived in San Francisco all your life?"

"I couldn't live anywhere else. This place nurtures my soul. And my family is here, well, near here."

Maybe they'd come and pick him up. "How near?"

"South. The hills. It's green, nice. But I communicate with the ocean, that's my mission. It takes a little while to get there from my house, but that's okay."

"Must have some pretty interesting conversations. The ocean's seen it all."

"I knew you'd get it. I'm heavily invested in mammalian sea life. They have been saving our asses, or trying to, for a long time."

I needed to leave, and not just because of Skip. I wanted to avoid the next whacko who happened by because they'd read my dumb article. I became bold.

"Skip. I'm sympathetic, but I'm busy. You have exactly three minutes."

"Straight to the point," he said. "I'm good with that. Can I meet the boy?"

"Even if I knew where he was, I wouldn't let you near him."

"After you hear me out, you may change your mind about introducing me to Jimmy."

His feet were bare and dirty, hugged by new Birkenstocks. Wearing sandals in San Francisco during the winter is either a strong fashion statement or the height of poor judgment. He fiddled with his feet, a fairly revolting sight. His toes were long and brown, and his toenails needed clipping.

"The dolphins," he said, "are our spiritual brothers and physical cousins. They sing to us, and they speak to us. The tragedy is that we can't understand one thing they're trying to tell us."

"Maybe it's something simple . . . *I'd like another fish from that bucket, please?*"

"True, dolphins are polite. But," Skip said, "they are so much more. They rescue people lost at sea, and they circle boats the day before a hurricane hits. . . ."

I tapped my broken watch at him.

"I respect people with boundaries," he said, giving me the thumbs-up. "We lost our shared language when we humans got up and walked out of the sea. Dolphin is our ancient tongue, and it may be the language that unites all people.

"I feel—I KNOW—that Jimmy could climb inside a dolphin's skin and tone with them. He could learn to make the same sounds they do. If he can translate cancer, he can probably pick up on our original language. Think about it. Dolphins do not make war upon their fellow dolphins. What if the language we lost teaches us how to get along with each other?"

"Skip, I'm worried about me because you, almost, make sense."

"Not many people understand my mission the first time I explain it."

"I told you I was worried about me. Leave your phone number," I said, "and I'll see if Jimmy wants to talk with you in a month or two."

"Man, that's really a long time."

"We abandoned the ocean a zillion years ago. Dolphin Communication 101 can wait for one kid's life to get back on track. If he's not interested, I'll let you know. End of story."

"You're not giving me much," Skip said. "Sometimes I feel pretty militant about this."

"You don't know the meaning of the word *militant*. Bother Jimmy, and you may take up permanent residence with your dolphin pals."

I couldn't believe I'd said that. At least I'd left out cement boots and sleeping with the fishes. Skip really had to go.

"I came in peace," he said. "I don't like threats."

"I know, you're about peace and water," I said. "Me, too. Bye, Skip."

Thanking me, for what I wasn't sure, and hugging me, Skip lit up like an aluminum Christmas tree. Whatever this man was about, I didn't think he was totally responsible for being a nut. His body chemistry was doing a woggy little two-step inside his head. Meaning that he was nowhere near safe and sane, and I hoped his family kept him well oiled on meds.

I walked him to the door, and I watched him disappear. It was time for me to hit the road, and time for Mina and Jimmy to flee to the Mystic Cafe.

"I heard the door close," Mina said. "Who was that guy?"

"You said you remembered meeting him a couple of weeks ago. He's a nut."

"In my line of business, I attract them. I'm asking what variety he is, because I forget."

"He's in a class of his own," I said. "Skip wants Jimmy to talk with dolphins and whales. Maybe we'll eventually get around to seaweed."

"Now I remember him. His feet smelled bad."

"We should introduce him to the doctor from Atlantis."

"Atlanta," she said. Mina pulled out her car keys and hollered to Jimmy. "Get down here and bring all your junk! Now!"

I didn't know how much padding she had on her, so I handed her cash. "That Caddy your old cowboy boyfriend gave you is too conspicuous. Take a cab."

"I love that car."

"Me too, but there aren't many silver Cadillacs with steer horns on the hood. I don't want you followed."

"I hate cabs. The drivers are mostly Russians, I have to tell them which streets are one-ways, and half the time they don't understand me."

Jimmy ran down the stairs, slipping into his backpack. Mina left the phone number of the café in case I needed to call. It was the familiar number that had appeared on my phone's tiny screen when E. B. had called me.

"Mina, tell my daughter I don't care who her friends are, and that I'm pretty bugged she thinks I would."

"You ever hear of killing the messenger? I'll give her a kiss for you."

"It makes me feel like I messed up the mothering deal on some essential level."

"Of course you did. But, concerning this particular issue . . . Okay, I'll level with you," Mina said. "Her friends are a Gypsy couple. The young woman is scared, and out to here with a baby, and they are sort of related to us. She hasn't got a mother—she was killed in an accident—no other family, either. The young man is your average male. They never believe sex makes babies until it happens, then they have to grow up fast."

"I don't understand why E. B. wanted to keep it a big secret."

"She knows how you feel about her Gypsy connections. Who doesn't? This pair is down on their luck, maybe she's embarrassed for them. I don't know," Mina said. "I do know she's helping out, giving them a little of the money she earned from those women who think too much and talk to plants. E. B.'s a good girl."

Seemed like a perfect circle. Scared as she was, the young pregnant woman was swimming in the middle of life's sacred river. The Isis women were sitting on a distant bank discussing rock formations, lizards, anything to keep from jumping in and getting wet.

E. B. was right. I would have been judgmental. I don't need

therapy to know that around certain things I am pretty screwed-up, but I understood the young woman. Long ago I was her. Sometimes life runs at you so hard that there's no time for anything but full-out survival, and that's where she was.

We locked Mina's place up tighter than a drum sitting on the Sahara and waited for the cab. Jimmy didn't pay attention to either of us. Fumbling with his backpack, he was focused on one thing—wrapping something shiny around a dull disk. He didn't budge when the cab pulled to the curb.

Mina climbed inside. Already frustrated with the driver, her voice was a quick wallop of words. I helped Jimmy zip up his backpack pockets.

"Jimmy?" He looked at me. Opaque eyes, waiting for the ax to fall. "Don't do anything scary until the driver takes you across town. Mina might have an attack."

He smiled and climbed in beside Mina, a happy and expectant look on his face.

I blew him a kiss. He almost humiliated his twelve-year-old self by catching it.

Eighteen

My bet for Hao's death was currently on Flora. There was no rational reason, and nothing essential such as evidence. But, evangelists have a history of wanting the entire trinity: fame, miracles, and money. With Hao out of the way, Jimmy could help her get the whole shebang.

With some notable exceptions, evangelists have lives littered with extramarital flings, regular affairs, and a taste for booze. I could understand lusting after Wagner. But Hao? Maybe Flora was falling for him, but it was hard to equate Hao and lust. More likely that she was using Hao to get to Jimmy. The picture made perfect sense: Woo Wagner to provide a good time and a great view, court Hao to get her hands on Jimmy, the little miracle-cure money machine.

I'd walk to my moldy building, then to the ocean and the Bay View Hotel. Thirty minutes to air out, and with a slight detour, the Church of All Light was on my way to the fungus tower.

I bought another bag of X-rated fortune cookies, this one for Flora. Visitors should come bearing gifts. I'd tell her that God must have a zany sense of humor; he'd created one wild carnival down here. Then I flashed on the Universal Life Source, seeing a large

Buddha with a Mona Lisa smile, hurling occasional thunderbolts, us humans being its divine 24/7 reality entertainment network.

Turning on Grant Street, I felt the familiar prickle of being watched. I spun around. The bozo in black.

I ducked into a store, pretending to look at stationery. I waited while he tried to squeeze himself behind a rack of postcards. The rack almost tipped over. I popped out of the store, and I walked. When I felt him again, a mosquito nipping at the nape of my neck, I made an abrupt turn and faced him.

I yelled to him. "Hey, you! Come here!"

He stuffed his hands in his pockets. Head down, he decided to walk past me.

A silly move. Four feet, three feet, two, almost in my face . . . I put my hand on his chest. "Tell me why you're on top of me." He stammered. I stood back, taking inspection. "Also, why you only own one coat. It looks like a holdover from the Cold War."

"I don't know what you're talking about."

"Come in here," I said, grabbing him by his flappy belt. "You're buying me coffee."

McDonald's, directly under the Red Pearl Delight, is a guilty little squatter, looking worried and out of place. No need. The golden arches blend in with everything else that's going on around there.

He pulled out a formfitting plastic chair for me, he waited in line, and he placed our order. His skin was very white. Looked like a local; not much sun pokes through San Francisco fog. He placed the tray gently on our table. Looking both ways, the man removed his coat, folding it tenderly over the back of his chair.

He was dark blond going to gray, wearing a black suit, white shirt, and a pop-eyed blue tie. Intense eyes, strong shoulders, no fat. Too thin. No noticeable guile. Fragile. It was like being in the presence of an aging Mormon missionary.

I sipped my coffee, black and scorched. I didn't care. It was buzzy fuel, and the quality didn't matter. He was about to tell me something, but his eyes shifted and his mouth froze. Sheer terror. I followed his line of vision over my left shoulder. An old Chinese man sat two tables over. It was the zither player of the duct-taped box. His clothes were rumply gray, but they could have started out life as any color.

The most extraordinary thing about the Chinese man was his complete spontaneity. He had unzipped his pants and was peeing on McDonald's yellow-tiled floor. The bathroom was twenty feet away, maybe less, and he'd decided to skip the formalities. His stream ran toward the front door. A woman came out, brandishing a mop, abusing him in Chinese. Not harsh abuse. I've been more soundly tromped for lifting a breakable item with a price tag of $5.95 off a retail shelf. By the time he'd fumbled his zipper back up, she'd finished mopping the floor. Mumbling under her breath, she brought him another cup of coffee. If I were the mop-up lady, I wouldn't have given him more liquid. Customers returned to happy gossip.

"This isn't my . . . I'm not usually in this part of town," my personal agent stammered.

"Don't tell me you work in the financial district. Not with that coat."

"I'm usually at my desk. Downtown."

"I hope you're better at pushing papers than you are at the spy game."

He colored. "I'm the best."

Not many people take pride in being a fantastic bureaucrat.

"What's your name?"

"Dudley."

"Dudley? Stop following me."

"I can't," he said. "Orders."

He pulled out a folded wad of old black leather. A shiny FBI identification badge tumbled out of its holder and onto the table.

"Why am I being dogged by a government employee who's at the bottom of the stack? By a man who stacks the stacks of paper?"

"It was requested that someone keep an eye on you. The bureau has bigger fish to fry, so . . ."

"So the small fish, me, got you. Do you know how to use a gun?"

"We have to requalify every two years in order to maintain our status as agents."

"You've only shot paper targets."

"I'm pretty good."

"Dudley, I've shot at real targets. And I'm not pretty good, I'm very good."

"This isn't the sort of case that's going to result in gunfire," he said, his skin descending to bleached-white beach towel. "I'm almost certain of that."

Dudley was soon to join the old Chinese man in losing bladder control right there in the middle of McDonald's. I didn't think the lady with the mop would be so nice to a white guy who wet on her floor.

"Dudley, breathe. Concentrate on moving some color back into your cheeks," I said. "Who wants me watched?"

His voice was a whispered breath. "I can't tell you."

"Has this got anything to do with Jimmy? With the twins?"

His eyebrows rose to meet his hairline. They started to stand up on part one of my question, they came to full attention on part two, then they fell. He looked at the table.

"The twins," I said. "I thought so. It was the first time I noticed you. You're hard to miss."

"Don't tell anyone about me. You know, don't write my work up in a story."

Why hadn't I thought of that? Great copy. My next article was itching to be born.

"You didn't get this from me, but the twins," he said, "are old friends of the bureau."

"I know. Are they on my side or not?"

"I wouldn't be following you if the twins didn't think you were valuable. And, of course, we know all about Jimmy."

"Can I get rid of you?"

"No."

"Someone is dead, and it may be because of a story I wrote. It may not. I could figure out some way to get rid of you—get that look off your face, I didn't mean permanently—but I'm busy keeping a kid, and myself, in one piece," I said. "Let's make a deal. Instead of trying to keep the wolf from my door, I'm inviting you to be my partner." I scrutinized him. "Brother, you are one sorry wolf."

"Your partner? I'm not even supposed to talk with you. I don't understand."

I tapped his skull. "It's not hollow," I said. "There's hope." Dudley was an ex-accountant. Had to be.

"Just keep following me," I said, "and keep doing a lousy job so I know you're there. Two things—if I'm having a hot time, beat it. If someone pulls out a real gun and points it at a real human, me, for instance, pretend that the shooter is a paper target—nail them. Forget they're human or you'll freeze. Got it?"

"Got it."

"And no peeking in my purse, ever, for charge card numbers or anything else that might be related to taxes."

"Hey! How did you . . ."

"You were supposed to act confused just then, not indignant. Dudley, you're lucky you got this assignment. By the time we're finished, you may know something about life without a desk."

He squared his shoulders and admitted that as long as I already knew about him, it seemed like a good idea for us to work together. He was sure the bureau would approve.

"No government agency has ever approved of me. If you'd done your homework, you'd know that," I said. "Don't mention our arrangement to your boss. And remember, you leave if an amorous adventure pops up. I'll do the same for you."

This time he went pure red. "I'm married. I don't have amorous adventures."

I stood up. "Give my sympathy to your wife. I'm going to Flora's. Don't lose me."

"Do you really think that's a good idea? She was under investigation even before. Before."

"Hao's death. Do I think it's one hundred percent safe to annoy her? No. Do I think it's necessary? Yes. We're also watching Wagner. There may be a jealous madman living inside that gorgeous body."

"Wagner Stipple is huge. He used to play for the Raiders."

"If trouble arises, you take care of Flora, and I'll take care of Wagner. Deal?"

He smiled weakly. I knew he was hoping that was exactly the way it would shake out. Now that he'd mentioned the football connection, I remembered Wagner Stipple. About a decade earlier he was all over the *Chronicle*. Top of his game, he was suspended for gambling, drinking, and heavy womanizing. Then he crossed the line and slugged his coach. End of career. He'd left with a chip on his shoulder and a giant dent in his lifestyle. Wagner was very nice to look at, but he was no one to mess around with.

Nineteen

A quick flicker of sunlight hit me from behind. I enjoyed its muted warmth all the way up the path to the church's front door. Dudley was creeping behind me, his dusty blur walking inside my gray-legged shadow. I tried to ignore him. Dudley dove into the bushes, I was not sure why, sending a flock of birds skyward. I put my ear to the church door. There was plenty of noise going on inside. No need to worry about Dudley arousing suspicion by having shattered the box hedge.

First words I heard belonged to Wagner. "I am *not* hanging around here while you grieve for that old Chinaman."

"I'm grieving for the way we treat each other"—it was Flora's voice—"the whole human race."

"You can hand that crap out to your congregation, not to me."

All quiet. I pressed my head closer to the door, it wasn't latched, and it slipped open an inch. I stepped backward toward an Italian cypress, waiting for them to inspect the creaking door. Didn't happen, and I was in good eavesdropping position.

Dudley, my federally funded knight in shining armor, was extricating himself from the greenery. I had no idea why the twins had stuck me with him. It didn't do much to convince me that they were in my corner. I hoped if Dudley was carrying a gun, it wasn't loaded. The man could turn into a major liability.

There was Flora, indignant, her voice piercing the hallowed walls. "You cannot possibly be jealous of Hao."

"Jealous of a dead man? You're right, I can't be," Wagner said.

Another stretchy silence. "I could never be with you in that special way again if I thought you had anything to do with Hao's death."

"*Special way?* We're alone, cut the baby talk. You pass it out here, there, and everywhere. That doesn't make love very special," he said. "I've never expected you to be faithful, but I need to know you're on my side. No matter what."

"I'm in no position to make such a promise."

"What happened to unconditional love? Another sermon that doesn't mean much to the real Flora?"

Her voice thinned, taking on the impatient edge of a loan officer turning a customer down for the fourth time. "Wagner. Get real. Unconditional love is a goal, not a reality."

Wagner's voice dropped half an octave, and I peered inside. He was holding his head between his hands, looking at the floor. "I didn't have anything to do with that old man's death."

I wondered if he was sorry about that.

She said, "Do you swear?"

"Cross my heart. It hurts you think I could do that, killing an old man."

Cooing sounds.

"You want to take this upstairs?" Flora, husky with wanting Wagner.

Wagner said, "In a minute."

"I must be losing my charm."

"Flora, I want to know what happened to that Chinaman. I didn't have anything to do with his death, and I'd hate to think you'd point the finger at me to get yourself off the hook."

"Get *myself* off the hook?"

"You used Hao to get to that kid, Hao finally told you NO, and there you were when the man died. As long as we've decided there's no such thing as unconditional love, maybe I'd better ask— did you kill him?"

"Whatever my failings may be, Wagner, I'm a messenger of God. God is love, not destruction."

"Been plenty of God's messengers who killed people that got in their way."

Back to her loan officer's voice. "Get this straight. I didn't kill Hao. I went over there to tell him I'd leave Jimmy alone until he was old enough to decide for himself if he had a calling."

"You tried to bring the boy here when the old man keeled over."

"Someone needed to take care of Jimmy. I wanted it to be me. Jimmy didn't want the same thing, so I left him alone."

"Truth?"

"Truth."

"Flora, we've got to stick together. We start tearing each other apart, and it's going to go hard on both of us."

"This conversation hasn't been pleasant, but at least we know that neither of us killed Hao."

"Good thing to know," he said, "and I hope you're going to do what you said—leave that kid alone. I'm sick of you treating him like the voice of God at the same time you're using him to fatten up the church's bank account."

"That was true at first. Things changed after I got to know Jimmy."

She opened her arms wide in a come-to-mama gesture. "Wagner," she said. "I'm all yours."

Wagner snorted. "That'll be the day. But I'm happy getting the largest percentage of you."

She gave him a playful smack on the behind. There was quiet of the stir-and-thicken variety. I backed out and away from the door, not so much as trampling one leaf of ivy.

Very informative. I'd learned they hadn't trusted each other, still didn't, and they were both pretending they did. They had every reason in the world *not* to trust each other. Each one thought the other might have caused Hao's death.

A tremendous clattering rang from the side of the church. Dudley. He'd pulled himself up after tripping on a piece of garbage by the church Dumpster, probably something the size of an ice-cream wrapper. I heard wild, fast, and heavy footsteps running to the church door. Had to be Wagner. I scooted into the shadows, leaving Dudley to fend for himself.

Wagner stalked out the door and saw Dudley covered with garbage. He went to Dudley, straightening the lapels of his horrible coat.

"What you up to, man?"

"Just trying to find my next meal."

Wagner pulled a few rumpled bills from his pocket. "Ten bucks. Get out of here, and buy yourself something to eat with that money, not a bottle of Thunderbird. You still look that terrible tomorrow, come back and we'll find you some decent clothes. You got to respect yourself, man. It's the first step in starting over."

He patted tall and thin Dudley on the back so enthusiastically that I thought Dudley might take another header. The church door closed, and the bolt slid into place.

When we reached the sidewalk, I said, "I told you—you need new clothes."

"I thought this outfit would help me fit in."

"Fit into what? Dudley, you look like a homeless guy. None of the people we're around are homeless. Eccentric. Crazy like a cage of foxes. But they are not covered with"—I picked a large coffee filter off his back—"garbage."

Twenty

I told Dudley to clock out. I considered giving him the address of the Mystic Café so he could do his bodyguard routine over there—after all, he was supposed to be concerned with my welfare *and* Jimmy's—but I thought they'd be safer without him. I considered telling the twins that the next time they wanted protection to hire private security. Their chips weren't worth much at the gaming table of the US government.

"All right, I'll leave you alone," Dudley said, "but call me if you have any problems. Even if you *suspect* a problem." He handed me a business card with at least four phone numbers printed on the front.

I told him I'd be at the Bay View. Telling him the truth was probably a mistake, but it was too late to take it back.

He walked away, got maybe five feet, and turned around.

"Now what?" I said.

"Remember, not everyone who works for the government is as well-disposed to you as I am. You're lucky the twins like you."

"Who else at the government knows I exist?"

"You can't work for an inflammatory newspaper and expect to go through life unnoticed."

"*The Eye* has many virtues, but being inflammatory isn't one of them."

"Okay, just don't trust everyone who tells you they work for the government. That includes cops. They're not all honest."

"You are such a Boy Scout. It's taken me most of my life to trust myself. Trusting a government employee, especially one in uniform, is not in the cards."

"Don't make those sorts of comments, either."

"Get out of here and be amorous with your wife, would you? I need breathing room."

I shoved the X-rated fortune cookies in his pocket, I hadn't had the opportunity to present them to Flora. Maybe one would inspire him. He looked puzzled. He always looked puzzled. I watched him walk in the direction we'd come from. Again. This time he kept walking. I imagined he drove a brown Mercury four-door sedan. Parked in Chinatown, someone would think a resident had gotten lucky. Parked on Columbus, someone would think a kid perusing adult book stores had taken off with Grandpa's car.

It was a tumbley walk up and down city hills to get to the wharf. The fresh air was wet and rich with brine.

I walked by my building that might, someday, be sold. I spoke with the pest contractor. They were putting up new siding, the buyer's lender required it, and I asked Pestman to send the escrow officer a complete rundown of his costs, including every inch of materials. He was annoyed. I asked when the work would be finished to the lender's satisfaction. Scratching his head, he told me there were more problems than he'd originally thought, and a lot of his crew had health problems or family emergencies. But he was sure it would be finished soon.

I should have paid more attention to the sale. When I inherited the place from my friend Jerry, I smelled lottery and figured whatever I received was found money. I hadn't been smart about this from a financial perspective—what else was new?

Five long blocks spent walking, breathing fresh cold air, and mold was almost off my mind.

I topped a hill and saw the wharf. Seagulls flew above a line of cars sniffing the curb for parking spaces. I made a loop through Ghirardelli Square. Sometimes looking at things I can't afford cheers me up. But window-shopping got old quick, and I walked down the worn steps to the lower level where Ghirardelli chocolate is made. My buddy Candy is king of their kitchen.

I stood outside, pressing my face to the steamy glass. Stainless-steel vats and gallons of hot fudge. Titan sterling mixing bowls and beaters spinning chocolate, the smell was an indescribable delight. Peeking around the side of the glass, I watched Candy. He wore a striped-cotton apron. Pulling the chocolate down from the upper chute, he poured it into the bottom bowl. Mixing and churning, the process began again. Candy sang and danced to his chocolate, completely at ease, unself-conscious. Boy, would I love to be that relaxed with myself, first I'd . . .

"Hey, come in here," he said, "and stop sneaking around."

"You got a treat for me?"

He hoisted a beater as large as my torso in the air. "You bet."

Always too good to be true. I sidled around the window, scrunching myself under his counter. He held out one of the beaters. It resembled a short canoe paddle riddled with slots.

"Enjoy!" Candy said.

The beater looked as if you'd need an instruction manual to learn every crevice. I held it, feeling the same guilty pleasure I would have if I'd stolen it. Guilt was part of the pleasure.

I closed my eyes, licking the warm dark again. It shot me into a whirl of childhood memories with mind-boggling speed. The best parts of childhood, the secret feelings, the hiding places. The pure enjoyment of being alive on the planet and spectacularly free, so many possibilities ahead. I figured I had licked my share of delight, and I handed the beater back to Candy.

He knew me in and out, at least when it came to chocolate. "Come on. You've got a little more smile left inside you."

"Not this time. I think I feel myself going into a diabetic coma."

"Okay, hand it over."

I started to stick the fresh-licked beater into a bowl of hot fudge. "Hey!" he said. "No one who buys a chunk of candy wants your cooties."

"Sorry," I said. "They're good cooties, though."

"Cooties are cooties. You want to buy some fudge and take it with you? You're looking kind of low."

"I feel low, and I didn't even know it until I walked in here."

"Twenty years I've been passing out beaters. Lots of times the taste sends people back to being a kid, maybe even to their first love."

"That wouldn't make me blue."

"Sure it would. One sudden lick, you're a kid. You feel the roads you might have walked and didn't. You're sad about the loss, even though the loss isn't real."

"Chocolate's an aphrodisiac, not a tour guide down roads not taken."

"Chocolate pushes your heart anywhere it's already going."

"Give me a half pound of fudge without walnuts. I have a night planned that'll remind me my present life is pretty good."

He put his head back and laughed big. "You walk in here, eat a little something, and I get to sell you a nice evening. Men should line up outside my door and thank me."

"Don't get too carried away with yourself."

"How're all your girls doing?"

"They are too grown-up."

Smiling, he cut off a chunk, weighed it, and put it inside a white bag.

Motioning with his candy cutter, he asked, "Is the man waiting for you on my bench the one getting the benefit of this fudge?"

He winked at me. He also waved at the man sitting just outside his window.

Damn, I'd told Dudley to take a temporary hike. Maybe I'd take Dudley for a ride and give Candy a hot kiss. I turned around, expecting to see my private agent.

No Dudley.

Candy looked in both directions and shrugged. "Must be playing hide-and-seek. Maybe he's going to sneak up from behind and give you a bear hug."

I said, "Tall blond guy? Bad clothes?"

Candy frowned. "How many men you got, Annie? This was a little guy, dark hair. Maybe Chinese."

I didn't say anything. I did feel alarm.

"Doesn't sound familiar?"

"No."

"He's got smart eyes, kind of like I saw last night on *The Nature Show*," he said. "I don't remember the animal, but it was wicked." More head craning. "If it was near my break, I'd walk you out and have a word with the man. He's been watching you the whole time you've been in here."

I told Candy thanks, said I'd be okay.

I decided to sit on his bench and pretend to enjoy my chocolate and a book. If the man was going to make an appearance, this was a safe place. I read. It only took five pages for him to sit down next to me. I turned, looking back at Candy. He nodded.

The man draped his arm on the back of the bench and grinned at me. If he saw Candy watching us, he didn't seem to care.

Irritation jumped from every cell of my winter-pale body. "What?" I said to him, slamming my book shut.

"Whooo . . . is that a nice way to talk?"

His voice was straight from a Savannah plantation porch. What was this creep doing with a honey-smooth accent?

I excused myself for sounding rude, told him I was carrying Mace, and I introduced myself using a phony name.

He sucked something loose between his teeth. "I want to talk with you about Jimmy."

"Who's Jimmy?"

"Annie, the fake name was enough. No need to get cute."

"In anything other than young children and dogs, cute is an affliction. I've never suffered from it."

"You're angry and stressed, I understand. Jimmy's a national treasure. It's as if you've taken on saving an old redwood grove or a wildflower habitat all by yourself."

"I don't know anyone named Jimmy."

He pulled out a wooden matchstick, and fa-whacked a long cigarette from its pack. Foreign. He struck the match on the bench and lit up.

"Let me tell you something," he said. "There are lots of people with amazing abilities. The government keeps track of them from the first moment we learn about them."

"Still batting zero. I have no amazing abilities."

"And when that person is threatened, we take action to make sure the national treasure is safe."

"I appreciate your candor, but," I said, looking for the second time that day at my broken watch, "I have an appointment."

"Unlike Dudley," he said, "I've done my homework. I know that you don't like authority—most particularly, I might say, of a government sort—but this time you're in over your head. You need our help."

My hands were icy. "Who are you," I asked, "and why have you dropped into my life?" I thought about the house falling on the Wicked Witch of the East. I was in the epicenter of all manner of falling houses.

"I'm from the Centers for Disease Control, Atlanta. We understand Jimmy needs time to grow up. We'll make sure he has it."

"If you find someone named Jimmy, I'm sure she'll be grateful." I stood to leave.

"Sit down and stop playing games." His voice was a snarl. "You have no idea what you're into. The CDC is more important than whatever knucklehead is currently in possession of the White House keys. We are a long-term, farsighted group, and our funding goes on despite changes in the regime."

"Must be nice to work in the twenty-third century for the Stepford Government."

I dug into my chocolate. Candy was still watching me, and I knew he could take this stranger down in a flash. Because I felt safe, and because I've watched far too much television, I said to the CDC guy, "May I see your credentials, assuming you have some that weren't purchased from Loonies 'R Us?"

He showed me his credentials and identification and secret password to the inner sanctum. If the whole shebang wasn't real, he'd paid one hell of a lot of money getting them made. They were perfect. I copied down every single number.

"I've known about Jimmy for some time," he said, "but I couldn't get to him—he has to trust us. Our grand government is full of incompetent boobs from the highest levels to the lowest. You cannot begin to imagine."

"Try me."

I was quiet, considering my options, slipping off my heels in case I felt like running.

He was introspective. "No good connection to Jimmy, then you happened."

"Dead end. Sorry."

"I called your mother-in-law, Madame Mina. Easy to find—not only was her picture in *The Eye,* so was her phone number. I told her I was from Atlanta and that I wanted to talk about Jimmy. I'm sure she mentioned me," he said. "Now here we are together, and Jimmy trusts you. It's a start."

The man from Atlantis. I hoped I was talking to the last nutcase who'd confessed an interest in Jimmy. This one seemed dangerous; he had working brain cells. I decided I'd better find out what the cells were up to.

I said, "What, exactly, do you want?"

"There may come a time when Jimmy wants to work on untangling the language of cancer, other diseases, too. If he chooses that path, we want to be there. Right now the biggest threats to Jimmy are you and Flora Light."

"Excuse me?"

"Flora Light because she wants to lure him into a bunch of hocus-pocus, offering him money, prestige, and popularity. You, because you want him to be a regular kid."

"Leave Jimmy alone."

"Not possible. But we can stay in the background." The man looked in the window at Candy. "That a friend of yours?"

"Don't know him."

He laughed, but it was cold, the kind of laugh that falls from a cynical mouth. "Remember," he said, "you're not the only one who gets paid for being nosy."

I sat on the bench, looking straight ahead, pissed off, chewing my cheek, keeping words back, feeling trapped. He smiled once to the sky, and he whapped his rolled-up newspaper on his thigh. Felt like the preface of an anecdote. I didn't want to hear it.

"I told you that I have an appointment." I stuck the strap of my purse over my shoulder and stood up. "But I lied. I'm sick of you, and I'm leaving."

His thin smile ran away. "One word of warning," he said. "Watch your step where Jimmy's concerned, and life will proceed without incident."

My life would proceed without incident? The man had, at least, given me something to look forward to.

I walked to the Bay View, eating goopy fudge, hearing Jimmy's haunting dream wish in my head: *I dreamed I was normal.* As far as I could tell, that wasn't a possibility. As far as I could tell, I was, in part, to blame.

Twenty-one

By the time Leo arrived at the Bay View, I was a mass of nerves and guilt. I sure as hell didn't want to need Leo, but I did.

We ate dinner across the street from the hotel. Finally, lobster. Leo ate my lobster's mate, plus a nice slice of grilled cow on the side. After a couple of margaritas I started feeling like myself. Like Jimmy, *myself* would never be normal, but it was familiar.

"What about Hao?" Leo said. "Should we see if there's anything we can do?"

"It's a little late now. The man is dead." Fully gorged on chocolate and shellfish and wine and margaritas, I only had room for the unvarnished truth.

"Annie, you look fried. Maybe you should see a trauma shrink."

"Because I saw Hao's body."

"People don't run into a dead body every day, and think about Jimmy—he could *really* use someone to talk to."

"Leo, you have a lot of confidence in shrinking than I do. I'm not saying no. I'm just saying I'm dubious about it working on me."

Maybe therapy works best for the normals. I'd hate to think of Leo as a normal, it would diminish the man. I liked Leo big and roaring.

Leo took my silence for introspection. "Annie? I'm pretty certain Jimmy needs help."

"I agree, but right now the prime objective is keeping him in one piece."

"How can people watch someone die without following up on it?" Leo said. "Not knowing if the death was natural or murder—it's surreal."

"But not unusual for Chinatown, especially if the dead person was involved with the tongs."

"This sounds like an old Charlie Chan movie."

"The tongs are alive and well. Very. People who were members have a hard time getting out—I don't know much more about them than that. In this case, ignorance is not only bliss, it's the key to a long life."

"So, we respect Ike's wishes, and Hao dies under a cloud of suspicion. Is he allowed to have a memorial service?"

"St. Theresa's is taking care of the details."

"Okay."

"Just a quiet good-bye," I said, working my way down my third margarita.

Leo looked into his dessert. "That's what I'd want even without a gang connection. Just a quiet good-bye."

"You're not going anywhere, Buster."

"We all go somewhere, sometime."

"Fine. If you drop dead, I'll wave my little hankie in your direction, bidding you a fond and quiet eternity."

The man did not even crack a smile. He said, "What about you? What would you want?"

"Gads, you're morbid on top of a perfectly good lobster and tequila."

"Someone died. It makes you think about things . . . You know."

"What would I want? I told you the last time we went through a death together."

"Yeah, yeah, the fiery motorcycle crash complete with natives performing semi-obscene ritualistic dances around your cranky old carcass. Do you have a second choice?"

"This is one of the advantages of having kids. They have to figure it out, and I won't be around to give a damn. You want another drink?"

"No, I want to get you back to the hotel room."

Leo had the hots. It had been a solitary month for me, too.

He said, "Know what? I'm damned sick of death and dying. It makes me want to sing and dance and laugh. Make love. Making love is like tossing sand in Death's wussy face. We'll tool around each other's curves, then we'll crash, a couple of gentle waves lapping an eternal shore, grinding shells to sand and dreams," he said. "Let's go."

The man was in a hurry. We left.

But the hurry would have to wait. Dudley and the CDC guy were arguing in the Bay View's parking lot, just beneath the stairs to my room.

and climbed mountains and he trained elephants and was a trapeze artist. Italian and angry didn't hurt, either.

He was almost on top of them before I heard his warrior whoop. They both turned, surprised. Rolling up his sleeves, he yelled again. The younger men wore looks of slight amusement. Mistake. When bears do that thing—opening their mouths wide, roaring, shaking their massive heads back and forth—that's when you know they're serious, and you've had it. Those two were about to get a load of the Animal Planet without the aid of television.

Even though he'd hollered loud enough to crinkle the yellow painted lines between parking spaces, Leo's assault took them by surprise. I heard thuds and grunts, and I saw one white-silk shirt circle and go down. Leo bent over the man on the concrete. Leo must have had ears in the back of his head—there was Dudley hovering over him, and there was Leo reaching back, turning on his heel, standing and slugging Dudley in the eye. Dudley held his eye, retreating into a recessed area between two small Japanese cars. Leo almost punched him again. He considered Dudley, and held back.

Leo dusted himself off. The CDC guy, still on the ground, worked himself up to a hunchbacked standing position, weaving back and forth. Leo turned once more to check on Dudley. He'd found the nearest load-bearing cement column to lean against.

Leo let the CDC man stand up straight, then he whacked him with the back of his hand. His hands are huge and strong. The guy fell flat. After the initial excitement wore off, I felt as if I was about to lose the lobster I'd been waiting one month to eat. Leo picked CDC off the ground, flapping him over the hood of a dark green Mercedes as if he were wet laundry. He ordered Dudley to move out of the shadows and stand next to the car. Dudley staggered back into the fray, his hands raised, as if Leo was carrying a gun. He took his place next to the limp man.

Leo leaned over, and yelled in the wet laundry's ear. "You want to tell me why you think you have the right to be all over our lives?"

The man was fishing around in his mouth, maybe he'd lost a tooth. He massaged his jaw, saying, "Give me a minute, will you?" I noticed the Southern accent was gone. Possibly the first time an accent had been beaten out of someone.

Leo shot him a look of disgust.

"Tall man," Leo said. "You're Dudley?"

"Yes, sir."

"Don't call me sir. I only gave you a black eye. If I beat the snot out of you, you're allowed to call me sir."

"All right."

"Dudley, we don't want you."

"I'll get fired if I don't follow Mrs. Szabo."

For a fleeting moment I thought he meant Mina. Then I realized he was talking about me. That was a cold splash of water.

"I don't care about your job security," Leo said, moving into his face. "For a few minutes, I didn't care if you were dead or alive."

Dudley's self-nurturing hand froze on his swollen eye. I was certain he wished he were buried beneath ten cartons of forms that needed to be filed.

I approached the dynamic trio. The testosterone levels were dropping, and the sweat was rising. I wanted out of there, but I had a few questions of my own.

I said, "What were you fighting about?"

CDC spoke up. "You tell us. It was your friend who attacked."

"The first fight, the one between you and Dudley."

Dudley's turn. He was starting to look tall again. Soon he'd be well on his way to five feet. "Jurisdiction. Procedure. You wouldn't understand."

"I don't want either of you anywhere near the jurisdiction that includes me."

"This is bigger than you," Dudley said.

"I know, it's a favor for the twins."

"And it's about Jimmy," added the CDC guy.

"When Jimmy is forty years old, find him, talk to him. By then he'll be able to chant you both to Mars. For now, consider this— Leo doesn't carry a gun. I sometimes do."

"Sometimes?" Dudley was growing paler, and his fat eye was growing darker.

"And I'm never sure when I'll be in the mood. Kind of like deciding to wear boots or heels. Got it?"

Dudley nodded his head *yes*. He understood.

The other man told us we were idiots. Then he found his bones and unglued himself from the hood of the fine car. He said to us, pointing to Dudley, "You have no idea who this man is."

"It's even. I have no idea who you are, either, but both of you have risen high above the mere nuisance level."

"I am a doctor. Dudley," he said, as if he were talking about a rash, "is an agent."

"Meaning you spent more time in school," Leo said. "Big deal. Get out of here."

"I'm already gone," he said. "By the way, I'm not worried about your Lone Ranger act and, Mrs. Szabo, I'm not afraid of guns."

He limped away, trying to collect himself, a difficult task when your white-silk shirt is wearing greasy tire marks and fresh blood.

I wanted to yell at his back, telling him he'd damned well ought to be afraid, but for some reason I was hoarse.

Dudley raised his hand.

"What is this?" Leo said to him. "Third grade? You have something to say, just say it."

"I've told you, all government agencies do not have the same agenda. Right now, my primary task is to keep an eye on Mrs. Szabo. She's the key to keeping Jimmy safe. At some point he'll be a great benefit to our country, and we don't want to lose him the same way we lost Ike."

Ike? Dudley had his brothers mixed up.

Leo scratched his head.

"Are you okay?" I asked him.

He dusted more of the parking lot off his clothes. "I'm fine. I just can't figure out how this whole mess started."

"Yeah, you can. It happened because of one article I wrote that paid less than the cost of the CDC man's silk shirt."

"I don't believe it. These people work for a very large ship, and ships do not spring into action quickly. I think you were caught in the middle of something that was already moving."

Dudley stood, saying nothing. A wise decision. Leo still had a little juice left. He was working one of his fists inside the other.

"I've already told you when I was brought into this and by whom." Dudley was forlorn. "I'm not high enough up the ladder to tell you anything else."

Leo asked, "How high up the ladder is the man I just pounded?"

"Mr. Lee? Very high. But CDC's a different ladder."

Mr. Lee. He was Chinese, and he was quite a foe. He wore expensive clothes and smelled like a man at the top of his game. I didn't buy an argument over jurisdiction. He was hassling Dudley for information, probably information Dudley didn't even know he had.

"Dudley," I said, "beat it. I trust you, mostly because you're too dumb to be nefarious. Mr. Lee's finished for tonight, but tomorrow is a different story. If you see him around, come and grab me or Leo. He's too much for you to handle."

Dudley apologized, and I wasn't sure why. Wearing a slight limp and a battered eye, he wandered to a nondescript car and started the engine. I pictured him driving home to an apartment full of beige furnishings and heavy draperies, and I almost felt sorry for him.

"Cut it out," Leo said, catching my expression. "Dudley is not a stray dog. He's a pest."

"But Mr. Lee is worse."

"Yeah, unpredictable. Strong."

"Feral. Predatory."

Twenty-three

Our arms around each other, we walked upstairs. I didn't know what we'd gained from the big bang, but I knew Leo was acting on instinct; he wanted the other men in the jungle to know I was not alone. Male language. I'm glad I don't have to speak it, but I appreciated Leo's instinct. I noticed that Leo's male language included the signs of leftover rage and frustration—he huffed and puffed up the stairs. I did him the favor of not mentioning it. He needed cooling-down time.

I was angry, too. The idea that government employees, regardless of their rank, were arguing about me as if I were a piece of territory in dispute. Liberty and justice for all, that was too much to expect. I'd settle for anonymity, for safety.

Leo climbed into the shower. I almost joined him, but one thing would lead to another, and I wanted to check in with the crew. I wanted to know that the violence and plotting and heated arguments had been confined to this part of town.

I called the Mystic Café. Mina answered. She confirmed that Jimmy was not only fine and dandy, he was standing right next to her.

"And E. B.?" I asked.

"You want to talk with her?"

"Yeah, I do."

Rattle, rattle, sound of laughter and my daughter picking up the phone. "Hi, Mom."

"Hi," I said. "Hey, whatever's been weird between us lately? Let's forget about it."

"Deal."

"Are you having a good time, and is Mina keeping her eye on Jimmy?"

"Jimmy is not a one-person job."

"Tell me about it."

"He's figured out things to do with the leftover herb teas that even Mina didn't know about. By smelling them and tasting them, he knows their Chinese equivalent."

"Be warned. That kid knows 101 things to do with almost any herb."

"I've found that out. We all have," she said. "You're really attached to him, aren't you?"

"It's odd, but I do feel connected to him. Who knows, maybe that's what love is—feeling the Big Connection and having no idea why."

"Maybe," she said. "I know very little about the secret language of the heart."

Artists often think they're clumsy babies on the playground of love, then they create something so beautiful that it breaks your heart. We'd been over this before, as I'd been over it with her dad. I let it go by.

"Any stray Gypsies still there?" I asked. *Stray Gypsies?* Please. No wonder my daughter didn't trust me to act decently around her people.

"No strays," she said. "Just family."

I couldn't comprehend my daughter having family that wasn't part of me. Family that I didn't know.

"Sounds good," I said. "Put Jimmy on, will you?"

I heard her call him. I heard her voice again, distant, calling him. My heart danced the worry-panic two-step until I heard him squawking, heard his footsteps running to the phone. My daughter's high-pitched screech was followed by laughter and *You little rat!*

"Hi, Annie!" he said.

For a kid who'd just seen his uncle die, he was awfully wound up. Leo was right. As soon as possible, we'd get Jimmy to a shrink. I wasn't making plans for his future, but I needed to tell . . . Whoever . . . what Jimmy would need.

"Having a good time?"

"Great. There are games and playing cards all over the place. Mina calls them tarot, and she's teaching me how to tell fortunes."

"Don't take it too seriously. A lot of it doesn't come true."

"I hope it does. She said I was going to be rich, and that a bunch of women will like me."

I wondered if Mina had stacked the deck in his favor.

"You know what else?" he said, his voice the whisper of one conspirator to another. "They've got the same herbs around here that Qi Dragon has. But they don't combine things in the same way. Hao never let me near his herbs."

"I heard you're making everyone's life pretty exciting."

"I can create smoke and colored clouds. Plus, they've got three things here that you can mix together and put in the toilet tank; it gurgles when someone sits down. I probably won't do that one."

"Good idea."

"How come they have all these herbs? It doesn't look like they ever use them."

"It used to be Mina's Mystic Café, a place where people went to have their fortunes told, drink tea, and buy herbs. Kind of like Hao's, but for rich white college kids."

"I guess the rich kids ran out of money. They haven't had one single customer."

Leo was out of the shower, wandering the suite, giving himself a tour. Easy to see he was stunned that I'd blown a colossal sum of money on this place before I actually had the big bucks in hand. I was fairly stunned, too, but I'd decided not to think about it. My mother's *It will all work out in the end* was tattooed on my hide.

Jimmy was yammering—excited, I didn't hear his words—as Leo, gape-mouthed, discovered the deck, complete with redwood hot tub. All that money landing on me in the form of debt had rendered him dumb. He'd recover soon; it was cold on the deck.

"Out of business . . . Now I understand what's going on," Jimmy said. "Nobody tells me anything. There's furniture, but no TV, so it didn't feel like a real house. No GameBoy, either."

He slid into the woeful, longing voice kids use when they want something, believing the pathetic angle will get them their heart's desire.

"Jimmy, knock it off. I'll be there tomorrow, and I'll bring your GameBoy."

"Hooray! Could you also pick up the latest Scrank for me? I really liked the first game."

"If I can find it without having to venture into a mall, I'll get it."

"The store two doors down from Mina's has black-market copies for ten bucks. The graphics are a little funky, but the game is just the same. I get my cell phones from them, too."

"I'll see what I can do."

His voice grew quiet again, muffled. Sounded as if his hand were cupped around the mouthpiece. He said, "Annie, a few times while I've been here I've wanted to be, I don't know, small."

"What do you mean?"

"I feel like everyone's looking at me. It makes me want to disappear."

"They're looking *out* for you. That's different."

"No, they expect something. It's like I'm a chunk of uranium, and they're waiting for me to glow."

"Jimmy, try to relax."

"It's not that easy. The young woman who's married to the handsome guy, the friends of your daughter's?"

"Yes?"

"Well, that lady's stomach is gigantic. I think she's about to have her baby any minute."

"They'll take her to the hospital, and the baby will be born. Birth happens all the time, it's not the same as dying. It's a happy thing."

"Everyone says *No Hospital!* I didn't know white people avoided them, too."

Why didn't this surprise me? "I guess it's none of our business."

"I hope not. I'm afraid if the baby starts happening, they'll want me to help. I did that once with a lady in Chinatown. It was kind of cool, but it was different. Hao was there."

All Jimmy had to do was survive this one night with the Szabo clan. He probably felt more normal than he ever thought possible.

I said, "Put your mouth on the lady's stomach and tell the baby to stay put. And no loud noises. The baby might get scared and decide to be born."

"I hadn't thought of that."

"Put Mina back on the phone. Wait a minute," I said, "Jimmy?"

"Yeah?"

"I love you."

There was a long silence.

"Okay," he said. "That's okay with me."

He handed Mina the phone. "What did you say to that kid? He's as white as a ghost."

"I told him I loved him."

"Oh. That. Hao's service is tonight."

"Already?"

"I don't know the details. I talked to Ike, and he has lots of friends with him. Even Jimmy's useless pig of a father is there. They found him peddling porn behind a restaurant."

"You going to the service?"

"No way. We swore off funerals together, remember? I'm doing something for Hao right here. I'm protecting the kid he died for."

I told her about the fight in the parking garage, and I described Mr. Lee in detail, her man from Atlantis. I told her she had my blessing to dispose of him if he came around.

She said, "Leo gave Dudley a black eye?"

"A doozy."

"I wish I'd been there. I'm telling you again, don't lose that man. I'd swipe him from you," she said, "if I thought I could, but I'm busy trying to find out how Hao died. I'm asking the tarot for answers, but so far all I've learned is that one day Jimmy will be a babe magnet."

"I was certain Flora killed Hao," I said. "Now I'm not sure."

"Maybe that boyfriend of hers. Jealousy makes people wild. I know this from my own personal life."

"I stopped by the church and overheard a fight between the two of them. It was about Hao, and it was loud."

"There's also the dolphin person," she said, "who thinks regular food from the supermarket is poison. I heard him say he was militant. Maybe he got kicked out of the army for being crazy."

"No military involved. Skip fell off a time machine midflight, and his brain hasn't been right since."

"I guess," she said. "Know what? I'd like to know what those government goons were arguing about last night *before* the big fight. Why were they waiting for you?"

"My guess is that neither of them knew the other would be there. Earlier, the CDC guy found me at Ghirardelli Square. He made it clear that he was my latest permanent fixture, and he dangled Jimmy's future in front of my nose like a threat."

Steel shot through her words. "He threatened you?"

"Basically, yes."

"This is worse than our mess with my ex-husband, rat-infested

Pinky Marks. Annie, for two people who don't want to be noticed, we get noticed an awful lot."

"We have dynamic personalities."

"We'd better knock that off and lie low."

"Mina, there's one thing you and I have in common—we will never be invisible."

There was a long silence.

"What are you thinking?" I said.

"I'm letting the horror of that settle in."

"Here's another news flash. The twins?"

"My old lady twins?"

"They're the ones who set Dudley on us. They called in a favor from the FBI. Dudley may show up at the Mystic Café. I hope not."

"Know what? Those women may want to cause trouble just because they can."

"That's what Leo said, but I don't think so."

"Sometimes when you get old, making trouble is the only way you get to feel alive. Who knows? Maybe they meant well, but Dudley started calling his own shots."

"Not possible. Either·one of us could think him out of a box of cereal."

"Okay, if he shows up, I won't poison him or lay enchantment on him, even though he *is* government," she said.

"At least he's safe."

"A safe spy. I guess the twins don't have much influence."

"It's probably gone the way of many things."

"What if my power does the big flush by the time I'm their age?"

"People who are three hundred years old are beyond clocks, Mina. You have nothing to worry about."

"I hope you're right," she said. "Now, let me get my job straight. I'm supposed to keep an eye out for the guy from Atlantis,

I like saying that, and I don't worry about Dudley. The dolphin man is nuts, meaning we try to avoid him."

"And if anyone asks, you have no idea where Jimmy is. None."

"Got it. Do I worry about Flora?"

"Definitely. It would be easy for her to charm Jimmy away from you."

"I also watch for her jealous boyfriend who was kicked out of sports, I make sure there are no tongs under my bed, and at the same time I take care of Jimmy. You want me to build a pyramid or hex someone straight to another solar system?"

"Nope. That's about it."

"What are you doing while I'm up to my elbows in worry?"

"You know. Bay View with Leo, and don't tell one soul."

"You have a hotsy-totsy time with a gorgeous man while I guard civilization."

"Right. Your job is to protect life on earth as we know it."

"How come you get the guy, and I get the work?"

"Because you wanted your picture in *The Eye* with Hao and Jimmy, and you got it, and I deserve one evening without having to think about any of you."

"You're right," she said, "and I can't figure a way around it."

"Get through tonight. Tomorrow Leo and I will come over and collect Jimmy."

I could almost hear Mina launch herself out of her seat and land on the floor. She had dropped the phone.

"Go to Chinatown," she said. "My place. I'll bring Jimmy there."

"Are you worried about me meeting those Gypsy kids, too?"

"Maybe."

This was really starting to piss me off. "I'm picking up Jimmy at the café."

She exhaled into the mouthpiece. "God, you're stubborn. You have to make a solemn promise to act decent when you come," Mina said. "No matter what."

"I promise. I'm not the one with a problem here."

"Fine, but remember one thing—never make promises you can't keep."

I hung up, disgusted with my whole family. They didn't mind bringing one hundred Gypsies to my house, uninvited, for a wake. But introduce me to a few Gypsies who were my kids' third cousins twice removed, and you'd think I hated the entire race. The only trouble I'd ever had from any of them had been dispensed by Mina and her wild batch of revenge after my husband's death. She and my daughter were stuck in a hazy past, taking their mental illness out on me. Tomorrow I'd tell them so, and I'd tell them at the Mystic Café.

Twenty-four

Leo was waiting for me in bed, reading a book. He looked comfortable, so comfortable.

He patted the covers, inviting me in.

His breathing had returned to normal, his color was there, too.

I said, "You okay?"

"I'm the best."

"No bruises, cuts?"

"From those two? Be serious," he said, smiling, stroking my cheek, a long stroke that rippled down my legs. "I've got a present for you."

"Is that what we're calling it now?"

He peered at me over his reading glasses. "I am talking about a *real* present. You have a wicked mind," he said. "I really like that."

He handed me a sheet of paper. "A poem," Leo said. "It's for you."

"Did you copy this from a book?"

"Hard to imagine, but I am not only a sex object, I am literate."

"Every time I'm itchy to throw you out of my heart . . ."

". . . because I've gotten too close."

"You pull a stunt like this. And this is not a mushy tear. I'm tired."

He brushed stray hair off my cheek, tucking it behind one ear,

and he kissed my forehead. I read the poem of black-lettered light
that Leo hadn't copied out of a book.

~Poem for You~

i want to twirl my
self
in your hair
and twirl and twirl
and dervish into your
mind
and spirit
and live there
in its infinite spaces
and energies crackling
like lightning
through the heavens
and blast out
my own
lightning
and dance
super-charged
eternally with you

i want to roll my
self
into your skin
and surround
me
with you
your flesh
your corpuscles
and the strokes

of your hands
and laughter
of your belly
and join hands
and bellies
and bonk
eternally
with you

I want to fold my
heart
into your
heart
and occupy
the chambers
of you
as you occupy
the chambers
of my loving
heart
blood mingled
with blood
one blood
one beat
and beat-dance
and beat-dance
and beat-dance
eternally
with you

Then I read it out loud to him, and we touched all the places inside the poem, tracing the thin roads on the map of a very important world until we fell asleep.

*   *   *

The giant bed. A comforter nicer than anyone owns in their own home was tangled around my legs. Half-asleep and I wanted to stay that way. His skin was mine. I could almost tell our breath apart, but not quite—I remembered stories of animal trainers trading breath with their animals to make them their own.

Leo, asleep in the off-season hotel light, was a place I loved to visit. To caress, smooth as polished stones, the curve of his back, his hardrock calves. Always a shuddering wonder.

Every once in a ridiculous while I've told myself that I was nuts, I was too old, I was too . . . to have this. But, if I were honest with myself, which mostly happens when I'm not fully awake, I couldn't imagine moving back to the shuttered suburbs of my heart. He was my big adventure—I appreciated him, and I didn't want to change him. He felt the same way. Unbelievable.

He yawned and rolled over, taking me with him. I caught a glimpse of my naked body in the double-mirrored closet door. A harrowing sight, far too much white skin. Those mirrors should be placed in rooms reserved for guests with masochistic fantasies.

"Leo, I'm fat."

"I guess we're waking up," he said, stretching. "You're fine, and no sane man ever gets into a discussion with a woman about body fat. Isn't it the middle of the night?"

I rolled over him and unplugged the clock. "This is serious. My body has decided to turn everything I eat into fat. I could probably eat an upholstered cushion and morph it into fat."

He sat up and opened his book. He tossed a pillow under the bed. "I'm saving the pillow. Just in case you get hungry."

"If there's another ice age, I'll be set."

He turned a page.

I used to be able to balance a wineglass on my stomach. I tried. The glass fell over. Leo, snuggling down, licked wine off the sheets, off my skin. He's a pretty basic waste-not model.

I surveyed the length and breadth of my body. "This is probably as good as it's going to get."

"Looks plenty good to me." He rubbed a foot up and down my leg.

I lifted the covers. "Already?"

"I'm in bed with you and we're naked. That's all it takes." Yes, a very basic model.

Our toes waggle-bundled together. I kissed him and rubbed his fur, and we rolled on our sides to see ourselves in the other's eyes, a much kinder mirror.

Marine middle night poured in, water rolling over streetlight towers, offering us crackling illumination. When time lost its last shoe, we ran barefoot through wet grass, we tumbled beneath a cool waterfall, we crawled on our bellies through a black tunnel to emerge into a sun-flooded underground grotto. Clear water, cold and shocking. The last languid, weightless laugh ran away.

Falling toward sleep to visit each other's dreams, without fear, no worries, I said, "Leo? Thanks."

"I know," he said. "Thanks back. What time is it?"

"Somebody unplugged the clock."

"Annie? Why don't you marry me?"

I didn't mean to, but I laughed.

"Was that a *yes* laugh or a *no* laugh?"

"A *what!* laugh. Marriage happened, once, so long ago it's like looking at someone else's photo album. I loved the man like crazy, he exited, marriage hasn't occurred to me again. I'm used to me."

"Look, I loved a woman like crazy, and I dropped her during trapeze exercises. An accident, but she died. It could have been me on that floor, and it could have been you who drove off a cliff. Just like life, death's a fluke."

"I don't remember how to be married."

"Great! We get to start from scratch—two aging virgins."

"Aging," I said, looking down at my white, "may not be a pretty sight."

"You think watching me crumble is going to be pretty?"

"You will be magnificent and graceful, even in decay."

"Maybe I asked you the wrong question," he said. "You want to watch each other get old and file joint tax returns?"

"I'll think about it."

"Good enough for me. Let's celebrate."

"Are there such things as sexaholics? Because I think you may be one."

"Should I seek professional help?"

"Not a chance."

Twenty-five

You can live your life in one of two ways. One is to believe that nothing is a miracle, the other is to believe that everything is a miracle.

—Albert Einstein

I learned tarot because I wanted to be prepared for miracles. Learning plants prepares you for miracles, too. Hops for dreaming about miracles to come, nettle to prepare for a lusty encounter . . . Someday I'm going to take off my training wheels, and give up all the preparations. Miracles feel more like miracles when they sneak up on you.

—Madame Mina

I'd gifted Leo with a deep wine robe, reversible, with dark gold and black dragons running loose from front to back. It looked large in the store, but it fit him perfectly. He was big in the spirit, I never thought of him as big in the body. I showered, steaming myself into a new morning.

I wrapped up in the hotel robe, and walked my dripping water into the kitchen. The *Chronicle* had arrived, just as it did every morning. Leo, seeing me, closed the paper, shuffling it into a messy wad.

"What are you hiding?"

"I'm looking for basketball scores."

"They're usually in the sports section," I said. "What are you hiding?"

Leo sighed. Opening the paper and folding it back to page three, between newsprint crinkles, was the story. Almost one full page, covering the death of Flora Light, San Francisco's premiere evangelical force.

A photo of Wagner, grief-stricken, floated in the upper right corner. He was named as head of her ministry for the poor. Shielding his eyes from the press, he appeared to have lost fifty pounds and gained ten years in one day.

I couldn't say anything, and I couldn't pull away from Wagner's gray-toned face.

Leo said, "What are you thinking?"

"That a person can love someone to death, and maybe that's what happened to Flora. Hao, too. And perhaps the horror of his actions has just hit Brother Wagner upside the soul."

"Doesn't wash. He'd go into hiding or run. He has enough money to buy a one-way ticket anywhere and settle in."

"When the horror sets in, sometimes the guilty party wants to be caught."

"No clues. With a crime of passion, there'd have to be a few. I haven't read the article yet. Maybe Flora fell off a stepladder." Leo pulled the paper toward him, lowering his reading glasses.

"It may be too early for clues. Could be that Wagner doesn't even remember the killing."

Leo skimmed the page. "Well, forget the ladder. Says here she was strangled, then her neck was broken. Flora's body was found in her own bed."

I couldn't find my glasses. Even the print on the bread box was a blur. "Anything else?"

"It happened late last night. If there was any evidence at the scene, SFPD isn't releasing it."

"I'm calling the twins."

"Why?"

"Because they seem to know about everything that goes down."

He looked doubtful, but handed me the phone. I dialed the Rafael, asking for the Duettes' room. The phone was picked up immediately.

"Jan?"

"Jean."

"Do you know what happened to Flora?"

"We just heard about it on the television news. Isn't it horrible?"

"Who did it?"

"For heavens sake, I wouldn't have a clue."

"Why do you sound like an old lady all of a sudden?"

"I *am* an old lady."

"An old lady who is gorgeous, who knows the FBI well enough to ask for favors, who smokes pot, and who knows, by her own reckoning, more secrets than the government. An old lady who introduced Flora to Hao—now both dead."

"Sheer coincidence. I told Flora her church was in a bad area. Squeezed between the old Italians and the gays, a rough neighborhood, and Chinatown, I offered to help her move. She wouldn't. I don't know what she was thinking."

"I do. Diversity is good for television ratings, and rich people like to go slumming in bum neighborhoods for fine music and God. For two hours they remember they are not their money."

She muffled the mouthpiece; soft words pinged back and forth.

"Hi again," the voice said.

"Jean?"

"Jan. Jean rattles easily."

"How well did you really know Flora?"

"Jean had come to know Flora quite well over the last few years. She had become enamored of her . . . philosophy."

"I don't see Jean as the religious type."

Long silence. "Neither do I."

"Then why did Flora happen to her?"

"Jean's ego is a Siamese cat, it loves to be stroked. Flora had the right technique, and Jean went for it. After she was hooked, we opened doors for Flora—power, money, fame—we were just a few of the people Flora stroked to meet the influential. Hao," Jan said, "was an accident, a nobody. Jean sent Flora there to buy her cosmetics."

The conversation made me sick. "Hao was somebody. Somebody important."

"Don't get sentimental. I'm telling you the facts. You have the stomach for them?"

"No. But I'm listening."

"I liked Flora, but if you have any bugaboos about religion, you don't want to like someone who's peddling God. Jean was hooked, I wasn't."

"You never fell for Flora's line?"

"No, but it didn't take me long to see that Flora was selling hope—not a completely terrible thing. And she had a gift for healing. That wasn't phony."

"Why did she need Jimmy?"

"A couple of years ago Flora was in an accident, it was a close call. She came out of it, but she suffered from terrible back pain. Lost her concentration, and her healing ability went downhill. Flora was running services, taking drugs, doing a pretty good job of keeping it all together. But she couldn't heal with any predictability."

"Did you ever see her in action?"

"Once, and it was truly something." Jan laughed. "Flora told me she could feel a person's broken parts, and, like a mechanic, she'd climb under their hood and repair the engine. Sometimes the person wasn't cured, but they'd experience deep peace."

"Sometimes there is no cure but there's a healing . . ."

"What?"

"Something Hao said to me."

Jan said, "That's why she wanted Jimmy—to heal her flock. She couldn't do it."

"And to keep her business running," I said.

"Of course, and if Jimmy could heal her, too, all the better."

"Our meeting at the Rafael was no accident, was it?" I said. "You agreed to talk with me because of Jimmy."

"We were already working on Hao. Some luck, but not enough.

Then he told us you'd written about Jimmy and that Jimmy really liked you. We wanted you to influence Jimmy, to help us get him to Flora's. We were willing to pull out the heavy artillery to do it—intimidation. But then we met you, and we liked you. That really gummed up the works."

"Sorry about that."

"You couldn't help it," she said. "We had to come up with Plan B—we'd provide you with protection, and you'd use it to protect Jimmy."

"The FBI agent you sent is nobody's idea of protection. Last night he got his clock cleaned by a Chinese guy from CDC and another guy twice his age."

More muffled conversation between the sisters.

"We'll get on it as soon as we get off the phone."

"Hey, I don't want a change in personnel—I have a deal worked out with him. I'm just letting you know in case you need help in the future."

"Suit yourself."

"Can I talk to both of you at the same time?"

Clickety, clackety, Jean back on the other line. "Hi, honey."

"Ladies, what—or who—do you think happened to Flora? Because if it hasn't got anything to do with Jimmy, I'd like to know."

"We think it had everything to do with Jimmy."

"Maybe it was Wagner. Flora's sexual shenanigans, their open relationship . . ."

"Wagner? Not a chance."

"He's a big man with a violent past."

"We are quite aware of his past. And that's what it is—the past," Jan said. "By the way, Leo is quite wonderful."

"You know about Leo?"

"Draw your hotel draperies when you're occupied," Jean said.

I wouldn't mention this to Leo. Sometimes he pretended life

had left him a small vestige of dignity. Hanging out with me had not helped him nurse that illusion.

"You tossed Leo into this conversation to distract me," I said.

"Sorry it didn't work," Jean or Jan said.

"I'm going to dig until I find evidence connecting Wagner to Flora's and Hao's deaths. Assuming the police aren't already on it," I said.

"Dear, it's a waste of time. Wagner did *not* kill Flora."

"I don't see how you can be so sure."

"Because," Jan said, "Wagner spent the night with us."

"With *both* of us," chimed in Jean, the God-fearing sister.

Twenty-six

"*L*eo, do not even think about laughing. Someone died. Now another person is dead."

"You're right, it's nothing to laugh about," he said, "but I really like those women."

"You don't know them."

"I admire their style."

"I'm never introducing you to them."

"I'm flattered."

Leo wiped a lone tear from his eye. He was laughing, but I was scared and trying not to be.

I said, "Did you ask me to marry you last night?"

"I don't remember."

I swacked him on the shoulder. "You are such a pain."

"Do you want me to have asked you?"

"Yes, and I want you not to know my answer. It's called suspense."

"You want me to keep working at this, don't you?"

"Not if it feels like work."

"I've always loved my work."

"You're excused," I said.

"For what?"

"Sort of a papal dispensation—a blanket forgiveness for the next dumb thing you say."

He pulled me close. "What now?"

"Grab Jimmy and take him to my place."

"You don't think he's safe at the Mystic?"

"I don't think any of us are safe," I said, "and I don't know what direction the danger's coming from."

"Let's hit the road."

When escrow closed I'd come back down, sign papers, and collect my check. I didn't want anything important, like my financial future, dependent upon my FedEx man.

We drove across town.

Haight and Ashbury Streets were thriving thirty years ago, now they're faded Day-Glo paint. We drove down Haight, passing a health food store, Amoeba Records, the Anarchist Bookstore, and two Thai restaurants. A store selling funky four-hundred-dollar T-shirts to German tourists, and the same tourists jiving with homeless kids lost in a time warp that had set them adrift in a techno-strange world.

Then all activity came to a screeching halt. Businesses on the west end of Haight were boarded up. Giant pieces of yellow iron crouched, ready to swallow the old Victorians. One earthmover chewed the pavement, preparing the ground for a new sewer line.

We pulled in behind the Mystic Cafe, now surrounded by abandoned dreams of people past. Mine was the only car in the lot. I'd seen Dudley sitting on an iron bench next to a skeleton construction crew. He was conspicuous, clueless, and wearing a bold shiner. Reading a newspaper, he was drinking from a paper cup emblazoned with Mina's logo.

I took Leo's hand and dragged him around to the sidewalk in front of the store. I didn't expect them to make up and shake hands, but I thought they should be in each other's presence in a way that did not involve heavy breathing and fists.

"I've been expecting you to show up here," Dudley said to me, looking past Leo.

"Your instinct is impeccable."

"You see the article about Flora this morning?"

"I don't get it. I thought Flora killed Hao," I said, "then I thought Wagner did it. Now I've found out Wagner has a pretty good alibi, at least in Flora's case. Unless the person I spoke with lied for Wagner."

"Persons," Dudley said, correcting me. "They weren't lying. Wagner spent the entire night at the Rafael with them."

"Dudley, I'm impressed."

"When they ask us for a favor, we wonder why. Doesn't matter if they're ex-operatives—we're going to tail them, too."

"Dudley! After that row last night *you* tailed them?"

"Someone else. They'd know I was watching them before I did."

"The twins have any reason to want Hao and Flora dead?"

"Doubtful, but people are full of surprises. Those women have messed with our heads for years. Usually just mischief, but you never know."

"Everybody's following someone," I said, "no one trusts anyone, and we don't have a line on why the same person wanted Flora and Hao dead. Their only connection was Wagner of the airtight alibi."

"As the wolf who's your partner, may I point out that their connection is a lot more obvious than Wagner? Flora and Hao's connection is Jimmy."

"Jimmy didn't kill them!"

"Of course not. But he's the connection. Keep that boy tucked inside Mina's building until we tell you it's safe for him to go home."

"He can't grow up in there with Mina," I said. "I was thinking of stashing him at my house."

"It's not a terrible idea, but let me run it past a few people. In the meantime, he stays here. A rural environment has its own hazards." I could see Dudley shuddering over a parade of spiders and snakes.

I said, "Okay."

No one named Dudley was going to tell me if and when I could come and go, or who was going with me. But I smiled at him like an obedient moron permanently tuned to FM station K-DUMB.

"Annie?"

"What?"

"Watch yourself. Whoever wants Jimmy is playing hardball."

Was I supposed to think this was news?

"Dudley, maybe you could run it by someone who is real protection, and you could merrily wrap yourself around your desk until retirement."

"You're stuck with me. Two deaths, the bureau thinks I'm on the inside track."

He toasted me with his yellowing paper cup. "Thank Mina for the coffee."

Only one positive thing I could see about being Dudley's assignment. If I escaped into the redwoods, or out to the ocean, Dudley wouldn't get in my way. A city boy, through and through, he would not risk direct confrontation with any form of nature.

Twenty-seven

I knocked on the Cafe's door, but first I looked in the front window. Faint television blue-light glow, Jimmy was watching Japanese cartoons, the kind that make characters look void and hypertensive.

Jimmy saw me out the window and ran to the door. He opened it, and quickly locked the door behind us. I introduced him to Leo.

"Mina told me not to let anyone in," Jimmy said. "Flora just died. Did you know that?"

"How did *you* know it?"

"Mina told me."

I was surprised she'd done that.

"Flora was very sick. I knew she hurt a lot, but I didn't know she was that bad," Jimmy said. "Mina said that Flora died in her sleep, and I shouldn't worry about her because now she's living in a big mansion in heaven, and wearing a lot of nice clothes, and she'll never feel pain again."

Whew! Mina had outdone herself. She'd been bombarded so often with the promise of salvation and the threat of hell that she had the drill down cold. Mina must have wanted to be the one to present Flora's death scenario. Easier on Jimmy. Considering she'd decorated the fairy tale with mansions and nice clothing, I agreed with her.

"Did you ever work on Flora?"

"Yes, but she wasn't easy. Too many layers, and the music inside her body was bad. Flora drank too much because she wanted to forget her pain," he said, "and that didn't help, either."

"I saw her after she'd been drinking too much," I said. "It made her puffy."

"She wanted to heal people, she couldn't, so she wanted me to heal them for her. That's what I think. Flora wanted me to work on her, like every single day, but I couldn't do it." Jimmy went from gleaming to dull. It made my heart ache. "I can't even remember to make my bed and brush my teeth half the time," he said, "but now I wish I'd tried harder to help her."

"Jimmy," I said, "it's okay. Keep saying no when you need to."

Leo said, "Yes is okay, too." I shot him a look. "Sometimes."

I said, "Have you talked to Ike?"

"Are you kidding?" Jimmy rolled his eyes around in his head. "Uncle's been calling every hour or two to make sure I'm okay, and if he's not calling here, Mina's calling him."

I didn't like the idea of Ike in his little home. An easy target. I'd wanted to take him with us to the country. Mina said he refused, insisting that he wouldn't be run out of his own house.

I went to what used to be the back counter of the café and picked up the phone. Mina bustled in, buzzing around me like a fly over potato salad.

She said, "You want to take Jimmy and go to your place in Sonoma? You could leave right now, out the back, before the FBI notices. I'll get up your way soon."

"I want to see my daughter, and I want to meet her friends or family or whatever, so she knows I'm over the Gypsy-hating disease she thinks I carry."

"How about if I just leave with you right now?"

I shook my head, *No*. I phoned Ike, and he'd heard about Flora. Hao's memorial service was large. Lots of people were still there wishing Ike well, asking Hao for favors from the other side. Ike confirmed what Mina had told me—as long as he knew Jimmy was safe, Ike wasn't going anywhere. I told him we'd try to sneak by before we left. I wanted Ike and Jimmy to know they still had each other.

Jimmy got on the line. They spoke Chinese, short and buzzy, with a quick good-bye.

Jimmy said to me, "You want me to distract Dudley so we can get out of here?"

"Yes. I'll tell you when, so don't pull anything until then."

"Know what? I think these phones may be tapped, and we'd better not talk about our plans on them. Same with your cell. Can I take it apart and check?"

"Jimmy, that's not necessary."

"Since you've been in the city, has anyone been near your phone? Did you lose it in a restaurant for a few minutes, leave it in a ladies' room . . . Anything?"

No purse left in a bathroom. No spare boyfriends where I could have left a trail of clothing and personal articles—my private possessions had been true-blue to Leo. Except once, at the twin's, when my purse fell on the carpet, tumbling the crud from the very bottom of my bag.

"Jimmy, I took a nap in the twin's hotel room. I guess they could have put a listening device on my phone. They know an awful lot about what's going on." I handed him my phone, hoping he'd be able to stick it back together again.

He caught my expression. "Don't worry. I have a bunch more cell phones in my backpack."

"Those ladies are too old to know about bugging and electronics," I said, although I didn't believe it.

"Those women," he said, "make me glad I didn't have a twin. The world couldn't have taken us."

Mina narrowed her eyes, leveling me with her disregard. It was a minuscule zap. Something was up. This time I had no idea what I'd done.

"What's wrong?"

"I'm standing here in my own place, minding my own business. Does something have to be wrong?"

E. B. walked in from what used to be the café, a large room to the side, surprised to see me. We hugged. A little stiff, but it would do.

"Grandma didn't say you were coming."

"Leave me out of this," Mina said.

"Out of what? You two have gone squirrelly."

Mina and E. B. looked at each other. One long, wordless, convoluted conversation passed between them.

"E. B.," Mina said, "we can't hold out forever. Better tell your mother the truth. And Jimmy, I want you in sight. When life hits the fan, I don't want to lose you in the tornado."

Melodramatic Mina. Whatever E. B. had to say wasn't as important, or as funny, as my probable marriage proposal.

I was blithering, oblivious, walking into the other room with them, telling E. B. and Mina that Leo, I believed, had proposed marriage, except that I'd had a little too much to drink, and so had he, and then we ate too much, and he was being pretty damned cute about popping the question and my nonanswer. But, since I hadn't heard a marriage proposal that hadn't sent me into fits of laughter for thirty years . . .

I realized I was talking to myself. When I stopped, I was looking across the room straight into my dead Stevan Szabo's dark brown eyes.

Twenty-eight

*B*ut unless Stevan had made a deal with the devil or the deep Pacific, the timing was off. This young man was about the same age Stevan was when he died, leaving me with two toddlers and another on the way.

He spoke first. "Annie?"

"Are you Mına's nephew or . . ."

My words weren't finding the English dictionary or any other.

"No." He looked at my daughter. "I'm E. B.'s half brother."

Leo put his arm around my waist. That was the only thing that made sense. I plunked down on a purple velveteen futon with a shirred moon and clouds. Leo plunked down at the same time. His hand was on my knee.

"Where did you find a half brother?" I said. "I think you have your family ties mixed up."

Mina said, "You want the truth?"

"Yes. I don't know. Do I?"

"No, but it's a little late to back out now."

Leo began patting a staccato of comfort on my knee. His high rate of comfort was about to drive me over the edge. I held his hand, tight, wanting him to slow down or stop. Waiting for an explanation, I had fine-tuned my hearing so that it approached that of a first-time burglar knocking off a ritzy estate. The air vibrated.

Jimmy sat on the other side of me. Unlike Leo, Jimmy was completely still.

Mina said, "You've noticed the resemblance between this young man and my son."

"A resemblance? Mina. He is as identical to Stevan as Jean and Jan Duette are to each other."

"Then this should come as no surprise—he's Stevan's son."

That didn't compute. I studied the young man. The room was expectant, but I had nothing to offer it. I noticed the young woman sitting next to Stevan's clone. Jimmy was right. She was ready to pop. The young woman didn't look a bit like me. That ruled out a few science fiction options such as alternative realties.

"When Stevan and I were married," I said, "he never mentioned having a child. You must have been just a baby. Where's your mother? Mina?"

"When you and Stevan were married," she said, "he had no other kids. Soon after the wedding, like about nine months to the day, E. B. was born. And this boy, he was born about one year, maybe a little longer, after your wedding."

"Mom. He's a few months younger than me."

I was leaning as hard into Leo as I was into the furniture. I couldn't tell much difference between the two. I shoved the things I'd thought were real and loving behind a massive stone wall inside my head.

I looked at him. I said, "What's your name?"

"Pavlik Szabo. This is my wife, Shirley."

I didn't say anything, I couldn't say anything. It was not this man's fault that my dearly departed husband had a fling while I was pregnant. Pavlik's life had probably been no bed of roses. But his life felt kind of irrelevant. At least he knew his true history, I assumed he did, but I'd been living inside a whopper of a lie for a very long time.

"Pavlik, when did you find out about the circumstances of your birth?"

"Seems like I was born knowing everything. No embarrassing details, of course."

I was thankful for that. The entire banquet of details would have been laid out before me. This family did not know the meaning of discretion.

"My mother was a bitter woman," he said. "She wanted my father to leave you. He wouldn't do it, saying his behavior was terrible. But he couldn't resist her. Looking back, I see it was unhealthy, destructive for both of them. I was their only child."

"You remember your father?" My husband.

"Little things, I didn't have much of him before he died. I remember him bringing presents to Mina's house. One was a six-foot painting of a flying bull, incredible drama. I still own it. I remember him singing to me in Rom, and Mina singing with him."

Stevan's frequent trips to San Francisco to visit his mother and to buy art supplies.

Shirley spoke up. "If I were in your place, I'd want to do something very bad. I'm sorry to meet in this way."

"You have nothing to be sorry about," I said. "Pavlik, neither do you."

He blushed red, blushed in the same intoxicating color his father had used to color his own face. "That's very decent of you," he said.

"It's real of me. You were born into a tough situation, and your wife is about to have a baby. It would have been easier if I hadn't shown up," I said. Turning to Mina, I said, "But YOU! I can't believe the deception, all these years . . ."

"In the vast, eternal scheme of things? It hasn't been *that* long."

"Mina, it's been a lifetime. Pavlik's lifetime, mine, and you've always known."

Mina fumed. "The truth was up to your husband, and he wasn't up to the truth. I kept thinking *someday,* and then Stevan was dead. I couldn't see more hurt coming from that direction. I knew Pavlik and his mother, and I knew they'd never bother you."

"E. B.," I said, "meeting your brother must have been a shock. When did it happen?"

"Mom, I've known Pavlik as long as I can remember. No one said *Don't tell your mother,* but I knew I was supposed to keep it quiet. I remember the feeling of loving my dad. He'd drive me to the city with him to buy canvas, to see Grandma. Handsome, dazzling smile, a brilliant artist. He smelled like tanned leather.

"By the time I was old enough to know it wasn't your average family situation, he was dead. I wanted to tell you, I didn't know how. My sisters and I talked about it. None of us could figure out the right time to tell you—every time was wrong."

"Your sisters know about Pavlik, too?"

"Yes," she said, in a little voice.

"Anyone else?"

"And my mother," Pavlik said, "of course."

"I assumed your mother knew. As long as everyone's running out of the closet like rats jumping off a sinking ship into a reunion raft, we may as well meet."

Leo's patting revved up.

"My mother," Pavlik said, "died several years ago. An early-spring day, she was sunning with the sea lions on the tarred floating barges at Fisherman's Wharf. She rolled off into the bay. A bull seal, believing he was jumping in to save one of his harem, caused her death. In trying to save her, he drowned her. Bull sea lions weigh eight hundred pounds, and it was breeding season."

"Are you making this up?"

"Of course not. It was very tragic."

Another perfect story for *The Eye,* right in the bosom of my own life, and I'd missed it. How many women are killed by a California sea lion while sunning on a barge in San Francisco Bay? I can tell you how many, because I Googled it—the number is one. The woman was Sala Salo. She died leaving a son, no other surviving family members.

Pavlik tried a smile. "I think my father had a thing for unusual women."

"That's exactly the kind of smile he'd give me when he knew he'd screwed up, and he wanted to charm me out of being mad. Exactly the kind of smile that tossed us into the sack, resulting in too many kids. Shirley," I said, "a warning—don't fall for The Look."

Shirley patted her belly, sporting an ironic grin. "Too late."

I sat back. I breathed.

Pavlik said to E. B., "Your mother's taking it well."

She answered him in front of her invisible mother—me. "No, she's not. She's calm and rational. Pavlik," she said, "Mom has completely lost it."

I heard the kids talking, Mina interjecting something, all of them discussing me and the unfortunate timing of Pavlik's birth, that it would have been better if I'd never found out. Leo was quiet, thumping my knee as if he were burping a baby. Jimmy jumped off the futon. I looked once in his direction. I was out of it, but I didn't want to lose Jimmy.

I watched as he pressed his ear against Shirley's belly. Cradling her baby-bundle with both arms, Jimmy's face was pure concentration. I wondered what underwater sounds he heard in there, maybe the same sounds Sala heard when she fell into the ocean, rocked by a sea lion.

Leo tried to hold my face, but I couldn't be with him. I saw yellowing photos, edges curling, of our happy, long-ago family. Never enough money, never worrying about it. Two little girls torturing their dad's back, squealing their delight clear up to the aqua sky. And, totally absurd, I could remember Stevan's taste.

I'd have to get real and face the fact that I had wasted part of me, wrapping it around his forever-gone heart, and unable to connect with someone else because it felt like a betrayal. The part of me that died in his motorcycle crash might have been rescued if I'd known there was another lover, another child, another set of family photos. If I'd known the truth about my own life.

Leo squeezed my shoulder. "Hey," he said. "You okay?"

"No. I hurt."

"Of course you do. It's . . ."

"So long ago. It really pisses me off to feel this. I want to punch in the wall."

"Don't take it out on the wall, you'll bust your hand."

"Blatant messages from E. B. and Mina about not coming here, and I ignored them."

"Annie. Stop."

I looked at Leo. Maybe I'd have more room for him now.

I looked at Pavlik and Shirley, her belly bursting with a new baby anxious to get born. Two pairs of eyes waiting as if I were the Red Queen. I couldn't take that.

"It's not your fault," I said to the kids. The Szabos.

I looked at my daughter. "It's not yours, either. I could never have talked to my own mother about something like this." E. B. was relieved.

"Mina, you're off the hook, too. I'm sure you'd wondered, more than once, if I'd kill Stevan when I found out. Then you didn't have to wonder about that anymore, because he was dead. Having one more child of his was probably a comfort."

"Annie," she said, "you're in shock. You need to lie down—there are two bedrooms upstairs. Leo, you better go with her."

"Leo," I said, "why is Mina being so nice?"

"Because," she said, "no woman in her right mind would be calm in this situation. I'll bring you up some tea."

"I did want to punch the wall."

"That's a good sign."

"I'm really okay." I stood up. I did a good job faking mental health. My knees didn't do anything embarrassing like crumpling beneath me, but I was not okay.

E. B. said to my back, "I'm sorry, mom. Thanks for not making a scene."

I waved at her over my back, Leo's arm still around me. "No problem, sweetheart. Sometimes life throws you a little curveball. You do the best you can with it."

Twenty-nine

We found a bed, probably not the one my daughter used—it was tidy. Mina tapped on the door, handing Leo my tea. I've been zonked more than once by one of her herbal teas. I thanked her, set it on the table, and didn't take one sip. The old movies were rolling, strips of umber film, behind my eyelids.

Soon I was bored with old movies and tired of Leo's ministrations. Appreciative, but tired of them. This stinky piece of history had to be placed on hold. I had a big present to deal with. I asked Leo to find a Coke for me—Mina is never without Coke and potato chips. He carried a few upstairs.

Leo handed one to me, huffing. "I don't know how Mina manages that climb. Pretty steep for an old lady."

"You could inform Mina that clients were waiting at the top of Mount McKinley, hand her a rope, and there she'd be—pink, rosy, and ready for commerce." I said, "That old lady is going to outlive my grandchildren."

"She was pretty upset about Stevan."

"She's waiting to see if I'm going to take his sexploitations out on her. I still might."

He ran his palm along my cheek. "You're starting to sound like you again."

"You want a sip of my Coke?"

"The caffeine's all yours. Tonight we'll be at your house, your real house, with the door closed. I want you awake."

"Leo, please. I can take care of you without the aid of drugs."

"You are very much of a which of a something."

I snuggled against him. I'd barely closed my eyes before Leo was snoring. I heard footsteps, tiny as a mouse, climbing the stairs, then a knock, tiny as a mouse, on our door.

The door opened a crack and Jimmy poked his head in. I motioned him to the bed. Leo was out cold. Jimmy and I whispered to each other.

"Hey," Jimmy hissed, "the lady with the baby about to be born is doing it."

"The lady is what?"

"That pretty lady with the baby is giving birth right downstairs!"

"Has someone called the hospital, gotten her into a car?" I studied him. "Anything?"

"E. B. was trying, but everyone else says *No birth certificates!* They want it born right here. They're fighting about it."

"Oh, for God sakes." I swung my legs off the bed, planting my feet on the floor. "Come downstairs with me." Leo, complete with drool hanging from the corner of his mouth, didn't budge.

"Jimmy, look at this man. Being with the family for part of one day has totaled him."

"That baby was really happy, I heard it laughing in its mother's tummy—it's a girl by the way—but when everyone started yelling, she got upset and curled into a ball so she didn't have to hear them."

We walked down to the living area. E. B. was holding her own against Pavlik and Mina, and the volume was turned on high. Shirley wasn't saying much, unless you counted groans.

"HEY!" I hollered. They shut up. I wished I'd known years ago it was that easy to turn them off. "Jimmy says everyone needs to stop yelling because the baby's upset."

"Mother, these people don't want to go to the hospital. They want to have the baby right here. I thought they'd change their minds when it actually started happening. Will you please talk some sense into them?"

"*These people,* as I have just discovered, are your family. You talk sense into them."

"No hospital," Mina said. "A baby born in captivity with one hundred percent Gypsy blood? They'll steal her and put her in an orphanage, or they'll make us give them a bunch of money so we can keep her. She might come down with a 'mysterious illness' and die."

Jimmy's eyes grew huge.

"Mina, I honestly don't know if you make this stuff up, or if you think being bonkers is a great hobby. But you're scaring Jimmy, and you're probably scaring the baby, too."

"Do you ever wish the government didn't know you exist?"

"We all wish that," I said.

Shirley yelled. It was strong and loud, and it had nothing to do with the government. It was a female animal in labor yell, clean and true, and it just about ripped the skin off the back of my legs.

Pavlik was in a state of terror tinged with guilt. "She's going to die!" he said. Here came the guilt. "I'll never touch her again!"

How many men had said THAT during labor? None of them remembered it longer than ten minutes after the birth of their child. It occurred to me that I was becoming jaded about men. An unattractive quality, but I sure as hell felt I had the right to be, at least for a little while. I envied Leo the luxury of sleeping through this.

This was the parents' decision, and the rest of us would just have to cope. Besides, I knew the pitch of that yell. We'd need an army to get her out the door. She had gone full-out, birthing ballistic.

Mina backed out of the room, saying she was going to make raspberry tea to ease the birth. I asked her who was going to help Shirley—E. B. was busy being outraged, and Pavlik was busy being useless.

"You've had three kids," Mina said. "You take care of this. My eyesight isn't good anymore."

"Baby's are too big to miss. You do it."

"I've helped enough human beings come into the world. I'm too old for this monkey business."

"What are you up to?"

"Do I have to be up to anything?"

"To admit you're old? Yes."

"Such a negative attitude. Stop before it becomes a habit."

Mina walked to her defunct kitchen, leaving the ball in my court. Felt to me as if she'd walked to the moon.

E. B. sat with Shirley, holding her hand, telling her to relax. Pavlik sat across the room with as much animation as a mushroom. Who decided men should be present when babies were born? In the old days, a midwife kicked the father out. A male animal sitting blind-eyed and empty-headed is no help. And they tend to forget that the event is not about them.

Shirley squeezed E. B.'s hand tightly. Her thin bones looked fused. "Stop telling me to relax," she spit into my daughter's face. "It's impossible!"

I stroked Shirley's back. E. B. shook blood back into her hand. "She started swearing at me about ten minutes ago."

"Transition," I said. "Means she's about seven centimeters dilated. She's not going to stop swearing until that kid comes out."

Jimmy closed in on Shirley, trying to stretch both arms around her enormous belly, which now squirmed like a burlap sack full of kittens.

"Pavlik," I said, "get over here and help me lift her onto the futon."

"How will we do that? She's kicking."

"Let's try this—you take one end, I'll take the other, and E. B. can handle everything in between."

Shirley screamed again. I gave her my hand. God, the woman was strong.

"Maybe," Pavlik said, "we'd better not move her."

"I need her off the floor so when the baby comes out it'll be easier to catch."

He was horrified. "Catch the baby?"

"If things go well, that's our main job. Catch the baby."

Shirley took my hand, again, and I waited for the bone-crushing. None. She told me she was glad someone with experience was with her. She gave her husband the evil eye. I knew how she felt. At that moment you feel men should be exterminated along with all other vermin.

"Shirley," I said, "the only experience I have with childbirth is at the other end. Your end. We're going to do the best we can. If things don't look good for the baby, or if you start bleeding, I call 911. Got it?"

She pressed my hand to her cheek and settled. E. B. gave Shirley ice chips, and I let her suck a few. Jimmy moved around me. He would not take his hands off Shirley's belly. I heard him humming, low and soft, two notes at once, a perfect fifth. If Shirley hadn't been cursing, she would have been astonished.

Jimmy climbed onto the futon, propping himself behind her. I didn't see how he could breathe. He wasn't listening to anything except the tones of Shirley and her baby. He scooched over a bit, lining up his heart with Shirley's, trying to support himself with his free elbow. Then he leaned away from the bed, away from Shirley, and he put his mouth above her belly.

"Hellooo, welcome to the world, Baby!" He kissed Shirley's belly, a most remarkable sight. After another contraction, he spoke to Baby Girl again. "Be kind on this earth, pretty baby, and be very happy. Love your parents." He pressed himself against Shirley's body, rigid with pain, and her muscles went soft for a few minutes.

Something about towels and boiling water. Thread, scissors. I told E. B. to gather those things, to boil them, and that I didn't have a clue why. She'd seen all the movies, too. We thought we'd know what to do if we needed them.

"You're brave, and you're doing just fine. Beautiful." Shirley started to pant, breathing in dry rhythm like a hot Saint Bernard. Humming in her ear, Jimmy slowed her down. Different tones, low and midrange, vibrated, invisible, along the fabric beneath her. Again her body relaxed.

When Shirley's contractions hit every minute, she looked as if she were fighting the entire Russian Army. E. B. brought clean towels. Thread and scissors were boiling. As if someone had handed me an instruction book, I suddenly knew what everything was for. I told her to hand me the towels when I said *Now.* And alcohol. Cleaning the scissors with it, dousing my hands with it— that seemed right.

I was scared to death. I looked at my husband's son, my new whatever-he-was. Stepson? I guess if I were generous . . . A handsome man, sensitive, serious. He was frightened beyond death, and fear had done a better job of numbing him up than a fifth of Jack Daniel's. I wished Mina hadn't decided to take a powder, but I realized, *She's this baby's great-grandmother, and she's as scared as the rest of us.* I'd rarely thought of her as a person capable of fear.

I pulled it together, and when I wished for someone, I wished for Leo. When Shirley wanted to push, I told her to stop. I didn't know why they'd told me that, but they had, so I told her the same thing. I was on my knees at the end of the futon, another contraction, and I understood why no pushing. Baby needed to slide down a little more. Next contraction, Shirley could push like crazy.

Here it came, I told her to let it roar, and she did. An animal birthing in the bushes could not have sounded more fierce. E. B.

cradled the towels in front of me on the futon. One more grand push, out came a glorious baby girl—fat and round, white and dark brown, a definitive Szabo infant. The baby started nursing before I cut the umbilical cord.

While the baby nursed, Shirley closed her eyes looking somewhere on the other side of ecstacy. Jimmy placed his hand on the baby's back. He said, "Kind girl with a big heart." Then he opened his eyes, and said, "Hey, she's a dancer and she loves music. She wants to meet her father."

Pavlik sidestepped to his wife.

Looking at him, Shirley said, "You can kiss me. I don't hate you anymore."

Mina peeked out from behind the door. I told her the baby was fine. When the umbilical cord stopped pulsing, I cut it and tied it off with a long piece of thread. When the afterbirth was born, Mina had a bowl ready for it.

I said, "What are you going to do with that?"

"Bury it under a tree. It's got to go into the ground—it plants the baby on this earth, good health."

She meant it kept the baby from deciding to go back to whatever ethers babies inhabit before they're born. Plant their afterbirths, and they hang around until they're little old ladies causing everyone a world of grief.

Mina came back in, wiping dirt from her hands on the back of her skirt.

I said, "Get the job done?"

"Yeah. Those nitwits who work for the city have loosened *all* the dirt. It was easy. Why are you smiling?"

"Was I? I was thinking about you, hoping I'd follow your example and live long enough to cause my family grief."

"Believe me," Mina said, "sometimes it's the only reason I keep hanging around."

Thirty

I lay down next to Leo. He was still sleeping soundly. I was wired, and I wanted to share my experience with him. I was also tired and ready for a nap. All was right with the world.

Watching Leo's face and drifting toward sleep, I didn't hear him coming, I didn't even feel Jimmy standing next to me, until he spoke and I opened my eyes.

He whispered, "They named her Jimmy."

"What did you say?"

"You forgot where you were, didn't you?"

"Kind of. They named her?"

"The baby. After me—Jimmy."

I put my arms around him and rocked. He let me hold him for a minute before he pulled back.

"Shirley said she couldn't have done it without me, so they named her Jimmy."

"I like it."

"It's a funny name for a girl, but I'm got going to tell them that. What's the matter with Leo?"

"Being around the Szabos, the fight last night, and possibly wanting to marry me—it's pooped him out. He needs a good rest."

"No. Leo's heart isn't working right. His rhythm is all off."

Jimmy was right. Leo was wrapped in a ball on his left side holding himself in a hug. He was the wrong color.

"Leo?"

Grunt.

"Can you hear me?"

Another grunt. Then, "help."

"I've got to get him to the hospital," I said. "Jimmy, distract Dudley. Get Mina, get Pavlik, too."

"No ambulance?"

"I'm getting us out of here, I don't want Dudley around, and I can drive faster than any ambulance."

Everyone running upstairs, Mina asking about 911.

"Forget it," I said. "I'll drive on sidewalks if I need to. They can only go five miles over the limit."

I told Jimmy to play a trick on Dudley—ditch him—and do it quick. A tall order, but I knew he was up to it. I told E. B. and Pavlik to carry Leo downstairs, carefully place him in my backseat. ASAP. Leo opened his eyes, tried to make a joke. It didn't make sense, but we laughed as if it had.

Mina and Jimmy were a team. She called Dudley to the door, engaging him in conversation. Jimmy did his thing.

Pavlik asked E. B. to step aside and he simply, but gently, flung Leo over his shoulder in a fireman's carry. He flew down the stairs two at a time.

E. B. was on my heels. "Mom, you're not thinking straight. Call 911."

"Stop wringing your hands behind my back, and get my purse. Call the hospital from my debugged cell phone, and tell them a critical heart patient of Dr. Johnson's is on the way."

"Who's Dr. Johnson?"

Pavlik was settling Leo into my backseat, E. B. stood next to me by the car.

I said, "I have no idea, but there must be one. I want a stretcher ready, I want drugs ready, and I want them to know Leo's coming. Bye." I stuck my head out the car window. "And don't go anywhere. Shirley can't be moved. Not for another five or six hours at least. Overnight would be best."

E. B. watched me, pale-faced, from the back door, a wan wave in my direction. Then she dialed a number on my cell. I careened around to the front of Mina's building, Leo lying on the backseat, slurring at me to slow down. I think he cursed at me. Leo groaned and rolled into a ball again, nurturing himself.

I screeched to a stop, Jimmy jumped into the front seat and we tore off, no Dudley in sight. Slight groaning from Leo, and there was no time to second-guess my decision.

I said to Jimmy, "Dudley's still in one piece?"

"I stuck an old windup clock of Mina's inside a leather suitcase. I locked the case. When Mina called Dudley to the door, I shoved it under his bench."

"He's probably got the bomb squad looking at it."

"No problem, I didn't leave prints." He looked back at Leo. "You're going to be okay," he said to him.

"I guess I'll believe you," Leo whispered.

I didn't say anything. I was crying, and I didn't know it until Jimmy handed me a Kleenex to blow my nose. We reached the hospital in seven minutes, a new crosstown record.

I told the nurses that this was Dr. Johnson's patient. A gurney waited for Leo in the drive of the ER. Nurses loaded him on, strapping oxygen to his face, taking his blood pressure. An injection.

"Dr. Johnson hasn't arrived," one of them said. "We've been paging him."

"Get another cardiologist."

"Dr. Johnson's associate is on her way."

Jimmy smiled, giving me a quick wink. Leo was rolled away on a metal table. It looked too much like an autopsy table. I followed as closely as I could without getting in the nurses' way. Jimmy held on to my purse, trying not to lose me.

Birth and death, death and birth, the divine blind dates, a match made in heaven. I looked to the fog-shrouded sky and I said, *Not together at my party. Not tonight.*

Thirty-one

I sat in recovery, pretending to be Leo's wife. Jimmy sat in recovery pretending he was our son. No one believed us, but they were kind. We'd told them what they needed to hear. Give nurses the truth or a loophole, and if it's for the patient's benefit, they'll work with it.

The new Mrs. Rosetti read a six-month-old issue of *People* magazine. The featured movie star marriage had already ended, and quintuplets had been born to a lesbian stand-up comic and her partner. Jimmy poked me in the ribs when Mrs. Rosetti's name was paged for the second time. Legal attachments didn't matter, the nurse knew that, and she knew the truth about Leo—I should have called an ambulance. He'd be fine now if I had.

I said, "He's dead, isn't he?"

"We've got him stabilized." She smiled at me, putting her arm around my shoulder. "He's a very lucky man—he arrived in time for us to help him."

She told me he was in ICU, that I could see him, but just for a few minutes. I followed her, and Jimmy followed me.

"Remember, not long, and YOU," she said to Jimmy, "are out."

"He's fifteen years old. Our son."

"Try that on me tomorrow. Today he's eleven and he's out."

Jimmy said, "But I can make Leo feel better."

I told Jimmy to wait in the hall, he refused, saying he just wanted to give Leo a kiss. The nurse sighed, but she didn't stop him. He gave her a phony and angelic smile.

Barely audible, but I heard Jimmy performing his eerie vibrating-stomach routine. When Jimmy stood close to the bed, kissing Leo on the head, I could feel it, running along the bed's railing.

"Heart chakra. Key of F," Jimmy whispered, tiptoeing out of the room.

Leo looked like the octopus man I'd first seen Jimmy with at the hospital near Chinatown. He was attached to an alarming number of tubes. It was difficult to see where the hospitalized man ended and the real man began. The real man was fleshy-frail. I felt tender and frightened for both of us. The bottom of my stomach was a nightmare of strangled nerves.

I stuck on my cheerful voice, keeping the tone light. "The nurse says you're a lucky man."

Leo cracked his eyes open. His lifeline was a thin tube taped to a mask covering his lower face, flooding him with pure oxygen, raising the sound and rhythm of his breathing. Watery drips clung to the inside of the mask.

"I don't feel so lucky," he croaked.

"You look good."

"It's the anesthetic."

He closed his eyes and put out his hand to me. I held it. Two IVs were taped to the back of his hand. They'd shaved the dark hair where the needles ran into his skin. I sat on the bed. He raised his other hand, touching my face.

"It's really you."

"It is."

More deep breathing. "I want opera. Verdi."

"I'll see what I can do."

I put an arm around Leo, keeping my eye on that heart monitor like a hawk.

Squeezing my hand, not strong, but he was there, and he said, "I think I'm going to pull through."

I laid my cheek against Leo's, keeping my head at an angle so I could monitor the damned monitor. When you're trapped with one of those things, it is the aging diva who walks into a room and IS the room. No way around it, straggly digitized lines and all, a heart monitor IS the whole event.

"If you checked out of my life," I said, "I'd hunt you down and make your death hell."

He closed his eyes. "You're nuts." And then he didn't say anything else.

The heart monitor coursed its ziggy path up and down. I didn't want *You're nuts* to be the last words he ever said to me.

Checking Leo's tubes and plug-ins and digital readings, the ICU nurse told me my fifteen minutes were up. Reading the tape that oozed from a machine, understanding its secret language, she frowned and scooted me out the door before I had a chance at good-bye.

I sat in the waiting room with Jimmy. He was communing with his handheld video game, undoubtedly killing a life-form that exists in the super-stratosphere. I was glad we'd brought it. There were too many things to get into around there.

He looked up at me, and quickly looked back into his palm.

"This GameBoy is new. How much did you pay for it?"

"Seventy-nine ninety-nine."

"Not bad. Probably could have bought it cheaper down the street from me, but their stuff doesn't always last long. I think they steal containers of electronics and sell them—sometimes they're broken. Thank you for buying it," he said. "I want to walk around the hospital, just this floor."

"Jimmy, they don't know you. It wouldn't be like visiting the hospital with Hao."

"It's neat to open a game that has the original shrink-wrap," he said. "All I want to do is look around. I won't touch anyone."

"Why don't you check out the cafeteria?"

"I've been there. They're getting ready for the next meal and cleaning up after the last one. It smells weird, just like my old hospital."

"I know the smell you mean—lumpy brown, day-old powdered gravy. Everything tastes like gravy, too, even the salads."

"I'd hate to starve to death in a hospital."

"Relax. We'll find real food."

"We can ask that guy who followed us here."

"WHAT! I thought we got rid of him!"

"Dudley? We did. This is the other guy who follows me. He was on my back before I even met you. Did I tell you that a girl who never knew I was alive spoke to me after she saw my picture in your paper? It was scary. She's, you know, popular," he said. "And developed."

I kept my voice level. "Do you know anything about the guy who followed us here?"

Jimmy shrugged his shoulders. "Most people who've followed me don't introduce themselves, but he did. Alan." Jimmy squinched his face up. "That's not true. Right after your article, another guy told me his name, I don't remember it, but he was funny. He wants me to talk to fish."

"That's Skip. Dolphins aren't fish."

"Everything that swims in the ocean is a fish."

"You're sure Alan followed us here?"

"He was in the courtyard outside the cafeteria, smoking a ciga-rette."

"Did he see you?"

"No. He was doing that thing adults do when they smoke and

try to look smart, blowing his smoke into the air as if he was thinking about something important."

"What does Alan look like?"

"Small guy, Chinese," Jimmy said, "but he doesn't act Chinese, not traditional, anyway."

"When he introduced himself, did he tell you why he was invading your privacy?"

"Since I'm a kid and he's an adult, he's allowed to do that."

"No he's not. Definitely not."

"Oh. Good. I think I'll tell Alan to get lost," Jimmy said. "He was a liar. He said my uncle Ike used to work for his company. He wanted me to know that after I grew up I could work for them, too. He said he wanted to make sure that I was okay, and he'd keep watching out for me."

"Your uncle Ike worked for his company?"

"That's what he said."

"I don't understand."

"Me either. Ike never worked for anyone in his life."

I thought about the tongs and Hao, about their lying in wait until Jimmy was old enough to pounce on him. About Alan being in the CDC—I didn't know what to make of that.

"Maybe he had Hao and Ike mixed up."

"When you're not Chinese, you think we all look alike. But it seems like Alan would know the difference between Ike and Hao."

Jimmy went back to his game. I looked down into the parking lot, wondering if anyone was waiting for us. My stomach growled.

I found a pay phone and called the Mystic Cafe. "Mina?"

"What?"

"Why are you out of breath?"

"I ran to answer the phone. I'm not having a heart attack. How's Leo?"

"He's kind of dopey. His color is gray, but he's alive."

"Of course he's alive, don't think different. Gray is normal when they fill people with medicine and fake air and mutated hospital bugs."

"How's Shirley?"

"Doing great! She just got herself a Coke," Mina said. Ahhh, a new mother's diet. I'd bet anything that E. B. was working very hard at keeping a sock stuffed in her own healthy mouth. "And, of course," Mina said, "the baby is perfect."

I couldn't see her, but I could feel Mina expanding, laughing from the inside out. New babies give off more glow than a nuclear power plant. They're hope. For a small time they make the entire world seem as if all is orderly and sane.

"Mina," I said, "could you do me a favor?"

"What?"

"Is Dudley back on the bench out front?"

"Yep. I don't know what Jimmy did, but the guy was gone for some time."

"Would you tell him where I am, and ask him to bring me and Jimmy some decent food."

"First you don't want him to know where you are, but now you do?"

"I don't care if he knows where I am. I didn't want him to talk me out of driving to the hospital."

"Okay. Decent food."

"Also, tell him an Alan is following us, Chinese, it must be Alan Lee. Tell Dudley that he's been following Jimmy for a couple of months," I said. "I haven't seen him here, but Jimmy saw him outside the cafeteria."

"What's this about? I don't like it."

"Alan told Jimmy that Ike used to work for him."

"Maybe Jimmy ought to move to Mexico with my ex, Pinky Marks, for ten years or so."

"Forget it. Jimmy would deconstruct Chichén Itzá, and Pinky would sell off the pieces."

"Okay, I'll get Dudley to bring you food and look for an Alan," she said. "Now. I've got a favor to ask you."

This was going to be a biggie. Maybe a pizza joint would deliver to the hospital. We could worry about Alan later.

I said, "What's the favor?"

"We want to get out of here. The twins just called. They said that because I know Jimmy, I may be in danger."

"Yeah, yeah. They told me the same thing."

"But this morning someone fired a shot into Ike's kitchen—don't worry he's okay, and don't tell Jimmy. Ike pretends he's not scared, but he is—exactly what the shooter wanted."

"Mina!"

"I know. If I was alone, I'd get the person to shoot at me, then I'd plug him. But I've got three young people and a baby to think of."

"Forget about us. Ask Dudley to pick up Ike and get you all out of there."

"Number one, Ike still says no one's running him out of his home. Number two, I know we like the twins and that they gave us Dudley. But I can't bring myself to put the life of my family in the hands of the United States government. Any government," she said. "Please don't argue with me. I'm not going to cave."

"Mina, this time I agree with you."

"You have any ideas?"

"Get out in a van or a truck, something Dudley won't notice. Maybe there's a set of keys in one of those city trucks. Easy to swipe, and away you go."

"Annie, I'm worried about you. That sounded like an idea I would have, but a really stupid one. I'm not spending my remaining years behind bars for stealing government property because I wanted to avoid asking the government for help," she said. "Go take a hit of Leo's oxygen."

"I'm off drugs. You'll need something big enough to hold all of you."

"This is why people own Cadillacs," she said. "Hey! The natural food store. They have a delivery van."

"Queen of Diet Coke and Pringles, do you know such people?"

"They used to make regular deliveries here. I never ate their cardboard junk, but the store owner owes me. I cured him of a bad case of body lice."

"How?"

"I read his cards and told him which girlfriend to dump. End of bugs, end of story," she said. "His store is three blocks away, he can get here in minutes. If not? His bugs return."

I thought about my daughter, wandering aimlessly, an eternal passenger on the streets of San Francisco in a van filled with flax fiber, organic carrots, and parasites. "Have you thought about where you want to go?"

"This entire city isn't safe for Szabos. We're going to your house."

"Why does my house always end up becoming your hideout?"

"Hey, it's partly mine. I bought a new trailer and left it there," she said, "and I never even charged you for it."

"I know. I have to see it every morning when I drink my coffee, plunked square in the middle of my old basketball court."

"When are you going to play basketball?"

"That's not the point."

"Here's the real point. You pretend you're mad when people move into your life, but you're not mad. You enjoy it."

"Not true. You invite half the Gypsy world to dance the fandango at my house, backed by a full band, and you act as if I should be grateful."

"Did I also invite giraffes to live at your house? Did I invite a crazy woman who killed her girlfriend to live at your house? Did I invite men to wrestle your nice garden into the dirt?"

"Okay. You win."

"Could we take one minute and be honest with each other?"

"Honesty takes longer than that, and I usually hate the outcome."

"What you hate," she said, "is that your husband got another woman pregnant while you were carrying his child, and there's not one thing you can do about it. I'm his mother, and I can get worked up over that one."

"So far so good."

"When Stevan died, I was mad at him, and I had no place to put it. He left behind two families, one knowing nothing about the other. As we know, family secrets don't remain secrets forever."

"What has this got to do with your crew using my personal I'm-Okay-You're-Not-Okay-Corral for a temporary hideout?"

"Everything. I took that anger at Stevan and rolled it into something different—love for his kids. You can do the same thing. You want a baby granddaughter? You've got one."

"You must be kidding."

"Not at all. Children need grandmothers, parents are so cranky and unreasonable. That little girl has nobody in your generation, it's unnatural," Mina said, "and you delivered her. Think of it! Connected from the very first minute."

Now I had the picture. "You engineered the birth."

"I was busy in the kitchen."

"You're full of it."

"You're right. I am. So what? She's a beautiful baby, and those are two nice kids. Family is where you find it and how you weave it."

Mina was the center of the web. Not in all myths is the spider woman bad. In many she is good. But no doubt about it—she is *always* weaving the world, spinning the web.

Mina said, "What do you think?"

"Maybe. Later. Do you think Mr. Natural will drive you all the way to Sonoma County?"

"Like I said, he owes me."

"Tell Dudley I want a large pepperoni and mushroom, and have Mr. Natural pick you up as soon as Dudley leaves," I said. "You're absolutely sure Ike won't go with you? I'm worried about the tongs."

"If Ike was involved with tongs, sooner or later he'll have to pay."

"That's harsh."

"It's the truth."

"Make a quick call to Ike. Tell him about Jimmy during the birth," I said. "That will make him proud."

"I will."

"And tell him not to worry about Jimmy, I've got him covered."

"Done."

"We'll get to Ike's as soon as we can."

"Let me light a fire under Dudley so we can get out of here, will you?"

One more time on the move. I wondered how often Mina had been in this position. I wondered if she ever got tired of it.

"Mina," I said, "are you really okay?"

"I'm a little worn-out. I was thinking it was because I don't usually have people being born and dying around me left and right, but I thought about it, and it seemed—I don't know—like I'd forgotten whose life I was thinking about."

"Maybe the life you'd like to have."

"Nah, I like mine just fine, but sometimes being me takes a lot of energy," she said. "Wouldn't it be nice to take a real vacation from your life for one week? I'd swap lives with a tax attorney, and go stupid over numbers, boring clothes, and dry martinis."

Thirty-two

Dudley showed up at the hospital, his feet clacking toward us, dull rototillers turning up the tile. I smelled food, and not the brown-gravy kind. Dudley had brought an extra large pizza with a family-sized salad and garlic bread. Three large Cokes. I'd have to peel Jimmy from the mint green ceiling.

We spread the food out on the coffee table in the ICU waiting room. God knows how many bacteria reproduce in that room, and how many tears have been shed there. For a small space, the room felt pretty full. I supposed it was full of everything, including smatterings of relief and joy.

Dudley flopped the pizza box on the table, telling me he did not appreciate the way I'd taken off when I knew his sole job was watching out for me and Jimmy. I apologized to Dudley, giving him an update on Leo—although Leo was not currently one of his favorite people. He listened with half an ear, keeping a sharp eye on Jimmy.

"Why do you keep staring at me?" Jimmy said. "It's kind of rude."

"I'm waiting to see what you're going to pull next."

"I'm sitting here eating my dinner, then I'm going to play with my GameBoy. I've read every issue of *Highlights for Children* in this room. I don't care for *Field and Stream*."

And Jimmy didn't care for Dudley, either.

Dudley laced his fingers behind his neck. "Whatever you say, Jimmy."

I didn't like his tone. "Dudley," I said, "were you able to find out anything about the man who's been shadowing Jimmy?"

"It's definitely Alan Lee. The guy I was arguing with last night."

"Parking lot and white-silk shirt," I said. "A menace."

"A minor disagreement over cases, it's not unusual. We would have settled it in a few minutes if Leo hadn't arrived."

"That was more than a disagreement, Dudley. He had run over your toes in a major way, probably turned up at the hotel while you were lurking around my life."

I hated to think of myself as someone's case, but I wasn't going to make a scene in the hospital, and not in front of Jimmy.

"Dudley, I don't know what alpha-dog game you two are playing, but Alan is dangerous. He followed me to Ghirardelli Square yesterday and he threatened me."

"Wow. Alan said he saw Jimmy. He didn't tell me you were there, too."

"I was there, but Jimmy wasn't," I said. "Alan's lying to you."

For one moment Dudley showed concern, but he got past it— just another woman gone hysterical. "I'll check it out, but it sounds standard. Alan's feeling squeezed, so he's covering his trail a little. No big deal."

"Maybe he's covering more than one trail. Hao may have died protecting Jimmy from the tongs. I saw Alan fight—he's tough."

"Alan's Chinese, so he's a neighborhood gang member? Annie, I'm surprised at you." Dudley shook his head in mock amusement.

"You sure Alan had no connection to Hao?"

He scrunched his face and leaned forward, tapping his fingers on his bony knees. "Look, I'm going to level with you," he said, "and I hope I don't regret it."

Dudley and I shared the same hope.

"Alan's connection," he said, "was with Ike. That is why Alan's too, shall we say, territorial."

"Here we go again. You guys have the Qi brothers mixed up."

"When Ike was young, he wanted to be an FBI agent, probably a reaction to his brother Hao's gang involvement."

"Dudley, somebody tossed you a line, and you bit. Wild guess—Alan."

"But joining the FBI wasn't possible for Ike. You need a college degree, not a music degree from some distant mountain in China."

Dudley chugged forward on the tracks with a sure hand—the signs of a psychopathic liar or a guy with a need to impress someone, anyone, with his mastery and volume of inside knowledge. If Alan discovered Dudley was spilling the beans, the next time around Mr. Lee might not be so easy to get rid of. And when Dudley came down from his thirty-two-ounce Coke, he might wish he'd kept his mouth shut.

Having polished off that Coke in a matter of minutes, and desiring dramatic effect, Dudley rose to buy himself a soda from the pop machine. A sugar junkie. Seems like a lot of thin people are. In matters of food there is no justice.

"Jimmy," I said, "did you know any of this about your uncle?"

"Are you kidding? If it's true, Ike would have been ashamed."

"About working for the government?"

"No, about the FBI not accepting him."

Dudley returned, popping open his can of soda, putting it on the floor next to him. He propped his long legs on the table next to our half-eaten pizza.

"And then," Dudley said, smug and happy to tell us more things we didn't want to know, "while Ike was banging on the FBI's door, not taking *no* for an answer, it was discovered that he had a unique ability. One we could use."

I knew what was coming next.

"So the bureau flew him to Atlanta," he said.

"Where Ike met Alan Lee," I said.

Dudley beamed. I was catching on. "There were no tests to quantify the impossible—they had to invent tests to give Ike. The results told them they could use Ike Qi to decode disease through the use of sound. Maybe work on high-security projects, too. Ike has great integrity."

"My uncle Ike?" Jimmy was amazed. I didn't want to hear one more piece of information. Tongs, government, disease—every one of them could make life a misery. I gave Jimmy a look that said, NO MORE.

Slumping into himself, he picked up his GameBoy.

"Jimmy," Dudley said, "Ike worked for the CDC, and there was great hope for him, hope of the miraculous becoming part of standard practice. I have a sheet from his old file somewhere." Dudley rustled through his briefcase as if he had no idea where that paper was buried. Amazing. He found exactly what he wanted.

"You and Ike are so much alike, this'll probably make sense to you." Dudley laughed, and, just like that, Jimmy wasn't a brat, he was Dudley's friend. "Ike transcribed the following for one of our researchers. If you understand this, kid, you can explain it to me. Here goes:

> *Every part of the body, right down to the smallest molecule, has a shape and a vibration. We are all bundles of electricity that create many vibrations. I follow a current with x-number of vibrations per second, and it is the same as music. Low sounds vibrate in long lines, and the curves are far apart. High sounds vibrate in close waves, and the length of the curve is shorter. So, listening to a healthy cell, and comparing it to a diseased cell, I understand where the problem is. I attempt to repair it through proper toning and renewal of the curve. Like the planets, our cells make music—there are many small uni-*

*verses inside us. Everything in the universe makes music because all
of it is energy. And everything includes the inner music of people.'*

"Says here Ike wrote two symphonies while he was in Atlanta.
He told his supervisor that they were merely notations of disease
into orchestration."

Last thing I wanted was a federal agent, suddenly freed from his
desk, thumping his chest and confiding in me. I had to make him
think I didn't believe, or understand, a word of what I'd just heard.
That wasn't difficult. Then I had to get rid of him, so Jimmy and I
could beat it.

"Dudley, please. You believe this nonsense?"

A nimbus cloud crossed his face, one holding the moist seeds of
doubt. But he shook his head, a swimmer shaking all signs of doubt
from both ears.

He pulled out another sheet from Ike's file. "Then we have another entry, one month later, from a physician:

*Ike Qi says his work environment is terrible and that he feels
sick. He states that it is conducive to disease, and he will become
chronically ill if he stays on. Psychological tests administered. Qi
deemed unstable. Sent home with strict orders to keep his work secret.
Agency will check on him yearly and report.' "*

Dudley flashed a smile, skeletal and empty. A man who'd left joy
far in the dust.

"I visited Qi Dragon every year as requested, just another white
guy looking for a tonic. But several years ago I heard chanting, and
it wasn't Ike. He was standing right in front of me.

"Ike laughed and played dumb. Their plumbing was old, sometimes a vapor lock filled the store with funny sounds, blah, blah,
blah . . . Then Jimmy walked in, carrying a scruffy kitten, his head
pressed against the cat's head, chanting. Ike, stern, told him to get

into the other room—they had a customer. Also, *No cats in the house. Bad luck.*

"Jimmy obeyed, but it was too late. We discovered Ike's gift ran in the family." Another smile, this one tight-lipped. "We have the ability to be patient, to wait for what we want—Jimmy working for us. Despite what Alan thinks, *us* does not necessarily mean the CDC."

I said, "We don't seem very patient in far-flung nations of the world."

Dudley frowned, waving away my remark. "International powder kegs. Jimmy's not a powder keg. He's a flower waiting to blossom."

This was over. The whole thing.

"Dudley, I have a message for Alan Lee—Leave Jimmy alone. Message number two—Leave me alone. And tell him if he ever sets foot on my property, he'd better come well armed."

"Careful. You're threatening an employee . . ."

". . . And you're next, Dudley. Out of our lives. The message to you about my property is the same as Alan's," I said. "*Another* thing—if you think someone, let's say Alan for instance, can't be in the tongs and work for the government at the same time, you are unbelievably naive. It's called playing both ends against the middle."

"Are you done?"

"Are you leaving?"

"I only follow instructions, and they don't come from you."

"Dudley, go look for Flora and Hao's killer."

"It's up to SFPD. It has nothing to do with us."

"You have no jurisdiction here?"

"Concerning their deaths? No. Concerning you and Jimmy? Yes."

I was not leaving that hospital, and I was not spending my worry-and-wait time with Dudley. I said to him, "Know what? I give up."

He cocked his head. "Why don't I believe you?"

"A man I love is fighting for his life. I'm taking care of a great kid. I may be responsible, at least in part, for two people's deaths, and I've had family complications."

"About your dead husband," he said. "I heard. That's a tough one."

Jimmy peeked under his eyebrows, waiting for me to explode. I didn't give Dudley the satisfaction. I played with my cold pizza, not saying one word.

The boinkedy-boink noise of the virtual creatures in Jimmy's hands, dying or flying to another level, banged against the glossy walls of the waiting room. I thought, *GameBoy is like religion. Do something right, you enter the orchestra seats of heaven. Blow it, and you've got a permanent seat with an obstructed view of the Almighty.* I wondered which seat had been waiting for Flora at the will-call window.

"Dudley, are you really sticking around? Because we might get hungry again."

"I'm not your delivery boy."

I made a couple of comments about his job, years spent pushing papers from one end of his desk to the other until a few forms fluttered into his waste bin. I gifted him with other kindnesses and gratitude. Suppositions about the sorry love life of a geek. Jimmy was wide-eyed. Dudley was disturbed. If I played him right, he would stomp away. I rattled on. His mother was next up for ridicule.

Whoops! There he went, up on his feet, and out with his voice. "This is a complete waste! I'm gone."

About time.

Bending over, he picked up his soda, storming to the elevator. Dudley had become the center of attention on the fourth floor. Nurses peered around corners, small smiles across their faces.

He yelled to me across the hall from the elevator, slowly making its ascent to his rescue. "You want to know something?"

I cupped my hands. "Not really."

"Jimmy is no saint. He needs a shrink, probably medication. He hid a ticking device under my bench. Do you know what that does to someone in my position?" He shook his head. "Textbook anti-social behavior."

"Want to repeat that, Dudley? A few people in the parking lot didn't hear you."

He fiddled with his soda can and pawed at the linoleum—a neutered bull in a field of heifers. He hoisted his pop can, taking a hearty swig. Jimmy broke into gales of laughter. I had no idea what was so funny until Dudley turned, facing me.

"Just two small holes about one inch below the top of the can," Jimmy whispered to me behind his hand, his eyes bright. "And notice? The soda was black cherry."

Then came the loudspeakers, booming their request down the halls. "Dr. Dudley Stone, floor one, urology."

I smiled at Dudley, shrugging, motioning my innocence.

"Dr. Dudley Stone, stat, to urology."

Dudley pulled out his cell phone and screamed into it, his face the same color as his cherry-splattered shirt. He gave me his back. I didn't understand the first part of his tirade, just piles of blithering anger. Then I heard him say, "Forget Alan. You tell those crazy broads I don't care what we owe them, I am *out* of here and back to work."

The elevator doors opened as he was being paged for the third time. He faced me, sending a wave of pure hatred. I might have felt frightened—I should have felt frightened—but the entire fourth-floor nursing staff broke out in cheers and applause, all for the departing Dudley.

I said to Jimmy, "Dr. Dudley Stone?"

"I told one of the nurses that he was an old boyfriend of yours and that he was bugging you. She said she'd get rid of him."

Our agent was over and out, and it was time to visit Leo.

Thirty-three

With full permission, Jimmy and I stood in Leo's doorway, grins smeared across our faces. Leo's grin was tired, but it was all peace. His face wasn't blue anymore, and it wasn't gray. Not pink yet, but white was better than blue or gray, and he'd been moved from ICU.

"I heard Dr. Dudley Stone being paged," he said. "Dump your protection?"

"We did."

I kissed Leo light and sweet. I didn't want that machine to start beeping. I was very happy that he had decided to stick around.

"Jimmy," I said, "stay outside, but no farther than the waiting room."

"I want to work on Leo."

If Jimmy worked on other people, okay. But this was my Leo. The heart monitor was oozing very little paper, and the lines spiked a regular rhythm—no more syncopation.

"Jimmy," I said, "later. You shouldn't be in here. Not yet."

"If this damned hospital hasn't killed me, he sure won't." Leo said, "Let the kid do his thing."

"Tell me exactly what you want to do," I said.

"I'll concentrate on Leo's heart, then move down the main arteries. If there are clots, the vibrations will break them up and begin healing any inflammation. I have to be very careful not to make a shrill sound—it may break something loose. If there's a clot in his brain or heart, he could have a stroke."

"Jimmy? Forget it."

Leo, with his eyes closed, smiled. "Give him a chance. It sounds great."

"You sure?"

"Positive."

I wasn't. But I wasn't sure about the miracles of modern medicine, either.

"I'll stand by the door. You do your thing, and I'll chat up passing nurses. Close the curtain around Leo's bed."

I stood in Leo's doorway, nonchalant, a cigarette smoker's pose without the smoke. Jimmy's shadow through the curtain, bending over Leo. Slim sounds waffling the room. Subtle, supernatural, similar to Tibetan monks chanting several notes at once. There are some sounds—death, making love, birthing, a wolf mourning her cub, a bird dying, a couple crying their final, soundless good-bye—that can't be replicated, and cannot be explained. As ancient as rock art, we're sent back through time in their presence. Such was Jimmy's voice.

I gave myself one moment, bathed in the mystery. Slipping away from the door, I peeked inside the curtain. Jimmy worked his tones down Leo's body. I could barely hear him, certainly no passing nurse could. Leo smiled, not in delight, but with deep relaxation. I eyeballed the monitor—nothing much different, a slight lowering of blood pressure. As I backed away from the curtain and turned, a nun appeared. Not just any nun, but the head honcho.

"How's our patient doing?"

"Sleeping peacefully."

"After thirty years, I'm tuned to inner activity. I thought something was going on here."

I pointed to the monitor. She checked it out.

"Glad I'm wrong. Looks terrific." She patted me on the shoulder, a disinterested gesture before moving on, prepared to witness the next miracle or ruin.

I stood inside the curtain and told Jimmy to wrap it up.

"Already finished. Leo sounds good," Jimmy said. "He likes you a lot."

Leo looked at him, and said, "Kid, I don't know what you did, but I feel great." And he gave me a hubba-hubba wink.

"I gave you an inside massage," Jimmy said. "Gentle and cleansing. You should drink a lot of water during the next hour."

Leo pointed to the solution dripping into his veins. "That's my limit."

Jimmy didn't like that. "It'll have to do. But when they give you a glass, really pour the water down."

Leo ruffled Jimmy's hair. "Who are you?"

Jimmy placed his hand on the back of Leo's neck, his face frozen serious. "You know who I am. Jimmy."

"I mean who are you *really*?"

Jimmy relaxed. "Oh. THAT. Leo, I've just been inside your body. You know exactly who I am, and I know you!" Laughing, looking more like Happy Buddha than a kid, Jimmy said, "Someone's coming. I'll be in the waiting room."

"Leo," I said, climbing into his bed, "I miss you." I cuddled into him, and he stuck his hand down the front of my dress.

"Cut that out. What if another nun comes in?"

"Who cares? I'm feeling better."

"Obviously."

"You know what? I'm not going to die."

"I told you that."

"But now I really know it."

"Good."

"Hey," he said. "I'm sorry."

"For?"

"You were smacked by a fresh view of the past—you needed me," he said. "I wanted to be your big brave bear, but my left arm started aching like crazy, and I thought, *Oh, Shit. Now I'm going to be another hole in her heart. We were supposed to do part of this life thing together.* I don't remember much after that. I thought a big guy threw me over his shoulder and carried me all the way here."

"Maybe your guardian angel," I said. Leo didn't need to know his angel was Pavlik and that his chariot was my old red car. Not yet. "Leo. You're wrapped around my heart, stronger than a ribbon, but never too tight. That's you."

"Nope. That's us."

He closed his eyes, his hand still down my dress.

"Leo, I have to tell you something, because I don't want you to find out from someone else and start worrying about me."

His eyes popped open. "Why am I worried already?"

"Jimmy and I are going to temporarily disappear. I'm sick of Dudley. I don't trust the twins, but I want them to think that I do. Alan Lee, the guy you tossed around the parking lot, is an angry unknown quantity. Wagner's in the middle of Flora and Hao—two dead people. And Ike? I don't trust anyone," I said, "except you, Mina, Jimmy and the rest of . . ."

"The rest of your family, Annie. They're nice kids. They want you, and you need them," he said. "Get as close to death as I did, and a baby seems like a miracle."

"Mina told me to be her grandma."

"Do it. I'll be grandpa. The baby's lacking in that department, too."

"I'll see."

"If you don't nurse the hurt, it'll go away."

Only the smart bears have a decent life span. I said, "I'll call you."

"Whenever you can," he said, "and that means often."

"I'm going to use a fake name. Dr. Verdi."

"Do you think that's necessary?"

"No, but I've got to make some kind of fun around here."

I turned his hospital-issue CD player on low. Opera, as ordered by Leo and by Jimmy.

He closed his eyes. Pavarotti singing Leo to bliss. Pulling his hand out of my dress, I kissed him. He dozed, and he looked okay. I didn't want him in that hospital.

I found Jimmy in the waiting room reading a *National Geographic*, intensely focused on its slick pages. Probably the same photos of topless women carrying water jugs that they'd been running since I was a kid.

"Jimmy, do you have a cell phone that works?"

Startled, he closed the magazine. "Sure."

He unzipped his backpack, pulling out four cell phones, a couple of walkie-talkies, batteries of various sizes, two packs of matches, thin copper wire, duct tape, and a newly acquired *National Geographic*. He handed me a tiny, off-brand model.

I dialed the Rafael and asked for the Duettes. The phone rang into their empty gin and smoke-filled room. The hotel guests' answering service clicked on. The twins' personal phone message wished me a nice day, requesting that I leave a message.

"Hi, Jean and Jan. Thanks so much. Dudley's been great, but everything's cleared up, and I've sent him packing. Bye!" I clicked off.

"Jimmy," I said, "you and I are going to be dead for a little while, and you're the one who's going to kill us."

"Cool."

Thirty-four

He said, "I'm hungry."

"Do you ever stop eating?"

"I don't eat that much. I eat lots of meals during the day. It keeps my weight down."

"Jimmy, you're a funny kid."

"I'm serious."

"So am I."

We dipped into the hospital parking lot, and there was my old Cooper, the paint half-on, half-off, a lady with her slip showing.

Jimmy buckled up. He was buzzed, and his legs were doing that jiggly thing boys do.

"Cut it out. You're making me nervous."

"I'm excited about killing us."

"Swell."

"Just tell me what's next."

"We duck into Chinatown. First to McDonald's, your favorite cuisine, to fill you up, and then to your uncle Ike's—a really quick stop to say hello."

"You must have been a great mom. I've never eaten so much

junk in my entire life," he said. "Do you think Uncle Ike should die with us?"

"If you can talk him into it, I'm all for it, but he said he would *not* be pushed."

Big sigh of resignation. "When he says *no,* he means it."

We found a parking place. No tall, skinny spies in sight. I didn't know about Alan. He was no Dudley, and he'd been on my tail long before I'd spotted him, same with Jimmy. I now thought of Alan Lee as the tong division of CDC.

I ate a burger that cost less than a can of premium dog food. That worried me some. There's a reason many Americans look as if we need a building permit for our butts with a variance from the county. Fast foods are it. Sad—only beautiful food should be fattening. But beautiful food isn't cheap, and it's not fast. Soon our oceans will rise and new inland seas will form due to our collective weight pulling North America down.

"I'm calling Mina," I said to Jimmy.

"Use the pay phone next to the counter. And tell Mina to unscrew the receiver and check your home phone."

I left Jimmy at the table, sketching boxes and wires. Diagrams. Stick people with O's where their mouths were supposed to be. Stick people running, pulling their straight hair, screaming their round screams to the skies. The kid had one wild imagination—we couldn't leave those drawings behind. I kept my eye on him while I stood across the restaurant, dialing my home. Mina picked up on the fourth ring.

"Don't even ask," she said, without saying hello. "I'm not having a heart attack. I was outside, and I always run to catch the phone. It could be a client in trouble."

"How did you know it was me?"

"Caller ID."

"Not this time. I'm at a pay phone in a restaurant."

More like a filling station than a restaurant, and what was that kid doing now?

She said, "Jimmy's still alive, right?"

"Of course he is." I gave her his instructions regarding the phone. She saw no odd devices inside the receiver, and she had a hell of a time putting it back together.

"But I'm glad you're being careful," she said. "Two deaths, and the worst is yet to come."

I don't discount Mina's intuition. Many other things, but not her intuition.

I said, "Are you tuned in to any particular disaster channel?"

"Nope. Just keep your eyes open. Jimmy's surrounded by black and you don't look so hot, either."

I had the same feeling, but there were too many possibilities, too many revelations, too much of the business of living and dying clouding my perception. I was doing my best, but my best might not cut it. Easier to stay on guard, trusting no one, no thing, and watching Jimmy.

I hadn't expected a baby in my life, but there she was, a girl named Jimmy. I wanted to know how she was.

"Fine," Mina said, "and I've put the kids in my trailer. I'm sleeping in your room. I figured they could use some privacy."

She had taken over my house.

I said, "No men over . . . at least not in my room."

"There aren't any men around, unfortunately."

"It's you. Pretty soon there will be one man, then another," I said, "and the idea of you and some guy rolling around in my sheets would turn me off sex for a long time."

"That's a nice thing to say."

"Mina, get out a pen and paper."

"You going to give me the name of a singles club?"

"I want you to call my nurse practitioner. Shirley should be checked. The baby, too."

"Forget it, we . . ."

"The nurse is a country midwife. She isn't going to make the baby get a birth certificate or haul Shirley over to County General."

"Are you done talking?"

"I haven't given you the phone number yet."

"E. B. called that woman as soon as we got here. She's finished examining both mother and baby, but she's still in the trailer with Shirley. She's giving her pointers about nursing the baby, you know. Also, she ordered a masseuse for Pavlik. He is a complete wreck," Mina said. "Szabo men are great at making babies, but after that part's done, they sort of lose their zip."

"Why didn't you tell me about the nurse to begin with?"

"You didn't give me room to breathe, never mind talk. Sometimes I think you work at exasperating me."

"Mutual."

"Your daughter's just as bad. Stubborn. Not one moment's peace until we had the baby checked," she said, "plus she has the Szabo curse."

"Curse?"

"The love curse, what else? The natural food guy who gave us a ride is following her around like a skinny dog. I've got to get rid of him before any leftover bugs jump off on us."

"Are we good with each other now," I said, "because it's time to move on."

"Do I forgive you for driving me nuts? Yes."

"Okay. I have something to ask you," I said. "That's not true. I have something to tell you."

"You're going to bad-mouth me until I die because of what my son did to you."

"The jury's still out on that one. This is about something else."

"Yes?"

"I'm going to destroy the Mystic Café."

"The place is closed down. What more can you do to it?"

"Destroy the building. And I want it known that Jimmy and I died inside the charred rubble."

"Listen, this thing with Stevan? It happened a long time ago. You don't need to kill yourself about it, and you sure don't need to take Jimmy with you."

"The building will be gone, it's going to look like we died in there, but we'll be fine."

I wished we were having this conversation in person. I'd already shooed two people away from the phone, receiving evil looks from one, nervous looks from the other.

I glanced at Jimmy, saw what he was up to, and shook my head NO in his direction. Oblivious, he scanned the condiment table, picking up several creamers.

I'd end the conversation quick. After Jimmy pulled this off, we'd have to make a run for it. I hadn't seen it in years.

Mina said, "You want to burn down the Mystic?" Her voice was a shrug. "I don't really mind."

"You don't?"

"As long as you don't hurt things like people and cats, I think it's a pretty good idea."

"Are we communicating? I want to wreck your building, make it disappear, take it down, send it up in flames and smoke."

"I approve. If you were here, I'd spit on your forehead, rub it in, and kiss you."

For the first time in days, I was glad I wasn't home.

"After Jerry died," she said, "a guy from urban development came by, explaining all the stupid reports they had to do before they could buy my building and write me a check. They asked did I have fire and flood insurance, and were my recent taxes paid. I said yes, but I didn't expect any floods, so maybe I could pay less and just have fire insurance. He said I have to keep the flood insurance. Do they expect the Pacific Ocean to come pouring down my street?

"Anyway, he smiled at me the way people smile at old people

when they're swindling them. I told him Jerry paid my insurance regular as clockwork, so they didn't need to worry about it."

"Good. We're going to blow it up."

"For God's sake, I don't have bomb insurance! That's something I'd remember."

"Look, as far as you know, it's an ordinary fire started by someone who hates you."

"I thought we weren't telling anyone the truth."

Jimmy strolled back to our table, his pockets filled with creamers.

"You know what?" she said. "This works for me. I won't have to wait for the city's money. I get it from the insurance people."

"And if they don't come through, I'll pay you."

"What would you do? Charge it?"

"The sale of my building is about to close. Pretty soon I'll have money to burn—pun intended."

"Remember the old saying *Don't count your coins until they're in your pocket . . . ?* Annie, I don't get wealthy vibrations from you."

"You're biased."

"Could be. Just make it a regular fire, and don't do anything dumb like getting caught or fried to death."

"I wish there was someone I could frame for this. How about you? Anyone you'd like to get even with?"

"I understand the feeling, but be careful. Karma happens, and you must trust the process. You don't want to marry some idiot in a future lifetime because you couldn't wait for the universe to jump in and do its job."

"You can't think of anyone to frame, either?"

"Not one single person," Mina said, defeated.

All the excitement of birth and near death had, momentarily, wiped her vengeance slate clean.

"Before you torch my place, do me a favor," she said. "I have an old set of tarot cards, they're next to the futon. Save them. They're not always accurate, but they have sentimental value."

"Used them recently?"

"When you were determined to butt into your marital past, and there was nothing I could do to stop you, I did a reading. You turned up as the Empress three times in a row. That's how I knew you should deliver the baby. Empress is Mother Earth. She's the queen of natural mysteries, but she doesn't have one dime."

"I think I'll let the cards burn. Uh-oh," I said. "Gotta run. Jimmy's about to do his number."

"Don't buy gasoline and pour it all over the place and leave the gas can behind. And don't charge anything on your credit card. On television," Mina said, "firebugs always get caught."

Jimmy was waiting for me at the table, and he was itching to get his show on the road. He took two creamers hidden in his palm and slammed them against his forehead, just above his eye. He started screaming. White goo oozed from his eye between his fingers. I improvised. Taking Jimmy by the hand, I led him to the door. "Dear," I said, "I told you not to pick the scab on your eyeball."

Jimmy moaned and groped his blind-eyed way through Mickey D's. We walked past a pair of tourists, German would have been my guess, and the man, getting a load of Jimmy, let loose a hefty dry heave. Jimmy turned to him and smiled, ooze crawling into his mouth. This time the tourist heaved with success. The Chinese lady with the ready mop ran to clean up his mess, yelling at him.

Jimmy and I tore out the door and up the block. We laughed loud, flooding our bodies with healthy little melodies.

I'd have to get word to Leo. Temporarily disappearing is not the same as being sincerely dead. Especially if the blazing building hit the six o'clock news, and Leo had the TV turned on in his hospital room.

Thirty-five

"Jimmy, you are a hazard," I said.

He found a crumpled Kleenex on the floor of my car and wiped the mess off his face.

"I was sitting by myself," he said, "and I got bored."

"How do you come up with this stuff?"

"Pure luck."

Forget the people who wanted to use Jimmy. The Qi brothers had also protected Jimmy from himself. I wanted to stay on topic before he thought up more mischief.

"Let's talk about how we're going to make us dead," I said.

"I've drawn a couple of different ways to do it. I don't know how to use plants or poisons. And I don't really want to use sound, although I probably could."

"You could use sound?"

"You know those women with high-pitched voices who can break glass? I have to be careful during healing sessions so it doesn't happen inside someone—I always hold back. I'm not sure what would happen if I really let go."

I thought about the battle of Jericho, Joshua blowing his wild and crazy horn. *And the walls came a'tumblin' down* . . . Maybe Jimmy and Joshua were on the same wavelength.

"Anyway," Jimmy said, "I don't want to use sound to break things. Maybe it'd turn into an addiction, thousands of times worse than smoking. First I'd do it to feel cool. Before you know it, I'm doing it all the time."

"Your uncles did a good job with you."

"I know," he said. "When are we going to see Mina? She has good sounds inside her."

"You're kidding me."

"I don't kid about important things. She likes herself, and that makes people sound good. Her body's very healthy."

Coke, cigarettes, potato chips. Why wouldn't she be healthy?

I took my eyes off the street traffic. Looking into his wide-open face, I noticed a small streak of cream across his forehead, a little furrow of worry beneath it. Chewing his lower lip, he wanted to say something, but he didn't want to say something.

"Out with it," I said.

"You know how I talked to you about being normal? I want to see Mina, but it's not just because I like her. It's because she's at your house. I've lived in a city my whole life," Jimmy said, "and I want to hear different layers of sounds. Bugs, plants growing, fish swimming in a river. Concrete is not normal."

"You are invited to listen to the grass grow at my house. Soon."

Just then, some imbecile cut me off, and Jimmy gave him the finger.

I said, "Where did you learn that?"

"Think about where I live."

"Well, don't do it again."

"Where am I going to make us die?"

"I was thinking of someplace kind of disposable."

"A burned-out warehouse in the Tenderloin?"

"No. Mina's place."

"In Chinatown?"

"Not that one."

"Because there are too many people on her alley. I might hurt someone there, including us."

"Mina's other place."

Jimmy's eyes went big. "Where the baby was born?"

"Right."

"If we do that, she'll kill us, and we won't have to pretend to be dead."

"She said she doesn't mind."

Jimmy wiped the remaining cream off his face. "You asked her if we could totally, and I mean totally, wreck her building?"

"Yep."

"I don't get it, but . . . It would be a big job."

"The building is over one hundred years old, and it's wood. Old wood."

"That's a good start."

"Nobody lives around there anymore, workers only there on weekdays, and today is Sunday."

"I've got to think about this."

"If you're scared, don't do it. I'll come up with something else."

"I'm not scared, but the size of that building . . . we need at least twelve yards to get away safely, and I'm not always great with clocks. I'm really good at math, but sometimes I get confused about time."

Oh my. "If you need to use a clock, I'll set the timer."

He didn't say anything.

"You sure you're okay with this?"

"Mina's got lots of fat books," Jimmy said. "Does she want them all?"

Future here, future there, future, future everywhere. Mina had a truckload of astrology books, tarot books, magic encyclopedias, and herbal cookbooks. She had never cracked a single one, and most of them came from garage sales. They were decorative items.

"Mina won't mind losing her books. There's not one she paid more than twenty-five cents for."

"Wow. I wasn't allowed to *breathe* on one of Ike and Hao's books until I was ten."

"Mina says she has more information inside her head than in all those books put together."

Jimmy said how glad I must be that Mina and I were related. She was so smart and fun. Like saying we could wreck her building? That was pretty neat.

When the tribute ended, I gave him a different view. "Jimmy, Mina's great when she likes you. If you get on her wrong side, she will chase you from one end of hell's eternity to the next."

Jimmy went flat. "You don't think torching her place will make her mad? Flora told me about hell, and I don't want to go there."

"If Mina curses anyone to hell, it'll be me, and I've built up an immunity to her."

"Okay," he said, "let's do it." But he wasn't as jazzed as he had been.

"Next stop, a quick hello for Ike."

He beamed. "Boy, Ike's going to like this thing with the building."

"He'll hate it. Let me tell him. I may leave out the major details."

Jimmy instructed me to drive into their little backyard. He hopped out, opening and closing a wide gate. I parked. Hao had died in that yard, and the place throbbed with his death. Because of that loss, Ike and Jimmy needed to see each other.

"Ike and Hao had clients," Jimmy said, "who parked back here if they didn't want anyone to see them. Like those rich twins and Flora, they came here for beauty supplies. One movie star used to fly all the way from LA to buy tonics from Hao and healing sessions from Ike. Nothing was wrong with her except that she was stuck-up. One man who'd been bald for twenty years . . ."

"Could I get out of the car?" I said. "You're talking an awful lot."

"I've never taken down a building before, not even by mistake. I blew up part of our fence once, and I wasn't allowed to leave the house for two weeks. I'm pretty nervous. I feel like a high A sharp. That's a musical note."

"I know what it is," I said. "Let's remember cotton balls. I don't want the blast to destroy your hearing."

"I don't really hear with my ears. I can't explain it."

When he heard us trooping through his bamboo, Ike opened the back door.

He stretched out his arms, and Jimmy ran into them, completely encircled. If Jimmy had been three years younger, he would have been crying. Age didn't stop Ike. He held Jimmy close. He rested his head on Jimmy's, the tears running into his hair. This visit was either a terrible idea or a brilliant idea. I wasn't sure.

I patted Ike's back. We stood in the small garden where I'd last seen Hao's body, and let ourselves feel happy. The sky went to shadow, a cloud passing overhead. I hoped it wouldn't rain. Looking over Ike's shoulder, I saw it wasn't a cloud, it was something bigger. Wagner. Towering over Ike, large enough to block the sun, Wagner not only looked like a stormy sky, he felt like one.

Thirty-six

"**W**agner," I said, trying to keep it light. "What are you do-ing here?"

"What are you doing with Jimmy?"

"Taking care of him. Ike didn't tell you where he was?"

"He mentioned a couple of places he might be. I didn't know what to believe."

"He have a reason to lie to you?"

"Of course he does. Ike doesn't want anyone to know where Jimmy is, and that includes me."

"Can I go upstairs to the attic and play?" Jimmy asked Ike. "I'm getting a headache."

Ike told him that, yes, he could go upstairs, and he told Wagner and me to stop acting like dogs, sniffing each other's behinds. We stopped sniffing, but we were still circling.

"What are you doing here?" I asked Wagner again. No light left in my voice.

"Ike called," Wagner said, "and his voice was worry all over. Something about hospital visits. I didn't want him to sit alone with that worry."

Which brought up a question that'd been nagging me. "Ike,

why didn't you visit hospitals with Jimmy? You're the one with the same musical gift."

"Almost the same," Ike corrected. "No one worked with me when I was young, and sometimes my mind has . . . difficulties."

"No one worked *with* you, but they sure worked *on* you," Wagner said.

Ike said, "I can't filter out the discord of an institution or the terror of an illness happening between narrow halls. When I'm around more than one sick person at a time, I have a headache for days."

Ike crossed the kitchen to make tea, a frail limp carrying him to the stove.

I said, "What happened to your leg?"

"Arthritis. On cloudy days, it gets worse. My body misses Hao's remedies." He turned the fire on under a teakettle.

Wagner was set on being angry with me. "Want to know what you did?" he said. "That little Chinese punk who works for Disease Control followed you, and you took him straight to the hospital. Then, somehow, you lost him," Wagner said, "and he came here looking for Jimmy."

"What did you tell him?"

"The truth. That we had no idea where Jimmy was. The boy needs peace and quiet," Wagner added.

"Jimmy needs safety."

"Exactly. Out in the country. With you."

How did Wagner know where I lived? I still appreciated Wagner aesthetically. I did not appreciate the full force of his Wagner-ness when it was aimed directly at me.

"Let's talk about a country outing later," I said. "I'm hoping the CDC guy actually left, that he's not hiding under a piece of furniture waiting to jump Jimmy."

"I escorted him out, but he'll be back. He's not going to do something stupid like use those crazy martial art moves on me, but he's hard to shake. Because he works for the government, I hesitate to give him what he deserves."

Wagner's voice skipped from ghetto to James Earl Jones in the course of one sentence.

"I don't understand why they're so interested in Jimmy right now," I said. "Why not wait until he's eighteen?"

"They think if they can get to Jimmy while he's young," Ike explained, "he won't be bothered in the future by the ethical dilemma of creating a disease. But they don't know Jimmy's heart."

"*Creating* diseases? This sounds like a bad episode of *The Twilight Zone*," I said.

"It is a great irony. If you can dream something now, in the present, it no longer belongs in the future. It *is* the now."

"How do we get Jimmy off the government's screen?"

"We don't write our congressman," Wagner said, "that's for sure. I'm thinking we make Jimmy disappear. That's where a healthy spell in the country with you comes in."

I didn't tell them that a disappearance was already in the works. I also didn't tell them that, once again, I thought they were slightly nuts.

Ike looked at Wagner, nodding his agreement. "I wasn't much older than Jimmy when a white woman walked in that very door," Ike said, "asking for pearl cream. My family was working in the back, and Hao was running around with friends. Next thing you know, my parents had money in their pockets, I had my first identification, and I was whisked out the door. I knew my parents were desperate for money, and I knew that Hao, as oldest brother, would feel responsible for my kidnapping."

Kidnapping? "Wait a minute. Has this got anything to do with Atlanta?"

"I was on an island off Georgia, but first in Atlanta, yes."

"Dudley told me you'd worked for CDC—I thought you were an adult. He said you wanted to join the FBI, you couldn't, then a research outfit attached to CDC found out about your gift."

"Did Jimmy hear this?"

"Yes."

Ike wiped his eyes. "Lies, all of it. I was a scared kid, and they grabbed me, wanting to use my skills. This," he said, spreading his arms to take in the distaff paintings, the tangy scent of green tea and jasmine incense, "is my world. I don't feel alive elsewhere. Certainly not healthy."

"What did they want you to work on?"

"Sex energy."

"You were a kid!"

"Chinese healing families don't think of sex as dirty. Sexual energy is your jing, your vitality. They wanted experiments to collaborate certain beliefs they held, but their beliefs were warped. My stomach cried, and my heart was tortured. I got sick."

"What were you researching?"

"I only knew a small part of the project I was working on—no integrity, completely unscientific. Wanting to know the whole, I pestered them until I learned other pieces of my project," he said. "Of course they didn't tell me everything, but when I learned the small truth they shared, my nightmare became worse."

Ike's face was a devastation. "I won't lose Jimmy to the same system that stole my innocence. I was a happy boy."

"How did you get out of there? Mix stray chemicals and blow a hole in your cubicle?"

"I wasn't like Jimmy in that way." Ike relaxed a little and smiled. "Our parents died, and Hao saved me. He worked for the tongs, they paid him well for making strong elixirs for success and strength. He talked to a connection in Georgia. An old Chinese man snuck into my building, found me, and brought me home to Hao," Ike said.

"The first months were hard. Hao made tonics to cleanse my mind and dreams. Eventually I healed, but he was never able to desensitize me. I startle easily."

"So," I said, "easy to imagine that Hao would rather have died than see the same thing happen to Jimmy."

"As I told you, Hao was a dragon. Fearless and loyal."

"Stashing Jimmy with me is a Band-Aid. Alan Lee, or someone else, will keep coming around until they get Jimmy."

"I wish they thought Jimmy was dead," Wagner said, "because it is one day at a time around here, and that gets old fast." His voice trailed off. "I've got to get some shaving stuff and deodorant."

I wondered why Wagner had attached himself to Ike like a junk-yard dog. Maybe his way of mourning Flora.

"Wagner," I said, "you have a life. You can't move in here."

He rubbed the skin on his forehead. The folds were sensuous, soft.

"Wagner?"

"I weigh a little less than a Buick Regal."

"And not many people are going to mess with you."

"Right, and if I have to move in here and protect Ike for the rest of my life, that's what I'm going to do. I had a talk with the Big Man, and that's what we decided."

The Big Man? Who could possibly be larger than Wagner?

Ike's eyes were small, strained, and moist. "He thinks God wants him to take care of me. I don't know why."

"Wagner, can I ask you something?"

His face closed up. "Not if you're going to fuss with me about God. Anything else, you can ask it. Doesn't mean I'm going to answer."

Having Wagner in the Qis' store would put a damper on Ike's steady clientele. Of course, he might attract new customers—

wannabe prizefighters, thugs, personal trainers, SWAT team members. . . .

I slipped my voice into an easy range, attempting to soften the question. "I had the impression that you and Flora were in love?"

"Correct."

Only one word, but it packed a punch. I had no desire to be run over by a Buick Regal, but I proceeded. "I sort of had the impression that Hao and Flora were lovers, too."

"I'm never going to love a woman the way that I loved her."

"You had an open relationship."

"I wasn't going to get my heart ripped out every time she walked out our door, but I was better off with her, in any way, than without her."

That was awfully gracious and evolved and sophisticated and stupid. Coming from Wagner, it was also hard to believe.

Smiling, he answered, shaking his finger at me. "You're wondering how a proud man could put up with that, thinking I might take my jealousy out on Hao's brother, maybe on his nephew, too. That I'm so crazy jealous I might spin out of control."

"Maybe I wondered that," I said.

"You can make fun of Flora and her God, I did plenty of times, but together they gentled me down," he said. "Love has nothing to do with me watching Ike's back."

I'd been looking around, wondering if I could get Jimmy out of the house without Wagner seeing us leave. I didn't see an escape hatch.

Wagner said, "Want to know why I'm really here?"

"You know what? You can fill me in on the details later. I ought to take Jimmy and get going."

"If you know what you're rescuing him from, you'll get the kind of mad I feel. It'll give you energy," he said. "It's more about Ike's work when he was a kid."

Wagner was solid, and he was as thick as a wall they use for crash-testing cars, the soft dummy-drivers crumpling over themselves upon impact. I was stuck.

"You have many black friends?" Wagner said.

"Not many." Felt weird to say, but it was true, and I wasn't going to mince words with him.

"You have friends who are gay?"

"Sure."

"Then you know about dying from AIDS. Fear, shame, agony."

"I do."

"Multiply the number of people you know by fifty, that's how many friends and family I've got who died of AIDS. I've done everything I could, at one time or another, to destroy myself, but I'm healthy. It doesn't make sense."

"This is about Ike's work?"

"Ike told me about the test subjects down there that they pump chemicals and diseases into. They're not what you would call the beautiful people," he said.

"One day, years ago, I'm having a beer with a buddy at a neighborhood bar. We imagine a similar scene, but this one's happening in Washington, DC, and the buddies are thin-blooded white guys wearing dark suits and too much schooling. They've gone to Harvard, Yale, some such noise. TV news is playing in their background—two more blacks down and another cop dead in a street fight.

"Another beer, and I've got this whole scene playing out inside my head: One Washington, DC, rich guy, drunk, says to his buddy, *Think how great our country would be again if we could get rid of the troublemakers—faggots, blacks, Mexicans. . . .*

"That scene," Wagner pointed to his head, "kept bugging me. Three days later, I go to the library. I find out that AIDS started in Africa from people eating monkey brains. This makes no sense at all. Whatever they're eating, they've been doing it for hundreds of years. Why AIDS all of a sudden?

"So, I imagine those grown-up brats and their idea of a better America. I see them pushing the right funding buttons, and inventing a disease to get rid of their troublemakers. This AIDS thing has got to be new, I figure. They don't dig up mummies carrying AIDS viruses."

"Not that I've heard."

"Government scientists think they're working on germ warfare, maybe they're not exactly sure what'll happen with their experiments, how it fits in with other experiments. They fiddle in their labs, come up with something, move to the next project.

"Meanwhile, the first batch of the nasties gets sent to kids stationed in Africa. They think they're inoculating people against typhoid, and they feel good about their jobs. People are dying, but they die over there all the time. Who cares? Nobody, except those white guys at a bar in DC who know that their new virus works.

"Vials of the AIDS virus go to clinics in Harlem. Doctors think that it's methadone, going to treat heroin addiction. Send more batches to the Castro District in San Francisco, tell those clinics that it's flu vaccine. The folks in Harlem, and the Mexicans who share needles, start dying. Gays join them, and a better America is just around the corner. It's so easy killing off the troublemakers, that it isn't even much fun.

"There's one thing they don't count on—how much blacks and whites mix it up, and how much the straights and gays mix it up. That disease doesn't know its place, and now, because it's chasing their brothers out of the family closet, they're stuck trying to find a cure for a disease they invented. A disease that was meant to be incurable."

"Holy shit, Wagner." I collapsed on the arm of the chair, sitting beside him. I took a couple of deep breaths. I moved to the logical side of my brain. "This is a conspiracy theory," I said to Wagner, "one of the millions. You're trying to make sense out of your friends' death. Find somewhere to place blame."

"It doesn't make the theory false."

"And it doesn't make it true," I said.

Wagner leaned forward, tapping his fingertips together. "Could it be a possibility?"

A possibility? "Yes."

"Meaning that you can imagine some highly placed blue bloods using Ike, and other good people, to brew up catastrophes. What does that say to you?"

"I don't want Jimmy around them, in capital letters."

"You got it. Ike told me what he worked on at CDC. Everything fits with the crazy scene that me and my friend, uneducated people, saw a long time ago."

"Ike," I said, "do you believe the scene that Wagner laid out?"

"People do terrible things and wondrous things. That's all I'm certain of. As far as my work, and other people's work, I can tell you this—even good people get tired when they work too hard, and they're not paid well. Pharmacy companies keep track of everything being researched, and sometimes a doctor is tempted once too often. He sells his research and makes big money. These people are called rogue—they are not bad. They are lost."

"You think they want Jimmy to work on curing AIDS now that they opened Pandora's box of horrors?"

"I doubt it," Ike said. "Many new issues have come along since then. I do know working for them made me feel as worthless as a lab rat. When people lose their humanity, anything is possible."

Spooky stuff. Wagner was sticking to Ike like glue, he'd given me a reason why, and I know very well that uneducated people are often brighter than book-smart. I could almost believe his theory regarding the birth of AIDS, and that scared me plenty. I had zero trouble believing a federally funded research arm could want

Jimmy, and other flukes, including psychics and time-travelers, to work on things that even *The Eye* would consider far-out. And I noticed something. Wagner had done a good job of distracting and scaring me. He'd done an excellent job of gaining Ike's weary trust.

I said to Wagner, "Don't jump out of your skin at me, but at the time of Flora's murder the twins said you were with them, both of them, all night. They're powerful and beautiful, they're connected, and they're damned fun."

"Not many people are going to question their word. They're a good alibi."

"Were you with them?"

Wagner grinned, nodding his head. "As I said, the Ivy League boys never imagined the many ways people mix it up."

Ike was planted, still as a stone, not resting, not anything.

"Ike," I said, "are you okay?"

"I'll never know peace, because I don't know what damage my work caused. My head hurts all the time, except when I see Jimmy."

"Then focus on Jimmy," I said.

"And suspect everyone," Wagner said.

"Including you?"

"Have you listened to one word I've said? Yes, suspect me."

"That's pretty easy."

"I hear Jimmy banging around in the attic," Wagner said. "What's he doing?"

"Boys," Ike said. "Up to something all the time."

"Ike," I said, "ignore anything you hear about me and Jimmy— we'll be fine. Wagner, you'll be glad to know that I'm not giving you a clue about our plans."

"Good for you."

"I need some clothes that will get us out the door, into my car, and through any part of town without being noticed."

230   *Meredith Blevins*

Ike was still doing his imitation of a stone.

"Ike, get your ass in gear. Oh, never mind," Wagner said. "Everybody around here could get killed while you're studying on it."

The sound of Jimmy's feet in the attic was dust hitting the floorboards, Wagner was a hailstorm.

"Ike," I said, lifting my purse off his counter. "Do you smoke?" Ike was a healer, but he was Chinese. His generation smoked as regularly as they breathed.

"No," he said. "It slows down the flow of oxygen, and it also plugs my inner ears."

I picked up a pack of cigarettes. It was next to the sink. "Are these Wagner's?"

"This brand is Xian, common on the Mainland, very expensive here. Must have been left by Alan Lee when he came looking for Jimmy. He also left this."

"How," I said, "did you get his wallet?"

"It fell out of his pants." Ike was sheepish and pleased. "We didn't steal it."

"Wagner held Alan upside down after he hurt your leg, didn't he?"

"He shook him, too, just a little. Wagner told me to get everything that fell out of his pockets while he held him."

"I hope you didn't laugh. I have a feeling dignity is big for Alan."

"No laughing. Wagner told Alan that he could smash his head on the floor and bury him in the backyard. He believed Wagner," Ike said. "I must do a prayer for this room."

"Ike, you have Alan's wallet and you have his cigarettes."

"Also a cigarette butt he left, and $238.00 that was inside the wallet. It makes me feel like a thief."

"Walk up the street, with Wagner, and give it to the organist at St. Theresa's. Tell her to give some kid music lessons with the money."

Ike brightened up. "Coins rolled out of his pockets. I found them under the cabinets." He handed me nickels, dimes, and a few pennies. "I'll give these to Jimmy in a red envelope," Ike said. "Tonight is the New Year's celebration. This is a hard way for a good boy to grow up."

"Ike, it's only temporary."

"I want him to be a regular kid, no worries except me getting mad about fast cars and fancy white girls."

"We all want the same thing for Jimmy—a good life, safety, laughs. But it's time for us to get real. Normal's never going to happen."

Thirty-seven

The Chariot, Tarot Card Number 7: Be calm now because the world has decided you're in control. Feelings are bashing all over the place. You must find the middle road between them, steering the chariot with a firm hand. Don't get nervous, but . . . Everything depends on you.

—*The Gypsy Guide to Fortune-telling*
Mystic Café Press, 2004

Ike made magic on us. No women's clothes in the attic were small enough for me, so I was given men's clothing. I resembled Mao on his way to an inauguration ball. It was not one of my better fashion moments. Jimmy didn't even look at himself in the mirror, and he was horrified. He was disguised in a sexy, red-silk number festooned with pink embroidered butterflies. The dress was closed on the side with frog fasteners. Jimmy was the picture of a child bride, one century earlier. Not one of his better fashion moments, either.

Wagner, with a delicate touch, slipped a pair of small, embroidered shoes on Jimmy's feet.

Wagner had a flair for cosmetics. My own mother wouldn't have recognized me. He placed one hand on each of my shoulders. His arms were heavy. I remembered him in the church, walking away from me wearing his silk robe, the way it hugged his body in a damp caress. A lot had happened since then.

"For a white woman, you're brave."

I decided to take that as a compliment. "Nothing brave about saving my own tail."

"You're saving Jimmy's, too."

"Which, at this moment, is connected to mine," I said. "And I owe him. He created healing for someone I love."

"I dig that, when life feels even."

"Doesn't feel close to even, not yet," I said. "You're staying with Ike?"

"I'm not letting him out of my sight."

"You're not telling anyone that you saw me and Jimmy."

"I haven't seen anyone except Ike."

I didn't tell Wagner that I had Alan's wallet. I hoped Ike hadn't seen me sneak it into my purse, along with Alan's cigarettes and the butt.

Wagner shook Jimmy's hand, one hard pump. Jimmy didn't so much as grimace.

Ike schruffled Jimmy's hair, kissing him once on each cheek. "You make me proud," Ike said, "every single day of my life."

Ike stopped us from leaving. He said to Jimmy, "I've surrounded myself with a sonic barrier. You remember how to do that for yourself?"

Jimmy looked embarrassed. Too much hocus-pocus right in front of Wagner, male to end all males.

Jimmy shrugged. Ike's voice rose to meet his resistance, sharp and loud. "No kidding around. You'll protect yourself with the barrier, right now, before you leave this house."

"Okay, okay," Jimmy said, "but I'm going in the kitchen."

"Sometimes you've got to be stern. Boy," Ike said, "it takes energy to bring up a kid."

Three minutes, maybe four, Jimmy said he was ready to leave.

I revved the engine, and Ike opened wide the garden gate. I thought there was plenty of room for a turn, there wasn't, and a screek followed me into the alley. I checked my rearview mirror. Wagner was smacking himself on the forehead, and Ike was laughing. One foot of green picket fence followed me for almost two blocks until it rattled into a gutter.

Thirty-eight

*L*ooking as if we were understudies for a Chinese version of *The Mikado*, I drove across town to the Columbarium. I thought we stuck out like a sore thumb, but no one gave us a second glance. I was an older traditional Chinese man with a hot date.

I was being a semi-considerate driver when a kid in a car that cost more than the budget of several third-world countries cut me off. Cheering and waving as if life were one big party, I was the butt of a joke devised for him by F. Scott Fitzgerald. I gave Jimmy a go-ahead nod. As one, we gave the driver the finger and made monkey faces at him, sticking our tongues out. Jimmy taught me a swear word in Chinese. Next time, I'd be prepared.

Just off Anza, in a refined neighborhood, the Columbarium waited for us on a cul-de-sac—One Loraine Court. It is a Greco-Roman beauty living in the wrong locale. It is the Neptune Society's largest repository for ashes, a classy place to spend forever, and I was willing to bet that some of the eternal residents had never stayed in a hotel so nice.

The building is muscular—it withstood the 1906 earthquake. In 1937, when San Francisco passed a law prohibiting all cemeteries within city limits, the Columbarium bared its teeth and held its ground. Its large copper dome, greened by years and weather, is barely visible until you turn onto Loraine where the building rises between two immaculate homes.

A circular staircase winds you 'round and around to the top, providing the opportunity to drop off the loop at any level. The interior is strictly old playhouse theater. Gold-leaf balconies, wine-velvet draperies, and tile mosaics dotting the ceiling. All that grandeur is not wasted on the dead. Occasional civic events and concerts are held there. Very occasional.

Jimmy grabbed his backpack as we were getting out of the car. He asked me to open my purse. He wanted all metal objects inside my purse. Other items were to be inside his backpack. I stuffed my car keys into my floppy-square pocket so I'd find them again someday. Satisfied, he swung his Jansport BigBoy over his shoulder. I told him the outdoorsy look did absolutely nothing to enhance the red-silk dress. He muttered in Chinese. If I'd been paying attention, I would have learned a few more words to use in traffic.

Above the front door was pseudo-Greek lettering—THE COLVMBARIVM. We'd been inside two minutes, tops, when a little gray man appeared, enthusiastic, in love with his job. I had the feeling this was more than a job: it was his vocation, the color in his life, the snap in his Rice Krispies. Seeing us enter, he glowed with gracious delight. In the land of the dead, the man with a pulse is the king of hosts.

"How may I help you?"

Looking puzzled, I turned to Jimmy. Jimmy translated the question into Chinese. I shook my head and smiled. The man told us that Chinese remains were placed throughout the building, and he asked if he could help us find our loved one. Jimmy said we weren't in a hurry, we'd just look around. The man handed him a map—those with famous names, and those of clustered ethnicities, were placed on the map with large square lettering. There was a directory with the names of every inhabitant. I smiled and bowed again. Polite.

The king of the dead said if we needed help to call his name—
Anthony. Great acoustics, he'd hear us. Apparently, the sound ran
through that building like water over boulders, and the domed ceiling bounced voices back and forth like a hapless ball over a net.
We'd have to whisper to each other.

Anthony spoke a few words of Chinese to us. Jimmy smiled, answering back, and I repeated the last two words he'd said, putting
everything I had into the intonation. Anthony was satisfied. The
chipper zombie was smarter than I'd thought.

On the second level, heavy bronzed-enamel urns huddled
against the south wall. They appeared to be the elite's final digs. I
read the names. There was no Mark Hopkins, no Leland Stanford,
no Lillie Coit or lesser dignitaries. The elegant urns were engraved
with a passel of German immigrants' names, each urn resembling a
Beethoven sonata or a Wagnerian opera—overblown, overstated,
dramatic.

Sizing up the rest of the floor, I peered over the rail. Yipes. The
height and spatial effect were woozy-making. I wouldn't do that
again. Jimmy buzzed in front of me, an efficient young woman.
Our sooty plunder would be Jimmy's choice, and his choice was
dependent upon the type of case that held the urn. The few that
weren't encased, such as the Germans, were the size and weight of
a television—not easy to transport. With luck, he'd find two small
neighboring urns to swipe. We perused, me clinging to the wall,
avoiding the spiraling view.

I stopped dead. A glass case held the photo of a laughing and
round black man. His ashes rested inside an ebony flask. There
were other reminders of things he'd loved—a toy Cadillac convertible, cream-colored, with burgundy upholstery. A pair of red
dice, a fat Cuban cigar. I wanted his remains to be me. Jimmy said,
NO! The metal in the convertible, the metal picture frame, and the
metal lip of the flask, made the black man's materials impossible to

use. We were not allowed one bit of metallic residue. This would be harder than I thought.

One aisle over, Jimmy found himself. The glass case held the drawing of an old Chinese man, a wooden bowl with uncooked rice, and a pair of bone chopsticks. His ashes were sealed in a slim teak box. Another aisle over, we found the real me. A photo of a housewife, looking as if she'd spent her life longing for a genuine Electrolux vacuum cleaner, was taped to the rear of the case. Propped in front of the photo was a Barbie doll, her plastic body sweeping the carpet, a picture of Lucille Ball taped to a pink-plastic television set. A wooden table with two wooden children eating cornflakes smiled as she worked. Her urn was Tupperware. Jimmy proclaimed her safe—no metal.

Reaching inside his backpack, he pulled out a small wooden bowl and naphtha soap. Using a Popsicle stick, he mixed the naphtha with rat poison and a product marked with Chinese characters. The consistency was stringy play-dough. Jimmy seemed to know what he was doing, and I had a sudden horrific realization—I was placing my life in the hands of a hormone-blighted preteen boy.

Jimmy stuck a glob on the lock of the Chinese man's case, covering the homemade plastique with a swatch of cotton fabric. He popped the fabric once with his fist, hard and fast. No smell, little sound, and the case opened. He pulled out the teak urn and repeated the procedure with my Barbie and her Tupperware urn. We closed both cases—no scratches, no shards of glass. Jimmy held his backpack open, and I stuffed the urns inside. He cradled the bowl with the leftover explosives. A smudge of soot on Jimmy's palm was the only evidence that we'd stolen the remains of two dead people.

We took off, but we didn't run. No point in arousing suspicion.

Anthony met us at the front door, an odd little vapor saying goodbye, appearing and disappearing without so much as the sound of one tootsie hitting the floor. He'd mastered the art of deathly quiet.

Jimmy and I settled into the car. My heart was beating as if I'd just knocked off a bank.

"Don't floor it," Jimmy said. "The way you drive . . . Wait! We need to get rid of this bowl. One pothole and we'd be history."

"Jimmy. Throw it out. Now."

"It's not that easy," he said. "See how gently I hold this bowl? When I blew up those cases I used pressure, but my major tool was low vibration in my throat. It traveled down my arm and pushed through my hand."

"We can't toss it out the window?"

"I read about a man who hit this stuff with a hammer to see if it worked."

"And?"

"His neighbors were ticked off about the mess he made all over their neighborhood in Ohio," Jimmy said. "We could always toss it out the window at the next person who cuts us off."

"DON'T EVEN THINK ABOUT IT!"

I drove in smooth circles around the small cul-de-sac.

"Sometimes you have no sense of humor," he said. "Stop right here."

"We're only two houses from the Columbarium."

"It's not like I've got a whole load of it."

I stopped, and he opened the car door. His ancestors had invented gunpowder—by now the love of explosives is probably genetic. I could only hope the kid would never go political. I could see him, ten years in the future, taking a little drive to Glen Canyon, armed with enough kitchen products and plumbing supplies to take an entire dam down to red dust.

He slowly shoved the bowl inside a curbside sewer grate. He pounded the pavement above with a small rock, and ran to the car. A minor rumbling, but not one house tumbled to the ground. I did feel the asphalt vibrate beneath my wheels. We took off, but casually. Speeding tickets place you at the scene.

"Make sure you keep it nice and slow. Some of the material for Mina's job is in my pack. It's not mixed yet, but, like I said, this is a big job. I'm smart, but I'm just a kid."

I was glad we had no intention of flying anywhere. Whatever was in his backpack would be enough to keep us going through airport security clearances the rest of my natural life. With Jimmy as a companion, that might not be long.

Thirty-nine

So far so good. We hadn't drawn attention to ourselves, and we were still alive. We puttered to Haight-Ashbury, and no one tailed us. At our rate of speed, they would have been impossible to miss.

A cell phone rang. Jimmy answered two of them before he found the right one. "It's your old one," he said, and he mouthed, *"It's some woman."*

"Hello!" I said, cheerful and bright. Sounded as if the remains of the Electrolux Barbie were seeping into my brain.

"You sound . . . different," she said.

"Hi, Jan."

"Good job. This time you got the right twin."

"Fifty-fifty chance."

"Glad you checked out our alibi with Wagner. It means you're keeping your wits about you."

I almost ran into one of those damned palm trees that breezed up the coast from Southern California a century ago.

"Wagner's quite a man," I said.

"Splendid."

"Yep."

"We wanted to talk before you and Jimmy disappear," Jan said. "Are you on the other end, Jean?"

"I'm on, but I'm taking the cordless into the other room. All I can hear is you, and that's about the last thing I want."

Jan said to her sister. "What's gotten into *you?*"

"You decided to call Annie while I was watching a *60 Minutes* rerun. It's not as if you couldn't have waited for Andy Rooney. I've loved that man since World War II—what a stud muffin. Brains, too! WOOOOO!"

"Jean, have you been smoking?" I asked her. If the gals were loaded, it would be a lot easier to maneuver a slice of truth out of them.

"One toke, that's all," Jean said, "but this new stuff! I have to learn to pace myself. It's not like the old days, when you could sit around with friends and pass a number, feeling a pleasant buzz."

"And it certainly doesn't do anything to shut you up," Jan said.

"Jan! Honestly. Why don't you make yourself a drink? It's been a long day." Jean said to me, "Dear, Jan didn't smoke. She wanted to talk to you while she was straight, and I wanted to watch *60 Minutes*. There you have it."

"There I have what?"

"Have what? Isn't it obvious? One of the women you're talking to is crazy, the other one is sane. Jean, why don't you hang up and catch the end of Andy Rooney."

A loud clunk, rattle, and click.

I said, "Why did you really call—other than to let me know, once again, your spyglass has a long lens."

"We want you to be very careful."

"Did you ever work with Alan, the CDC guy who wants Jimmy? He's had a slight mishap with Wagner. Unfortunately, it's not enough to keep him from returning to Qi Dragon."

"You're clever, especially for a lady on the run. No, we don't work with the Weasel—that's our pet name for Alan. Something about those eyes. We *did* work with his father. Sometimes above his father."

One more hard plastic clatter on a tile floor. Jean was back on the phone.

"Andy's over," Jean said. "Would it have killed you to wait until my program was finished?"

A long-suffering sigh from sister Jan. "Annie, as I was saying, we know Alan. Avoid him."

"I think Wagner can take care of Alan."

"Alan needs an exterminator. We were grooming Wagner to be just that before Flora died."

"You may have succeeded."

"We can only hope, but remember what we first told you—grow eyes in the back of your head and don't trust anyone."

"Including you."

"Including us."

"You've done a better job fashioning Wagner than you think."

"Only time will tell. One more thing—you haven't heard from us," Jan said.

"We're packed," said Jean, "and we're leaving town until this blows over. It's going to get big."

"Life will do that," I said.

"And the wrong people often take the heat," Jan said, "when the you-know-what hits the fan."

"Put another way, we've survived because we know when to take a powder."

I said, "I've got a new cell phone. Several. You want a number, in case there's any late-breaking news?"

"No. We won't have a cell, or a landline, and don't try to contact us."

"Okay by me."

Jan said, "Hey, tell Mina she was absolutely right. She said we'd take a long journey. We were hoping for a month of white sand and a bevy of beach boys."

"But," Jean said, "she *was* right about the long journey. Thanks for turning us on to her. *Au revoir.*"

Jean, you are an idiot supreme! plus other fond sisterly remarks, flew over the air waves before we were cut off.

Forty

Jimmy needed a few supplies. We visited the market at Fillmore and Haight, the beginning of the end of the old neighborhood. I followed Jimmy through narrow, dusty aisles, watching him check items off his list, putting them in our cart. Seltzer water, five limes, three large bags of mothballs, a few fat-sized dry-cell batteries.

He said, "Do you think this store has pencils?" We found an aisle with three shelves of yellowing stationery items.

"Pencils aren't made with lead anymore," I said. My costume didn't match my voice. If we weren't the only people in the store, I would have felt out of place.

"I need graphite, not lead."

More items in the cart: a roll of heavy string, lighter fluid, and there, behind the laundry products, he'd found an ancient box of 20 Mule Team borax. Looked like it had been fading on that shelf for thirty years.

Jimmy pointed to the label, saying "Sodium borate," as if that was supposed to mean something to me.

"Are you sure you know what you're doing?"

"You have two urns in the backseat of your car, and we're in one piece, although I don't know how well those sewer pipes held up. Annie," he said, "I know what I'm doing, and if I mess up, we won't really care."

That was a chunk of rough reality. "You need anything else?"

"A deck of playing cards."

"No time for Go Fish, Jimmy."

"Ha-ha. I need to scrape red ink off the hearts and the diamonds."

Jimmy emptied the cart, placing items on the counter in front of the cashier. She looked as if she'd been in that store longer than the borax. Adjusting her glasses to read every single price, she tapped them into the register. Her reading glasses rode low on her nose. I expected to be arrested any moment.

"You never know if string is going to really catch," Jimmy said. "That's why the lighter fluid."

The woman peered at us over her spectacles. I gave Jimmy a fast elbow in the ribs. He wasn't thrilled about that, but it shut him up.

I paid cash. I didn't want the purchase traced to me through a check or credit card, assuming there was a trace of me left after the big event.

After we left the store Jimmy said, "You didn't have to break my ribs. Chinese fireworks are made with a little dynamite around the fuse so they stay lit. When you're doing it yourself, you have to soak the string in lighter fluid. I'm not stupid."

"Don't talk about trouble when you're about to cause it."

"That old lady was practically blind, she wouldn't be able to identify us, and I'm the one who has to walk around dressed like a girl. What are *you* so upset about?"

"The anticipation of my favorite body parts, which means all of them, flying around Haight and Ashbury is starting to get on my nerves."

He patted me, forgiving me. "I understand. Hao was always a little worried about me during New Year's celebration, which is, HEY!!! Perfect! New Year's is tonight, and about what time is it, anyway?"

He looked at my broken watch, shook his head, and checked out the time on a billboard. "Four o'clock," he said. "Our project will blend in perfectly with the other fireworks."

"Number one, there aren't many 'projects' going off in this part of the city."

"You've probably never been in San Francisco on Chinese New Year's. Fireworks are everywhere."

"Really?"

"Kind of. Anyway, most of the fire trucks will be in Chinatown, and the rest will be busy in other parts of the city." Anticipation wiggled him like a three-year-old junked-up on Twinkies.

We placed the bags in the backseat, next to his backpack. I turned the engine over, and he looked into my face, serious now, not one ounce of play.

"Annie, we need to find inner calm. I really have to think to get us out of this alive. I can't do that if I'm nervous."

"Believe me, the last thing I want is you with a case of nerves."

"One more thing. There are potholes, and then there are POT-HOLES. The ones the city made on this street are huge. Really pay attention when you drive, okay?"

"Jimmy. I'll do the best I can."

Two turtles crawling over lumpy asphalt inside one shell, we turned left and pulled into the lot behind Mina's café. There was my café parking space. Next to my space another car waited in the empty lot.

Forty-one

*A*ctually, it wasn't a car, it was a van, and it looked as if it had blasted straight out of 1968, using Mina's parking space for its landing pad. Flowers and a peace sign were painted on the hood over an ancient VW cream yellow body. A little rust on the bottom, its windshield was divided in half by a stainless-steel frame. They built those babies to last.

"Whose van is that?" Jimmy asked.

"I don't know."

"Maybe if we drive around the block, it'll go away."

"Give me a minute to think."

"You want me to be quiet?"

"Yes."

"I can do that," Jimmy said.

I could see his eyeballs running back and forth under his closed lids as if he were reading. I felt tender toward Jimmy, a kid who'd seen too much, an orphan in many ways. I hadn't heard about his mom, just his useless dad. Maybe his mom was dead. I might never know.

I'd destroyed his anonymous safety blanket by plastering his face across tabloid pages, billing him as the latest and greatest Wonder

Boy. Now he'd been exposed to two deaths, and I had asked him to blow a building to smithereens and get us out alive. I was also going to frame someone for the destruction. I hadn't let Jimmy in on that one. If we lived through the explosion, I wasn't sure I'd make it through the frame job. The less he knew, the better. Who had trusted me with a kid? It was a fluke that my own had survived my mothering.

A lot of my life was an explosion right then, making me feel as if I'd pressed the *pause* button on ordinary life. I'd delivered a baby—that was a first. My emotions around the situation were jumbled, whose wouldn't be, but I was clear about several things: I'd like to see her, I'd like to hold her and touch the soft baby part on the back of her neck. I'd take it from there and decide later about buying her baby clothes.

Stevan. I'd forgive him, I always had. Why should a little thing like death change a relationship? But I'd never stop being pissed at him, not entirely. He'd just have to deal with that.

Leo loved me, warts and all, and wanted to marry me. At least he thought he did—his near-death experience might have distorted his common sense. He was lying in a hospital bed waiting to see which number came up when life rolled the roulette wheel again. That's where I stopped, because that's what I wanted—to be in Leo's narrow hospital bed loving him well.

There was no movement from inside the cafe; maybe the van had been abandoned. I decided to call Leo in case this didn't go well.

Keeping my eye on the van, on any signs of life, Jimmy opened his eyes a crack. I told him to go back to whatever meditative world he was visiting, told him I was calling Leo and wanted an inch or two of privacy.

Jimmy smiled, closing his eyes again.

The hospital switchboard transferred me three times before I hit the right place. I asked the nurses' station for Leo Rosetti, telling them I was Dr. Verdi.

They put me through to his room.

He said, "Hey, beautiful. Come up with an answer?"

I'd just called to hear his voice, not to determine my future. I wasn't even sure if I had one.

Oh, what the hell. "Leo, the answer is yes. I think."

"You think?"

"I think I might marry you someday if you really meant it when you asked."

"Gee. I'm feeling all warm and rosy. It must be the drugs. No one has ever received a more romantic answer to a marriage proposal."

"You're the Italian. Romance is your department."

"You don't know yourself very well."

"Right now I'm hoping I have time to learn—cooking, relaxation, real writing . . . I always kind of wanted to learn geometry, too."

"Annie, am I having a minor stroke, or are you not making sense?"

"I'm not making sense."

"That's a relief. Where are you?"

"Sitting outside Mina's café in my car with Jimmy and wondering who the hell that flowered van next to us belongs to. Wondering how to get rid of the person, and hoping Jimmy can get us out of this in one piece."

"Don't tell me what you're talking about. I'm recovering. I'd like to keep it that way."

"Leo, you will see me tomorrow night."

"Not sooner?"

"No."

"If I don't hear from you," he said, "what should I do?"

"One way or another, I'll make contact with you. Be open to any form of communication."

"If I weren't already in the hospital, that remark would have put me here."

I pictured climbing inside Mina's body, channeling through her to Leo. I wondered if I'd need an appointment in advance, or if she'd work this out on the spur of the moment. I was losing it. There was no way in hell I'd climb inside Mina for anyone.

"Leo. I love you."

"I love you right back. Get here as soon as you can."

"Okay, but don't worry," I said. "I've got to go. Jimmy's getting antsy."

"I really like that kid."

"Leo," I said, while looking at Jimmy dressed as a mail-order bride, "you like him because he's all boy, every man's fantasy of the trouble they used to get into."

"Exactly."

We hung up. There was an empty good-bye echoing down a hospital corridor, tat-a-tatting its heels across a linoleum floor. I could hear it. I was about to tell Leo to hang in there for me. Considering the circumstances, that didn't seem fair.

Jimmy and I lifted the grocery bags from my car.

The back door was unlocked. The Szabo crew didn't get it together to lock up when they'd left. We walked into Mina's. Skip the Dolphin Man was sitting on a rickety chair, drinking a cup of tea.

"Yo, I wondered when you two were going to show up."

He'd recognized us, didn't blink twice at Jimmy's dress or my Mao-gone-gaudy pantsuit.

"What made you think we'd be here?"

"I went to Mina's in Chinatown, the place where I met you, but she wasn't there. Then I figured maybe you were over here—I used to come here all the time. I knew you'd be where she was and that Jimmy'd be where you were. Aren't families cool?" he said. "They are so symbiotic."

Cool? I wasn't sure about that. Symbiotic? Maybe. So are parasites.

"I liked this place," Skip said. "I'm sorry to see it so empty."

"Things change, people move on." The place wasn't nearly as empty as it was going to be.

"I met the first woman I ever loved in here. She became a realtor."

"I'm sorry."

"All water under the bridge. Who knows, maybe next time around we'll come back as a couple of humpback whales and hang out together again."

I don't care how environmentally minded a woman is, she wouldn't want to return as a whale. It's too close to the way we sometimes feel, especially when trying on bathing suits.

"Hey," he asked, "where did you get those clothes? I haven't seen Mao gear since, I don't know when, but it's been a long time."

"Skip, you've got to leave. This place isn't ours anymore. The city bought it from Mina." It was close to the truth.

"Bummer."

"A genuine bummer."

I didn't see Jimmy. Panic climbed up my throat. Then I heard rattling outside near the cars. Skip stood up to investigate.

"Wait here, Skip."

"I hope the little guy's okay."

I opened the door. A wedge of tofutti light struck Jimmy. He was rustling around inside Skip's van. "What are you doing?"

"Giving Skip a method to contact us. He's not a bad guy, just crazy. We might be able to use him."

"Get in here this minute."

"Okay, okay. I'm done."

Jimmy and I walked inside, two smiling people, hiding the strain of our tentative future.

Skip said, "Hey, kid. I know what you're up to."

Jimmy turned vanilla, I went straight to white linen.

Skip said, "You're sick of adults wanting things from you. You want your freedom."

We were so relieved that the color jumped back to our cheeks.

"They treat me like a baby," Jimmy said, "and you know what? I have my own bus pass. I can go anywhere I want in this city at any time."

"Little dude, that is *so* not cool. You need to let people know where you are. There are evil people in this city."

Shuffling his feet, Jimmy, contrite, said he'd try harder. Then his eyes did that narrow, thoughtful thing.

He said, "Skip, what do you want from me?"

"One last shot. I want you to go to the ocean and listen with me. You might be the only one who can understand why dolphins stayed there, and why we decided to take a walk. They have it pretty together, and we've screwed up royally." Skip turned to me. "Don't you think so, too?"

"I've lost sleep thinking about it," I said. "Skip, I don't want to get caught here by the cops. You probably don't want them running down your identity, either."

Skip was the pale yellow of his VW. I'd pushed the correct *exit* button.

He stood, and then he stopped, gazing longingly at a chair with a laminated seat. The King of Hearts. "I was sitting right there when I kissed Linda."

"Why don't you take it?"

He brightened up. "It's weird, she's not the only Linda I've known who turned into a realtor."

"Must be the vibes of the vowels," I said.

"Don't fall for any more Lindas." That was Jimmy.

"Right on, little guy."

Skip hoisted the chair above his head. Jimmy said, "Hey, Skip. You're right about the dolphins. They're our higher selves."

"I knew it!"

"Skip, if I ever get into real trouble," Jimmy said, "I'm going to contact you, don't worry about how, because I know you'd do anything to help me."

Skip was out the door, chair overhead, a happy man. We heard the unmistakable sound of a VW van starting up.

"They're our higher selves?" I said to Jimmy.

"I told you that Dragon Qi had rich people from LA who came to our store. I learned how they talk," he said. "And about the dolphins?"

"Yes?"

"It might be true."

Forty-two

1) Put red chili sauce in your enemy's Twinkie.
2) When someone is asleep, shave off one of their eyebrows.
3) Put Tiger Balm in the seat of a man's pants. Don't do it to girls.
4) Slip an egg into the end of someone's shoe.

—Copied from Jimmy's notebook

"Jimmy. Jimmy?"

"I'm up in Mina's attic."

"What are you doing?"

"I'm watching the dolphin guy drive off, you know, making sure he's really gone."

"Is he?"

"Yeah, he just turned the corner. I stuck a tracer in his van. Something else, too. It's a surprise."

"Skip's not driving around with something hazardous, is he?"

"Of course not. I'm a healer, not a killer."

All five feet of Jimmy were dressed like a little Chinese house-wife, but that disciplined voice, firm, mildly outraged—I knew ex-actly what he'd be like at the age of forty. A strong man who knew what he wanted and wouldn't be swayed from his path. Sometime between now and then he'd achieve a remarkable center. I remem-bered Mina saying she'd seen his future. I'd only had the tiniest glimpse down his road—his was a future worth saving.

"What else are you doing up here?"

"I need a few scraps of wood," he said. "I'm tearing apart this old lath and plaster. Some is redwood, no good. It won't burn fast enough."

Opening the attic hatch, I scooted inside, batting spiderwebs from my hair, itchy all over.

"This building isn't very sturdy," he said. "I'm surprised the city wants it."

"They don't care about the structure, they want the land."

"Good thing. Land is all they're going to get." He checked out a few strips of lath with an appraising eye, cracking them into short chunks.

"This is my night," he said. "It's the year of the monkey, end of my first cycle. And this," he said, holding up a rotting piece of lumber, "is a lucky way to start my second cycle."

He pulled out a pen. Wrestling with his sketchbook, moving it odd-angled on his lap, he drew.

"Could I ask you a favor?" he said.

"Sure."

"This has to be perfect, and there's a lot of confusion inside your head." He placed one of his hands on my cheek; he placed the other hand on my heart. Closing his eyes, he hummed. When he stopped, I felt as if I'd downed a mug of mulled wine.

I kissed him, just a tiny peck, and he almost didn't pull away. I held his chin, and I looked into his eyes. "I am crazy about you."

"I think you're just crazy," he said, trying not to smile.

I left him alone, gathering his supplies, free of my interior clutter. Stairs creaking with every downward step, Jimmy was right. There wasn't much about this building that was solid. But it was sweet, and part of me loved it. Like Skip, I'd done my first falling in love there, too. Stevan and I had snuck in one night, late, carrying bottles of cheap wine. There were a couple of ratty couches that customers sat on while enduring meaningful conversations. But it was late, and the place was empty. One bottle of wine, half of another, I fell in love right on the ratty couch. A couple of weeks later, this time in Stevan's upstairs room, we decided to get married.

Maybe my oldest daughter started there the same way many babies start—too much alcohol and not one ounce of common sense.

Maybe Pavlik had started out the same way in the same place. I didn't feel any pain about it just then. My husband was dead, I didn't have to go to the trouble of killing him for cheating on me. I was going to annihilate the place where I'd fallen in love with him, and where he'd probably had a fling with someone else. Closure. How many women get to enjoy that?

Jimmy walked down the stairs carefully, balancing large books in each arm. He asked me to help him. We stacked *Moby Dick, War and Peace,* books filled with plant magic and spells, the R and the M volumes of the World Book, plus other fatties.

I left him cutting the centers out of the books. Outside, looking to my left and right, except for one scrawny cat, I saw no one and nothing near my car. I got out our his-and-her urns. One more check—still no one in sight.

Jimmy was placing a dry-cell battery, three powders wrapped in red tissue, and the contents of a large Chinese firecracker in the middle of each book. He took thin copper wire and cut it into pieces. He wrapped the wire around the tissue, keeping it stable inside the book with a smidge of chewed gum. One end of the wire was attached to the end of a battery, the other was attached to a piece of the attic lath. Two dimes were on either end of the wire, separated by the wedge of wood.

"When a book falls off the shelf, the wood will move, the dimes will touch, and they'll complete the electrical circuit. The electricity will make the powder GO!"

"I cannot believe we're doing this."

"We're not. I am."

"What's going to shake the books off the shelves?"

"Simple pipe bombs. I'm using cardboard tubes from inside paper towel rolls, they'll burn in the fire. PVC pipe is for the larger explosions."

"Why all the damned books if you're making pipe bombs?"

"You're getting rattled again," he said, and he was right. "The pipe bombs will set off several large fires and detonate the books. The books will create small fires all around Mina's building. This place is big, and we want it to go up fast. Even the paper in the books will be fuel. Nothing wasted."

"Are we going to get away with this?"

"That's why the building's got to go fast—we want a really hot fire. Did you know that bodies are cremated at a temperature of seven-hundred degrees?"

"Don't tell me how you know that."

Humming, building his pipe bombs, Jimmy looked pleased with himself. Too pleased. "See? Only things that anyone would ordinarily have here—batteries, dimes, books, cleaning products, paper towels. I've made a diagram of where we should set the books. Again, we do it carefully."

"Jimmy, we can't forget the evidence that proves two humans died in this fire."

I opened the lids of our urns. Placing a mug in front of each stool pulled up to the counter, I began sprinkling our ashes. Jimmy had died on the east side of the counter, I had died on the west. Human ashes will turn you symbolic if nothing else will. Most of our ashes were sprinkled on stools, the places we'd been sitting while we enjoyed our final cups of tea. I sprinkled a little dust on the counter next to the cups. A Stephen King tea party.

Jimmy said, "None of that stuff is going to be here after it blows."

"They'll investigate, and the lab will recognize human bits and bones."

I was given the map and charged with placing books. I only made one change—*Moby Dick* was moved to the front window. I thought Captain Ahab would enjoy a parting look at the street, a different kind of ocean, but a rolling swell just the same.

I wandered around Mina's, trying to keep my noisy head from crowding Jimmy. Next to the birthing futon, I found the deck of tarot cards Mina wanted me to save. I cut the deck. The Empress. Probably one of those decks where each card was the same. Mina was a grown-up female version of Jimmy. Her techniques had simply become subtle over time. I fanned the deck. Every card was there. I stuffed the deck in my pocket.

I'd never had the opportunity to snoop around Mina's life, and probably wouldn't again. I opened the small chest that her tarot cards had been lying on.

Legal papers, piles of them, waiting for her signature. No wonder she'd encouraged me to torch the Mystic. The city wasn't holding up the sale of her land, it was her lack of ability, and desire, to sign papers and mail them someplace as official as a County Recorder's Office.

Below the legal mess were kids' drawings, cards, and letters written in large crayon print. I opened one card covered with heart-shaped balloons. My daughter's signature was on it, circa third grade. A large envelope stuffed with other cards and letters. Floods of Mother's Day cards, Christmas cards, Valentine's Day cards from all three of my daughters. An Easter card with three bunnies hopping across the faded newsprint, picture albums . . . I carried the small chest outside and put it in my trunk. Jimmy didn't hear me come back in. He was sliding the last pipe bomb together, using a finger of Vaseline.

"I brought both lead pipe and PVC. I checked Mina's plumbing, and her pipes are PVC—it's not original. I wanted to make sure the pipe bomb matched her plumbing. I'll keep the lead pipe in case we have to hit anyone."

"Don't say that."

"Hao told me to take care of myself, not to depend upon others. That's what I'm doing."

A pretty tough way to grow up, but Hao was right, especially in

Jimmy's case. He needed to know how to take care of himself. There was no mommy or daddy with a fat wallet waiting to bail Jimmy out of trouble.

He placed two of the pipe bombs, complete with lighter-fluid-saturated fuses, a little off to the right, next to a wall.

"This wall is load-bearing," he said. "We want it to go down in a big way. It'll start the building falling, and that'll get the books going," he said. "Did you put the books in the right places?"

"Except for *Moby Dick*—it's in the window. I kind of wish we'd saved that. It was a nice edition."

"Please don't start picking up nice books and throwing them in your car. Those two dimes touch, and you and I are out of here. *Really* out of here."

I was frozen, sweating, nearly afraid to breathe. I wouldn't get sentimental over one single book.

He shuffled through his backpack.

"What are you looking for?" I said. "I want to leave."

"As long as we walk carefully, and don't knock anything over, we'll be okay. I went pretty light on the powder."

As I scanned the café, it was hard to imagine that he'd gone light on anything, hard to imagine we weren't about to take down half of the city and part of the Bay Bridge for good luck.

Jimmy pulled off his Chinese dress, leaving it behind to become part of the charred ashes, and he pulled on clean sweats. I hadn't brought a change. Mao and I were stuck with each other.

He took one last look around, rubbing his hands together. "Okay, let's roll."

I set the clock that would light the first fuse, and he attached the fuse to a piece of guitar string. A high E, he told me, the thinnest wire. Jimmy wanted seven minutes, but I gave us fifteen. I had something to do, and I wanted to live through it and be some distance away before we became part of a spectacular fireworks display.

Jimmy left first, and I locked the dead bolt on the back door behind us. It would be a fine, starry night. Crisp and clean.

I told Jimmy to hold tight—one more detail to attend to.
Opening my glove compartment, I pulled out Alan Lee's wallet.
I searched it: platinum credit cards, his health insurance card,
courtesy of the US government, his driver's license, AAA tow
card, and three photos. I tucked a few twenties inside. Tossing
the wallet carelessly, a few parking spaces away from mine, it
looked as if it had fallen out of a pocket when he'd climbed out
of his low-slung car. I almost lit up one of the Xian cigarettes—
I wanted it to look as if Alan had been smoking and waiting.
Jimmy had a near heart attack. I left the cigarette pack by the
wallet, took the butt I'd swiped from Ike's, placing it near the
doorway of the Mystic.

It was easy, too easy, to imagine Alan getting out of his Italian
car, his wallet falling from his pocket, leaning in our doorway, having a smoke, spying on us, wondering if he'd just about had
enough of us . . . I handled everything with the corner of my
shirt. I took one can of gasoline, empty, from my trunk. Stuffing a
rag in it, I placed it in Mina's doorway.

"If we were going to use gasoline," Jimmy said, "why did you
have me go to all that trouble? Gasoline is crude, no art to it. Besides, it wouldn't do much except set the kitchen on fire. Unless it
hit the natural gas main."

"Perfect."

"I just went to a bunch of work so that we wouldn't leave one
trace. Why?"

"Jimmy, I'm giving the police evidence for arson, and I'm pointing them in the direction of a possible suspect. Maybe our deaths
were accidental, maybe they weren't. If nothing else, it'll cause
confusion."

Jimmy scrunched up his face, scratching his head. "That's pretty
good."

"I'm going to pour out the last smatter of gasoline from the bottom of this can. Will that make anything go off?"

"From out here? No, I don't think so."

"You can relax. This is going to work."

"How do you know?"

"I know everything."

"You do not."

"You want to bet?"

He didn't want to bet. It's good to bluff a smart kid into thinking you're ahead of the game.

"Annie, remember I told you that I wasn't scared?"

"Yes."

"Now I'm scared. People don't usually trust a kid to do something this dangerous."

"Jimmy, believe me—I had no other choice."

"You could have left me with Ike and Wagner and gone home."

"I'd like to catch the guy who killed Flora and Hao before I go home, and I don't want them to get you. I'd just as soon be dead while I take care of that."

"You must think Alan Lee killed them, or you wouldn't have put his stuff in the parking lot."

"This will keep Alan busy explaining himself and keep him off our tail. If he's innocent, he'll be cleared." I said, "Jimmy, we can't find the killer until they stop looking for us. I don't want the next dead body to be Ike's. This buys him insurance, too. Why are you looking at me like that?"

"You have a very devious mind."

"Between that and knowing everything, I am one dangerous babe. Let's hit the road."

"I want to go to Coit Tower."

"Why?"

"When this goes, I want to see it. Lots of the high places in town are hotel bars, and they'd notice a Chinese kid."

"While we're there I can figure out what we're going to do next."

"You don't know?"

"Not a clue."

"Awesome."

Jimmy reminded me to drive carefully. I told him there was only so long that I could be careful, and he'd better defuse his backpack or prepare to become a tiny particle of dust drifting through the universe.

"Forget it," he said. "I haven't had a chance to be a large particle yet. Tiny isn't happening."

Forty-three

*L*ive near any large city, and you're drawn to it and repelled by it. San Francisco is stuck-up, politically correct, and a feast cooked up by Bacchus. Los Angeles is a trashy little sister wearing too much jewelry, too many cosmetics, and she's a blast. Sometimes you love a city in spite of its unique characteristics, not because of them.

Jimmy said, "I've never been anywhere but San Francisco, really not outside Chinatown. Except down to Castro Street—Hao takes me there to see my dad."

The light around Jimmy glowed dim and went out. "I'm never going anywhere with Hao again."

"I know, Jimmy."

"Okay. Take care of myself, I can do that. I'm tired," he said. "Can I take a nap for a few minutes?"

"Sure, why don't you put the seat back?"

Only about two minutes, six long city blocks, and he was sound asleep. I pulled out my own cell phone, the one Jimmy checked for bugs about every three minutes. I couldn't believe the thing still worked. I called Mina.

She picked up on the first ring. "What's happening?"

"It's me."

"Of course it's you. I'll call you right back."

She called me back. Her San Francisco number came up on my screen, with the hot cell number Jimmy had given her. I was tired of squeezing tiny phones between my mouth and ear. But Jimmy enjoyed handing them out, and I enjoyed seeing him happy.

I said, "I saved your stuff from the café."

"Thanks. Those tarot cards aren't worth two cents professionally speaking, but, like I said, they have sentimental value."

"I saved other things for you, too."

"You rummaged through my belongings?"

"I saved the cards and letters my girls sent you. Years of them."

There was a long silence. "I guess the cat's out of the bag."

"It should never have been in the bag. They shouldn't have had to sneak around my back to write to their grandmother."

"We've been over this. We both acted dumb with each other, and, given another chance, we'd do exactly the same thing. You being you, and me being me."

"I guess."

"Anyway. Thanks. I meant to take them, but what with the baby . . . Is my building dead?"

"No sirens, yet."

"Is that good or bad?"

"Jimmy set the explosion to go off fifteen minutes from the time we left. It hasn't been that long."

"What a kid."

"Mina, the man from Atlantis, Alan Lee, went to Ike's house. He was looking for me and for Jimmy. He hurt Ike's leg. Wagner taught Alan a lesson."

"Didn't I tell you? Alan Lee was the first person sniffing around after Jimmy. His eyes are too close together," she said. "I'd call him a snake, but snakes have a certain charm. Alan Lee does not."

"I took his wallet, cigarettes, a stray butt he left behind, and left them at the scene of the crime."

"It's strange to think of my café as a crime. . . ." she said. "I don't know if leaving that stuff was such a hot idea."

"I don't know, either."

"You're not a pro. It's big enough to set one fire with the owner's permission."

"Jimmy built a string of bombs, two different kinds. I left a one-gallon can of gas that, I'm hoping, will point the cops to arson."

"I told you that I don't want the details. I'm already breaking out in hives and wishing I had a passport," she said. "Annie, about Alan Lee?"

"Yes?"

"What if he didn't do anything except hurt Ike's leg?"

"You think he's in the clear?"

"Absolutely not, but it's my intuition, it's not hard facts."

"My intuition also, and I trust it over hard facts any day. Intuition takes what your mind can't grasp, makes sense out of it, and gives you an answer. You just don't see the middle process."

"Did you inhale fumes? You sounded like me."

"One problem at a time."

"Time to go home and take Jimmy with you."

"Also, the twins called. They told me not to trust anyone, including Wagner, and to suspect everyone," I said. "They are going to, and I quote, 'take a powder.'"

"This is too complicated for us. Turn around and get that gas can and Alan's ID. Somehow you're going to get blamed for the whole mess and end up in jail. That's what always happens on television, and you know what?"

"What?"

"You'll spend the next ten years trying to stay away from a fat woman who wants to be your girlfriend, and when you get out of jail you'll knock off a Stop'N'Rob because you won't remember how to live on the outside."

"Mina, we're cutting off your cable TV."

"Go get that ID."

But behind me the earth shook, just a bit, maybe the size of a 2.9 earthquake, something you'd never notice if you weren't expecting the mini-cataclysm. And sirens, half a city's worth of sirens.

"It's too late to go back, Mina."

"So I hear. What now?"

"We drive to Coit Tower and watch your business go up in smoke."

"Wave good-bye for me. I had a lot of good times there."

I turned on the radio just as the local oldies station interrupted their bebop with a report stating that there was a fire in the old section of the now defunct Haight-Ashbury district. Cause unknown, too early to know if there were victims.

I turned off the radio. I thought for several blocks, blurry cars drifting by. I came around when someone honked—I had stopped at a green light. The honk woke Jimmy up.

He wore his last sleepy dream like a peaceful down comforter. Looking at me, trying to remember who I was . . . Sometimes when I wake from deep sweet sleep, I think I'm a kid waking up inside my grandmother's quilted world.

"What are we doing?" Jimmy asked.

That question was a pretty tall order. I stuck to the near present. "We're driving to the tall building you requested. Coit Tower."

His seat flew upright with a whamp. He was wide-awake. "Did it work?"

"I guess so. They're talking about it on the radio."

"Wow," he said, his voice hushed to the point of reverence. "First I was in *The Eye,* now I made the news."

"This isn't news anyone will ever know about, not in connection with you and me."

"I know. I just wanted to pretend that I was famous again for a minute."

We found a spot off Filbert, and we walked our butts off getting to that idiotic tower. There was the lobby, and there was the elevator waiting to take us to the top. There was my fear of heights, jumping out of the closet, laughing in my face like Jack Nicholson on speed, sticking its foul tongue in my face. Coit Tower is 210 feet tall; 210 feet above a sea-level city you experience breathtaking views. That's what I've heard.

The lobby art is spectacular. Another public works project, it was commissioned before anyone knew what they were getting. Twenty-five artists working together, portraying the struggles of the Bay Area's working class, it seemed that every artist was in love with Diego Rivera. Fine with me, I could look at his . . .

"That elevator is not going to be open forever," Jimmy said.

"It doesn't close until, I don't know when, but it's not for a while."

"You want me to go up by myself and come back down after I see the smoke and, if I'm really lucky, a few flames?"

"I don't want you to be alone."

"I really want to see it. I want to see where I live, too," he said. "Maybe you could pretend not to be scared."

Time to suck it up, but it wouldn't be easy. Me and my neuroses have a pact—I don't push them, and they don't bother me. Twenty-one wavering stories would definitely make them feel pinched.

"Scared?" I said. "Are you kidding? I'm enjoying the art, and now I'm done enjoying it. Let's go."

An old docent said to me, "The young man seems very interested in the view from above. Is he a native?"

Taking his hand, I pushed the elevator's buttons, a line of stainless numbered noses. "No, he's imported," I said to her.

"What did that mean?" Jimmy said to me, inside the elevator, already one flight above land.

"It means until we reach the ground again, I am no longer responsible for anything I say."

"Can I cuss?"

"No. You're still responsible for what you say."

We saw the smoke, and, as they say, where there's smoke there's fire. My stomach hurt, and it wasn't from the heights.

He said, "You look funny."

"Have you seen enough?"

"Show me where I live."

I waved my hand in the general direction of Chinatown. A place tightly packed with lots of colors. I wasn't sure it was Chinatown, but he was, and, excited, he said he could see his own house. I thought I'd felt terrible a few minutes before—not even close. Two hundred ten feet above the earth, I could see the real picture: Mina's property was billowing smoke and bits, thanks to me, and I'd asked a boy to do it. There were good reasons for getting Jimmy involved, but I couldn't remember a single one.

"Jimmy," I said. "I'm sorry. So very sorry."

Turning, he looked at me, genuinely puzzled. "Sorry? Is that why your face is funny?"

"I asked you to do something terrible, and you're a kid, and I had no right to ask you to do it."

"Then why did you ask me?"

"At this exact moment I don't remember."

"Well, I do," he said. "Being dead gives us a better chance of finding out who Hao was protecting me from. Maybe we'll find out about Flora, too."

"But you shouldn't have . . ."

There came that expression again, roaring like a fine racehorse across the finish line. "By doing this I'm taking care of myself, my family, and you. Mina didn't want that building. We helped her, too. I'm doing what Hao taught me to do, what I know is right. It's not easy, but there's no other choice. Okay?"

I sat down on a bench, telling Jimmy I needed a little air. Who was I kidding: I needed a lot of air, and I had an entire city of it up there. I was perfectly fine as long as I could feel the building pressed against my back.

"This might make you feel better." Jimmy sat next to me, and he leaned his head on my shoulder. "You and me," he said, "we go back a very long way. Hao told me that, so did Mina, but I've seen it myself. We're tied to each other with an invisible string that comes from here"—he put his hand over his heart—"and goes right into here"—he pointed to my heart.

"Two hearts," he said, "but when we're quiet together—which isn't often, we both talk too much—there's a sound between us. One heart beating. Do you hear it right now?"

I listened. "I don't hear anything but blood pounding against my head. An ugly throb."

"You listen with the wrong part of your body," he said, "and it's time to be strong now. We're walking down a dark path."

I told him five more minutes, only five, and I'd have a plan. I didn't have an idea where to start looking for one, and I felt sick to the soles of my feet.

Jimmy gave me his hand, willing my insides quiet. We looked out over the city, and he read me the brown signs with white lettering. "Think about it!" he said, trying to cheer me up. "A woman got this whole building named after her. Oh, wait. That's because she paid for it."

"Lillie Coit."

"It says the building is shaped like a fire-hose nozzle because she loved fire trucks. She started hopping on them when she was a kid. I'd like that, too."

"I think she loved firemen."

"They're brave and wear cool clothes and everyone respects them."

"That's not the kind of love I mean."

"Oh."

"But that's only a guess."

"I think she and I were alike. Most people think fires are exciting. Annie? What are you trying to worry about now?"

"I want the radio to say we're dead, but they won't find our ashes for days. Someone has to report that we're missing and say they saw us in the building."

"Is that all?" he said. "No problem. We tell the dolphin man to call the cops. He tells them he saw us at the café, and says he's afraid that we burned up."

"I have no idea how to get in touch with Skip."

"Pretend we can find him. Do we trust him?"

"Do I think he wants to hurt you? No. Do I think he'd like to kidnap you? I don't know. He might if he convinced himself it's for the good of mankind."

"Do you think he killed Flora or Hao?"

"I don't think he'd hurt a fly."

"He's a bighearted man, and his inner sounds are smart . . . that's very strange. I'll get in touch with him and tell him we're dead."

"You connected to the dolphin switchboard?"

"I play jokes on funny people, right?"

"Like when you set off the stink bomb in my car the first time I met you."

"Yep. Remember when Skip left the Mystic, I said I'd left a surprise for him in his van, and you said that you didn't want to hear about it?"

"And now I have no choice."

"You'll be proud of me."

I imagined Jimmy, rigging up batteries, wires, old coins, and laundry detergent, sending our planet back to its origins, wearing that same self-satisfied grin. The few forms of remaining life would resemble cockroaches and Keith Richards.

Forty-four

*T*here was only one person we knew who'd think he could drive and carry on a conversation with the dead at the same time. We got in touch with him.

Skip said, "This is so incredibly cool, I can't believe it. Why did you choose me?"

"Because," I said to Skip, "you're a bridge between the ocean and the earth. This means you're also a bridge between the living and the dead."

"Oh. Wow." The sound of many honking horns.

I said, "Watch your driving. We need you."

"I'll pay more attention. What can I do?"

"First of all, be aware of your immediate environment. It's very important that the energy, meaning the molecules, inside and around your van is exactly as it was when we last saw you at Mina's café—the place we left this dimension. Do not clean out your van."

"I haven't cleaned it in years."

"If the molecules become disturbed, we'll lose contact."

"No sweat. I won't touch anything."

Jimmy had supplied me with the details of his surprise. When I'd found him in the parking lot horsing around Skip's van, he had just shoved one of his Chinatown walkie-talkies under Skip's passenger seat.

Jimmy said they had new batteries, his walkie-talkies were the most expensive set you could buy—assuming you'd paid for them—and you could use them all over the city. He had experimented with them twice on Hao. The first time Hao was scared to death, thinking the spirit of a dead ancestor was speaking to him. The second time Jimmy was grounded.

I still didn't have a plan, so there we were, driving around the city on our way to nowhere-in-particular, two dead people waiting for a revelation. And there was Skip, driving around the city talking to the newly dead through a hidden walkie-talkie, ready to do their bidding. Skip was a perfect messenger. If he'd been a straight-and-sane suit, the whole deal would have laid down flat.

"Here's what we need you to do," I said to Skip.

"Wait," he said, sounding nearly normal. "I know this is corny, I don't even know if dead people can lie, but before I do any favors I'd like to hear Jimmy's voice. I'd be so bummed if anything had happened to him."

And here I thought Skip was nutty enough to understand this the first time around. "Skip. I just explained it to you. He's not alive. He's dead."

"So are you, but I can hear you," he said, "and I think I can smell you. You smell like electricity."

I handed our end of the walkie-talkie to Jimmy.

Jimmy lowered his voice, a deep Chinese Casper. "The woman's spirit said you'd like to speak with me. Skip, I am truly dead."

"No offense or anything, but you sound funny. Are you sure you're Jimmy?"

I could feel a string of Chinese curse words about to roll through one of my car windows and out the other. Jimmy took a deep breath and controlled himself.

"You have been chosen, Skip. You must exhibit gratitude for that extraordinary gift."

"Okay, don't get mad. Gee, I thought being dead would be a mellow experience."

"You ever see those paintings of God throwing thunderbolts?"

"Sure."

"This place doesn't make anyone mellow," Jimmy said. "I'm putting the woman back on. She has a name by the way. Annie. I'd appreciate it if you showed respect."

Jimmy was the voice of radio-free ChinaGod.

Skip apologized. I wasn't sure for what. I guess it was just for being alive.

"No time for apologies," I said. "Jimmy's an old soul with a short fuse. Most people up here try to avoid him." Jimmy stuck his real-life tongue out at me.

"Skip," I said, "here's what we need. Call the police and tell them you saw two friends at the Mystic Café just before it caught fire. Tell them you saw the boy playing with matches, and that I'd asked him to stop, he didn't, and we argued. Tell the police you're worried because we'd had several cups of tea, you had one cup with us, and it made you drowsy. Make sure you tell them our names, but don't tell them yours."

I gave Skip our full names.

He said, "I'll make up the details."

"Just stick to the facts. Not the real facts, but the facts I just made up. By the way, you were there picking up a chair, and we were there hiding out. That's all you know."

"Got it. I saw you both at the café, and I'm afraid you're dead. But . . . you are dead. What's the problem?"

I hadn't thought about that. Well, I had, but I didn't think Skip would.

"Let me confer with Jimmy. He is the older, wiser energy force."

I put the walkie-talkie in the palm of my hand, muffling honk-ing horns, sirens, the general clutter of urban cacophony.

"Here's the problem," Jimmy hollered in the direction of the hand set. "We want a decent memorial service. Unless our families are convinced that we're dead, they won't give us one. With no service, we'll have little rest."

"Also," I said, "this may seem minor to you, but you know Mina, so maybe you'll understand. The cops need to *know* there are human remains inside, otherwise, it'll be a while until Mina gets insurance money for her building."

"Uh-oh," Skip said.

"That's right. When she gets to this side, she will make our lives a living hell."

"That's really funny."

"Skip. I'm not joking."

He gulped. "Okay, I'll do it. I'll call the cops, an anonymous call, and tell them to look for your leftovers. Hey, what if they think I caused the fire?"

I sighed. "Jimmy was playing with matches, and your call is anonymous, remember? Hey, one more thing. You saw a suspicious-looking character hanging around the back smoking cigarettes. Maybe Jimmy got the matches from him."

"Is your voice coming from the center of the earth? It's like I can hear you through the floorboards of the universe," he said. "Oh, never mind, I've got enough to think about. Matches, anony-mous call, cigarette. I hope I can remember all that. Maybe you'd better contact someone else."

I boomed into my walkie-talkie. My voice was hot enough to start another fire. "Skip, your eternal soul depends upon doing this."

His voice was a mousy wisp. "I'll try."

Still a tiny voice, but Skip wasn't giving in, not entirely, until he'd cut a small bargain. "What about the dolphins?"

If I hear one more word about dolphins, I thought, *I'll start buying chunk light again instead of solid albacore.* Jimmy read my face and grabbed the handset before I flung it into oncoming traffic.

He said to Skip, "I'm researching dolphin souls and language for you. I'll keep you posted, but don't hold your breath—this may take your entire life. Or longer."

I could almost hear Skip clutch the worn corduroy shirt covering his bony chest. "Oh my God . . ." Skip gasped for breath. "Thank you."

Three times through, and Skip had the story down. Given the double threat—Mina's wrath concerning her insurance money, and the state of his eternal soul—his memory was scared into attention. Not for the first time, I wished Lawless were in town. Without a cop who's willing to bend the rules, lying to the law is dicey.

"Skip, proceed. Feel free to contact us if necessary."

"How do I do that?"

Beat the hell out of me. I'd gotten caught up in the moment, and the invitation slipped out. I looked at Jimmy.

Jimmy took over, saying to Skip, again using the voice of ChinaGod, "Go to Clarion Music in Chinatown. Play the largest Tibetan bowl. Because we are newly arrived souls, the tone will reach us."

Jimmy clicked the *on/off* switches back and forth, blowing static into the speaker. He'd ended the connection.

"Good save," I said to Jimmy.

"Those bowls are a low G, same as giant pipe organs. Entire towns hear the organ, but what they're really hearing is the note. Its wavelengths are long. Low frequencies travel miles." He said, "I can hear that low G anywhere."

"I don't know who's crazier, you or Skip."

"Annie, you've got us both beat. Hands down."

For one moment I was more alarmed than I'd been standing at the top of Coit Tower. I had the slightest glimmer that Jimmy was right about me.

Forty-five

An hour or so passed, and we'd each had a large cup of coffee. Jimmy assured me that he'd been drinking coffee since he was three years old. I didn't know if it was true, and I didn't care. As we stepped into the car, with coffee number two and a bag of glazed doughnuts, a cell phone rang. Jimmy gave me the go-ahead, meaning answer it.

"Forget it. I am not talking to anyone. My fear and exasperation levels are both through the roof."

"Look at the call number. It's from Mina."

"You take it. When you're done talking, I am tossing every cell into the nearest Dumpster—I'm sure you can get more—and I am never going farther from home than my telephone with the old-fashioned curly cord can reach."

"Boy, death has made you cranky." He shook his head. "Hello?"

"Jimmy. Let me talk to Annie."

"Okay."

"Mina, this had better be a matter of life and death."

"It is. I just talked to the cops and they gave me the bad news. Burning up is a pretty drastic way to diet."

"In the end, we don't come down to much. What did they say?"

"That my building is kaput. A man called the station, saying he'd been with you and Jimmy at the Mystic Café. They wanted to know if I'd seen you, I told them no, last I knew you'd gone to the Mystic." She said, "Annie? The dolphin guy called the cops."

"How did you find out that it was Skip?"

"He told them his name, and they told me."

"He was supposed to make an anonymous call."

"He improvised," she said, "and it's too late to change that, so we'll use his mistake for leverage."

"Leverage?"

"Sure. People are always nervous about the dead laying curses and boils on them. We can probably use his goof to scare him, or scare a cop," she said. "Why did you ask *Skip* for help?"

"It just happened. Mina, I want to ask you a question."

"You know what else? Dead people lose all sense of decency. I've seen it happen many times. There's a good reason to do what they want."

"Are you listening?"

"You wanted to ask me a question, but I wanted to finish my story. Go ahead, I'm done now."

"When Jimmy was about to launch Spaceship Mystic Café, I started to worry."

"That makes sense."

"Do you really believe dead people can pass messages to the living, assuming that they have the right messenger?"

"Is the sky blue?"

"If something happens to me, let me tell Leo that I love him, you know, through you."

"You'd want me to channel you to Leo?"

"I guess so."

"I'm not crazy about having your spirit inside my body."

"That makes two of us, but . . ."

"You feel bad because Leo doesn't know that you really love him—I mean a lot. I'm crazy about him myself, so if you can stand me, I guess I can stand you. I'll channel."

"Would I have to make an appointment or something?"

"Sure, what's another hit on your credit card?" she said. "Annie, are you nuts? This kind of work is done for free."

"Something else, too."

"For someone who didn't want to talk to me, you've got a lot to say."

"I told Leo I'd be at the hospital tomorrow night. If I'm not there, start tuning in."

Not even one insult. "You're spooked, aren't you?"

"Seriously spooked."

"I don't blame you. The body they found at the Mystic Café belonged to a wicked man. Black is swirling around you like hot fudge over ice cream."

"What body?"

"The CDC man who isn't from Atlantis."

"Alan Lee? He's dead?"

"They found him right next to my building, and his wallet with a bunch of his ID was near him, not on him. It must be the wallet you left behind," she said, "and a gas can was tossed in the bushes. Did you kill him? Not that I'd blame you, but we'd have to do some soul-unwinding to get you straightened out."

"Mina, we checked the place before we took off, the gas can was in your doorway, and there was no one around, not even one stray cat or wino."

"Alan Lee has followed you more than once without you seeing him."

"The fire couldn't have killed him if he was outside."

"How do you know? Maybe something exploded out the back door."

"They're sure he died at the same time the fire occurred, that he died from smoke or burns?"

"They didn't give me details. Just told me the man's name and said they'd found him dead outside my place. He was positively identified, so there must have been something left of him besides his wallet."

"Did they find our remains? Mine and Jimmy's?"

That stumped her. "How could they have done that?"

I told her about our trip to the Columbarium. At first she was horrified, telling me what a terrible thing I'd done—disturbing the dead—and how they'd come back to make my life a hairy ordeal. Big deal. Seemed like they already had.

"These people were already cremated," I said. "What difference do you think a second cremation makes?"

"I thought you were joking about the puny amount of ashes you'd left behind, or I never would have made that comment about losing weight. We don't know the lady you swiped, but I don't want to be on any ghost's hit list." She said, "I wish I had some of my old books, this situation is beyond me."

"Me, too."

I held the connection open between us, my stomach screwing itself into an ever-tightening knot. My lungs were suddenly three sizes too small and heavy—a wet-jeans-on-a-laundry-line pair of lungs.

"Go home," she said. "That guy who followed you, threatening everyone, is dead. Case closed, no more loose ends."

"What if Alan's not the killer?"

"We may never know the truth," she said, "although . . . Skip was the last person you saw over there. Maybe he hung around and killed Alan."

"Skip? Why would he do that?"

"Why? Because in some demented way he thought he was taking care of you, and maybe he was, and maybe he took care of Flora, too. Hao—we'll probably never know about him."

But in some deeply instinctive place, I did know that Hao had been killed, and I also knew there was not one chance Skip was responsible for anything, including himself. More silence between us, growing denser.

Mina said, "I've never depended on a man for one single thing. Now I wish Lawless was around—a cop for God's sake!—and I wish Leo were well enough to punch everyone out."

"Lawless and Leo are our friends, and we could use their help. Just don't think of them as men."

She tried that on. "Okay, that makes me feel less pathetic."

"We've got to go," I said. "If you get the urge, call Leo and tell him the reports of my death have been . . . I can't remember the quote. Just tell him I'm okay, and I intend to make my date."

"Hey, if you don't make your date, I will."

"Do you want to give him another heart attack?"

"I know, I'm too much for him," she said. "Annie, I just thought of something. You said the twins left town. It was pretty close to the time of Alan's death."

That wrinkle had not occurred to me. "Maybe the timing's a coincidence."

She sighed. "As I've said many times, nothing is a coincidence. I may have to do something drastic."

"Don't rattle any cages."

"Trust me on this."

Mina was now one of the few people I *could* trust. How had that happened? While milling that wonder through my mind, a realization ran over me like two trains chugging from opposite directions down the same track—the standard algebra word problem. When would the two trains collide? I had no idea, but I had set up a sweetheart of a situation for the man at the switch.

"Mina," I said, "think how easy it would be to kill a dead person."

"I'm not following you."

"Whoever killed Alan could kill me, snatch Jimmy, and get away with it. The cops already think we're dead. Or they will soon."

"They heard you were dead from a man who talks to fish. It wouldn't be hard for them to un-believe Skip."

"Maybe I'd better return to the land of the living."

"Don't rush into anything. Death has its advantages."

Forty-six

I wanted to go home, put Jimmy in a plump bed loaded with blankets, feed him, and turn on the TV. *I dreamed I was normal.* I hoped Jimmy had a shot at staying alive long enough to experience some variation of normal. I hoped the same thing for myself. I wanted him to experience the old-fashioned kind of normal that really isn't normal at all. A cozy home with people who take care of you, a place to be safe. A place to be alive and well.

Three people were dead, that was the last count, five if you included me and Jimmy.

Jimmy needed a treat, and I needed a friendly face, one installed in a very large person. It would only be an intermission from trouble, but I could stretch my lungs and breathe, possibly even think, eat chocolate, and wait for the sugar rush. We headed to Ghirardelli Square. I hoped it was Candy's shift, and I hoped Jimmy could lick the beaters.

We turned the corner at Bay and walked down a steep block. People laughing and chattering—big excitement. Maybe a movie star had shown up at Ghirardelli's, maybe Danielle Steele. One time I'd seen a current number-one box-office siren lounging by the fountain, packing at least ten pounds of chocolate on her hips. A photo would have been worth big bucks, but is there a great photo of a woman, forty pounds overweight, eating her blues away because her husband dumped her? Not in my book.

I could smell the chocolate, but this time it was different: dark and bruised, pungent and bitter, almost sickening.

Descending the stairs, we were catapulted into an area resembling the target of a terrorist attack. The epicenter was the chocolate factory.

KRON news was wrapping up, a cameraman rolling snaky blue wire around his arm. Tight jeans. All those guys wear tight jeans and loafers. The cops closed their notepads, talked to a last investigator. Candy stood in the eye of gooey brown carnage.

He shooed the last reporter away, and the cops straggled off. Candy shook his head, yakking, cursing nonstop at an infuriating universe. The crowds remained, but they did not press in. Candy was a pacing lion behind mighty slim bars. Two guys in jumpsuits from the Square's janitorial team were cleaning the devastation.

Jimmy scooted as close to me as he could get.

I said to Candy, "What the hell happened here?"

"You tell me."

"How would I know?"

Chocolate everywhere. Chocolate on the bench where I'd sat with now-dead Alan Lee, slinky and smooth. Chocolate on the sidewalk and on the brick path. Inside the factory, the white high-gloss walls were a newsworthy event.

"If I ever catch the SOB who did this, I'll kill him."

"Why would anyone *want* to do this?"

"That man, the one I thought was your boyfriend, but you didn't know him?"

"Yeah . . ."

"He sat on that bench, got into a fight with somebody, then he walked in here. This was maybe three hours ago. He said to tell my lady friend, meaning you, that if she didn't stay away from some kid, the kid was going to look the same as a chocolate factory that had exploded, mush and ooze everywhere . . . He told me to use my imagination. I did. It was ugly.

"Making threats about a poor kid—I told him he was sick, told him to get out. He said to make sure I passed the message along to you.

"I watched him after he left my store, thought about calling security. Now I wish I had."

Jimmy was attached to me like a thin layer of liquid bandage. "Candy," I said, "can you find something for Jimmy in this mess?"

Candy salvaged a beater, whapping off two inches of chocolate from a pot in the sink, handing it to Jimmy. He patted Jimmy on the head.

He bent down until he was eye level with Jimmy. "A kid sees all this, he might start licking the walls. God knows how much lead is in this old paint," he said. "Chocolate's good, but you don't want to go lead-pipe stupid over it."

Jimmy's eyes were huge. I told him to go ahead. He unstuck himself from me, but strayed no farther than three inches.

Candy studied Jimmy. "Is this the kid that guy was looking for?"

"Probably."

"What he want with a skinny little Chinese kid?"

"Jimmy can work miracles. The kind that could make someone very rich."

"Can he clean up this mess with a magic wand?"

"Not his field."

"That's a shame."

I said, "Just to make sure . . ."

"We're talking about the same man. Chinese, muscles, he bothered you. I don't forget people."

"How long was he going to hang around waiting for me? It doesn't make sense."

"When I first saw him, I wondered if you two were meeting here. But I think this was just a convenient place and he wasn't looking for you at all. It was only five minutes before a tall, blond man showed up. They exchanged tight smiles. The blond man smacked him on the shoulder, like *Job well-done!* There were words between them, then the words stopped. They sat another minute or two, not saying anything, even their tight smiles gone. The blond man, still no words, smacking his newspaper against his leg, got up and left."

"You hear anything they said before the silence set in?"

"No, but stand in front of a window for twenty years, and you learn people. They had so much to argue about that it got stuck in their throats. The blond guy, he acted like he was the other one's boss, but who knows? Tall men are hard to figure—they get to acting all big shot even if they're scrubbing your floor.

"When the blond man turned and walked off, the other guy looked right through his back, giving him a look that was cold devilry. Then he sighed, sat a little longer, looking through my window. That's when he came in, saying all that sick stuff to me. He was carrying a fast-food bag. I notice when people bring food in here.

"He went back outside, sat a couple more minutes—that's when I should have called security—and he stuck that bag under my bench. I thought he was too lazy to use the trash can."

"Then?"

"Then everything. He smiled at me, waved, and left. I went into the back to get more fixings, and my whole front window blew. Cops say it came from the bag, they made a joke about cheap food and gas. I didn't laugh. I've got to deal with this mess and I'm pretty shook up."

Wringing a rag in the sink, he started to wipe down the walls.

"This place was a wreck after the 1989 earthquake," he said. "I'm moving back to St. Louis. I've got a brother works at a perfectly safe candy store, and they sing while they're making fudge. They'd hire me in one minute, what with my experience."

"Candy, for what it's worth, you don't have to worry about killing that SOB."

"They catch him already?"

"He died in a fire in the Haight, would have been right after he left."

"Over at Mina's old place? I just heard two cops talking about it. Radio's saying that probably three people died, but radio's not saying this—only two were killed in the fire. If the third person was your stalker, it definitely wasn't the fire that killed him."

"How do they know?"

"Man had a bullet clean through the head. Killed execution-style, they said. No mugging, his ID and money were all there. Name of Alan Lee."

Lee murdered . . . I reshuffled my deck. "Any line on the killer?"

"Good thing I had an alibi," he muttered, turning to take another swipe at the wall. "The two cops laughed, they always do when they're nervous. Their guess is someone got mad about Mina's burning down, taking it out on some guy who happened to be in the wrong place at the wrong time. You know how crazy-high white folks in the Haight can act. Cops certainly know it."

Jimmy had almost licked the metal off the beater. I handed it back to Candy. Jimmy was very quiet, and he thanked Candy.

"You're welcome," Candy said. "He's a nice, polite boy, Annie."

Nice, polite, quiet. Kids act like that when they're scared to death. "Candy, if anyone asks, you didn't see me, and you didn't see Jimmy."

"No problem."

"Because the bullet in Lee's head had to do with us. And there is more than one suspect on my list."

"Such a nice-looking boy. Who'd do such a thing?"

"Someone who has underestimated their enemy."

Candy looked at me, standing back, his hands on his hips. "Big mistake on their part," he said. "You've got no brains when it comes to flat-out mean, bullheaded, mama bear. 'Member, I've known you since your kids was small."

"What am I going to do without you?"

"I may stick around for a little while. I'd like to see the fool who made a rather bad enemy of the Wicked Witch," he said. "Are you carrying?"

"Are you nuts? You can get arrested in San Francisco for wearing a nonunion sweater."

I trusted Candy. It was my fault that he had the grossest walls in town, and I stuck around a few minutes, helping him wipe the walls, repositioning myself for offense instead of defense, gaining momentum. And I shouldn't have been doing any of those things because while I was talking to Candy, I wasn't paying attention to Jimmy. Candy was midsentence before I realized that Jimmy had disappeared, leaving his backpack behind.

Forty-seven

Speaking into the handheld gizmo again, I said, "Skip?"

"Yo."

"Problem in this sector."

"Are there sectors in the afterlife?"

"No, but I like sci-fi. I used to."

"Me, too. A lot."

I'd counted on that. "Skip. I can't find Jimmy. I want you to look for him."

"Whoa! I like Jimmy, but I don't want to die for him. Don't they, like, have a lost and found up there?"

"Jimmy squeezed back through a portal. He's on earth. San Francisco."

"Jimmy's a troublemaker, isn't he?"

"I'm afraid he didn't want to go back to earth, and someone down there snatched him, pulling him through time and space."

"Pulled him right back here to San Francisco?"

"Yep." I paused, then said, "You haven't rearranged the molecules in your van, have you?"

"No way. But I'm going to need gas pretty soon."

"You can do that."

"Where do I look for Jimmy?"

"If someone grabbed him, I think they'd take him to his uncle Ike's, maybe they'd grab Ike, too," I said. "If Jimmy ran away, I've got a line on that one."

"Where is Ike's?"

I gave him the address. "Skip, time is critical."

"What do I do if I find him?"

"First, tell Jimmy you're operating under my instructions—he'll trust you. Next, this is your city. Come up with a meeting place, somewhere safe, uncrowded."

"The Anarchist Bookstore. I can handle anything that goes down there."

"Address?"

"It's at the end of Haight Street."

The last building left on the far end of Haight standing in the way of progress. The Mystic Café and the Anarchist Bookstore had many things in common—they looked into the future through two cuts in the same wavy prism.

"I'm surprised the city didn't want it."

"They did, but I refused to sell. I don't need the money."

"You own it?"

"Yeah," he said, "my grandmother on one side was Richmond, on the other side I'm Stanyon." I could hear his shame. "I've got money."

Two of the snootiest families in San Francisco, and when their DNA collided, *voilà*, Skip! He'd been given a unique gift. He could roll around heaven all day, counting his women and scheduling manicures, or he could create a unique life. He had gone for unique in a big way.

"Okay," I said, always amazed by life's little worms. "You go to Ike's. I'll find a portal, I think I saw a kiosk with free maps when I got here, and I'll come back down and look, too. We'll stay in touch."

"Be careful. If the cops think you're still alive, they might think you torched Mina's."

"I'll find some snazzy clothes—some sort of disguise."

"Dump the Mao threads, good idea," he said. "And Annie? This is embarrassing, but when I called the cops, it wasn't anonymously. I used my real name. It works for me. If I get into trouble, my old man pays my way out. I asked him to stop years ago, but he won't."

An off-center guy from old family money, unconcerned with the law, no accountability, and owner of the Anarchist Bookstore—purveyor of books concerning peace, love, and artillery. I had taken him into my confidence. This was one of my all-time lows, and there have been more than I care to remember. Candy had just run down the nature of crazy white folks in the Haight, and I may have walked right into the lion's den, dragging Jimmy with me.

And still, there was something about Skip that I trusted. Maybe as much as I trusted myself at that point.

"Skip, don't let anything happen to Jimmy. If I don't show, get him to Mina. I carried a lot of baggage up here with me, and it might not be so easy getting down there."

"Bet you wish you'd dumped it just like I did."

Most of my baggage involved people and experiences and relationships and birth and death, and all I could think to say was this: "No. My baggage is me, and I am my baggage."

"Cool. I'm all over Jimmy."

"Skip? The dolphins have a message—they love you very much."

"Man, I have tears in my eyes."

"And Linda's giving up real estate and moving to Mendocino, she's painting again. Track down Jimmy, then get up there," I said. "The city is bad for you."

"Right on. And don't worry, I'll get the little dude."

Mendocino. Skip would be out of our hair, living in a land where no one was as rich as he was, and everyone was just as loony.

Forty-eight

$\mathcal{T}$ ime to blend in with real life. I found an outfit at a woman's store in Ghirardelli Square. It cost a fortune, another wham on my credit card, and a trail I didn't want, but my cash was gone. I didn't think the saleswoman would remember me, just another customer dumb enough to spend a month's rent on a handwoven tunic and pants. It was gorgeous, the color was great, and if I ever had real money, I'd go back and buy a few more by the same weaver—gossamer rayon duds with thick threads that shone with silver slicks. A table was placed in the corner of the boutique, offering fine cheese and wine. One glass, two, of Chateau St. Jean to wash away my worry about the cost of the clothing. I'd still be able to drive, but it made handing over my plastic practically painless.

"I'll just wear it," I told her.

"You'll want to leave . . . those." She hated to call what I was wearing clothes. "Want me to put them in a Salvation Army bin for you?"

"It's my Chinese New Year's costume. Ugly but warm."

She smiled. We were friends again. "OHHHH." It was okay to dress like crap as long as it was theater.

I carried my bag of Mao duds out the door. I should have hurried, I had a missing kid, but I only had one or two ideas about where to look for Jimmy. The cops would be no help. Report a missing person who had no birth certificate? Forget it. Mostly, I hated to leave the area where I'd lost him, thinking that he might be hiding in a toy store, the kite store, wandering dazed . . . I stepped it up, walking through rows of shops, peeking inside, asking if anyone had seen a little boy. Everyone wagged their head, a series of sorry *nos*.

I'd done everything I could at the Square. If my next stop didn't pan out? I refused to go there. Walking up the hill, I stopped at another shop and blew $150 on a pair of shoes, comfortable ones, wide ones. The wine had benefited that merchant, too. If I owned a swanky shop, I'd keep everyone tanked on fine wine and set up a little nook that aired romantic comedies. I'd provide a muted peach toile ambiance, creating the impression that everything in the world was simply perfect. All newspapers within fifty feet of the store would be banned, and no husbands rustling the sports section allowed.

My new clothes did not match my car. I finessed her into what was left of reverse—boy, I hoped my building sold—and the gear ground in a way that made my teeth ache, including crowns I'd had since I was sixteen years old. I knew where I was going, but I'd have to skirt Chinatown. That wouldn't be easy on this night of revelry. Traffic was already building to a crescendo.

I plowed through, slow and steady, parking in a garage that was urine-soaked and packed. I squeezed into a nonspot painted with yellow diagonal lines. It was a holiday. No one was going to tow my car. No tow truck could fit through the streets.

I cut through Portsmouth Square, San Francisco's original center. Excitement buzzed and danced, kids were dressed as monkeys. Old men shouted at them to get away from their mah-jong games. Old men pretending they hadn't loved this holiday when they were kids. Old men pretending they still didn't.

One yahoo monkey-man ran out of a bush straight at me. Nobody paid attention. I ran away from him, dropping my purse. He disappeared. I ran back, scooping up my belongings: wallet, credit cards, phone, and Estée Lauder lipstick, a new tube, and my car keys. Once again he hurled himself in my direction, a missing link on the move. I hollered back at him, nothing that made sense, just noise. He fled to his cave inside the bushes. A quick check, nothing more of mine was lying on the sidewalk on top of loogies and dried wads of gum. The old men and their mah-jong, the old ladies and their gossip, and the little kids chasing each other with backscratchers went on as if monkey-man and I were invisible.

St. Theresa's was my bastion, my center of peace in a skewed world gone baffled. I'd lost a lot in the last few days. Trust. I'd gained a lot. The knowledge that betrayals can happen where you least expect them. But I'd also gained the friendship of a great kid, and I'd delivered a baby. Someday I might get used to my daughters' relatives. Anything was possible.

St. Theresa's is worn red brick and very old, as many bastions are. One woman knelt, praying. Hat on her head, veiled netting, she was not Chinese. No priest in sight, and six o'clock mass was long over. Services were given in English and Chinese, one service per week in Latin for traditionalists who didn't want to understand what they were hearing. That's the service I would attend. Peace and glory without the details.

I'd never gotten lucky in a church, but that evening I did.

Jimmy was hunkered under the organ, sound asleep, sucking the first two fingers on his right hand. His other hand was pressed upward against the mahogany soundboard. I wasn't surprised to find him there, but my relief was electric. Jimmy was so vulnerable; I didn't know what to do with him. I was tired to the inside of my bones. If I'd been smaller, I would have climbed under the organ with him. Instead, I got on my knees next to Jimmy.

I soaked it up—the Stations of the Cross, the altar, the praying woman mumbling her hopes and fears to an unseen God who made very little sense to me. If there was some Great Plan, I'd never understood it. Not because of disasters, plagues and wars, all the usual biggies. The small and daily inhumane behavior, the greed, the lack of kindness, that's what I didn't get. It takes a huge dose of faith to believe in balance and to see the invisible good. To know that somewhere a stranger is taking care of a stranger, that someone is risking their life for a cause. I supposed I was taking care of a stranger, but Jimmy didn't feel like a stranger. We were war buddies, we were family. Sometimes life's a picture puzzle with all four corners missing, chewed by the neighbor's dog. It had been a long day.

I scooched as much of me as possible under the organ, touching Jimmy lightly on his shoulder.

This time when he awoke he knew me. He smiled, sweet and gentle. "Are we okay?"

"I don't know about you, but I'm great."

"I knew you'd find me. I had to get out of Candy's place. It was terrible."

"Next time you run? Don't do it."

He smiled again. "You're silly." Then he stuck his fingers back in his mouth. With luck, he'd forget that he'd done that in front of me.

"Jimmy, we're going to your uncle Ike's house."

"To my house."

"That's right. Something big's going to happen, I don't know what, but we need to be there," I said. "I can feel it."

Jimmy went still as a mountain pool. He pulled his fingers out of his mouth. "Okay, but I can't take care of us both, Annie. Right now, I don't know if I can take care of me."

"Why don't you slack off a little and let me do the work for a change?"

His body plunged into relief. He was letting it go, willing to breathe. I swore to myself that I would never ask anyone to break into a crematorium or blow up a building again.

"You ready?" I said.

"No."

"You want to stay a little longer?"

"Not really."

"Sometimes being in the middle place feels good, doesn't it?"

"Yeah. You know the bad stuff is over, and you got through it. You know that more bad stuff is waiting, but you don't know if you'll be as lucky the next time."

"I've felt like that lots of times."

"See the lady who's praying?"

"Yes."

"She's very sick and she's going to die. There isn't anything that anyone can do about it."

"Miracles happen, Jimmy."

"That's not true. Sometimes the right thing happens, and because we don't understand it, we call it a miracle. Sometimes disasters happen. We don't understand those, either. Miracles and disasters are the same coin, flipped. Take your choice."

"Birth and death."

"Yes."

"It's time to stop stalling. Time to stop being in the middle."

Giving me his hand, he crawled out from under the ancient organ carved with beasts and gargoyles, saints and nightmares and dreams.

We walked up the aisle. I gave him the backpack he'd left in Candy's store, and he slung it over his shoulder.

Sudden and still, he tilted his head to the right.

I said, "What is it?"

"Coming from Clarion. It's the Tibetan low G. Skip. He wants to get in touch with me."

"I asked him to look for you. The walkie-talkie's in your pack."

"Good." He scuttled through his accumulated junk, top to bottom. "Here it is. You still think Skip's okay? You know, safe for us?"

"I have absolutely no reason to believe he is, but I do."

Jimmy handed me the walkie-talkie. "Hi Skip," I said.

"I guess you made it through all right."

"It was a very close call."

"I have a line on Jimmy."

"It's covered. I've found him."

"I know you don't have much time, but could I say hi to him?"

I hoped I would never be odd enough to understand Skip.

"Hi Skip," Jimmy said.

"Hey, you rascal. Were you really pulled back here, or did you come back on your own?"

"On my own. It was a real pain finding my way out of the portal, there are millions of gates. Thanks for playing that G."

"Any time. Listen, there are pictures of you and Annie all over Chinatown."

I yanked the set from Jimmy. "Why?"

"It says you're missing, possibly dead, and there's a reward offered by the FBI, an agent named Dudley DoRight, something dumb like that. If anyone sees you, they're supposed to call the cops or DoRight. There was a phone number on the poster. You want it?"

"No thanks."

"You'd better get out."

"We have one stop to make before we can get on with the business of being dead."

"Tell Jimmy not to come back until he gets born all over again. Too many people want him, including me. I'm probably a pain, but . . . Man it must be hard to be a spook on the loose."

"You have no idea," I said. "Skip?"

"What?"

"I have a present for you. It's a dream I had, but it's for you. It was about a place where fish, people, and other creatures live together, go shopping together—you get the picture. If you apply for a special license, you can marry another species. So far, you can only get the license in the space above Connecticut and California. Tell Linda to paint the place. It's beautiful."

"This is big, but I'm not surprised," he said.

"Welp, this is it. Thanks for tracking down Jimmy."

"You'll stay in touch if something big happens?"

"No problem," I said. "Skip, you're a good guy. Get yourself up to Mendocino."

"Pronto. And tell Jimmy to be cool, just until we're sure he's safe." Then he said, "I have a present for you, too."

"Yes?"

"I believed the portal deal at first. It's been great to play along. I don't know exactly what you're up to, but I know, without a doubt, that you are both as alive as I am."

"And?"

"And nothing. If you need me, click the handset and speak loud enough to tell me where you are, what's going on. Something. I'm here for you."

And I, with a most tremendous leap of faith, believed him.

Forty-nine

Chinatown was heating up. Tempers were fine-edged, lovers spiked, taunting laughter set flutes crackling, fireworks whistled, moondogs sang with sewer rats. Everything out of whack. I spotted our first *WANTED* poster in the underground parking lot. I tore it up.

I intended to grab Ike and stuff him in my car. I could play the stubborn game, too, and I was bigger than Ike. Despite any misgivings I had, and there were plenty, I was taking both Ike and Jimmy to my house. Maybe after three days of solid sleep, I'd convince the Sebastopol Zen monastery to house them. Maybe they could hide out at Leo's women's shelter. But they had to leave Dragon Qi. I wished I could kidnap Leo, but that might be equivalent to killing him, and I didn't want to do that.

The street behind Ike's house, and to the north of Ike's house, was jammed with cars. Cars parked on sidewalks, double-parked in front of fire hydrants, cars pinched up tight. One small foreign job was surrounded by men pounding the hood, a Jamaican drum chorus of fists. The car was blocking their driveway. Hoisting it into the air, they plopped it down near a stoplight. I drove into Ike's yard. Since I'd taken out part of his fence, getting back in was easy.

No need to knock on the door, it was Jimmy's house, too. We walked in the kitchen, and Ike didn't hear us. That worried me; anyone could have walked in. The sound of satellite TV from China, hundreds of excited voices, parade noises, festivities, hilarity, and singing danced through the room. Jimmy, looking around his empty kitchen, said, in a small worried voice, "The show is not a success until the audience claps."

The mundane aspects of the holiday, cleaning the house, weren't televised. Ike could have used some New Year's enthusiasm; his place was a mess. Too much of a mess.

Canned voices boomed the kitchen walls. Jimmy whispered to me, "Ike doesn't like to admit how much he hears the world through his heart. His ears are practically shot. That's why the television's too loud."

In the living room, electronic light bounced up from the floors, and the doors were festooned with red paper, some of it torn and hanging in shreds. Popcorn covered the floor. Hao must have been the spit-and-shine member of the fraternal duo. A bag of chips, a Diet Coke can tipped over. Telltale signs of a Mina visit. The back of Ike's head was pointed at the television. Sitting across from Ike, was Wagner. He wasn't moving an inch, except for his eyes, darting in every direction. Mina—what was she doing there? She started to open her mouth, but didn't. I didn't speak, either. The room was eerie, a wax museum of living figures. In the corner of the room, I saw the cause of our wax buildup. Not moving a muscle, Dudley, my Secret Agent Extraordinaire, was pointing a .357 Magnum at Ike's head.

When Dudley saw us, he moved his eyes in our direction, saying, "I wondered when the fuck you'd get here."

I put my hands over Jimmy's ears. He pushed them away.

Jimmy surveyed the scene in his living room. I expected him to be frightened. He wasn't, and that's really what I should have expected.

He said to Dudley, "This is my home. May I ask what you're doing here in such an impolite and dangerous manner?"

He not only tried to sound like an adult, but a member of ancient Chinese royalty. He didn't quite get the phrasing, but the tone and dignity were dead on.

"Don't talk to me, Pest. You've caused too much trouble."

"I'm not afraid of you," Jimmy said.

Dudley slid his gaze in the direction of the gun, then back to Jimmy. "You should be."

"No. You want something from me. If I'm dead, you're not going to get what you want. I love every person in this room. If you harm any of them, you come up empty. I would die before I'd help anyone who hurt my family."

I imagined Hao saying the same thing. It hadn't worked out well for him.

Jimmy pulled his backpack off his shoulder. He rubbed it nervously against his legs a few times, then he laid it gently on the floor.

"Well, here we are," I said, "and there you are, Dudley, macho weapon in hand. What do we do?"

Dudley straightened his shoulders, trying to shake the sick, twisted effect he wore closer to his skin than underwear. He said, "Exactly what I tell you to do."

"Nice try, Dudley," I said. "You can correct your posture from here until doomsday, and we'd still be listening to the gun, not you. Respect doesn't come easy to a longtime paper-pusher."

Dudley turned red. He wanted to slug me, but he couldn't do that and hold his .357 at the same time.

I said, "Back out gracefully. Jimmy says he won't perform for you like a trained seal. I believe him. And if you hurt any of us, what little chance you may have with him in the future, is completely gone."

"He's a kid," Dudley said. "I can buy him things, then he'll do what I say."

Jimmy said, "What kind of things?"

"An electric guitar, a boom box, video games. An expensive skateboard with an extra set of wheels and new Etnies sneakers. You'd like that, wouldn't you?"

"Actually, I would like that."

"Look at the way they dress you—old sweat suits. It must be hard to get girls dressed like that."

"Girls think I'm a shrimp and a dweeb."

"See? You need cool T-shirts and jeans. Your uncles may not have been interested in a love life, but you may feel differently."

Their words, a Ping-Pong of nonsense, were background snow. The real event was happening in a place without words. I didn't understand it, but I felt something low. I smelled ozone and ammonia the same way a dog smells chemical changes before an earthquake. The words continued, Jimmy and Dudley negotiating. I looked at Mina and Ike, and I knew they felt it, too. My instinct told me to tuck my head between my tail, and search for cover. Something was about to come down, and I hoped it wasn't us.

Sulfur and fireworks blasting over seven square blocks, rocking the pavement and old warehouses beneath the street. I'd never experienced this part of the holiday. Time to end this before Jimmy believed he'd soon hold stock in Sony and TiVo—the world according to Dudley.

I said, "Why did you kill Alan?"

Calling his bluff, throwing Dudley off-balance, seemed important.

"Because," Dudley said, not batting an eye, no denial, comfortable with the truth, "when we started out, we were in this together. One thing went wrong, then another, and Alan thought he'd be better off on his own. I told him to be patient, but he wouldn't."

"I've often wanted to bump someone off because they didn't like my rate of speed," I said. "I believe they call it road rage."

"And you . . . What a pain. You weren't supposed to be in this equation at all."

"I was never good at math." I stood up, hoping a benign wind would blow me out the door.

"Sit down."

"No, thanks. I'm fine just where I am."

Jimmy said, "I'll sit down. She's not good at following directions."

Only three steps to the couch, but Jimmy tripped over his backpack, making weird clicking noises with his tongue when he fell. His eyes fluttered, and he looked up at me and grinned. He closed his eyes. Low undertones were still present, but barely discernible. Not much different than street traffic, neighbors squabbling, cats fighting.

"What's that, what's wrong with the kid?"

"Seizures," I said to Dudley. "Stress causes him to seize."

Helping Jimmy up, I stuck my hand in the side pocket of his backpack and double-clicked the walkie-talkie. We were open to Skip. Soft whining sailed from the handset around the room. Jimmy whined even louder to cover the sound. He fell over again, more groaning.

"What's *wrong* with that kid? If you've killed him . . ."

Jimmy spoke toward the walkie-talkie, "I just need to get a drink of water from my uncle Ike's kitchen." He looked pathetic, as if he weren't sure he could make it all the way, but now Skip knew where we were and that Jimmy needed an exit.

"Get a drink. And you," Dudley said to me, "sit down next to the crazy old woman and don't move." *Crazy old woman?* That comment, made to Mina, proved beyond a shadow of a doubt that Dudley was playing with a short deck.

Jimmy inched his way toward the kitchen on his hands and knees. He was crawling for time. I peeked around the kitchen curtain and saw Jimmy up on his feet.

I heard the water running, and I noticed the unmistakable sound of a German auto engine rolling—*merrily, merrily, merrily, merrily, life is but a dream* . . . VWs have sung that song for more than forty years.

"What's that noise?" Dudley asked. Every frayed nerve was smoking.

"Jimmy's comforting himself."

Dudley did that quick, turn-on-his-heels move that they must learn during week one at the academy. He ran to the kitchen, while trying to keep us in his sights. It was all too much, and Dudley was showing the strain. He was a border collie with sheep running in every direction.

"Jimmy," he called into the kitchen, "where are you?"

"Check the floor," Mina said. "Maybe he passed out and rolled under the table."

If I was right, Skip's van was scooting around the cars on an obstacle-course alley. The merry putt-putting grew dim, the kitchen door opened out to the yard, then it slammed shut. The sounds of Dudley swearing.

He said, "Some damned nut took off with the kid!"

"Did you get a look at him?"

"No, but the kid is definitely gone."

"Maybe he just walked away. And after you promised to buy him all that preteen paraphernalia. Ingrate. Maybe you'd better call the police."

"I don't think Jimmy'd get very far on his own steam," Mina said to me, "and it sounded like Stevan's old van out there. Did I tell you I just sold that thing?"

I shot her a look that would melt holes in steel.

"Don't look at me like that! I'll toss it right back at you magnified a million times. There will only be a small pile of ashes sitting in that chair, wearing your name. Even smaller than the ashes you swiped."

"Mina, Jimmy could have wandered off and gotten lost in the crowd."

"Nope. The stupid agent is right—someone took off with him. Probably King Nut."

304 . *Meredith Blevins*

Then she went blank, realizing she was blabbing in front of a man who'd killed several people, and that he'd just lost the reason for his crimes. Jimmy. Dudley was not a happy person.

"What nut?" Dudley asked Mina. "Who took Jimmy?"

"How do I know, every person I've met in the last few weeks is a nut, including you."

I wished she would just be quiet. No internal editor. The woman had absolutely none.

"Van? Probably the guy who still thinks it's 1968."

"Him?" I asked as if I were pondering the mystery of life itself. "What in the world would he want with Jimmy?"

"Dolphins," Dudley said.

"You need a scorecard to keep track of all the crazies who want Jimmy," Mina said. "Poor kid. Dudley, do you think we could get some food around here? Annie told me you were good about getting food."

Dudley was disassembling inch by inch. If I read him correctly, nothing would get him to complete his self-destruct faster than being in the presence of two average women chatting with each other.

"Mina," I said, "Skip's not one of the crazies."

"Since when? Hey! If you fall for Skip, I get Leo."

"I'll let you know," I said. "Skip's very bright. He believes Dolphin is our original language, and that Jimmy can translate it, thus teaching us our mother tongue."

She put her hand to her cheek. "This is huge, and," she said, leaning forward, "it makes complete sense. Do you know that among mammals, a dolphin is the only female animal, other than most of us human females, who have orgasms?" She leaned back. "Think of it."

"The more you know," I said, "the more Skip makes sense. Let me ask you something."

"Shoot."

"You were supposed to be at my house. How did you end up back in the city—I even talked to you on the phone."

"On my cell phone. You've got to get into the twenty-first century," she said. "Like I told you, Mr. Natural was hot after E. B., so I got a ride back here with him. That relieved her, and it got me back to Ike. As far as I'm concerned, Mr. Natural's bugs are gone forever."

"I'm glad you're here. Do you believe I just said that?"

"I was going to ignore it."

"SHUT UP." The sound of Dudley erupting. "No wonder neither of you is married. You would drive a husband to suicide. Or homicide." He said that to scare us, but it didn't work.

"Just between us," Mina said to Dudley, "we've had a number of husbands and boyfriends. They can't keep up with us, and they decide to check out. Annie's got one guy who's in the hospital right now, he's about to . . ."

"SHUT UP! I MEAN IT!" The sounds of Dudley derailing.

Shrugging, Mina did as she was told. She didn't consider Dudley's .357 any more menacing than a pink-plastic cap gun. I didn't either. Another display of faulty judgment.

Ike and Wagner. I'd kind of forgotten about them. Ike still hadn't moved, and Wagner was still a junkyard dog on a short chain. I've never seen anyone's eyes blat back and forth so quickly, taking in every inch of every detail. Wagner's dignity was not shattered, but it had seen better times. He'd set himself up as Ike's protector, and he had failed.

It suddenly occurred to me to wonder why I was in that room with Dudley. I might die there, the thought of dying with Dudley was horrifying, but I didn't want my lifeline to stop without understanding why.

"So, the plan to turn Jimmy into your private agent was sidelined by a man who got greedy and cut you out."

"Skip's not going far," Dudley said. "Jimmy will walk in the back door any minute—the van probably has about three blocks left in it."

Dudley's walk through the straight side of life had left him with holes in his knowledge bank. VW vans never die, they just need their oil changed every three thousand miles and a rebuilt engine every hundred thousand. Occasionally their fenders fall off. That's about it.

But, the longer I kept him talking, the farther Jimmy and Skip would get in the limping van. I sat on Jimmy's walkie-talkie, swiped from his backpack before he headed to the outside world, just in case Dudley became less self-absorbed and decided to check me out.

Dudley said, "I could kill all of you."

"Dudley, you don't have to go all Neanderthal over your big gun."

"Maybe I'll kill you one by one."

Trapped in a cheesy Chinese Arnold Schwarzenegger movie rip-off.

"Kill one of us," I said, "and the rest of us will jump you before you've savored the moment."

Wagner could snap Dudley's neck in a matter of seconds. I didn't want him to, but I knew he would without hesitation.

"Dudley," Mina said, "you'll probably kill Annie first. I've wanted to kill her lots of times, I certainly wouldn't blame you. You may as well do what she asks—tell her what plans you and Alan had for Jimmy. Then you can kill her, and she'll shut up."

Dudley squirmed. He was sure Jimmy would be home soon. The plans would have to change since Alan was out of the picture, but Dudley wanted to share his excitement. We were a captive audience, and his need for praise won out. It always does with these clowns.

"Alan used to be with CDC," he said. "We grew up in this neighborhood, me just a few blocks outside of Chinatown. We went to St. Theresa's High School together. You know how Asians are, good with math, good students. Alan became a research scientist, and we stayed in touch."

I reconfigured Dudley's lunacy quotient, and I'd come up with a new number. He had killed someone he'd known since he was a kid. Dudley was the kind of man who visits his grandma every weekend at the nursing home, but whose freezer is filled with the neighborhood's missing pets.

"Alan and I had a plan," he said. "I wasn't making any money, not enough for the years I've given the FBI, and Alan was smart, too smart for a low six-figure income. So we went rogue. No big deal, it happens all the time.

"I had my ear to the ground in the city, looking for an opportunity. Alan kept his eyes open in the research department. We got lucky. I walked into this shop and I heard Jimmy."

"What did you have planned for Jimmy?"

"As I said, Alan was a real brain. He created an electronic chip. We decided to use Jimmy to make the sound of health, one that would balance any known disease. We'd record the healthy sound on the chip. Cancer, heart arrhythmia, Parkinson's . . . Alan was right on it, and closing in on AIDS."

Wagner's ears went perky, and his head flew up. I hoped he wouldn't say anything. We needed to get out of that room alive, and we needed to keep Dudley calm. I caught Wagner's eye and held it. I hoped he received my message.

Dudley shrugged. "Easy plan. Implant the appropriate chip into a patient and cure their illness. Not much different than a pacemaker."

"Ike," I said, "is this possible?"

Ike brought me into focus, saying, "I have no opinion." Then he was gone again.

Dudley brushed Ike's words aside. "Of course you do. I have a paper here written three decades ago. It was written by you, Ike. It reads, *'For every disease there is a corresponding sound that pulls the cells, on a molecular level, back into shape. Every disease has its own shape and pattern.'*

"Alan decided that for a terminally ill patient, the chip should be inserted directly into the right hemisphere of the brain, front lobe, the part that processes music. Not sound, but music. Specifically."

"The big picture was?"

"Jimmy would orchestrate the correct sounds, we'd sell the technology to a pharmaceutical company and make billions of dollars from the patent," he said. "We already have three companies bidding on the chip process."

"But with Alan dead . . ."

"The research is finished. Now it's just a matter of recording the proper sounds and manufacturing the chips. Any electronic company can do that by following his plans and reading the music Jimmy will provide."

"You want to know something really sad?"

"Your future?"

"Funny, Dudley," I said. "If Jimmy could have stayed home, he would have done this, gladly, for free, for the joy of healing people."

"Nobody's that good."

"Yeah, they are. It's not unusual," I said, "but Jimmy will never trust you now."

Dudley sat, still holding his gun, but it was flaccid in his hands. "It never occurred to us."

"To talk to his uncles?"

"They would have wanted part of the money."

"Plenty to go around."

"You can never have enough money." But Dudley didn't sound sure, and when the crazies start doubting themselves, the unraveling begins. I wanted Dudley together, tightly wrapped in his psycho-world of spies and rogue agents and billion-dollar schemes.

"I lost the kid, didn't I?" he said. "Alan, too."

Dudley was a Macy's Day balloon gone flat, losing height, about to suffocate the humans massed below.

Faint, but I picked up a sound again, whirring, this time high-pitched, a refrigerator on the blink. Wagner settled, and he no longer looked like a Doberman, wondering who to bite first. His eyes were on Ike. His gaze so intense, so deep and intimate, that it was as uncomfortable as getting stuck between two lovers' eye lock. Wagner had found a life raft and he wasn't letting go. It was a lot to put on small, nervous Ike.

Mina scooted closer to me, walking her index and second fingers across the couch cushion to my leg. She rested her hand on my knee.

"Hey," Dudley barked in Mina's direction. "No moving."

"I'm an old lady and I'm nervous. Do you mind?" Then she said, turning to me, "Nice outfit. Where did you find . . ."

At the word *find*, Ike rose straight out of his chair. The front window, all six feet by six feet of it, crashed to the floor, sharp shards flying in every direction. Wagner was on top of Dudley before the final icicle chunks landed. Ike, ten sopranos and a bass rolled into one, had rumbled the glass, delicately and slowly. He'd created an earthquake of high pitches, almost beyond hearing, but not beyond feeling. Wagner had reacted to it, he had no clue what he'd been reacting to, but it had made him as shaky as the shattered pane.

Wagner rammed Dudley to the floor, and I moved my foot out of the way as Wagner pinned both of Dudley's arms behind his back. Ike found rope and handed it to Wagner. There was one hell of a struggle—Wagner trying to truss Dudley, Dudley's long legs escaping and his arms flailing.

In keeping with tradition, Ike clapped his hands for a successful New Year's entertainment.

Unless there was an accident involving Dudley's welfare, we had a problem—the trussing was not permanent. As long as Dudley was around, Jimmy would have a large blond shadow protected by the US government. I didn't want Jimmy to be tempted to tone Dudley to dust because he grew tired of the me-and-my-shadow routine. When this was over I'd teach Jimmy that song—we'd turn it into a joke. I'd have to figure out how Jimmy fit into my future. I didn't want to lose him.

While Wagner was roping Dudley, his .357 skittered across the floor. Ike picked up the gun. He was surprised he'd picked it up. Maybe he'd also been running down Dudley's permanent presence.

As if he were reading dialogue from an old movie, Ike said, "Don't make me use this."

Sweating, Wagner said, "Ike, hand that gun to me. Real easy, because it'll blow a hole through the middle of someone if you keep waving it around. Just hand it . . ."

Midsentence Dudley rose and hit Wagner in the jaw. Wagner rolled, collapsing in a corner, and Dudley yanked the gun away from Ike. Ike wore surprise again. We all did. Wagner bested by Dudley? It seemed impossible.

Dudley wanted to laugh—he had reclaimed his gun! But he couldn't. He was sore, his future options were wearing thin, and he was scared. He wouldn't get off so easily with Wagner next time, and with Wagner there'd definitely be a next time. He decided to split before Wagner found his pride and started raging.

Dudley's face was clammy wet, and he wore his desperation like a badge. He said, "I'm following that van, and none of you will see Jimmy again!"

Dudley ran out the door to his government-issue Buick. He was on a mad fool's mission. In traffic packed tighter than noisemakers in red paper, he wouldn't get far.

Mina was fanning herself, and her color wasn't good. I didn't want two people in the hospital. Even if I had to carry Mina, we were gone. Life would lose its spice without my nemesis.

I hefted Mina onto her feet, pulling her by one arm.

"I can't go anywhere," Mina said.

"Do *not* argue with me."

Gads, she was a load when she was deadweight. She'd probably become a much bigger pile of ashes than the Electrolux housewife.

"Wagner," I said, "you okay?"

"Yeah. That stunt of Ike's with the window was good. Now he's got to work on busting up things, or people, that really matter."

We both knew he meant Dudley, and we both didn't say it.

Ike said, "I considered causing the implosion of Dudley, but I didn't think it would be healthy for me. Probably a mistake, but at least the window created a diversion," he said. "Mina, please go. You and I play at love, it's good fun, but now is not an appropriate time."

He kissed her on her pale cheek. "Let Annie find Jimmy for me, and let her keep you safe."

I grabbed Jimmy's backpack, and Mina pulled herself together. We ran outside, both of us jumping into my car. No arguments from Mina. Small miracles are everywhere you look.

"If this heap gets us from point A to point B," she said, "I will be amazed."

"Stop griping and buckle up."

She screwed around with the seat belt, and couldn't make it click. She discovered the writing on the fabric. "Look at this! It's from an old Ford Fairlane."

"I had the belts installed. They didn't put seat belts in cars when this was built."

"I can't believe my grandchildren grew up driving around in this car."

"They all survived."

"I wasn't thinking about their safety. I was thinking about their dignity."

"With me for a mother, that was never going to happen."

"That's true," she said.

"And if you'd been running in and out of our door, it would have been the final knife in the corpse of dignity."

"Actually, dignity is a nuisance," she said. "Where are we trying to go?"

"We're chasing Dudley."

"We have no idea where he went."

"Mina, if we can push through this automobile mudflow, it won't matter where we go. We'll find him."

She made that face, the one that looked as if she'd just eaten a large spoon of expired cottage cheese, and it was too late to spit it out. Then her expression cleared.

"He's waiting until we leave," I said, "because he's hoping we'll lead him to Jimmy."

"Of course," she said, "he has no idea where Jimmy is. Do we?"

"Absolutely." I pulled out the walkie-talkie. "Hello, Skip. All well with you and Jimmy?"

"Boy, this kid is something. If I were still acting like a nut, I'd think that death had enhanced his personality. This," said Skip, "is about the best thing that has ever happened to me."

"Skip, thanks," I said. "Have you taken your medications today?"

That question came out of nowhere, and it sure wasn't meant to make him mad. It didn't.

He said, "Yeah. Some people say they can't tell the difference, but I can."

Probably why I'd asked him that question . . . "Where are you? I'd like to get us out of the city."

"Well, this is kind of a bummer. My van broke down."

He had to be kidding.

"I hadn't changed the oil in a while," he said, "and I guess it overheated a couple of times."

My voice was that of a mother who'd just caught her kid jumping off a three-story building wearing rollerblades. "SKIP! It overheated in San Francisco?"

"I preferred your attitude when you were pretending to be dead."

"I'm doing the best I can. Where are you?"

"Not far away."

"There's a guy who knows your van. Dudley. He wants Jimmy, so I have to get him. Quick."

"Chinatown is a zoo, we're about a block from McDonald's. I don't think anyone named Dudley will find us."

"Bad news. Dudley is FBI, and he has snapped."

"Ohmigosh."

"Get to McDonald's and do not leave. The man is tall and blond—Jimmy knows him. If Dudley finds you, don't leave, stay in the crowd. Tell Jimmy to make Dolphin sounds," I said. "It disturbs Dudley."

"You recognized the noises?"

"Right, Skip. I'm learning the language at the JC up here in Deadville. They've reserved a place in class for you."

"If I wasn't taking my meds, I'd think I was part of history that hadn't happened yet."

I had been to fast-food heaven more times in the past week than I had in my entire life, and it was becoming pivotal to my health and well-being. Who could imagine *that?*

Fifty

He who sacrifices his conscience to ambition burns a picture to obtain the frame.

—Confucius

It is later than you think.

—Confucius

First I'd heard the phrase, *Don't make me use this,* spoken by Ike, an old Chinese man. Then I heard, *Keep the engine running,* coming out of my own mouth. I had died, and come back to life inside an old gangster movie.

We'd parked as close to McDonald's as I could get. Looking at my car as if she'd never seen it, Mina said, "Do I have to drive it?"

"Maybe. When you get behind the wheel, stay there." I wanted the option of a fast departure.

Mina tried stuffing herself into the driver's seat. No luck. It took one hard whack, and a shove from both of us, to get the seat back. It had rusted to the runners. She heaved into the driver's seat, steering wheel not far in front of her.

She said, "I never think of myself as being bigger than you are."

"You're not. This thing always gets stuck." A crumb of kindness here, a crumb there.

I'd left her in my car, engine running, sitting in the middle of Chinatown, looking more than doubtful. I tore up the street wearing my soft shoes. I don't know how people in wheelchairs handle San Francisco. The entire city should be fined for being inaccessible to those who are physically challenged.

Throngs of rattling people banged pots, beat drums, lounged on sidewalks, drank beer, and spilled off the curbs. Other folks were hanging out their upstairs windows, waving to friends. Cheering grew to a tsunami when the dragon came into view.

Dragon always leads, and in his wake follows prosperity and good luck. An extraordinary animal, part lion, part snake, red-and-gold fabric and paper, he was beneficent and intimidating. He moved from side to side, shaking his giant hula-skirt head, swaying in the foggy night. Ten sets of legs carried Dragon through the streets, coins dropping on the pavement from his belly. He was a majesty and a magnificence. Kids rushed to grab the coins. Everyone walks in the wake of health and good fortune.

I squeezed close to the dragon, finally climbing inside him. It was the only way to cross Grant Street. Also, there was the obvious—Dudley was awfully big and awfully Anglo to climb inside the dragon with me. My entrance caused angry chat, skittering along the cardboard spine. I wasn't welcome, but I was small. I was given coins, and told to toss money on the street. I was a natural. I'd been tossing away money for as long as I could remember.

Dudley wasn't going to have an easier time maneuvering through this mess with his Buick than I had, and at least my Cooper was pointed . . . Mina. What had I been thinking? I pictured her fuming, trapped in my car, smelling hot-scented food cooking in outside stalls. Fuming, because she'd missed the dragon. Angry because she had a lot of clients in Chinatown, and she'd rather be caught dead than be seen in my car. It was no one's idea of a successful person's wheels. Worse than that, alone, she was an easy target for Dudley. I experienced one-half second of worry—*What if I've lost her?*—but that wasn't possible. I'd been trying to lose her for years.

McDonald's squatted like a guilty lover caught under a neighbor's bed, and the place was hopping. Jimmy saw me before I saw him. Standing on a plastic chair, he waved his arms back and forth.

"ANNIEANNIEANNIE . . . Hey, Annie!" he yelled above the crowd.

So much for Jimmy's cover. I waved to him, and I waited. No Dudley leapt out and grabbed Jimmy, and there wasn't a Dudley worming his way through the crowd. That night there were as many blond and redheaded humans in Chinatown as there were Chinese, maybe more. As with many other things, the fire department applies different regulations to Chinatown than the rest of the city.

I spotted Mina. Wearing her signature loud clothes, she'd elbowed her way to the front of the line, and was ordering up a couple of Big Macs and a Diet Coke. I'd had a head start, and she'd beaten me. I should have known. I hoped she had cut the Cooper's engine.

A scrawny white guy had his arms around Jimmy, still standing on the chair. I squinted. Skip. I worked my way toward him.

Skip lifted Jimmy off the chair and gave me a hug. "Thanks for letting me in on this."

"We'd have been lost without you."

A man who owned the Anarchist Bookstore and spoke with ocean life had saved our bacon. That was our current reality.

"Sometimes," he said, "I act whacked out, I know that, but I really do care about Jimmy."

"You have a good heart. It's impossible to miss."

He was sheepish. "I was off my meds when I first met you and Mina. I can tell the difference when they've kicked back in, you know, really kicked back in. I'm okay now."

Jimmy jumped on Skip's back, and Skip boosted Jimmy to his shoulders, flung him upside down, turning him in a tight space, and hoisted him back to his shoulders. Jimmy giggled.

"Thanks again, you know, for going along with me." Skip said, "If you ever need anything, let me know."

Jimmy said, "Skip saved me at Ike's house, so I made him a promise."

"What was the promise?"

"I don't know if Dudley will find us."

"I understand," I said. "What was your promise to Skip?"

"I told him I'd go to the ocean and ask the dolphins to be patient, tell them that we're working on it."

"Working on what?"

"On cleaning up their home. We appreciate everything that they've tried to do for us, and we'd like to get together again."

"Jimmy," I said, "the ocean may have to wait."

"Ocean is everywhere. Unless we have a plan, why *not* go to the ocean?"

Why not, indeed? We could take the back highway to my house, cruise past the ocean, and let Jimmy say . . . whatever. Let him repay a debt.

"Okay, but you've got to talk to the ocean fast. And where we stop is my call."

Jimmy and Skip shook hands, and I gave Skip my home phone number. The real number. I hoped I wouldn't regret it. What the hell, it wouldn't be the first dumb thing I'd ever done.

Mina joined us, the remaining bits of her burger wrapped in yellow paper. She tossed her leftovers into a plastic trash can. Her mouth full, she told me that she'd walked, a shortcut, and locked up my car. She handed me the keys.

"Okay! Let's go," Jimmy said. He lifted his backpack, and I helped him into the shoulder straps. His pack was getting heavy.

Dudley chose that precise moment to barge through the golden arches and go deranged right in the middle of McDonald's, repository of all that is right and wrong with America.

"Everybody," he shouted, motioning with his gun, "get into that corner." No one could see the corners.

Jimmy and I, Skip and Mina, bent low, easing our way toward the front door. The customers were a swarm. No one noticed us, and no one yelled when one of us stepped on a foot. A few people laughed when Dudley pulled out his gun. It was a little extreme, but everyone clowns around on New Year's.

We snaked closer to the door, making ourselves short, trying not to joggle someone's extralarge root beer down their shirt. Once I poked my head up, ducking again, quick. Dudley was scanning the room, looking for us. For the second time, Dudley barked orders. It was a fool's mission. A few customers tittered in his direction, then they turned, ignoring him.

Intolerable. He shot his .357 into the ceiling. Bad move. Dudley didn't know what was up there. A bunch of Chinese people, not white people, were enjoying a classy holiday dinner with friends and family, and this was their neighborhood. Screams and curse words sailed through the ceiling, pouring down through the bullet hole into McDonald's. A stampede of footsteps, running down the stairs, charged out their front door and into ours. We froze, awaiting the onslaught. Three white guys backed Dudley against the counter. They weren't going to pay for his stupidity. The diners upstairs could eat him alive for all they cared. The gun was useless, but Dudley managed to hold on to it. The crowd wasn't interested in Dudley's gun, just his hide.

We fled to my car, but we were stopped halfway by Dragon. Roaring, he looked into our eyes. Sounded scary, but I'd seen the inner workings—smoke and mirrors and a good-sized megaphone. I was born in the year of the dragon, but enough is enough.

The three of us held hands, and we crawled inside Dragon. It flows like a river, you go with it. I slithered toward the front, Jimmy and Mina behind me. I whooped and jumped. A few minutes passed, I heard Mina whoop. A frisky guy full of Tsingtao beer copped a feel as we passed him. We were nearing the dragon's head, and free of him. The smell of papier-mâché, glue, and sparkles, the guts of this dragon, was powerful. Outside the dragon's skin, Jimmy flicked his Bic, tossing a small firecracker near the dragon's tail.

"People are going to notice us," I said. "Cut it out."

"Notice fireworks? I don't think so. The dragon was rude to you and Mina. I was teaching him a lesson."

He pulled out another one and hurled it.

"Jimmy. Really."

"Traditional. Fireworks scare away the monster Nian."

"This year," I said, "our monster has a different name."

"A monster is still a monster."

"Fine, keep tossing, but save a few. We might need them."

We crossed the Grant Street tide. A cluster of fireworks arced skyward, frightening the veins down my left arm and the arteries inside both legs. Maybe this was my big break. I'd have a heart attack, and they'd haul me to the hospital where Leo slept peacefully, peeing into a plastic bottle. I'd be out of this whole mess.

Rounding the corner, there was my car. And Skip. What was he doing there?

The stray dog syndrome. I wondered if we were ever going to shake him. I am only good for so many good-byes.

"Don't forget, Jimmy," Skip said to him.

"I know. The ocean."

"I called my parents. They're going to pick me up. Not here, it's too crowded. A place I like up on the coast."

"I can't give you a ride there. If I can cram Mina into my car, it'll be a wonder."

"What did you say?"

"Nothing, Mina."

"My folks will probably never believe me, but I did take my meds, and you guys are not the voices in my head," he said. "You're strange enough to be, but you're not."

Skip looked serious. "Can I give you some advice?"

"Sure."

"If you need to pull the dead routine again, you've got to seem less worried about getting killed. It's a pretty obvious tip-off."

I promised to swear off being dead. In return, he said he wouldn't have any more conversations with dead people.

Skip looked happy, more substantial. I wondered how many friends he had, how many he'd lost along the way. Assuming we made it home in one piece, we wouldn't lose track of him.

"Mina, get into the backseat," I said to her.

"There was barely room in the front seat!"

"Now you'll be able to stretch out."

"Maybe a poodle could stretch out, not me."

"Sorry. I need Jimmy in the front seat."

She grumbled and she groused, she did her best to squeeze in, and she didn't ask questions.

"And," I said, "if anyone gets carsick on the curves, roll a window down. I'm not pulling over."

Skip stuck his head in my car window. "I'm going to tell my folks how kind you've been, and that was before you knew who they were. That doesn't happen to us very often."

"I'm sure your friends like you for yourself—same with your folks."

"Most people want something from them," he said. "My dad is Wrightwood Stanyon, my mom, Millicent, is his wife." Jeez, not only a Stanyon, but Skip's dad was head of the entire clan.

"Tell them they did something very right—they have a good son."

Skip whapped our hood just like a regular guy sending off his buddies. I would have asked him to check on Leo, but our date wasn't until tomorrow night, and I was pretty sure I'd make it. If not, I didn't want Skip to be the one who delivered the bad news.

I pulled out carefully, trying not to drive more than the few inches I'd need to flip a U-turn and vamoose it out of San Francisco. The night was foggy, and the fog was getting worse. Dudley was out there somewhere; but with this cover, maybe I'd lose him before I left the city limits. With any luck, the hordes of celebrators had demolished him. I should have hollered into the crowd, telling them he was an employee of the US government. That would have put an end to our troubles. We always think of the perfect thing to say when it's too late.

I made it over to 19th Avenue, no traffic there, people were stacked on the magic end of town. I caught every green light and zipped north to the Golden Gate Bridge. I imagined that, standing on a low hill, across the bridge and above the city, Chinatown looked like a pulsing Christmas tree with fuzzy crayon-colored lights. The fog and the mist sat still, one strong and angry wind blew, leaving a quick patch of clear sky. The mist wheezed back, swallowing us, leaving only blurred orange lights on the towers and cables.

The metal railing was clear, that was about all, until a set of headlights, looking very Buick-like, appeared in my rearview mirror. I was either about to get another ticket—unlikely because I was under speed, and I was pretty sure my registration was current—or Dudley was manifesting his eternal devotion.

I drove, waiting for him to pull some dumb stunt. But the smeared headlights passed me. The car held laughing kids, rocking back and forth, listening, top volume, to the sort of crap that clogs up your head for hours.

"Could you hear that car shake?" Jimmy said.

"I *felt* it shake."

"When babies are inside their mother's bodies, and they hear that kind of music, they kick, and flail, and have a most miserable time. They are trapped by their parents' poor judgment."

"Jimmy, where did you learn English?" Mina asked.

"From my uncles."

"That's what I figured."

"But I learned regular talk from watching commercials. I don't know why companies think women are stupid, but they use very poor grammar when making household-product commercials."

"Why do they always aim the cleaning commercials at women," I said. "Men clean. I read it about it all the time in women's magazines."

Groan from the backseat.

I said, "Are you going to get sick?"

"No. I never met a man who cleaned house," Mina said. "Have you?"

"Not regularly. Wait. There was one . . ."

"*The Eye* is more real than women's magazines. And all those dumb articles."

"Is this a compliment aimed in the direction of my work?"

"It's the truth. In every woman's magazine there's an article about losing twenty pounds in time for Christmas so you can look sexy. It's next to an article about baking Christmas cookies. Summer it's barbecues, next to diets, next to swimsuits. They don't think we're stupid, Jimmy," she said. "They think we're schizo-you-know, and that all we think about is food and sex."

"What else do you think about?" I asked.

Silence from the rear. "Forget I brought it up."

Jimmy said, "You're a lady, Mina. You're not supposed to say the word *sex* in front of me. Annie, did you know there was a car following us?"

"Yeah," I said, "the kids. They passed us and took off."

"No, this car has the same headlights, but it's not filled with bad music."

I checked my rearview mirror, but I couldn't see much. A car eased up beside me. Dudley smiled, waving his gun at me, a friendly greeting, his face lined with jangles, nerves, and a Halloween soul. He'd driven onto the wrong side of the road. I wished for an approaching big rig. No luck. Dudley slowed, and fell behind me.

"Damn that man," I said.

"Jimmy," Mina told him, "as long as the nut has found us, and I'm curled up back here like a stupid dog, I've decided to go with the poodle mentality. Meaning, I'm glad you're in the front, and if it looks like we're going to die, don't warn me."

"Okay. Annie, Dudley was driving right next to us. Why didn't he shoot?"

"If he hits me, I go off the road and you're dead or disabled."

"I become something he can't use."

"Right."

"What do we do?" he said.

"I'll slow down until he's on my bumper, and you're going to give us a minute of cover by lobbing a firework at him. We're getting off this road and onto a smaller one."

"This is a pretty small road."

"It's a superhighway compared to the other one. You ready?"

"All set."

The Mina poodle groaned again. As she requested, we ignored her.

I drifted into the wrong lane, to the left of Dudley. Jimmy, now directly in front of Dudley, opened his passenger window. We were close enough to see his white knuckles wrapped around the steering wheel. Jimmy tossed a firecracker out the window. It vomited a cloud of crackling white light on Dudley's hood. His Buick staggered to the left, then swerved to the right. I turned off the highway onto a county road that would meet up with Highway 1. We'd drive north from there, up the coast. I awaited the ocean, one of the great spiritual homes and safety zones. Somewhere on that coast, when and if I lost Dudley, Jimmy would do his bit for Skip.

After Jimmy spoke to the sea, we'd head home and batten down the hatches, not to mention the windows and the doors. Home, the dirt that nurtures me, the trees that breathe my name, my nest of people. My weapons. My two giraffes. If I had a few more, I'd stampede them into Dudley, but I didn't think a two-giraffe stampede would do much. Buffalo? I could get a license for them. Talk about a stampede . . .

Fifty-one

I wound around dairy farms, lush places populated by fourth-generation Portuguese families who've remained there to ranch and fish. I should have married into one of them. My life would be secure, possibly even sane. It's alluring land with a memory like an elephant. Stick a trendy restaurant in there, and the place is out of business before the radicchio turns brown. Tomales Bay, holding its steel thunder-gray, unrelenting basin of salt water—part of me belonged to it.

We continued north, driving through fog, about as bad as it gets and getting worse. Occasionally I saw a headlight approaching, then vanishing, eaten quickly by wet air. I turned a corner past a ranch, taking a right up their drive. I turned off my headlights, waiting. Three minutes, maybe it was four, Dudley drove past me, up the coast. I exhaled in honest relief. I'd lost him. I was shaking. I gave myself time. No one knew this weather, or this road, better than I did.

I pulled back slowly toward Highway 1. I could barely see the damned road, and I sure as hell did not want to drive over a stump, or into a ditch. I stuck it in first gear. Five miles up Highway 1, we were doing okay, not a light behind us. Once we were home, it wouldn't take Dudley long to show up. I'd deal with it—him—then.

South of Jenner, I relaxed. I turned on the radio, humming along with a song I'd never heard. With a sudden hard-glint piercing light, headlights shot into my rearview mirror. I knew the shape of those lights, and I recognized the blinding intent. Dudley.

The Russian River was coming up. If I turned east, the jig would be up. Two miles up River Road, and the fog would dissipate. Dudley would follow, on my tail, right to my front door. I needed time, not much, but some. As long as I kept moving, staying inside the fog belt, I had it. Time to make plans, time to decide what to do with Jimmy. What to do with Dudley when we met. Not what do about Dudley, but with him.

Made sightless by wedge-thick slices of hazed night, I nearly lost the road. When a house light or cafe fixture pierced the fog, I knew exactly where I was. Not much to go on. This place was mine, but Dudley held the advantage—my red taillights were his tiny beacons.

Plenty of guts around the curves, but my car had zero guts up the hills, and my transmission wasn't happy. I had to come up with something. I didn't plan to spend eternity, or even the rest of the night, driving on Highway 1. I considered driving to a police station, but the nearest one was miles away from the cover of fog, leaving too many places for Dudley to crowd me off the road and get nasty. And, if I made it through the night, that was still a temporary solution. I know a relentless man when I meet one. My mind was busy, turning over permanent solutions to Dudley.

By then I had little idea where the ocean was, other than somewhere to my left. I hadn't seen the few oncoming cars until they were practically on top of me, and often it looked as if they were driving toward me in my lane. In each case, I pulled far to the right, hoping not to run my tires into a ditch.

A brainstorm hit, the voice of a tangy loudmouthed god pulsing a past experience in my ear. Many years before, I was driving while in a state of—let's say—altered consciousness. The whole world looked pretty damned nice, even though it was the middle of night. The sky was fog-beaten air, and I couldn't actually see one real thing. I had been chosen as the designated driver because, among my friends, I was deemed the least warped. Now, this was not your ordinary night, driving on a decent road while messed up. This was driving south through Big Sur in a February fog at three in the morning.

Driving south, you're on the ocean side. There is nothing between you and the Pacific, with the exception of seriously rugged cliffs. I had lost all sense of the road, when my guardian angel—overworked and underpaid—hatched a plan. I placed my left tires, front and rear, on the speed bumps planted in the center of the skinny road. When I'd stop hearing those bumps, I knew I was headed into the ocean or driving on the wrong side of the road, neither being desirable. The plan was brilliant, it worked like a charm, and, except for a few deviations, our behinds rattled safely for seventy-eight winding miles down the coast. I had lived long enough to breed and grow wrinkles.

No reason it wouldn't work again, and no reason I couldn't work a variation that would shake Dudley. I hated to think of the word *permanently,* but that's what was bubbling hopeful on the top layer of my mind.

Dudley suddenly turned off his headlights, and he rammed my rear bumper. He slowed and backed off. I could feel him, breathing down my neck. Another ram, this one harder, as if we were playing TAG, YOU'RE IT.

I've never enjoyed being the IT.

"Hey!" Mina said. "What was that? I thought another car was going to drive right through us. There's no cushion in your backseat."

"I'm going to take care of it." I said, "Jimmy, if you're scared, now's the time to swallow it. I need you."

"Who was trying to drive through us?" Mina asked. "Was it Dudley, the man who is scum in the bottom of a bathtub?"

"The very same."

"He almost killed us at Ike's," Jimmy said, his voice colder than the sea, "and I believe he killed my uncle Hao and Flora." Jimmy was not scared. He was smart, cool, and he was moving straight into fight mode.

Mina said, "Did Dudley ever think that by getting us into a wreck he could get in one, too?"

"No, but I've thought of it," I said. "He just wants to rattle the women and children."

"How's he doing?"

"If I weren't so mad, he'd be doing a good job."

"I was afraid of that."

The large picture—our solution—had come to me, but I still needed the fine details. I asked Mina and Jimmy to be quiet so I could think. This was like asking two brown trout to live out of the water. They did their best.

It didn't take long, and it was beautiful.

"Everyone, unbuckle your seat belts. Jimmy, slip your backpack on. I want you wearing that thing."

He didn't argue, he didn't once ask why, he just did what he was told. Unlike my own kids.

"I cannot believe that moron," Mina said. The next few words bumped out of her mouth, thanks to a small series of jolts and rear-ramming attacks. "Jimmy, my Ford Fairlane seat belt is stuck. Help."

Jimmy turned around, unfastening her. Some of her dress was stuck in the buckle, and he had to pry it out with his teeth.

"Don't look back here," she said to me. "Keep your wheels on those speed bumps."

"Both of you," I said, "open your car doors, but just a crack."

"Jimmy, take the wheel and drive. Annie's lost her mind."

"Just open your door one damned crack, would you? Hold on to the door handle until I tell you . . ."

Mina said, "Until you tell us what?"

"There's a house just beyond a steep curve to the right. If I head straight, instead of taking the curve, we're in the ocean."

"Great, you've figured out where the ocean is."

"Better than that. I have a plan."

I saw the taffy shack, shop of the widow who supported herself by pulling out people's old crowns and giving them diabetes in return. The curve was coming up.

When Dudley had rammed me, I didn't know if it had happened the first or the second time, he'd broken my taillights. Fine by me. No red stars to guide him, he'd flipped on his fog lights. Dudley was very close. It would work.

"Will you tell what you're planning? I might not want to join you."

"When this road takes a hard curve to the right," I said, "we're taking a left."

"A park trail?"

"No."

Mina said, "Has the geography changed, because what I remember to the left is cliffs and the ocean."

"That's right." I suffered from utter clarity.

"Jimmy," Mina said, "do like I told you and get into that driver's seat."

"Jimmy stay put," I said. "There's a carport to the south of a house. If I work this right, we'll catch some help from a dim porch light to the north. The light spills between the carport wrought-iron bench for watching sunsets."

"We're a little late for the sunset."

"We're missing the bench and we're not changing enough time."

"Why," she said, "do we have to do this?"

"One of two things will happen. When we leave the highway, we'll jump out of the car, it will careen past the bench, the car will fly off the cliff, and Dudley will drive past, thinking we all died. Or, number two, we'll jump out of the car, it'll go off the cliff, and he'll follow. Not knowing what's there—the ocean—he won't jump out of his car. That, as they say, will be that."

"You're crazy."

"Mina, can you think of a better way out of this? And fast?"

"I can't think of *any* way out of this. All I heard you say, and you said it twice, is that this car is going over the cliff."

"Right. Jimmy, can you think of a better idea?"

I had hope for real help from him. He had a bold and devious mind. This time he came up empty. They both told me their car doors were open, and they were holding on to the handles.

"Annie," Mina said, "in case we don't make it, I want to tell you what a good job you did with that baby. It's fine."

"Thanks. We're going to make it. If we're lucky, Dudley won't."

Dead silence from Jimmy, also from Madame Gypsy sprawled in the backseat.

Dead silence because that's what I'd just wished on someone. Death. I would have preferred that Dudley disappear from Jimmy's life, and from Ike's life, but relentless is a quality that does not mellow with time. It only grows sharper teeth.

The right curve approached, and I didn't turn into it. I needed to drive a little farther, straddle the line before I crossed it, and I'd will my car to work up some guts. I told everyone to hold on to their door handle, that there'd be no time for the count of three. One quick command—'OUT'—that was all they'd have. The turn came hard, I drove straight, then I pulled my car directly to the left, iming just to the left of that yellow porch bulb and an eternity of mist. I was driving as if there were a highway exit, and we etting on it.

T!" I yelled, and we rolled. Oomphs and grunts. No loud

screams. The silence worried me more than screams would have. I was cataract blind—the world was milky white, gray, and cold. Metal hit hard rock, granite cliffs, end over end. My old friend Austin Cooper told her stories with each bash.

I heard trips to Little League games, and every dinner out with a friend. Mornings spent taking my kids to school, and, years later, mornings spent driving home from a lover's. Miles and years hitting the rocks, tossing off small choruses of memories as she dashed to meet the sea, sounding happy, ready to leave me. The car was wiser than I was—it had a lifetime of wear, lifetimes of laughs and junk-food wrappers, too many kids piled inside with cats hiding under its seat. Its natural time was over, and I'd have to say good-bye. One final glug, the ocean swallowing my car. Below the surface one more whale was chowing down another used Jonah.

Up on my elbows, squinting through the fog, I saw a small shape, definitely not a Mina shape, lying at the end of my feet. Jimmy.

"Jimmy? You okay?"

I realized he was holding my ankles, holding them with both hands. I didn't know how close we were to the edge, he probably didn't either. No matter, wherever we were, it was too close. I stretched my arms in front of me—what would I feel? I held Jimmy's wrists and pulled him up to me. I hurt. The gravel had done a decent job of chewing chunks off both my hips. This was no way to diet.

Mina said, "I am alive. Is there anyone here who cares?"

Jimmy and I groaned a *yes* in her direction. Not much enthusiasm, but it was the most either of us could manage.

"Annie," Mina said. "Do you have your arm around me?"

I felt both my arms. I felt Jimmy's.

"No arms around you, Mina."

I heard a groan, another groan.

"Is that you?" I said to her. "Are you okay?"

She whispered. "I think we've got a problem here. It's sort of like waking up with someone you hadn't meant to sleep with. It's Dudley, and I think he's coming around. I'm afraid if I sneak out from under his arm, he'll wake up, but I gotta get away from him."

I whispered back. "Wait a minute, Mina."

"What are you doing?"

"I'm looking for Jimmy's backpack."

Mina said, "I think it's on my lap."

"Can you hand it to me?"

"Not without waking up Dudley."

I crawled out of the gravel and rescued Jimmy's backpack from Mina's belly. Part of it was looped around her neck. We'd never know exactly how that had happened, but I was glad it hadn't flown into the ocean with my car.

I fumbled in Jimmy's pack. I found what I wanted and his Bic.

"Annie," Mina said, "what are you doing?"

My words were a snake's hiss, unfamiliar to me. "I don't want this man following Jimmy for the rest of his life. We know he will. If I have to pay, spiritually, for this, I'm willing."

Jimmy said, wringing his hands like an old woman, "Dudley sounds hurt. It's terrible."

"Mina," I said, "roll away from Dudley."

"What are you going to do?"

"Move far away from Dudley. Now."

She did. He stirred. I took a Roman candle. I flicked the Bic and lit the Roman. I stuck it in the front pouch of Jimmy's pack, placing it on Dudley's stomach. Dudley stirred again, this time smiling into my face. I wrapped one of his arms around the backpack, and he cradled it like a lover.

"Whoever he thinks he's holding," Jimmy said, "he's in for a surprise."

"Jimmy, the man is holding justice," Mina said.

Dudley opened his eyes, locking into my eyes. When the smell of sulfur surrounded us, we sat in that death-dervish together. Dudley smiled at me, evil, empty, and not the least bit surprised.

A fizz, a hissle, more fizz. We forgot our aches, we all ran from Dudley. Nothing happened. I thought, *I should have used two or three, just in case* . . . Then an explosion blew me backward against the carport I'd nearly hit. The boom sealed Dudley's fate.

Fifty-two

I didn't feel so hot, and I was sure I had gravel in places where gravel shouldn't be. My eyes, for starters, and the gravel had nibbled large patches of my skin raw. The pariah was groaning. Despite all odds, it sounded as if he were still alive.

Dawn would soon wake up. When she saw what was going on, she might decide to stick her head back under the clouds. With her first pale prelight came a faint sun, burning off the fog.

Jimmy's face was bunged-up, and his hands were scraped. I decided not to look at myself. I felt pain in many different places, but if I saw myself, the pain would be worse. Mina was rolled into a ball.

She said, "Are we alive yet?"

"I'm alive. I can't speak for you."

"What about Dudley? Is he dead, or is he standing over us waving that gun around? Doesn't the government have tests they give people to see if they should have weapons? If they do, Dudley passed, and the test failed."

Mina was talking too much, and it was for the same reason I wasn't talking at all. We were two ragged bundles of bones and nerves.

Dudley's Buick had made sounds going over the cliff, but they were nothing like my car's stories. No music in them, no memories. Too new. The Buick sounds held nothing but those of a piece of machinery that had been used and discarded. Same sounds as a bad relationship. I got brave and looked in his direction. Dudley was mostly in one piece, but his middle part was a mess. There were things sticking out that shouldn't have been.

He saw me looking at him, and he started crying. Something about his guts.

"Maybe he's on the way out," Mina said. "First that man tried to catch a child in his web. Then you and I became so desperate to save the kid that we jumped out of a car to lose him. Not to mention that your classic car," she said, "was destroyed because of his greed."

Classic car?

"And Dudley, the car was minor," she said to him. "You killed a couple of slightly tweaked, but perfectly good, human beings. Some actions are not forgiven."

Dudley stopped crying about his guts. "I only killed Alan Lee. He did the other two."

"You're lying," I said. "Hao was respected in the community—an impossible hit for Alan. And Flora? Wanting to get rid of a woman and a minister rolled into one, that was really the end."

"Flora was no saint."

"She didn't deserve to be your victim," I said. "I'd guess that Alan was ready to let the money go, you railed, and he was ready to turn you in."

He cried about his guts again, then he stopped crying.

"How do you know all this?"

"Truth is written in the groans of a dying man," Mina said. "In this case, the man is you."

My skin hurt like hell. Several cars had passed. No one stopped, but they could have called 911. If someone *did* stop, what would I tell them? Under normal circumstances, I can come up with a colorful lie, no problem. But pain doesn't help the creative process.

Jimmy moved close to Dudley, and he was very still. "Mina," Jimmy said, "don't get mad, but I don't think he's going to die."

"What? Listen, if you can fix him, don't."

"I can't fix him."

"Thank God."

"He's going to need what hospitals put into people, bags and tubes, but only if we can get him there on time."

"We don't have any cars left."

I checked my purse. "Out of cell phones."

"Stuck," Mina said. "You know what, Annie? Before you start feeling bad about what you've done, besides saving us from a lot of grief, this man made you burn my building down. And then he killed Alan. If you hadn't burned up in that fire, you might have been blamed for Alan's death."

"Mina, you're not making sense. Maybe you have a concussion."

Another groan from Dudley. Mina looked at him as if he were the absolute and elemental end of the line.

"Maybe," she said, gently shaking her head, opening and closing her eyes. "How long do you think it's decent to wait before I ask for my insurance money?"

"It's not like having a first date after a funeral. I guess you can ask them today."

"Too soon," she said. "I need to get emotionally prepared to deal with beige people wearing beige polyester clothes walking in and out of my life. When surrounded by beige, I need to wear red, and I'm not up to red."

"Mina, I think you took a big whack on the head. Is it bleeding?" She checked herself out.

"No blood, and it's not like I've got anything else to do here except talk. I think my leg is broken."

"Are you kidding?"

"I just noticed that it's pointing in a brand-new direction."

Jimmy left Dudley's side. He straddled Mina, doing his thing over her leg. "Nope. It's a strain," he said, turning it carefully until it pointed in the old direction.

"Can you make it stop hurting?"

"I'm so tired," he said. "I think it would take a lot more energy than I have."

"I understand completely," she said to him.

He flopped off her leg and lay down next to her. There were rivers of quiet, punctuated by groans. I dozed, and woke up to sirens screeling, several of them. I lifted myself to my elbows and saw a long black car behind the ambulances. The license plate on the black car read STANYON1.

Skip stepped out of the car, holding the elbow of a refined-looking gentleman. Then Skip broke loose, running to Jimmy.

"Hug carefully," Jimmy asked.

Mr. Stanyon introduced himself, saying, "This scenario is horrifying."

And I hadn't even had to invent anything.

Two policemen cuffed Dudley, and he screamed. The paramedics yelled at the cops to pull off the cuffs, promising them that Dudley, should he survive, wouldn't be going anywhere. Not for some time. After that, the police could do what they wanted with him.

They picked Dudley up and slid him on a gurney. His groaning had turned to muttered and moist burbling. Terrible. They launched the gurney into the ambulance, and it headed south, sirens blaring, lights flashing.

Then I noticed something was wrong. They were trying to roll me onto a gurney, too.

"Hey! I'm absolutely fine."

"Lady, you don't look fine."

"No hospitals. If I get home and I feel sick, I'll call you."

"Ma'am, just relax now." One paramedic said to the other, "She's probably in a state of shock. Look at that mess."

Jimmy interrupted. "I don't think you'd better tell her what to do. She doesn't like it. I think she needs to rest and heal."

They mumbled something about kids these days, how their parents let them talk as if they were adults, and what does a skinny Chinese kid know anyway.

I interrupted by threatening to bite one of them.

"I told you so," Jimmy said to the men wearing pale green outfits.

Mr. Stanyon stepped in, offering home nursing care. They left me alone. They left.

Mr. Stanyon said that he appreciated our befriending his son.

"Your son saved Jimmy's life," I told him. "He's a terrific young man."

"I know," Mr. Stanyon said, tears in his eyes.

He put his arm around Skip's shoulder, a loving, tender father. Sometimes I want to dislike rich people, but it is one more wrong-minded prejudice. They're regular people who got lucky or worked hard or both. Mr. Stanyon was okay. Better than okay.

Jimmy stood at the edge of the cliff, staring into the ocean. He wore his timeless expression, the look that he'll wear until he's a little old man singing deep inside the mystery. He motioned for Skip to come to his side. Skip broke loose from his dad and heeled like a dog.

"Skip," Jimmy said, "listen carefully. Not with your ears, but with your stomach. Do you hear them?"

Mr. Stanyon sat on the gravel next to me. I wasn't doing so great when I was on my feet. We watched them together. They looked like old friends.

Mr. Stanyon picked up a small handful of gravel, letting it run through his fingers. He peered into the new morning.

"Skip was in school, studying to become an ocean biologist. Very gentle. We noticed he didn't seem right, small things first, then the big things. Medication helps, but it's been a long road."

"I'm sorry."

"So are we. We're lucky, though. We have the means to keep Skip at home with us, and he's maintained his love of the ocean. We love our son."

"We all like Skip." It sounded lame, but it was true. And I was in a lot of pain. Words weren't working very well. I wanted bed.

I watched Jimmy and Skip being together. Inside their world, my pain decreased.

Jimmy said to Skip, "Anything yet?"

"No, and I'm trying really hard."

"Sit on the ground and place your palms on it."

Skip did that. Dismal and sad, he looked up into Jimmy's face. He was missing the experience he'd been waiting for all his life.

Morning broke the clouds into streaky orange, glorious and loud, outrageous and boisterous bubbles. The ocean's surface turned oil-slick pink and lavender.

Jimmy laughed. It was as loud and boisterous as the sky. He bowed low, hands together, smiling at the ocean. "Thank you," he said. And then Jimmy stood, spreading his arms wide and high to the sky.

Jimmy helped Skip up. He put his arm around Skip's waist. Skip turned to join his dad, but then he turned to face the ocean again. Tilting his head, he didn't move for several minutes. It almost looked as if he'd stopped breathing.

"Dad," Skip said, "come here!"

I stayed in the gravel. Mr. Stanyon ran to his son.

"Dad, I heard the dolphins talk."

"Mr. Stanyon," Jimmy said, "don't be scared. I heard them talk, too."

Skip laughed. "And I heard you talk back to them, Jimmy."

"It's a secret," Mr. Stanyon said, "just between the three of us."

Jimmy looked into Mr. Stanyon's face, "They have a really funny sense of humor. Skip can teach you how to hear them."

Fifty-three

I woke up because I felt someone staring at me. Jimmy. Every part of my body hurt, including my hair.

He said, "Do you feel as bad as you look?"

"Do I look like I was run over by a cable car that jumped its tracks?"

"And then rolled you into the pier. Yes."

"Don't show me a mirror."

"I'm glad you're home. You need rest. You *don't* need hospital bacteria crawling inside your lungs, making you sick."

Hospital. Leo. I told him I'd be there tonight. I had to start getting ready. It would take me at least five minutes to slip my shoes on.

Mina was standing behind Jimmy, grown pale with concern. I must have really looked terrible. "What is that movement?" she said. "Are you having a fit?"

"I'm trying to get out of bed."

"Tell me a joke that's funny."

"This is not a joke. I told Leo I'd see him tonight."

"Love is one thing, killing yourself over it is another. I've been telling people this," Mina said, "for two centuries. Why does no one believe it?"

"I don't want Leo to worry."

"You go to the hospital looking like that, and you"! be in the next room."

"You think they'd take me? I'd like to be in the hospital with Leo."

"Hospitals are not hotels, places where you check in and check out . . . They don't work that way."

"No mileage points for staying there, no nothing."

"Just the bills," she said. "I was real proud when you said *no* to the hospital."

Jimmy stood next to Mina, a VACANCY sign hung over his face. I knew he was working on me. I wished him sonic luck.

"Mr. Stanyon," Mina said, "was so happy that we'd been nice to his wacky son, he would have torn off his expensive jacket and carried you to the hospital in his arms if you'd asked him to."

"Skip isn't wacky. He's eccentric."

She thought. "No, he's wacky, but he has a good heart. These days that's very important. We'll invite them over for dinner when you're well enough to cook."

"In the meantime, I'm going to invite Mr. Stanyon to help us. I was out of it, but I did hear home nursing care offered."

"Every time someone helps you out it turns into a mess. For you."

"Not this time. Hand me the phone, so I can call Mr. Stanyon. After I get that squared away, I'm calling Leo."

"Okay, get you the phone. I can do that."

"You can do something else."

"What?"

"I want to see Jimmy. Baby Jimmy."

Mina glowed. "Nothing is better for good health than a new baby."

After she left the room, I picked up the phone and had a nice chat with Skip's dad, then I called Leo.

"Hiya, Toots," he said. "You on your way over?"

"Leo, no details now, I'm not up to it. You only need to know one thing—we're busting you out of there."

Fifty-four

Before there were bodies, music was the sound of the soul.
When there aren't bodies anymore? Music will still be the sound
of the soul.

—*The Gypsy Guide to Wisdom*
Zlato Milos, 1902

—The Lantern Festival—

When Mr. Stanyon set up two hospital beds in my living room, they came with a protesting cardiologist. Mr. Stanyon convinced the doctor that we were only eight miles from a hospital and that Leo would languish if left in San Francisco alone. I liked Mr. Stanyon very much.

The doctor almost had a heart attack of his own when he discovered that, prior to his big event, Leo had not seen a physician in twenty years. He put Leo on blood-pressure medicine. Leo looked at the bottle and read the label. I could hear the wheels turn inside his head . . . *I wonder if I can get my prescription refilled without going to the doctor for another twenty years.*

Jimmy took care of us, too. I told Mr. Stanyon about Jimmy's gift. He smiled at me indulgently. He believed Leo and I could help each other heal. He understood the power of love—he didn't need to understand everything.

But it had been two weeks, many doctors had come and gone, and now it was time for the beds to go home. The last nurse—no uniforms, please—was leaving. Three days after the accident, we received a huge bouquet of tropical flowers from the twins. They were sent from a florist in Cincinnati, Ohio. Between the *au revoir* and the tropical flowers, they'd wanted to tell me they were somewhere French and tropical. Tahiti? There are many French-speaking tropical places. And a florist will take a credit card from anywhere. It was a nice gesture, weird but nice. The flowers were fading, and they were heading out the door with the beds and the nurse.

It was the day of the lantern festival, and a celebration was in order. Leo had passed his EKG with flying colors, and I was growing new pink skin. I still took a painkiller every day, but that's mostly because I liked the way it made me feel.

Jimmy put on a CD. It didn't sound much different than the old man who played zither on the streets, painful, except there was an entire orchestra of the musicians. Ike clapped his hands, pulling Mina to her feet, an invitation to dance.

"Mina," he said, "it's a simple rhythm, but you must follow me."

"Follow you?" she said, as he spun her around. "When you step all over my feet, I can't even move."

He stood back a little, doing his best to keep her in his arms.

"Annie," Mina said, "do we look like the king and queen of the idiot's ball? Because that's what I feel like."

"Beautiful women are often impossible, but you," Ike said to her, "take the cake."

Mina was about to say something in response, but Jimmy cut in. "Ike, dance with me for a minute. I don't mind being the girl as long as I don't have to dress like one."

They stood in a line of two. With their hands on their hips, they stomped on the fifth beat. It felt off, but it looked great. Ike spun Jimmy, and he landed back in Ike's arms. The last time Ike spun Jimmy, he kept spinning until he hit the Barcalounger, a dizzy whirl of laughing. He started to tickle me, but he caught himself. My new pink skin could only party so hard, and he knew it.

I said, "Jimmy, you looked great."

ne."

"I was born knowing that dance. It's in my bones."

"I don't know how anyone can dance to music that sounds like a cat with its tail stuck in a door," Mina said.

Mina loved to dance, she loved music, and she was not impressed with the lantern festival. Not until Ike pulled out a black-market video. It was a tape of lantern shows made for this holiday, this holiday that was born in the mist of a lush valley, halfway around the world.

Every lantern show sang of dreams and illusions. Lights danced behind puppets, poking them through with shadowed speckles and rays. The puppets loved and fought and acted silly. They mocked the foolishness of kings and the foolishness of peasants. One tall puppet, a monkey-man, winked at the audience saying, *We're all part of the joke, and even the money in your purse can't save you from the joke of being human.* Then monkey-man ran in crazed circles. I looked at E. B., wondering how she was doing. If there was a word for monkey fear, she had it good. Primateophobia?

E. B. excused herself, going into the kitchen, bringing back two handfuls of vitamins. She had shoved every nutrient known to man down our throats. They tasted bad, and I hated them.

"Can you just take these without arguing? Leo takes his."

Leo palmed his. He'd gotten away with it until I caught him. Now he took them.

"Why do we always have to go through this? I don't want them," Leo whispered to me.

"On the off chance that these things work, I don't want Mina to be the only person I know who's still alive in the next century."

"I'm only doing it for you."

"Just swallow the damned things."

He did.

"I smell something good," Leo said. "It can't be one of Mina's inedibles."

"Ike is cooking. Tang Yuan, rolled dumplings made of sweet rice. I think it's like eating turkey on Thanksgiving. Traditional for the lantern festival."

"I appreciate Mina, but there were a few times I thought she was practicing death-by-cooking."

"And," I whispered to him, "E. B. is just as bad. At least my crippled jaw saved me from solid food. One time I thought she was feeding you pet chow. Why does health food look as if a barnyard animal should be eating it instead of a human?"

"I don't know, but that particular bowl went under the bed."

After two weeks of soup and Jell-O, the dumplings smelled as if a corner of paradise had taken up residence in my kitchen.

"Leo, you want something to drink?"

"Ask Jimmy to get it."

"No more being waited on." I stood up. My legs were shaky, but they worked. "This may take a while."

He rolled on his side, fluffing a pillow someone had stuck in the chair for him. "Take your time." The trip out of bed and into the Barcalounger had pooped him out. Mina pulled up a chair for me as I walked into the kitchen.

"Don't move around again," she said, "not yet. I got enough to take care of around here, and I do not need you in traction. Someday I've got to get back to work."

"Mina, how long until the next lunatic comes around? I'm tired of this."

She sighed, and it was a mighty one. "I don't know. I think when you live big, you attract big people. Most of them are good—look at Leo—but you're going to attract big lunatics, too," she said, "and not the simple ones who wash their hands two hundred times a day."

"I guess."

"At least Dudley's gone."

"Thanks to Skip's dad, he'll stay gone."

I don't care what anyone thinks, justice is not blind. Justice has a little black book containing the phone numbers of the rich and powerful. Mr. Stanyon's name was highlighted in yellow. He made many calls to people in many places. He assured me that when charges against Dudley were pressed, he would not be able to wiggle out of them.

Dudley was not going to wiggle for quite some time. He'd survive, but he'd never win a mambo contest on the Love Boat. And the only cruising he'd do after a frail form of recovery was straight to jail, do not pass go. The city wanted him, and the feds wanted him. I discovered the CDC had wanted Alan Lee long before he'd wanted me, but in the matter of Alan Lee they were out of luck.

There were questions about the human remains found at the Mystic Café. Too many questions—even my painkillers didn't send me to BlissWorld for a few days—but in the end it was decided that Alan Lee had killed a couple of people who'd gotten in the way of his empire building. Unless they tracked down Anthony, king of the dead, and he played connect-the-dots successfully, the mystery would remain unsolved. I doubted that there were any laws against burning dead people. Theft, yes, but I was confident Mr. Stanyon could handle it. He liked handling things. He might someday be sorry that we'd become part of his circling orb.

I watched Mina and Ike cook together.

"You want something?" she said.

"I'm giving my skin a break before I stumble back into the living room, carrying water glasses. I never thought of this as a big house. Right now it feels like an over-stuffed and over-large museum."

"The moon is full," Ike said, stirring orange fruit into his rice. "A fortunate time for the lantern festival. Moon is the kindest lantern of all."

Full moon. It was time. "Mina, do you have any cigarettes?"

"Of course I have cigarettes."

"Give me one."

"E. B. will kill me if she finds out."

"She won't," I said. "I want to forgive Stevan."

"For that I'll risk your daughter's anger." She pulled a pack out of her pocket, handing me a book of matches. She said, "Don't expect much. I only have these natural things E. B. bought me. Still, I guess tobacco is tobacco, chemicals or not."

I wobbled to the door, Ike holding my elbow. I had almost been eaten alive by pavement, but my wobble had more to do with matters of forgiveness than the condition of my sad and sorry butt. Forgiveness does not come easy.

Moon, giant moon . . . I pulled out a cigarette and inhaled. I blew smoke to sky. I played with it, swirling a smoke ring around the moon, a misty necklace of pearls. Sometimes I really do believe that people we've loved can hear us after they die. Like dolphins, they just speak another language. I'd do my best.

I tried a prayer, couldn't pull it off, and so I talked to Stevan. He hadn't always been such a great listener. I hoped death had changed that, at least a little.

"Stevan," I said, blowing smoke into a cloud resembling a biscuit, "thanks for my kids. They're terrific, all of them. And thanks for Mina. When I feel nuts, I have often blamed it on her. That's handy.

"Down to business. I guess I have to thank you for your son and his wife. They're good people. Did you know Pavlik's mother died while sunning with a crew of sea lions? Call me mean, but I really get a kick out of that.

"Mostly thanks, because their baby girl is in the range of stellar. I may let them keep her, I haven't decided. She feels like mine. I love the way she smells.

"I came out here to smoke and forgive you. I'm trying, but I'm not sure if it's working. When eternity rolls around, I hope I'm more evolved. If not, start running. I can love your kids, but still be pissed as hell at you.

"That's probably the best I can do right now. And it's probably more than you expected."

I didn't know how to end the conversation. I did feel lighter, and I did feel as if this were one more bump in the road. Inconvenient, but not something that would slow me down. The truth was hard, but I was glad to have it.

One more truth needed saying. "Stevan, I hate to tell you this, but I still love you. It feels different, but I still do. Okay, over and out."

I gimped back into the kitchen. Mina and Ike were two kids playing house.

"What do you think of this guy?" Mina said, laughing.

"I think he's one of the most honorable men I've ever met."

"Me too. That could be a real problem for us down the line."

He swacked her on the behind with a wet dish towel, she made a weak effort at retaliation. You either have the towel-snap down, or you don't. He stopped playing and looked at me.

He said, "You have no more wobble."

"I'm tired, but I'm good."

He held my face. "Did you find answers out there?"

I thought about it. "Sometimes there is no cure, but there's a healing."

He nodded to me, eyes glittering, quiet as a tortoise. *Yes.*

I sat with Pavlik on the couch, watching the baby on the blanket. Watching her do nothing but be, because that's what a new person does. Be. Mina joined me.

"You know what? You may have to add on to this place."

I was about to tell her that I didn't intend to have everyone live with me forever, but when someone leaves my house, they're replaced by someone else, so I didn't bother.

"Maybe," she said, "with that fat check you got from the sale of your building, you can buy a different house. Bigger. Is the check good?"

"It cleared."

"How much? Exactly."

"None of your business."

"This is probably why I thought the sale wouldn't go through. You are totally closed down to me on this subject."

"Because it's none of your business."

"With family, one person's money is everybody's money."

"Mina, our views vary slightly about that."

"Up to you. But why not buy a bigger house?"

"This house has too much juice in it. Good or bad, it's all been good."

"I think that you've mistaken yourself for a tree and you're afraid to move."

"Nope. I'm a bird. I fly into the world and I always come back to my nest. It's here."

She looked at the people sprawled around, comfortable, and she stuck her lips out—thoughtful. "You know how much I hate to agree with you, but this time I think you're right."

"You're not going to start kissing up because I've got dough, are you? You acting humble and sweet would really put a strain on our relationship."

"Not a chance. And when those people get done rooting around in the Mystic Café's ashes, I'll have my own big check. You won't have any idea how much money I've got."

"I already know. I filled out your paperwork."

Mina sighed. Crawling on all fours, she lay on the blanket, putting her face into Baby Jimmy's. She said, "If that woman ever drives you nuts, remind yourself that you two are related by the heart, but not by blood. I know all about that with her."

Leo was asleep, a comfortable heap inside the Barcalounger. After sparse meals of Jell-O and chicken soup, I'd lost fifteen pounds.

I wasn't feeling sexy

my corner. I climbed into

scooched close, laying one arm across m

I fell asleep in my nest inside my bigger nest,

afghan that someone had crocheted during a visit.

laughed, healed, loved, feasted, and then they had moved on.